“Who is this mad vagabond?”

Trimesqua asked a nearby courtier.

“I am Elhathym,” said the stranger. His voice was deep and cold. “I knew this city when it was called by another name . . . but I have lingered a great while in distant lands. Tonight is my homecoming.”

“Say again, Elhathym, what you said to me when first you caught my eye,” said the King. “If you dare.”

Elhathym nodded. “I said that your reign has come to an end, Trimesqua.” He glanced about the crowded hall. “Step down from your marble seat. This city belongs to me.”

Publications by John R. Fultz

Books of the Shaper

Seven Princes

BOOK ONE OF THE BOOKS OF THE SHAPER

JOHN R. FULTZ

SEVEN PRINCES

www.orbitbooks.net

Orbit
Hachette Book Group
237 Park Avenue, New York, NY 10017
www.HachetteBookGroup.com

First U.S. Edition: January 2012

Orbit is an imprint of Hachette Book Group, Inc. The Orbit name and logo are trademarks of Little, Brown Book Group Limited.

Library of Congress Control Number: 2011935842

ISBN: 978-0-316-18786-2

10 9 8 7 6 5 4 3 2 1

RRD-C

Printed in the United States of America

For Darrell S.

The Giantlands
Far Sea
NEW UDURUM
Vod's Passage
Grim Mountains
Uduru River
LAKEHOLD
Vod's Lake
Western Flow
The Stormlands
River Orra
SHAR DNI
MURALA
Isle of Iardu
Eastern Flow
UURZ

The Great Earth Wall
ALLUNDRA
Golden Sea
Cryptic Sea
to the Jade Isles
The High Realms
Western Steppes
MUMBAZA
ZAASHARI
KHYREI
Eastern Marshes
YASKATHA
River Tah
to the Southern Isles

Prologue

Sunset in Yaskatha

The stranger came to Yaskatha at sunset.

The city had taken on the color of blood, a mound of rubies stacked beside the blue-green mirror of the sea. Shadows glided through streets and gardens. In the royal orchards weary harvesters carried bushels of lemons and pomegranates. Along the wharves a flock of trading vessels folded their sails for the night. Mariners prowled the taverns in search of red wine and the red lips of women.

In the airy palace of King Trimesqua the Feast of Ascension began with a legion of musicians, a flourish of dancers, and a quartet of fire-eaters. Before the throne sat a long table piled high with delicacies. Prince D'zan sat at the head of the board, looking far more regal than his sixteen years would suggest. Behind him, as always, stood Olthacus the Stone. The solemn warrior wore a massive blade on his back. It had served him well in three wars, but he seldom drew the sword from its jeweled sheath. A glance of the Stone's gray eyes sent fear fluttering into the hearts of brave warriors. To D'zan, laughing at the antics of a fool who juggled flaming brands, his fearsome bodyguard was little more than a stiff-lipped uncle. Yet no man could have been safer at court than the young Prince. Not even the King himself.

In the midst of the revels, as the sun poured the last of its lifeblood into the sea, a stranger appeared before the throne of Trimesqua. No one saw him enter the palace gates or move between the ranks of armored guards. He flowed like a shadow across the motley crowd and stood before the King. When first he spoke, the music overpowered his words so that only the King could hear him.

Trimesqua set down his golden goblet, raised a hand heavy with rings, and commanded silence. All eyes fell upon the stranger. He was a tall man, gaunt, and as pale as the jungle dwellers of Khyrei. His hair fell long and gray down his back, and his robes were black as pitch. An arc of rubies hung across his chest like drops of frozen blood, mimicking the cold moon with a red smile. The nails of his fingers were long and sharp, making claws of his hands. Shadows rimmed his eyes.

"Who is this mad vagabond?" Trimesqua asked a nearby courtier.

"I am Elhathym," said the stranger. His voice was deep and cold. "I knew this city when it was called by another name . . . but I have lingered a great while in distant lands. Tonight is my homecoming."

"Say again, Elhathym, what you said to me when first you caught my eye," said the King. "If you dare."

Elhathym nodded. "I said that your reign has come to an end, Trimesqua." He glanced about the crowded hall. "Step down from your marble seat. This city belongs to me."

A flood of gasps and muttered curses filled the hall. Prince D'zan stood up from his feasting chair and stared at the stranger. His guardian, the Stone, did not move or even blink an eye. A moment of silence fell across the assemblage.

The exquisite tension was broken by the King's laughter, which spread like bubbling water throughout the courtesans, nobles, entertainers, and servants. The stranger stood mute and grinning as the laughter surrounded him. Guards along the walls drew their curved blades and moved closer to the throne, but the King raised his glittering hand again, halting them.

"Surely you are one of the fools sent to amuse me?" said the King, regaining his composure. He quaffed red wine and chuckled again. "A rare jest!"

"I assure you," said Elhathym, "I am no fool, and this is no jest. This land is mine by ancient right. I could bring your city to its knees with sorcery and shed the blood of all these beautiful soldiers, but I am not a cruel man. Therefore I give you this chance to surrender the throne without any deaths on your conscience but your own. I will make your execution quick. You will feel no pain. Deny me . . . and all will suffer."

Now the King did not laugh. Nor did anyone in the hall. A deathly silence hung between the pillars with the smoke of feasting, broken only by the crackling of torch flames. D'zan drew the long dagger that he always wore and moved toward his father, but his silent bodyguard placed a hand on his shoulder. Despite the nervous twitching in his stomach, the Prince stilled himself.

The King stood up and tossed his wine cup down the steps of the dais, turning white marble to crimson. Guards rushed forward, but a third time Trimesqua raised his hand, and they halted. "My father, and his father, and all their fathers before them ruled Yaskatha from this high seat," said Trimesqua. "Neither men, wizards, demons, or tidal waves shook them from this throne. Here is what I think of your threat, Elhathym the Sorcerer."

In the blink of an eye Trimesqua, who was seasoned in the same wars as Olthacus the Stone, drew his silver sword and swept it down upon the stranger's head. Elhathym's skull split with a meaty crack that rang the length of the hall. He fell backward in a shower of gore, staining the fine carpet at the King's feet.

"Remove this trash!" commanded the King. He tossed his

soiled blade to lie upon the chest of the dead man. Guards rushed forward and dragged the body away; one of them would clean and anoint the sword before returning it to him. Servants exchanged the ruined carpet for fresh one, and the Festival of Ascension resumed. Music and wine flowed through the heart of the palace like blood through a living man's body, and the corpse of Elhathym was thrown into a deep furnace. Later, his charred bones were tossed into the midnight sea.

That night Prince D'zan fell asleep after exhausting his passion with a comely courtesan. Instead of the sweet oblivion born of drink and exertion, his rest was plagued by nightmares. He found himself wandering through the ancestral burial vaults deep below the palace, where lay the bones of his grandfather, his great-grandfather, and all the generations of his family going back a thousand years. He was cold and without garments as he wandered those lightless, musty catacombs, and the eye sockets of decaying skulls glared at him from the shadows.

Somewhere among the vaults he knew his mother lay, for she had died when he was an infant, and he did not remember her face. Still, she must be here in this realm of chill darkness and creeping grave mold. Royal families throughout the centuries filled the numberless rows of niches, and sometimes favored servants and war heroes earned the honor of burial in the royal crypts. In terror, D'zan wandered this mansion of the dead, calling the name of his father into the dark. Only echoes answered him.

He called, too, the name of Olthacus, his bodyguard. Not even the Stone came to help him navigate those dark depths, and he could not find his way out. He found only chamber after chamber of mummified ancestors, the population of the city's long history, and the crumbling, engraved sarcophagi in which they lay. Here was a city of death that slept beneath the living city, and at last he gave up looking for the exit and lay down in the dust near a pile of bones. It seemed to him then that he heard a faint laughter ringing through the tombs.

He woke to a sweltering bedchamber, lying next to the senseless girl who shared his bed. He could not sleep again so he walked along the open balcony of his room and let the ocean breezes dry his sweat. The girl joined him on the balcony and soon lured him back to bed.

The following day was like any other in Yaskatha's thriving capital. D'zan arose early and walked the palace garden with his fair-haired cousin Lysinda. He spoke to her of his nightmares and she comforted him like a mother with gentle kisses on his forehead and cheek.

"I've dreamed of my mother before," D'zan told his cousin. "But never of the place where she lies."

"There is nothing to fear," said Lysinda, taking one of his hands in her own. "Dreams are only passing fancies. They cannot hurt us."

"Do you truly believe that?" he asked.

"Of course," she said.

"But . . . this dream seemed so real. It was . . . a warning of some kind. I know it."

"Don't be silly," said Lysinda, ruffling his hair. "Look about you: the sun is shining, the sea is laughing, the blooms of the garden rejoice. The stranger is dead and forgotten."

"I'm afraid," he whispered. She cradled his head in her lap awhile. She did not have to tell him that Princes of the royal house were not supposed to speak of fear or weakness. He knew that well enough.

D'zan forsook his studies for the day, and the two cousins went riding along the pounding surf. They rode twin mares the color of honeyed milk, and Olthacus the Stone rode some distance behind on his black charger, a single shadow for them both.

When sunset fell on Yaskatha once again, the King sat on his throne listening to reports of trading galleons from Mumbaza, Murala, Shar Dni, and the kingdoms of distant continents. D'zan reclined nearby on a lesser throne; his father was grooming him in the ways of statecraft. Behind D'zan stood the vigilant Stone, his eyes hidden beneath the hood of a heavy cloak. Olthacus scanned the throne room for potential threats among the comings and goings of the court.

Despite his keen sense for danger, not even the Stone saw the stranger's second arrival. As before, the dark-robed Elhathym simply appeared before the King's throne without any warning. His hoarse voice interrupted and overpowered the voice of the King's viceroy, who read a cargo list from an unfurled scroll.

"Trimesqua," interrupted the sorcerer, his sallow face looking even more skull-like than yesterday. "You have spurned my offer of mercy. As you can see, my death is beyond your power to grant. I give you one more chance to abdicate your throne. Since you refused my first offer, now it falls upon your people to suffer if you refuse a second time. Everyone inside this palace will die if you deny me again. Blood will flow through your streets and orchards. The shadows of your own past will tear you from your throne. What say you?"

Olthacus the Stone drew forth his great two-handed blade, and D'zan rose from his own chair to unsheathe his ceremonial scimitar. He felt again the terror of his dream . . . For a moment he was lost in the lightless crypts. Then he was staring at the broad back of the Stone, and guards rushed forward to encircle Elhathym in a thicket of bronze spear points and shining blades.

King Trimesqua did not rise from his throne this time, but his wrath was great.

"Charlatan! Chicanery will gain you nothing! Your fatal mistake was in returning to the scene of your previous treason. Now your death will be slow and agonizing. You will scream and beg forgiveness on the rack! Take him!" Spittle flew from the King's lips to fleck his dark beard.

The palace guards swept over the sorcerer, a vast wave of silver and gold drowning a single black pebble. Olthacus the Stone did not move, but kept his place shielding D'zan in case the sorcerer unleashed some dreadful magic in his direction. But Elhathym did nothing as soldiers loaded his limbs with heavy chains and dragged him from the throne room. He did not even scream as they dragged him down below the living levels of the palace and into the sulfurous glow of the torture chamber. Here, among the half-dead relics of political prisoners, murderers, rapists, and traitors, he endured the worst of torments the torturers could envision. For hours the hooded ones plied their trade, but not once did Elhathym scream. Instead, he *laughed*. As if all the processes of his own bodily pain and dismemberment offered some private delight.

In the throne room far above, the condemned man's laughter drifted like a fetid smoke. D'zan, sitting at the arm of his father, shivered in his cushioned chair. He recognized that hollow sound from his dream of the tombs, and a nameless terror swelled in his heart. He could not speak to his father of his true feelings. He must be as brave and valiant as his sire, as grim and unfazed as the Stone. So he hid his quietly growing horror, and stuffed his ears with pieces of silk to drown out the faint laughter of the tortured man.

That night D'zan dreamed himself into the tombs again. He wandered, naked and alone as before, looking for the sarcophagus of his mother. In the living world he had visited her grave a thousand times, and such a familiar landmark might give him some hope of egress from the nightmare maze. But he could not find his dead mother, only legions of those who had died before his birth, a necropolis of winding corridors leading nowhere. At last, he saw a pale light and ran toward it. It seemed to draw away from him in the ever-lengthening distance that only occurs in the midst of dreams. Finally, he came close enough to realize the glow came from a single face, gleaming in worm-pale moonlight. It was the face of the sorcerer Elhathym, and it smiled at him in the darkness, floating wraith-like before him, bodiless. The face laughed, and the flesh sloughed away like that of a leper, leaving only a cackling skull that hovered in the endless dark.

D'zan woke screaming, and seconds later the Stone came into his bedchamber.

"It's all right, Olthacus . . . I'm fine." D'zan waved his guardian away, but the big man would not leave the room. He stood in the corner while servants dressed D'zan. The Prince called for a cup of morning wine, but could eat no breakfast. He spent the day in the library, poring over ancient texts from Khyrei detailing legends of sorcerers and necromancers who had haunted the Old World. In one of these tomes, after hours of meandering through moldy pages, he discovered mention of a wizard bearing the same name as the one who'd come to plague his nightmares. "The Tyrant Elhathym," said the *Book of Disgraced Savants*, "ruled a southern kingdom before the Age of Serpents." Nothing more than that brief passage.

Such texts were widely discredited by Yaskathan sages, because there were no civilizations that existed before Giants out of the northlands drove the race of fire-breathing reptiles from the earth. According to D'zan's history tutors, the Giants then claimed the north for themselves, forcing the Four Tribes of humans to flee southward to ultimately form the five kingdoms: Yaskatha, Khyrei, Uurz, Mumbaza, and Shar Dni. How could there be a southern empire before any of this happened? Unless history was wrong . . . a lie invented to cover up horrible truths. And why would this present-day sorcerer take the name of a tyrant from an age of mystery?

It did not matter, he told himself. The sorcerer was finally dead now, tortured to death last night by order of King Trimesqua.

Or was he?

As the sun slipped once more into the sea, D'zan closed the musty volume and walked with urgency into the lowest level of the palace proper. Behind him, a second shadow, came the imposing figure of the Stone. The Prince hated the reek of the torture chamber, a blend of feces, sweat, blood, and fear. Even more he despised the terrible sounds that resounded among the boiling furnaces and intricate devices of torment. He usually avoided this part of the palace. But the sorcerer's laughing had finally stopped, and he had to be sure that Elhathym was dead.

The smells of scorched flesh and decay drowned all others as D'zan entered the chamber. There was no sign of the sorcerer. Only the bodies of the three hooded torturers lying across the floor, blood pooling about their split bodies, their limbs askew in impossible angles. All the racks, cages, and shackles were empty, even those that had encased rotting corpses to terrify victims.

The sound of screaming came from somewhere above. D'zan raced back up the steps and ran toward the throne room, the Stone pounding at his heels. Courtesans, servants, and soldiers fled the great hall, mouths agape, eyes wide with terror. A cacophony of shrieking filled the arched corridors, and the odor of ancient decay was everywhere. The stench from D'zan's dreams . . . the acrid reek of the tomb.

D'zan raced into the throne room to see his father the King surrounded by a trio of grasping mummies. The smell of long-rotten flesh filled the chamber like a fog, and two of the mummies grasped the King by his arms, holding him immobile while the third decomposing corpse raked its claws across his flesh, spilling royal blood across the dais. D'zan heard his father scream, and his legs were frozen; he could not move forward or backward, but only stood staring at the tableau of impossible slaughter.

On the King's throne sat black-robed Elhathym, a grim smile on his lips, his skull nearly visible through the tight, pallid flesh of his face. He bore no marks of torture on his person; not even his black robes were disturbed, and his necklace of blood-drop rubies hung gracefully upon his emaciated chest.

A legion of the dead swarmed the hall. Already several guards lay bleeding on the flagstones, their throats ripped out by fleshless fingers and the teeth of withered skulls. Swords and spears clove into dry breastbones with little effect. The mummies of previous dynasties were now ravening ghouls, splashing gouts of blood across fine tapestries as they tore the palace guards to bits. D'zan recognized the tattered raiment of the ghouls, and saw on the head of more than one a royal diadem or crown out of Yaskathan history. These were the inhabitants of the royal necropolis crawled up from the underworld beneath the palace.

The shadows of your own past will tear you from your throne.

More lurching corpses poured into the hall; the screams of women and children rang from the walls in every wing of the palace. A grinning mummy rounded the corner and reached for D'zan's throat, but the Stone's blade took off its moldy head. Olthacus' booted foot crushed the corpse against the floor; as he tamped its ribcage into dust, its fleshless arms kept grasping at his legs, tearing through his leathern leggings and drawing blood. D'zan backed away, inspired by the Stone's bravery to draw his own weapon; a reeking cadaver grabbed him from behind, pressing its rotted skull against his ear. Its jaws snapped like those of a turtle, and he dropped his sword clattering to the floor as horror suffocated him.

The Stone tore the mummy from D'zan's back and pulverized

it with blade and boot. His big hand slapped D'zan across the face, ending his paralysis. "Come, Prince!" growled the Stone. "I know a secret way."

"No!" shouted D'zan. "We can't abandon my father!"

"Your father is *dead*, boy!" said the Stone, pointing his blade at the cluster of ghouls who tore at a mess of scattered flesh upon the royal dais. Above the horrid feast sat Elhathym, the bloodstained crown on his head now, smiling at the devouring of Trimesqua. Still the ranks of blood-hungry dead things continued filling the chamber, the last of the guards falling before their voiceless assault.

The Stone grabbed D'zan's arm and they ran through milling clouds of grave dust. They never stopped running, all through the winding corridors of the servants' wing, the Stone's great blade demolishing one desiccated corpse after another. Everywhere the dead feasted upon the living. None in the palace were spared the bottomless hunger of the corpses; royal and servant alike died under the raking of bony claws. So Elhathym had promised, and he had delivered on his ultimate threat.

D'zan wondered if his mother's corpse was among the hungry dead. *Would I recognize her? Would she tear out my throat with the same hands that gave me life?* Stifling a bottomless scream, he drove such thoughts from his mind, closing his eyes and mumbling a prayer to the Sky God.

The Stone brushed aside a wall hanging and opened a hidden passage, leading the Prince along the dark and narrow way. D'zan, fearful of dark places now that his nightmares had come to life, closed his eyes while Olthacus dragged him along that winding route, up and down seldom-used stairwells, through crawl spaces, and finally out into the night air. Once again the screams of the dying filled D'zan's ears. He dared to open his eyes and found that the Stone had brought him to an outer palace garden. They ran for the orchards beyond. Behind them flames danced among the towers and courtyards. The dead were heedlessly knocking over braziers and torches, spreading flame and death throughout the royal domain.

Where can we go to escape this damnation? His unconquerable father was dead and there was no safe place left in the world. The Stone grabbed his arm and pulled him onward.

Once in the deep shadows of the orchards, they seemed free of the undead plague a while, steeped in the tangy aroma of hanging citrus. But when they crossed the outer wall into the seaside quarter, they saw again the terror and panic that had claimed Trimesqua's house. Here, too, corpses walked the streets and tore at living flesh. It seemed every graveyard and mausoleum in the capital had vomited forth its dead at the command of Elhathym. Citizens fled for the hills or locked themselves inside their houses. The Stone smashed another mummy to powder as he drew D'zan on toward the wharves, where towers of flames writhed and flickered. All across the city, walls of orange-white fire leaped toward the sky. *They must be fighting the dead with fire*, D'zan thought. *But they will burn their own city to ash . . .*

Many ships in the harbor had already launched, heading out to sea to escape the apocalypse of Elhathym's making. Citizens jostled and fought one another for passage on one late-embarking galleon which flew the Feathered Serpent of Mumbaza among its white sails. The Stone hacked his way through the crowd, leaving a bloody trail in his wake, dragging D'zan by his elbow. The panicked Yaskathans gave way before the big warrior. Without a word the Stone gained passage from the ship's captain at the point of his dripping blade.

The deck of the galleon was crowded, and the sailors had to beat back the mob with oars and clubs before they could cast off. D'zan collapsed on the deck, near the prow. The pitiful cries of women, children, and men – all doomed – filled his ears even when he clasped his hands over them. When he dared to look out over the railing, the capital was a flaming, screaming mass of chaos separated from him now by an expanse of dark water. The horned moon hung pale and implacable above the dying city. Towers gleamed brighter than rubies in the glow of the roaring fires.

Those who had escaped by securing passage on the galleon were weeping, or cursing, or both. A few had brought entire families with them. D'zan stood in the prow watching his inheritance burn, thinking of his father's bloody crown sitting upon the sorcerer's head. Hot tears burned his cheeks. Behind him, as always, stood the Stone, silent and still as the moon.

In the blood-spattered throne room, Elhathym drank wine from Trimesqua's goblet as his army of undead Yaskathans preyed on their descendants. He smiled at the irony of using the past to remold the present in such a way. Among the entrails and filth littering the hall, a great white panther glided toward him. The beast licked at Trimesqua's blood, and the snapping ghouls ignored it as they wandered off to find fresh victims.

The white panther came close to Elhathym's knees and rubbed its silky fur against him. His thin hand caressed its head between the ears, and it growled.

"You see, my dear?" the sorcerer told the panther. "I told you my birthright would be easily reclaimed."

"So you did," said the panther. "But what of *my* desires?" Now the cat was a pale-skinned lady sitting at his feet, her voluptuous body draped in strings of chromatic jewels. A thick mane of hair, gleaming white as silk, fell across her shoulders. Her eyes were as dark as his own.

Elhathym, the new King of Yaskatha, smiled at his lover.

"Patience," he whispered. And he kissed her ruby lips, which tasted of royal blood.

1

City of Men and Giants

In the twenty-sixth year of his reign madness came to the King of New Udurum. It did not fall upon him like a flood, but grew like a creeping fungus in the hollows of his mind. At first he hid the madness from his Queen, his children, and his subjects, but eventually he could no longer steady his shaking hands or hold the gaze of his advisors during council.

Udurum was a city of both Men and Giants. The power of King Vod had fostered an era of peace between the two races for almost three decades. Vod himself was both Man *and* Giant, and therefore the city's perfect monarch. He was born as a Giant, grew into a sorcerer, and became a man to marry a human girl. He slew Omagh the Serpent-Father and rebuilt the fallen city of Giant-kind. Now, twenty-five years after he forged a path through the mountains and began the reconstruction of New Udurum, his children were grown and he felt the call of an old curse. This was the source of his madness.

The children of King Vod and Queen Shaira were neither Giant nor human, but a new breed all their own. His first son Fangodrel was pale of skin, with sable hair and the anguished soul of a poet. These were altogether human qualities. His second and third sons likewise stood no taller than average Men, but they carried the strength of Giants in their modest frames, and their skins were the color of tempered bronze. These were Tadarus and Vireon, whom many called his "true sons." His daughter, youngest of the brood, was named Sharadza. She took after Queen Shaira, almost a mirror image of her mother, yet in her fifteenth year was already as tall as her brothers.

When Vod began ignoring his royal duties, his court began to grumble. Both Men and Giants feared his dissolution as an effective monarch. His uncle, the Giant called Fangodrim the Gray, tried to quell the fears of the court as best he could. But even he knew that Vod's rule sat in peril.

When the chill of early fall began to invade the warmth of late summer, Vod called for his children. "Bring them all before me," he told Fangodrim. A cadre of servants ran along the gigantic corridors of the palace in search of Vod's offspring.

Sharadza sat beneath the spreading arms of a great oak, listening to the Storyteller. The leaves had turned from green to orange and red; the rest of the courtyard's lush foliage was following suit. All the colors of the rainbow revealed themselves in this miniature version of the deep forest beyond the city walls. She was not permitted to exit the gates of New Udurum, not without the escort of her father, and he had not taken her into the forest since last season. Here, beneath trees grown safely within the palace grounds, she got a taste of those wild autumn colors, but in her heart she longed to walk among the colossal Uyga trees once again. The sun shone brightly through the turning leaves, but had lost its heat. The faintest breath of winter blew on the wind today. She sat on a stone bench as the old man finished his tale.

"So the God of the Sky had no choice but to recognize the Sea

God as his equal. But still sometimes the Sky and Sea fight one another, and these battles Men call hurricanes. Doomed is the ship that ventures across the waves while these two deities are in dispute." The old man turned his head to better meet the eyes of the Princess. "Are you troubled, Majesty?" he asked.

Sharadza had been distracted by the varicolored leaves blown upon the wind. Beyond the tops of the palace walls, gray clouds poured across the sky. Soon the season of storms would be upon them, and then the crystal purity of winter. She did not mind that chilliest of seasons, but fall was her favorite. Each tree seemed hung with fabulous jewels. She smiled at the old man. It really was not fair to invite him here and pay less than full attention to his stories.

"Forgive me, Fellow," she said. "I am somewhat distracted these days."

The old man smiled. He ran a hand through his short white beard and nodded. "You are growing up," he sighed. "Mayhap you do not care for my stories any longer."

"No, don't think that," she said, taking his wrinkled hand in hers. "I treasure your visits, I really do. You know so many tales that I could never find in the library."

Old Fellow grinned. "Would you have another?" he asked.

Sharadza rose and walked about the oak tree, trailing her fingers along its rough bark. "Tell me what you know of my father," she said. "Tell me about Old Udurum. Before I was born."

"Ah," said the Storyteller. "You had better ask the King for stories of his youth. He would tell them better than I."

"But you know he won't talk to me," she said, blinking her green eyes at him. "I hardly see him . . . He's always in a meeting, or in council, or off brooding in the forest with his Giant cousins. He forgets I even exist."

"Nonsense, Majesty," said Fellow, rising from his stone seat.

His back was slightly bent, and he supported himself with a tall, roughly carved cane. His robes were a patchwork of motley, as if he wore all the shades of the fall leaves, a myriad of colors spread across the fabric of his flowing raiment. Yet Fellow wore such colors all year round. He had very little taste when it came to matters of style. She had given him gifts of silken tunics, delicate scarves woven in Shar Dni, and other garments worthy of a nobleman's closet, but he refused to wear any of them. He would, however, accept whatever jewels or coins she managed to wheedle from her parents. Even Storytellers had to eat, and Fellow was little more than a vagabond. Yet he was so much more.

"Your father cherishes you, as does your kind mother," said Fellow in the tone of an encouraging schoolmaster, which he was not. Sharadza's tutors were never so informal with her, nor did she relish spending time with them the way she savored her every rendezvous with the Storyteller. He wandered the streets of the city between visits, telling his stories on street corners and in wine shops, earning his daily bread by weaving tales for the weary Men and Giants of Udurum.

"What do you know of him?" she asked, challenging Fellow to spill any secrets he might possess.

The old man licked his dry lips. "I know that he built New Udurum on the ruins of the old city, after the Lord of Serpents destroyed it."

"Everyone knows that."

"Yes, but did you know the young Vod was born a Giant but was raised by human parents?"

Sharadza nodded, sitting back down on the cold bench. Thunder rolled low in the distance, like the pounding of great breakers at the edge of a distant sea. She had heard rumors of her father's human parents, but he never spoke of them to her.

"Oh, they did not know he was a Giant at first, just a very large baby," said the Storyteller. "But they soon found out when he grew too fast." His voice sank to a whisper. "They say his human father abandoned him, but his mother never did. She died not long after the building of the new city."

"She would have been my grandmother," said Sharadza.

"Not entirely," said Fellow, "for she was never related to your father by blood."

"What about the Serpent Lord? Is it true my father slew him?"

"Yes," said the Storyteller. "By virtue of his sorcery, the same powers that make him both Giant and Man, your father destroyed the oldest enemy of Giant-kind. His magic made him tall as the Grim Mountains, and he wrestled with the Great Wyrm, his flesh burned by the great fires that it spit in his face. Their battle took place right here, among the ruins of Old Udurum. Nearly all the Giants had been slain and their city toppled. When young Vod crushed the life out of the monster, he vowed to rebuild the city. That is why we have this capital of Giants and Men. Your father brought peace to the Great Ones and the Small Ones. He is a hero. Never forget that."

Sharadza nodded. How could she ever forget the legacy of her father? But there was much she still did not understand. The wind caught up her long black curls, and she brushed them away from her face.

"Is it true the Giants are dying?" she asked.

The Storyteller frowned at her. "Since the destruction of Old Udurum, no Giantess has borne a child. Some say the dying Serpent Lord put a curse on his enemies, and that is the reason why the she-Giants are barren. If your father had not fallen in love with your mother, a human, you and your brothers might never have been born at all! The Giants who live among us now are old.

Yes, they are a dying breed, and they know it. Little more than a thousand still walk the world, and by the time your own children are grown someday, they may all be gone."

"Is there nothing we can do?" Sharadza asked. Such finality made her want to cry. Her cousins were Giants, so if they died a part of her died with them. Her father's best friend was his uncle Fangodrim, who was uncle to her as well.

"Likely not," said Fellow. "These things are decided by higher powers than you or I. But remember that it is not death that counts in the end, but a life lived well."

Sharadza smiled through her brimming tears. Fellow was always saying things like that. "Jewels of wisdom" he sometimes called them. It was one of the things she loved about him.

"Fellow," she said, "I have another question for you."

"Of course, Majesty."

"How did my father learn sorcery? Was he born with it?"

Fellow sat quietly for a moment. Sharadza heard the moaning wind and a peal of approaching thunder.

"I'd best tell that story another time," said the old man.

"Why?"

"Because your mother is coming."

"Oh! You must hide. I'm not supposed to be listening to your tales. She says you're a liar and not to be trusted."

Fellow smiled at her, the skin about his gray eyes wrinkling. "Do you believe that, Princess?"

She kissed his cheek. "Of course not. Now go. I hear her steps along the walk."

Fellow turned toward the tall hedge and disappeared into the leaves. He would find his way back out onto the streets of New Udurum by a hidden path she had shown him months ago. She could not explain her mother's distrust of the Storyteller, but she knew in her heart it was baseless, so she smuggled him into the royal gardens whenever she could, at least once a week. She began to think of him as her grandfather, albeit a grandfather she could never publicly acknowledge. She had learned much from his stories, and there was much more to discover.

Queen Shaira rounded the corner of the hedge maze with two palace guards in tow. Shaira was not a tall woman, but her presence loomed as that of a Giantess. Her hair was dark and her eyes bright as emeralds, both like her daughter's. Looking at her mother, standing there in her gown of purple silk and white brocade, a crown of silver and diamond circling her brow, Sharadza knew exactly what she would look like when she was grown. There could be no doubt that she would be the spitting image of her beautiful and regal mother. At the age of forty-five, Shaira retained every bit of her beauty, and this gave Sharadza no small comfort.

Her mother called her name, and smiled at her in that loving way that nobody else could ever smile. In the warmth of that smile, the day felt a bit less cool. The blaze of summer lived in her mother's green eyes. Maybe it was the fact that Shaira had grown up in a desert kingdom, or maybe her love itself was the source of the heat.

Sharadza ran to embrace the Queen.

"What are you doing out here, Little One?" asked Shaira. Even though Sharadza stood taller than her mother already, Shaira still called her by that nickname. She felt comfortably small in her mother's arms. It had always been so.

"Admiring the leaves," she answered. "Aren't they beautiful?" She cast her gaze upward at the splendid fall colors.

Her mother gave her a quizzical look, as if suspecting that she told only part of the truth. "Your father summons you before the throne," she said, running her hands along Sharadza's hair, smoothing the dark curls.

"Me?" Sharadza asked, stunned by the news.

"You and your brothers," said her mother, and the Princess saw a worried look pass across her face like a shadow passing across the face of the sun.

"What is the matter?" Sharadza asked.

"Come," said the Queen. "We shall soon know."

She followed her mother across the grand courtyard as big wet drops of rain began to fall. The sound of the drops hitting the leaves was a chorus of whispers. Then a blast of thunder split the sky, and she entered the palace proper.

Mother and daughter walked toward the King's hall as the storm broke against monolithic walls built by the hands of Giants.

Not far from Udurum's gates, beneath the branches of enormous trees, a gathering of Giants stood in a circle about two struggling figures. By the purple cloaks and blackened bronze they wore, these Uduru were known to all as the King's Warriors. They howled and leaped and shouted curses, but their great axes, swords, and hammers hung sheathed on their backs. Their eyes focused on the two man-sized combatants at their center.

Among the brown leaves lying big as shields on the forest floor, two sinewy, broad-chested youths rolled in a contest of power and stamina. Straining muscles gleamed with sweat, and the wrestlers breathed through gritted teeth. A pulp of leaves and mud smeared their bodies. The Giants, each standing three times the height of the wrestlers, shouted and waved bags of gold above the peaks of black war helms.

"Tadarus!" some shouted.

"Vireon!" cried others.

On the ground, Vireon stared up into his brother's face, feeling the weight of him like a boulder against his chest. Their arms locked together like the trunks of young oaks. Vireon's legs shot upward, his heels dug into Tadarus' abdomen, and his brother went flying. The giants roared. Now both brothers stood on their feet, coiled in the manner of crouching tigers. Tadarus laughed. Vireon smiled back at him.

"My little brother!" roared Tadarus. "You know I will beat you. I always do."

Now Vireon laughed to show his defiance. "You are but one year my senior. And youth has its advantages."

Shoulders slammed together and the Giants reeled from the sheer force of their collision. Once more the brothers stood locked in stalemate.

Vireon wondered who would tire first. If he could simply outlast his brother, he would win. The Giants would never underestimate him again.

They might have been twins, these two, but for Vireon's more narrow face and slightly lesser height. They shared the same jet-black hair, the same sky-blue eyes, and the strength of raging Uduru.

Tadarus slammed Vireon's back against a tree trunk. The monolithic Uyga trunk trembled, bark exploded, and the last of the tree's faded leaves fell in a slow rain about the brothers as they wrestled. The Giants howled at this display of strength, and Vireon leapt forward, flipping over his brother's head. They rolled together longwise through a debris of branch, bark, and leaf. Dead wood cracked beneath their bodies.

At the end of the roll, Vireon arose first, his arms still locked on his brother's shoulders. He took advantage of Tadarus' split second of disorientation and hurled him through the air, screaming after him. Tadarus crashed through a pine tree as thick as his waist, shearing it in half. Both he and the upper half of the tree fell with a double crash into the forest beyond the ring of bewildered Giants.

Vireon stood panting in the center of the chattering Uduru. The thrill of victory was a momentary sensation, replaced by instant worry for his brother, who lay somewhere in the shadows of the great trees.

"What excellence!" growled Boroldun the Bear-Fang. "The younger triumphs at last!"

"Hail, Vireon the Younger!" bellowed Danthus the Sharp-Tooth. "I knew your day would come!"

The Giants exchanged bags of gold, precious jewels, and other baubles as the supporters of Vireon claimed their winnings. Vireon payed them no attention, but leaped across the stump of the felled tree to find his brother. Tadarus lay among a knot of big ferns growing about a wedge-shaped boulder. Vireon feared the big rock had brained his brother.

Gods of Earth and Sky, let him be well.

Vireon bent low over his brother. "Tadarus?"

Without opening his eyes, Tadarus sprang up and knocked Vireon off his feet with the force of his shoulder. Vireon's posterior met the ground, and he stared up into the grinning face of his brother.

"Did you think you had actually *hurt* me?" Tadarus said. A few Giants came tromping near, flattening the undergrowth with their every step. Some of them shouted to their fellows that Tadarus was fine – of course. The elder brother offered his hand, and Vireon took it. Now they stood together as the Giants looked upon them with admiration.

"I beat you," said Vireon.

"So you did," said Tadarus, smiling. "And you killed a tree."

The Giants laughed, thunder among the redwoods.

"I say your next bout should be fought on the plains of the Stormlands, or perhaps the top of a mountain!" said the Sharp-Tooth. "To avoid more casualties of nature!"

The Giants and Tadarus laughed. Vireon saw no humor. He regretted the felling of the pine. He would carry it back to the palace for the woodcarvers, or at the least to stoke the fires of the kitchens. Even a tree's death must serve a purpose.

"I am proud of you, brother," said Tadarus. Once more he placed his hands on Vireon's shoulders, warmly this time. His white teeth showed in the forest gloom as he looked his brother in the eye. "You have proven yourself my equal this day. And won a ton of loot for old Sharp-Tooth!"

Vireon at last smiled. His beefy chest swelled. He loved his brother. Only praise from his father could find more currency in his heart.

"I stand amazed, yet again," said the Sharp-Tooth to his fellows. Most of the Giants wandered toward the city gates as drops of rain began to fall, but three of the Sharp-Tooth's fellows lingered, his steadfast drinking companions, Dabruz the Flame-Heart, Grodulum the Hammer, and Hrolgar the Iron-Foot. "These whelps are sturdy as Uduru, though they could pass for Men in any kingdom south of the Grim."

"The True Sons of Vod!" said the Iron-Foot. "They are both men and giants."

"Perhaps we're neither," said Tadarus, sharing a gourd of cool water with Vireon. "Perhaps we are something new. Mother said we carry the best of both races in our blood. Perhaps there is no name for what we are."

"Aye," said Danthus. "You speak with your father's wisdom. But here, Vireon, take you this hammer won from Ohlung the Bear-Slayer." He held the great weapon out to Vireon. The length of it was greater than half the youth's body, but he grabbed its haft and lifted it above his head, testing its balance. It was a Giant's weapon, forged in the smithies of Old Udurum, before the coming of the Serpent Father. Its pitted head was carved into the likeness of a grinning demon, and a band of beaten bronze wound about the dark stone.

"It is a good hammer," said Vireon, admiring the ancient signs of the Uduru carved into the back of the demon-head. "But too unsubtle for me. I think my brother should have it."

Vireon passed the hammer to Tadarus, who grinned at him again and took the war hammer, swinging it about him a few times playfully. "A fine weapon," said Tadarus. "But you won. It should be yours!" He offered it back to Vireon.

"And as mine, it is also mine to give!" Vireon rammed his elbow into Tadarus' tight stomach. Tadarus grunted, then laughed. He nodded, and the argument was done.

The rain fell now in pleasant sheets, so the brothers washed the earth from their bodies while cold winds blew through the upper leaves. The Giants stood counting their loot, heedless of the rising storm.

"Now," said Tadarus, banging his fists together with fresh vigor. "Which one of you Uduru will challenge me and my brother? Let's have a *real* wrestling match!"

The Giants roared their mirth at him, and Vireon went to fetch the felled tree. "None will wrestle you, Prince," said the Sharp-Tooth. "For there is the off chance that you might win. And no Giant could stand being bested by such a small thing."

Tadarus laughed. "Then flee, Giants! Or face my wrath!" He lunged at the Uduru, and they scattered among the trees, laughing at his temerity, dropping coins and jewels in their wake. Vireon joined his brother, the slain tree slung over one shoulder. Tadarus took up his hammer.

"Thank you, Brother," said Tadarus. "For the hammer."

Vireon grinned. "It was the least I could do after humiliating you in front of the Uduru."

Tadarus looked at his brother with a semblance of anger on his handsome face.

"Do you imply that you could best me twice?" he asked.

Vireon grinned. "Three times, even."

Tadarus threw down his hammer, and Vireon his tree trunk. Again they faced each other, crouching ready to spring. The rain pelted them and thunder rolled among the deeps of the forest.

A different thunder, that of a horse's hooves pounding the wet earth, met Vireon's ears. He turned his head just as Tadarus slammed into him. They rolled through the mud for a short while until the voice calling them rose above the sound of the storm.

"Prince Tadarus! Prince Vireon! The King commands your presence!" The hooded cloak of the King's Messenger shone brightly violet during a brief flare of lightning. A black steed, caparisoned in jewels and silk, had carried the rider to them. His name was Tumond, a good man. And he only carried important messages for the King of New Udurum. For Father to summon them in such a manner, the matter must be of great urgency.

Tadarus knew these things as well as Vireon. The brothers rose from their mud-fight, took up hammer and tree, and ran beside the horse as it galloped across the field toward the black towers of the city.

Lightning bolts hurtled madly across the black sky as the brothers ran. Orange watch-fires burned along the city wall in gigantic braziers. The Princes followed the herald onto the wide street called Giant's Way. All eyes large and small turned to catch a glimpse as they jogged toward the spires of jet and basalt that marked the palace of Vod, living heart of the City of Men and Giants.

The eldest Prince of New Udurum stood near a north-facing window high in a tower of the gargantuan palace. Fangodrel watched the thunderheads rolling in and casting their shadows across the great forest. The rolling landscape was a panoply of colors as far as the eye could see, an ocean of autumn leaves in every shade of the rainbow save one. All the green had bled away from the world, and the myriad hues of autumn stood triumphant. A chill wind stole through the open window and raked his chest with icy fingers.

The wide chamber lay shrouded in the gloom of a small brazier topped with low-burning flames. On the bed behind him the servant girl Yazmilla lay senseless among the silken pillows. Her flesh had not been enough to quench his restless hunger. At least her ceaseless yammering had stopped, now that she was unconscious. Now he might have chance for concentration.

He turned his attention to the parchment on his writing table. The poem was almost finished. A few more lines would bring the piece to a transcendent climax. Forty-two lines were ideal. The first thirty had taken a month of agonizing introspection . . . long walks beneath the cold moon . . . a hundred meditations in the moldy air of the city graveyard. Every line was a piece of his soul, a shard of truth, jagged and dangerous to the touch. The splinters of his essential self. This would be his greatest work, a poem that would shame all the hundreds that came before it. His crowning achievement in the realm of verse. If he could only finish it.

He took up a white-feathered quill and dipped its point into a cup of black ink. The point hovered over his parchment. His mind reeled with blank frustration. He hesitated. A drop of ink fell onto the page, blotting like black blood. His left fist clenched, fingernails digging into his palm, and he bit his lip until it bled. His red eyes watered, and he threw the quill across the room like a dart. He stuffed the unfinished poem into the drawer of the table, slamming it shut.

Inspiration is a fickle whore.

The sleeping girl would wake soon, whimpering and crying, begging for more of the bloodflower. He lifted to his lips the long pipe, carved from white oak into the shape of a many-legged

Serpent of legend. Touching a candle's flame to the round bowl in the back of the Serpent's skull, he inhaled the sweet crimson vapor. It sang in his veins and sent sparks flying behind his eyes, so that he imagined it was his skull, not the Serpent's, to which he touched the flame. Leaning his head back, he slumped onto a divan of burgundy velvet. From his reclining position he watched the stormclouds moving toward the window. A few wet drops blew in to kiss his naked skin.

The lights of the city were kindled below as the day turned to night; a million tiny jewels spread in secret patterns far below the tower chamber. He drew another lungful of the bloodflower smoke into his lungs, and watched lightning caper among the thunderheads. He enjoyed the advent of a storm, the casting of light into darkness, the warm air growing cold, the faint stench of fear that rose from the streets as the commoners fled for shelter. He brought the Serpent's tail to his lips once more. Now thunder rang inside his skull, shaking his very bones with its violence. He fell prone on the divan, trembling, moaning his pleasure to the corners of the dim chamber.

The girl must have heard him. She raised bleary eyes toward him and staggered to his side on the narrow couch. She placed a long-nailed hand upon his white breast. He flicked it away. He would touch her only when he pleased. She was merely a servant, and should know better than to touch him when *she* chose.

"My Prince," she mumbled, her pouting lips close to his ear. "Let me taste the smoke with you again."

He passed her the pipe and the candle. She inhaled, coughing, and lay back on the couch beside him. The candle fell from her fingers and singed the rug. He rushed to grab it, but its flame had scored a black mark into the vermilion fabric. He grabbed her by the neck and slapped her face. She awoke, staring into his black jewel eyes, timid as a cornered hare. Her fear reignited his desire.

"I could have you whipped for that," he whispered in the breathy tone of a lover, but his threat was a bludgeon of iron. "Or thrown from the roof of this tower."

"I'm so sorry, My Prince," she muttered. Silly wench, nothing but a scullery maid he'd pulled from the kitchens a week ago. She made an interesting plaything for a while, but he had grown bored of her. She was barely seventeen years and knew nothing. He was Fangodrel, and had celebrated his manhood at fifteen – ten years ago.

"Perhaps," he told her, "you can earn my favor once again."

He took her, this time on the divan, and far more roughly than before. The rain fell in silver sheets beyond the window as the black clouds moved in to separate palace and sky. He wrapped his hands about her throat, the bloodflower singing in his veins. Flames seemed to burst from his eyes as he took his pleasure. His body moved of its own volition, while his mind floated in a miasma of swirling crimson. The bloodflower danced in his vision, telling its tale of endless secrets. He listened . . . at the edge of awareness . . . he burned . . . he almost, almost understood. The flames faded.

When he was finished, cold rain blew in through the window and the storm still raged. The girl lay limp in his hands. He pulled away. Her neck bore a purple ring, and his fingers were numb.

Lightning threw mock daylight into the chamber, and for an instant he saw himself in the oval mirror on his far wall. A pale, emaciated figure bending over the pink and lifeless carcass of a slain animal. He stared into his own eyes for an eternal instant. Then the chamber plunged into darkness again. The coals in the brazier had burned out, moistened by the big raindrops blowing through the window.

He stood and fastened the obsidian panes into place, shutting out the storm. He re-lit the candle with a tinder stick and held it over the body of Yazmilla. So beautiful she was, even in death. More beautiful even, for the absolute stillness of her features, the cool pleasantness of her pallid skin.

A pounding at his chamber door brought him out of the trance, and he turned from the dead girl to face the oak-and-bronze portal.

"What is it?" he bellowed.

"My Prince, your Lord-King Father summons you." A thin, reedy voice. "Even now he gathers in the Chamber of Audience all those of his household."

Fangodrel watched the candle flame dance in the dead girl's eyes, twin rubies captured in orbs of glass.

"My Prince?" came the voice again, through the heavy door.

"Rathwol, is that you?"

"Yes, My Lord. So sorry to trouble you. The summons comes from the King's Viceroy."

He stumbled to the door and unfastened the heavy chain. Opening it just enough, he motioned his body servant inside.

Rathwol entered, a slight man with a hawkish nose, his lavender tunic reeking of turnips, sweat, and sour ale. His bald pate was covered by a leather skullcap, and his tunic bore the fine gold trim of a palace servant, though it needed a good washing. He appeared to have crawled out of a gopher's burrow somewhere. The man was an offense to royal sensibility, but he was very useful.

"Light a brazier," Fangodrel commanded him, handing over the candle.

Rathwol followed the order, using a fine oil to ignite some coals in a dry bowl of hammered iron. His close-set eyes immediately fell upon the body of Yazmilla, lying on the soiled couch. Another man might have screamed in shock or revulsion, but Rathwol had seen much worse. He had prowled the streets of Uurz for twenty years before finagling his way onto the palace staff in New Udurum. Most likely he had fled his native city to avoid imprisonment. Fangodrel had never asked what crimes he may have committed, and he did not care. He only knew that Rathwol was a loyal subject, and a man who could keep his many secrets.

Fangodrel scrubbed himself with a towel and bowl of lemon-water. Rathwol bent to examine the dead girl's neck, checking for a pulse.

"Oh, My Prince," he muttered. "Here was a tasty bit of flesh for the nobbin' . . ."

"Get rid of her," said Fangodrel, pulling on a pair of doe-skin leggings and boots of black leather. "*Discreetly*."

Rathwol looked up at his master. "Into the furnace? Same as the others?"

"Need you ask, fool?" Fangodrel pulled on a high-collared tunic of green and silver, fastening it along the sternum with engraved buttons. "There's a palm-weight sapphire in it for you."

"My Lord is generous," said Rathwol, his eyes turning back to the dead girl's face.

"Get rid of that carpet, too," said Fangodrel. "She *burned* it."

Rain pelted against the window panes, like claws scratching at the inner hood of a coffin. Such thoughts made him wince, but it was only the lingering effect of the bloodflower. It always made him a bit morbid.

Rathwol laid the girl's body gently on the ruined carpet and rolled it up.

"Get her clothes too," said Fangodrel, motioning toward the bed.

Fangodrel checked himself in the big mirror. He combed his narrow mustache and groomed his short black beard into a single point in the style of Shar Dni. He wore his dark hair short, and he brushed it back from his forehead, running a handful of lamb grease through it and wiping his fingers clean on the towel. He hung an amulet of opal and emerald about his neck, and placed a thin circlet of platinum set with a single onyx on his forehead. This was the crown of the Eldest Prince, the Heir-Apparent to the throne of New Udurum. A cloak of green and silver completed his raiment.

His pale skin did not matter, he told himself. It did not matter that his lean, V-shaped face in no way resembled the broad, rough-hewn visage of his father, nor that his physical strength was a mere fraction of Tadarus or Vireon. None of these things mattered, for he was the Eldest Prince. *Let men continue to call me Fangodrel the Pale*, he told himself, *for my skin will never be the umber shade of my brothers. But none can deny that I am the heir to Vod, King of Men and Giants.*

Rathwol carried his burden to the door. There was no sign of the girl now inside the thick roll of carpet. Fangodrel, grimacing at the faint touch of dirty nails, slipped a jewel into the man's sweaty hand just before he exited.

The Prince waited a moment after his body servant left, lingering just long enough to drink a gulp of red wine from a crystal goblet. Lightning flared outside the opaque windows, bolts of fire dripping from the Sky God's fingertips.

Thunder boomed above the soaring towers as he left the chamber and descended a spiral staircase. As he walked he thought one last time of pretty Yazmilla. The girl had been a simpleton but she was not entirely without charms. Tonight he must find a replacement for her.

But first an audience with his noble father.

What could the old fool possibly want of him?

2

Words of the Giant-King

The Giants of New Udurum welcomed the storm as they would welcome an old friend. They stood in the streets while the driving rain caressed their faces and shoulders, and the thunder greeted them in its booming voice. Every human soul fled toward hearth and home to put a roof between himself and the storm, but the Uduru came forth from their tall houses in great numbers. They loved the storm in all its fierceness, and they celebrated the rule of their King, Vod of the Storms, whose shifting moods often brought these tempests upon the city.

Within the black palace Queen Shaira sat waiting for her husband. The fires of twelve hanging braziers dispensed steady heat and dancing light. The walls thrummed and pulsed to the rhythm of the squall outside, and she knew the six Giant sentinels lining the hall would rather be out in the rain and wind.

Vod's man-sized chair sat beside the Queen's own, both of these before the single Giant throne that glittered with the light of precious stones. Vod would only take the Great Throne when some matter of weighty import was to be discussed with the Uduru; then his magic swelled him to the proportions of his Giant kin. Mostly he sat beside Shaira in his accustomed man-form. All three thrones sat upon a dais of black-veined marble. On the highest step of the dais sat Sharadza at her mother's knee.

"Where are my brothers?" asked the Princess, taking her mother's hand. Shaira stared into her green eyes. It was like staring into a mirror, looking at her daughter. A mirror that showed herself as she was twenty years ago, back in the days when Vod's love for her had been an all-consuming fire. Before the weight of time and wisdom had settled on her husband's shoulders, the heavy chains of kingship.

"Summoned from the wood's edge," she answered. "They will be here presently."

"Fangodrel too?" asked Sharadza.

"Yes," she said. "Even Fangodrel."

As she spoke his name, she saw him enter the hall in a flash of green and silver. Fangodrel was her first-born and her greatest secret. She spent her life trying to hide the truth from him, but as he grew he seemed to sense the imperfect nature of her love, and it spoiled him. He was the fruit of a cruel man whose domination left a scar on her heart and a life in her belly. Vod had raised him as his own, but with the same reserve and detachment as Shaira. The pale, quiet boy grew into a hard-hearted and distant young man. Despite his grim nature she tried her best to love him.

"Evenbliss, mother," said Fangodrel. "Sister." He took each of them by hand in turn, kissing their knuckles with his cold lips. Everything about him was Khyrein; nothing of her had invested his appearance or mood. He was entirely the son of his dead father, and he could never know it. The eldest of her sons, and the weakest, yet the most human. It was not his fault that his progenitor was a tyrant and a savage.

"Why does Father call us?" asked Fangodrel. "Is some new war in the offing?"

Sharadza looked at her mother. Her oldest brother's moods and temper had frightened her more than once. As far as Shaira knew, he never abused or threatened his sister. Yet his presence was a quiet threat, a storm that simmered behind clouds of courtesy.

"The King's mind is his own," Shaira said. "We must wait to hear his words."

"Of course," said Fangodrel, looking toward the main entry. "And here come the Twin Brutes."

Tadarus and Vireon entered the hall side by side, broad shoulders mantled in fresh cloaks of violet and black, dark manes slick with rain. Shaira swelled with pride at the sight of them in the hall. They were heroes in every step and mannerism, every word and deed. They were her strength and her glory.

Sharadza ran to embrace them both. Fangodrel stood atop the dais, hands behind his back. How he must envy his brothers' great strength and heartiness. How he must despise the way their father doted on them. Shaira wanted to love Fangodrel in the same way as Tadarus, Vireon, and Sharadza . . . and she had tried for twenty-six years. It simply was not possible.

Tadarus and Vireon hugged their mother, kissing her cheeks, and took their places next to Fangodrel. The senior brother offered a courteous half-bow that was returned by his two juniors, and this was all they ever displayed in the way of brotherly love. Tadarus and Vireon were nearly inseparable, and neither had much to do with sensitive, book-minded Fangodrel. He wrote verse while they wrestled Giants. Perhaps he feared they would murder him one day for the right to claim the throne. But Shaira knew her boys better than that. They would support their elder brother even to their deaths.

A flourish of trumpets announced the approach of King Vod. Shaira stiffened in her chair. She had not spoken with her husband since he arose in the early morning. Something troubled him deeply. For two moons' time now he had not slept a full night. When he did sleep, he tossed and turned, rolling on the mattress like a man drowning. He mumbled strange things in his sleep, too. Curses, or incantations. At times he woke screaming, "Take the Pearl! Take it!" or, "Too deep! It's too deep!"

When she asked him about his nightmares he grew quiet and stubborn. There was something he could not bring himself to share with her. Something that haunted him. In his youth he had demanded her body every night, and even as they grew older – he now in his forty-sixth year, she in her forty-fourth – his hunger for her had persisted. Since his nightmares began, Vod had not touched her.

What secret guilt or terror tormented him so? Would he finally share his dread tonight?

The King sent away his train of human chancellors, advisors, and attendants before taking his place beside her on the man-sized throne. His face was grim beneath the heavy crown of gold with its eight stones of onyx; his puffy eyes were dark, full of secrets. The years had turned his flowing hair from sable to gray, and his thick beard was of that same distinguished color. All these years and she hadn't come close to plumbing the depths of those eyes. She had learned to accept his mysteries, as she accepted his twin statures, Giant and Man. Everyone knew Vod was a sorcerer, but she suspected that he did not know the true depth of his own power. Tonight's storm, for instance, was the direct result of his troubled mood.

The King looked upon his children. Flames crackled in the braziers as the Princes and Princess sank to their knees before him. He took Shaira's hand and looked at her with those restless eyes. It was a look that said, *I love you, and I wish I could avoid what I have to say now.*

Shaira smiled at him, and her eyes said, *You are my husband and my love, and whatever you do I will honor and accept.* But it also said, *Let me share your burden.*

Vod turned to his daughter and sons.

"My sweet children," he said. "Dearest of all the treasures in my realm, I love you above all others. It fills my sad heart with pride to look upon you."

Their eyes sparkled in the firelight, perhaps Fangodrel's most keenly.

"For twenty-five years New Udurum's walls have stood strong, and I have ruled from this seat of power. I watched you grow from tender infants to young men and a woman. You are the pride of giant and man alike, the future of this realm built by the hands of both races."

He paused, as if to weep.

Fangodrel broke the silence: "Father, why speak of the future now? Surely you are not so old and feeble as to give up the throne." Yet his glimmering eyes said, *Yes, give it up now. Give it to me! I am the eldest, and I will take this great chair from you. Gladly will I take it!*

Shaira dismissed this as her own distorted fancy.

Vod sighed. "Hear me, son," he said. "You will know my mind."

Thunder moaned above the high vault of the roof. A black hound came loping into the hall and settled itself at the carved base of a pillar.

"Many years ago," said Vod, "when I was young and foolish . . . before I knew what power truly was, or the sorrow of a thing done in haste . . . I did a great wrong.

"Below the waves of the Cryptic Sea lives a people little known by those who walk the land. With sorcery I went into the depths of that coral realm and stole into the Temple of Aiyaia, where the Sea-Folk kept their holiest treasure. A great sea-stone it was, which some call by the name pearl. Of purest whiteness it was. It gleamed and shone like a drowned sun in that dim kingdom.

"While the guardian of this pearl slept, I . . . I stole it. My Giant arms carried it back toward the land, but the Sea-Folk came upon me in great numbers, assailing me with spear and trident. I hauled the stone away from them as the points of their weapons broke against my thick skin. I knew then it was an evil thing I did, but I had a reason that outweighed all proper thought. Perhaps it was only my lack of maturity. Heedless of right or wrong, I took the Pearl of Aiyaia from the Sea-Folk.

"Seeing that their tiny warriors could not hinder me, they called from the deep a leviathan which wrapped its terrible arms about me. I nearly drowned in its black embrace. But instead . . . instead I used this holy sea-stone as a weapon. I smote the leviathan with the Pearl of Aiyaia and shattered its skull. And I carried the pearl away.

"Yet before I left those waves there came to me one unlike all the other mer-folk. By her crown of coral and jewels I knew her as their Queen. She spoke to me then and cursed me, saying, 'The people of the sea are now your enemies. If ever again you enter our waters, you will surely die, for such is the curse I lay upon you. By the Sacred Pearl, let it come to pass.'

"She swam away, back to her watery palace, and a great remorse fell upon me. I had never stolen so much as single coin or crumb of bread until that day. Now I was the sea-thief, the enemy of the Mer-Queen and her aqueous nation. So I would ever be.

"I gave away the pearl soon after, and for many years I forgot this curse. I brought rain to the desert, opened the course of rivers, avenged the Giants of Old Udurum by killing the Serpent-Father, and united the races of Giant and Men. I rebuilt this demolished city. I raised a family and ruled a kingdom unlike any other.

"Now . . . now the Curse of the Sea Queen has come upon me at last. She has stolen my sleep away with visions of the briny deep and its waiting horrors. No longer can I sit idle and pretending on my throne, wearing the semblance of an honest man. The time has come for me to accept my doom. I must go to the Cryptic Sea and surrender myself to the Sea Queen's justice, else I'll never know peace."

A pall of silence fell upon the great hall, and Shaira heard the Giant sentinels rustling and restless on either side of the throne. They had heard the King's words, and they liked it not. The children must be horrified.

He is leaving me. Just as I feared. Her eyes grew moist, but she kept her silence.

Sharadza's eyes swelled with tears. "Father, *why* did you steal the pearl? What was your reason? Surely the Gods will forgive you even if this Mer-Queen never will? Surely your reason was just?"

Vod looked at his daughter, reached a heavy hand to touch her cheek. "I was selfish," he said. "Selfish and foolish . . . a dire combination."

"But . . . " Sharadza wiped a sleeve across her cheeks. "If you go back to the sea, will you not *die*? So says the curse you uttered."

Vod looked into the shadows of the rafters. "Failing the Mer-Queen's mercy . . . yes, child. I will perish for my hated crime."

Now Tadarus leaped upon the dais steps. "No!" he said, his breath quickened. "Let us lead an army of giants and men to the sea. We'll battle this Sea-Queen and depose her. We cannot abide such a fate."

The six Giants grumbled, ready to start warring upon the Sea-Folk this very moment. They would march into the waves behind their King if so commanded.

"No, my brave son," said Vod. "Such a course would only bring more dishonor. You must understand . . . This is a debt I must pay.

I alone will go to the sea. And I alone will face the fury of the depths and she whom I wronged. It is just, and the Gods will not support an unjust war."

Vireon the third-born stood near his brother, but his eyes were like those of his sister, wet with tears. "Is there no other way to avoid this doom?"

Vod shook his head. He turned to Shaira; she wept freely now. She finally understood his distance from her these past months. He must either do this thing, or stay here and waste away, a prisoner of guilt and visions that would drive him truly mad. She squeezed his hand.

Fangodrel stood tall, unfazed by the tragic scene. "Great Father, I respect your dedication to justice. Your abdication will bring much honor to our house. With terrible sorrow, I accept the rulership of New Udurum. I will build a mighty statue in your honor, to stand in the heart of the city. Of iron, steel, and diamond it shall be wrought, for such is the composition of your heart."

Vod raised his hand. "I have more to say," he spoke. "The time has not yet come for a Son of Vod to sit the throne."

Fangodrel's eyes flared. He breathed through his nostrils, his mouth clamped tight. His hands were fists at his side, crumpling the folds of his verdure cloak.

"Although the King of Udurum must go," said Vod, "its rightful Queen shall remain." His eyes turned to meet Shaira's again. She saw him through a watery haze, thinking of the deep ocean and its harsh secrets. "Queen Shaira shall rule when I am gone. She is beloved of the Uduru, and there is much strength and wisdom in her. I ask all of you to honor your mother in this new office. She will stand above men and giants, and she will need the strength of her hearty sons. Yes, and her daughter—"

Fangodrel could contain his outrage no more. "This cannot be!" he shouted, hurling spittle from his lips. "The Uduru will not settle for a frail woman to rule them! Nor should Men, if true Men they be! I am the rightful heir to this throne, Father. I am your eldest son and I *demand* you name me your successor."

Vod rose from his throne. The children stepped back from his terrible gaze . . . all save Fangodrel, who stood now on the top step of the dais. He stood nearly as tall as Vod, yet his bulk was less than half of his sire's. Shaira had seen Fangodrel's anger before, but never this blatant, never this directed and never aimed at his own family. He was at times a terror to the servants and the lesser folk of the palace, but now he stood before his father as an equal. No, as a rival.

"I have spoken," said Vod.

"You have gone mad," said Fangodrel. "This is a city of warriors, hunters, and builders. And I am within my rights as first-born to claim it . . . even before my own mother."

Thunder broke the sky above the palace, and the walls trembled. The black hound whimpered and pranced into the shadows.

Shaira felt Vod's rage building like a typhoon in his breast.

"You are not—" he began, then stopped himself.

Will he say it? Will he declare the truth of Fangodrel's bastardy? Will he disown this impudent boy? Will he slay him? Oh, Gods of Earth and Sky, grant my poor husband wisdom in this moment.

"You . . . are not . . . ready," said Vod. His anger died as quickly as it was born. He sat back in his chair and stared at his adopted son. This son who thought his blood was true.

Thank you, merciful Gods. Shaira gripped the arms of the throne to calm her trembling hands.

"Many will support my claim," said Fangodrel. "Both men and giants will rally to the cause of my inheritance."

"I think not," said Tadarus the second-born. He stood now between Vod and Fangodrel. Gallant soldier versus brooding poet. "The Uduru like you not, for they respect only the *strong*. You have not a tenth of the strength of Vireon or myself. And you dishonor us all by standing against our father."

Vireon stood calm at the side of his father's chair, with Sharadza on the other side. Always it had been thus. The two youngest would never confront Fangodrel in his tantrums; it was always Tadarus who rose up to defend them, and anyone else, against the eldest.

"Enough," said Vod. "You will both obey the Queen's will. Someday, when she is too old and feeble to rule . . . then may Fangodrel take his inheritance. But there are many years of good life in your mother, boys. Your argument does her dishonor. Go to her now and beg forgiveness."

The eyes of Tadarus and Fangodrel stayed locked together. They did not move.

"Now!" bellowed Vod, and his voice shook the flames in their braziers.

Tadarus tore himself away from Fangodrel's gaze, and kneeled before Shaira. He kissed her hand. "My mother, my Queen," he said. "Body, heart, and soul are yours, as they always have been and ever shall be."

Fangodrel stood his ground. He stared first at Vod, then at Shaira.

Does he hate me now? Poor boy . . . poor, misplaced soul. We cannot tell you that your father was a monster and that you've no claim to this throne. It would destroy you.

Fangodrel said not a word, but strode across the hall, his cloak flapping like the wings of an incensed bat. He stalked through the main arch and was lost in the shadows beyond.

"Little does *he* care about the loss of his only father," spat Tadarus, staring after him with disgust. Vireon said nothing.

Sharadza wept aloud, and Vod pulled her to his lap and hugged her.

Shaira did not know what to say, so she sat in her royal chair and wept as well. *I will be alone now . . . the burden of Queenhood on my back. O Vod, my love. You have cursed me.*

Vod's sons, his true sons, stood with their hands on his massive shoulders. They wept also, though silently, as Men do to hide the shame of it.

Above the hiss of the burning braziers, Shaira heard a strange, low sound. It took a moment to recognize. Even the six Giant sentinels who stood guard in the hall were weeping. Their tears glistened like great diamonds in the glow of orange flames.

The black hound slipped quietly into the night to weep alone.

3

Sea, Storm and Stone

Murala was a tiny city, a collection of gray stone dwellings without a single tower or rampart to protect its inland borders. For less than a league it stretched along the western coast, a town built upon the convenience of its busy wharves. There were no other ports north of this place, so Murala was gateway to the Stormlands for the southern kingdoms. It was a passing place, a weigh station on trade routes that ran to Uurz and New Udurum, the metropolises of the north. Dozens of galleons were moored here in various stages of loading and unloading. The sky was full of rolling thunderheads. The sun rarely broke through that eternal layer of cloud, and a day without rain here was as rare as an eastern jewel.

D'zan was glad to put the ocean behind him with its endlessly rolling face and unpredictable temper. For thirty-three days he had endured the lurching decks and sodden quarters of one trading vessel after another, on a diet of dried fish, hardtack, and stale keg-water. He would never take ship again if he could avoid it. The weeks were spent in nausea and misery, nights in silent despair or nightmares. The Stone hardly left his side, and D'zan would not weep in sight of the big man. So he let his tears flow only in the dark of night, among the moldy blankets of whatever cabin they had secured. The Stone slept lightly, and sometimes not at all. For a time D'zan wondered if his guardian was human, but eventually he saw the man give in to weariness, and his snores were undeniably mortal. The one thing all their cabins and berths had in common was the ever-present odor of fishy brine. It was a reek D'zan was glad to escape along with the pitching decks and foul-mouthed sailors.

Nine days out from Yaskatha they had approached the white cliffs of Mumbaza on the merchant vessel *Lion's Heart*. The capital city stood proudly atop the precipice, a cluster of pearly domes and spires glaring down at the sea with arrogant beauty. D'zan marveled at the Upward Way, the staircase road cut into the bare rock leading up to the city's towering sea gate. The trip had been a torture, and his inability to sleep made it worse. The Stone said they would find sanctuary in Mumbaza with the Boy-King Undutu. But it was not to be.

When the *Lion's Heart* drew into port, an inspector boarded the vessel. He wore a cloak of sable feathers and a helm of beaten gold. His skin was as dark as his cloak, and his eyes were nuggets of onyx, cold and hard and without mercy. He spoke to the Stone in a tone that no man of Yaskatha would ever dare to use, and D'zan thought the two would draw their blades and settle the matter right there on the foredeck. Yet the Stone only walked away, his great hands balled into fists, and came to stand near D'zan as the official continued his inspection.

"Will the Boy-King let us stay?" D'zan asked his guardian.

"No," said the Stone, his eyes still focused on the strutting inspector. "This man serves the King's mother, Umbrala. She is the power behind the throne of Mumbaza, and she refuses to give us sanctuary."

"But how can she overrule the King?" D'zan asked. Even here, with the ship tied to the stone quay, his stomach churned. He wanted to sleep, but feared what sleep would bring.

"The King is only eleven," said the Stone.

"Oh," said D'zan. "But why does she refuse us? We have a treaty with Mumbaza."

"She fears Elhathym . . . and she is fool enough to think she can maintain neutrality in what is to come."

D'zan closed his eyes. He had almost forgotten – his father was dead. A new power set on the throne that should be his own.

"What . . . what is to come, Olthacus?" D'zan asked.

"War," said the Stone.

The Mumbazans would not grant sanctuary, but they would not hinder the Prince of Yaskatha either. Therefore, Olthacus booked passage on a series of northbound galleons. They stopped at various dismal trading ports along the coast every few days. D'zan's nightmares eventually subsided under the weight of sheer exhaustion, but his nausea never entirely faded. He dreamed of speaking with his father often, but he could not hear the words of the dead King. Visions of the walking dead still came to him, but infrequently. Sometimes he dreamed of dead men marching along the deep sea bed, staring up at the keel of the vessel in which he slept. Could there be an army of drowned sailors following him at the command of black-hearted Elhathym? He tried not to think about such things, and a cup of strong wine before bed each evening reduced his morbid night fevers. He still wept in the dark, hoping Olthacus did not hear.

The Stone's pouchful of precious jewels served them well for passage and foodstuffs, but there was little to no luxury to be had on these austere vessels. D'zan used to stare at the ocean dreaming of adventures among the waves, discovering fabulous islands full of monsters and recovering lost treasures. But now he hated the gray-green expanse of roiling, capricious chaos. The farther north they sailed, the more storms they encountered. The skies grew black and the rain nearly drowned them, not to mention the great waves that swamped the deck. D'zan learned to stay below during the squalls.

One evening he stared at a dagger, the one his father had given him for his sixteenth birthday, and contemplated opening his throat while the waves tossed the ship to and fro. He studied the tiny jewels set into the hilt, the traceries of silver and gold in the burnished bronze. The pommel was a griffin's head, its eyes miniscule emeralds. The blade was nearly as long as his forearm, and sharp enough to shave a man's beard. He could draw it across his throat in one fluid motion, using all his strength, and in a few short moments his life would be over. Blood would flow out his neck, seep through the cracks in the cabin floor, and join the brackish bilge water down below. If he killed himself now, his blood would ultimately rejoin the sea, the place where all men came from, if legends were true. The sailors would likely throw his body overboard, completing his journey back to the source. He would join those armies of drowned dead who crawled along the sea bottom like brainless crabs.

It was that last thought that made him sheathe the dagger. Could he even escape Elhathym by dying? If he killed himself, might that be giving the usurper complete control over him? The thought of this deathly surrender made him set his jaw. He must stay alive, no matter what. This was the only way to defy the necromancer. The only hope of freeing Yaskatha from a tyrant who used the dead to dominate the living.

"We'll go to Uurz," the Stone told him. "The Emperor there is kindly and wise. He was once a soldier, a friend of your father's."

"Will he grant us the asylum that Mumbaza denied?" D'zan asked.

"If the Gods will it be so."

"What then?" D'zan asked. "What can we do against someone like Elhathym?"

The Stone stared at him. His rough face was craggy, unshaven, his eyes twin diadems of blue ice. "We make alliances. We build an army. We prepare you for the role you must play."

"What role is that, Olthacus?"

"You already know," said the Stone. "Avenging son. Liberator. You must take back Yaskatha."

D'zan thought on those words often during the voyage. Of course he must do these things. Of course he must slay the monster who had slain his father, and take the kingdom that was rightfully his. But how?

A few days after their conversation, he posed the question to Olthacus: "How can a mere boy hope to gather an army and oppose a sorcerer with such terrible power?"

Olthacus did something then that D'zan had never seen before, though he had known the big man since infancy. The Stone smiled. "There are *other* sorcerers in this world, Prince," he said. "And there are many men hungry for glory. Men who are willing to die for a cause they know is just."

D'zan contemplated this. "And all of this . . . begins at Uurz?"

"At Uurz," said the Stone, looking across the leaden sea where stormclouds flared and rumbled. "And at New Udurum. And at Shar Dni. These are the cities of the north. The Stormlands. It is a land of Giants and legends. It is where the Gods drive us. We must trust in Their wisdom."

D'zan could say little more about this. The Stone knew what must be done, and where they must go. Was Olthacus now his father? This common soldier, this man without a drop of royal blood in his veins? He would sacrifice his entire life to ensure D'zan's return to the throne. There was no denying it.

A glimmer of hope showed through the churning clouds at that moment, and D'zan breathed deeply of the salt air. For a slight moment, his future seemed secure, as if predetermined. *I will do this*, he told himself, and his dead father.

Late that night a hail of flaming arrows set the sails alight. Under cover of a raging storm, a reaver ship drove alongside the *Lion's Heart* and men boarded the galleon. From his doorway D'zan watched Olthacus draw his great sword and cleave the skull of a howling boarder. The Stone led a party of sailors against the ragged pirates, who had not expected to find a true warrior among the seamen.

D'zan locked himself in the cabin and listened to the sounds of battle, his dagger drawn in case some pirate came crashing through the door in search of plunder. He heard men die, squealing like animals, and watched blood leaking through the planks above (as he had imagined his own blood doing before). The reek of burning wood and rigging choked him. Sooner than he expected, it was over. The Stone came into the cabin, gore smeared across his silver breastplate, a smattering of brains clinging to the blade of his sword, and gulped down a bottle of yellow wine. The reavers had been a desperate bunch, he told D'zan, not a worthy swordsman among them. Still they had killed nearly half the crew. The captain survived with a wounded arm, and his men had succeeded in putting out the fires. The ship would hold together long enough to reach Murala . . . assuming no more pirates appeared. D'zan stayed below as the survivors scrubbed blood and offal from the deck with buckets of seawater.

Olthacus and three volunteers stove in the reavers' ship and left it a sinking, empty hulk for the angry waves. He tossed five captured reavers overboard, each chained to the corpses of their slain brothers. They sank like boulders, screaming as their lungs filled with brine. D'zan imagined them joining that undersea army of tireless marching dead, but he kept such thoughts to himself.

A few days later they saw the green coast again, and there stood Murala, as unimpressive as a city could be. Yet she represented dry land, an end to the terrors of the sea, and D'zan had never been more elated to reach any destination. Beyond this humble township lay the Stormlands with all their mystery and promise.

The streets were cobbled and muddy, and the air stank of horseflesh, manure, and woodsmoke. Walking on solid ground felt strange, and D'zan stumbled. Olthacus' strong hand was always there to grab his shoulder and get him upright before any of the scattered commoners noticed. They both wore black cloaks which hid their southern clothing, and the Stone impressed on him how important it was to stay unnoticed until they reached Uurz. But the busy folk of Murala hardly seemed to see them; foreign sailors and merchant crews were common here, and when they entered the central bazaar the noise and spectacle of commerce made them entirely indistinguishable among the masses.

Now D'zan's stomach growled and his mouth watered at the smell of baking bread, roasted beef, braised pork, and a heady blend of raw spices. He wanted to stop at the first meat vendor's table, but the Stone drew him onward, ignoring the booths of brightly colored silks, the wine shops, the armories, the spice barrels, the sweetmeats laid out like delicious jewelry. Goats and sheep bleated on the auction block, and somewhere a band of musicians played a strange northern song with drums, flute, and lyre. Dancing girls swirled in masses of diaphanous silk, smacking tambourines as eager sailors tossed them coins.

Olthacus ignored all of these temptations and many more besides. He drew D'zan into a narrow street where the signs of a half-dozen lodging houses hung from poles over wooden doors reinforced with strips of greenish bronze. Beyond each door rang the sounds of revelry, drunken sailing songs, and female voices raised to enchanting pitch, or simply the jovial bellowing of drunkards. The Stone chose a house carved with the unlikely sign of a golden skull with imitation sapphires in its eye sockets. Inside the smoky den a profusion of tables and commoners ignored their entry, and the smell of cooked food was overwhelming.

D'zan hardly remembered the Stone paying for their stay, or his long conversation with the southern-born innkeeper. He dove into a steaming bowl of pork stew with potatoes, carrots, and other northern vegetables, served with slabs of warm bread. It was the finest meal he had ever tasted. He drank too much of the wine that accompanied the meal, and soon found himself in the comfort of a warm bed, in a room whose decor he didn't bother to inspect. The Stone laid himself down on a rug near the roaring fireplace, and that was the last thing D'zan remembered. He slept without dreams, warm and dry for the first time in what seemed like forever.

A serving girl woke him the next day well past mid-morning, and the Stone was gone. At first D'zan knew panic, then he realized the girl had run a hot bath for him. She did not speak the southern dialects, but his father had insisted he learn all the major languages of the realms, so he thanked her in her own language. This made her laugh greatly, and she left him a plate of fruit and cheese for breakfast.

He bathed before the water grew cold, then dressed in his laundered clothing and broke his fast. The girl did not return. *Too bad*, he thought, *she was quite beautiful*. A simple beauty, dark of skin and hair. These northerners were dusky-skinned like his own people, but their hair was almost always black or heavy brown. The folk of Yaskatha were fair-haired. He thought of the many palace girls whose attentions he'd enjoyed before . . .

before Elhathym destroyed his world. How many of those golden lasses had perished in the takeover? How many had risen again as—

No. He must put such thoughts out of his head.

There are other sorcerers in this world, the Stone had said. Elhathym's magic could be countered with another, stronger magic. But how would a deposed Prince gather such great powers to his cause? Olthacus would know.

As if summoned by D'zan's thoughts, Olthacus the Stone opened the door and stepped into the room. His breastplate and helm were polished to a silvery sheen, the embossed standard of the sword and tree bright upon his chest. His beard was still unshaven, but clean now, and he appeared much refreshed. Yet he still seethed with that same air of urgency that had driven him since the fall of Yaskatha.

"Majesty, I've found us horses," he announced.

D'zan nodded, drinking a cup of honeyed milk. "When must we leave?" he asked.

"Now."

D'zan pulled on his boots. "Can we not stay here a bit longer? It is . . . comfortable."

"No, Prince," said the Stone. "It is not safe. Nor will it be safe for us anywhere until we find sanctuary. We are for Uurz, and right away. You always liked riding, eh?"

D'zan nodded. He was a good horseman. When he turned twelve his father had given him White Flame, a highbred steed. For the first time, he missed the horse. He wondered if the royal stables had burned when the palace caught fire. *Don't think of that; think of the road ahead.*

The horses were pale imitations of the champion stallions bred by Yaskathan horselords, but they were strong and swift. In the inn's muddy courtyard Olthacus loaded both animals with packs of hastily prepared food and gourds of water. D'zan climbed into the stirrups and introduced himself to his steed.

"Does it have a name?" he asked, petting the horse's mottled neck.

"I didn't ask the seller," said the Stone, pulling himself up into his own saddle.

The horse neighed and stamped the mud lightly beneath D'zan, and he decided the beast was good-tempered enough.

"I'll name him then," said D'zan. The Stone was silent, adjusting the sword belt over his shoulder. A brand-new crossbow hung from his saddle, and a quiver of bronze-tipped bolts. Was Olthacus expecting trouble on the road to Uurz?

"You are Northwind," D'zan told the horse, rubbing its neck.

"And mine?" asked the Stone. Every now and then he indulged the Prince in a boyish whim or two.

"Yours is Stormcloud," said D'zan.

"Very good," said the Stone, looking at the steed below him as if truly seeing it for the first time. "Then may Northwind and Stormcloud speed us to the City of the Sacred Waters."

Olthacus steered his trotting horse through the courtyard gate, D'zan and Northwind following close behind.

Thunder split the air, and a soft rain began to fall. The horses carried them slowly through the crowded streets until they reached the eastern edge of Murala, and the green plain stretched away toward a gray horizon where lightning danced between heaven and earth. The wide unpaved road cut across the plain with hardly any curves. There were no hills here to speak of, hardly any trees . . . just wide-open flatland and tall green grasses waving in the winds. D'zan smelled fresh rain on the air. He spurred his horse and galloped away from Murala with Olthacus riding alongside him. A grassy wind caught up his hair, and he found himself smiling for the first time since leaving home.

He glanced back at the gray-green ocean and the black roofs of smoky Murala one last time. He would not miss the ocean.

But he might miss that girl in the Inn of the Skull and Sapphires.

Each day on the road, it rained. Sometimes the rain came in gentle sheets, other times in driving squalls, when thunder and lightning split the sky. They rode between blue lakes surrounded by groves of slim green trees. Often farmhouses sat near the lakes, and on the second day the road ran through a tiny village. Olthacus and D'zan did not stop to ask the hamlet's name, or to see if there might be a dry public house in which to sleep. They slept instead well off the road, nestled among the tall grasses. The thrill of traveling on solid ground soon disappeared for D'zan. His cloak and garments were soaked through with rainwater, and at night he sat shivering by the campfire, drinking brandy. It warmed his bones, but the damp was an ever-present nuisance.

Along the road itself they met scattered traffic. Small groups of riders or single horsemen, the occasional ox-drawn caravan bound for trading in Murala. Most wagons bore the green-and-gold sun banner of Uurz. Once a merchant rode by in a chariot pulled by three white stallions, his servants riding behind on a covered wagon filled with kegs of Uurzian wine. Behind the wine wagon came a cloistered carriage where the merchant's wife and daughters rode, a guard of five armed horsemen surrounding them. The merchants of Uurz were among the wealthiest folk in the northlands. D'zan caught only a glimpse of the merchant's daughters, dark eyes above gossamer veils as they peered at him from narrow windows, and then they were gone.

On the evening of the fourth night Olthacus killed a hare with his crossbow and roasted it over a small fire. D'zan sipped his brandy and tried to get the Stone talking. If left unprompted, Olthacus would remain silent for days at a time. Tonight the rain had died to a warm drizzle, and D'zan was tired of silence.

"Is it true what they say?" he asked the Stone. "This place used to be a desert?"

The Stone nodded, turning the hare on its spit. Its flesh crackled and smoked, emitting a pleasant aroma. "When last I was here, it was nothing but sand and rocks for hundreds of leagues," he said.

"You were here?" D'zan asked. "In the Stormlands . . . When?"

"Before you were born, Majesty," said Olthacus. "I accompanied your father to visit the Emperor. The old one . . . Iryllah. They say he was killed by Giants. Some say his death caused the rebirth of the land."

"Is it true?"

Olthacus shrugged. "Others say it was Vod the Giant-King, Bringer of Storms, Child of Thunder."

"I know that story," said D'zan. "Eikus, my history tutor, made me read about it in the *Book of Northern Histories*. Good old Eikus . . . he's probably dead now."

Olthacus ignored this last comment. "The way I hear it, the Serpent-Father burned this land to ash a thousand years ago, turned it to desert. Used to be some fairly big lizards here as I remember. Tasted terrible." He licked some grease off his finger and adjusted the cooking hare once again. "Vod was raised by humans, or so they say. When he found out that his true father was devoured by the Lord of Serpents, he took up his sire's axe and marched north beyond the Grim Mountains. There the Serpent had conquered the City of Giants, killing most and driving away the rest. Vod used his father's axe to slay the Serpent, and when the beast died the rains returned to the desert, the grasses began to grow. The land came to life again. It used to be called the

Desert of Many Thunders. Now they call it Stormlands. With all this rain, it's no wonder."

"In the book," said D'zan, "Vod was a sorcerer. He grew to the size of a mountain, strangled the Serpent-Father, and drank his flaming blood. Then he marched southward, and his footsteps cracked open the earth. Rivers poured from the underworld and an ancient curse was lifted. In a single year the desert blossomed into a green paradise. That's what the book said . . . but I never truly believed it."

"Do you believe it now, Prince?"

A peal of distant thunder moaned across the sky. "Yes," said D'zan. After witnessing the terrible power of Elhathym, he would never again doubt the tales of sorcerers.

"Olthacus," D'zan said as they devoured the crisp hare-flesh. "Can we not go to this Giant-King and make him our ally? Surely he has power to rival Elhathym."

"Aye, and an army of Giants to boot," said the Stone, smacking his lips.

"Then why go to Uurz?" said D'zan. "Eikus told me King Vod rebuilt the City of Giants and invited men to live there. Why not go to him instead?"

Olthacus frowned and guzzled a cup of brandy. "New Udurum is much farther than Uurz, Prince," he said. "The Grim Mountains lie between us and Vod's city. And they say those mountains are haunted by the ghosts of all the Serpents slain by Giants . . . and even worse things."

D'zan sat quiet. He knew precious little about the Emperor of Uurz. Only that he came to power twenty-some years ago, at the time of the land's rebirth. Would Dairon give him sanctuary, pledge to aid him? For that matter, would the Giant-King be any easier to sway?

"Perhaps we will go to Vod's city eventually," said the Stone.

"But Uurz is on our way. The Emperor Dairon rules there, and the Giant-King is his fast ally. If we gain the support of Uurz, we will gain the support of New Udurum and the giants. Be sure of that, Prince."

"And why would either of these monarchs aid us?"

The Stone shrugged. "Perhaps they won't. Perhaps they will. This is for the Gods to decide." The big man laid himself down on a sodden blanket, his greatsword unsheathed and lying across his chest. "Sleep now, Majesty. Tomorrow we ride until we see the gates of Uurz."

D'zan finished his wine and lay down. Moonlight found its way through the cloud cover, sparkling on a million drops of rain along the edges of tall grass blades.

If each of these green blades was a sword, I would have my army. Though perhaps it would be better to have a single sorcerer at my side.

At dawn they awoke and remounted. Storms gathered quietly in the pink and purple sky as they galloped the final leagues toward Uurz. Near midday, in the midst of a steady rain, they came within sight of the city's outer wall. It rose upon the horizon and gleamed like wet gold. Above it a hundred gilded towers shone against the clouds, and the sun struck brilliant sparks against those spires.

Here the road was paved, and the first of many great estates lined the way. Orchards, grazing pastures, and croplands stretched across the plains as far as the eye could see. Giant palm trees sat alongside the road at regular intervals, and side avenues were numerous. These were the agricultural plantations that gave sustenance to the gleaming city and grew the grapes that made the famous Uurzian wines. The workers on these farms wore loose-fitting pantaloons and leather vests, though most went barefoot through the muddy fields. Their children ran free and laughing in the gentle rain.

They seem happy, D'zan thought, watching the adults at work and the children at play. *How long has it been since I knew such happiness? Will I ever know it again?*

Now was not the time for such thoughts, so he locked them away.

Six days on the road had brought them to the Great Gate of Uurz, and now they approached its massive open slabs. A perpetual crowd of commoners and noble folk came in and out of the wall's single portal. The two southern riders joined the crowds seeking entry at this hour and found themselves in a great line of mounted travelers, horse-drawn carriages, and wagons pulled by oxen or wetland camels. As they waited for ingress, D'zan studied the brown faces of the guards. Their bronze armor shone like gold, and their spears stood twice as tall as the men themselves. Their swords were straight-forged in the northern manner, and they wore cloaks of green stitched with golden suns. That same emblem decorated their round shields. Along the top of the wall, guard towers watched over the surrounding lands for many leagues. The wall was taller than any D'zan had seen, and he recalled the legend of its impenetrability. Even the Giants, long ago, had tried to tear down this wall, and failed.

He saw no Giants outside the gates today, and felt a bit disappointed.

Just before sunset D'zan and Olthacus crossed the threshold of the Great Gate and entered the city proper. The first thing D'zan noticed here was the sound of music. It seemed a dozen minstrels were playing on every corner, strains high and lilting, or low and throbbing. The stone buildings were on top of each other, often literally, and roof gardens rang with merriment, dripping with vines and living blossoms. The streets were paved with flat cobbles, black stones that rang beneath the hooves of a thousand thousand horses, and the gutters ran heavy with foaming rainwater.

Gigantic palms stood sentinel over taverns, manors, and common houses. The smells of blooming orchids, spiced pastries, and perfumed ladies nearly overpowered the more pedestrian odors of animal dung and hearth smoke. Not even in Yaskatha had D'zan smelled such clean streets. Uurz might indeed be a paradise. Or as close to it as any earthly place could be.

Everywhere Uurzians walked and laughed and danced and haggled and shouted. D'zan spied a trio of girls atop a lush roof garden as he rode past, and each of them seemed to be winking at him. Olthacus ignored the women of Uurz as he ignored all the city's wonders. His eyes were fixed upon the golden towers at the city's hub, and D'zan knew they would find the Emperor's palace there, at the very center of this great hive of green and gold.

Night fell softly upon Uurz, and the lights of the city came alive. A hundred thousand lanterns cast their warmth across the damp streets, and cheerful groups of youths gallivanted along the lanes. Olthacus, who had been here when the land was dry and parched, had no trouble finding the gates of the royal grounds. The palace stood taller and wider than Yaskatha's own. Its hundreds of windows gleamed in all the colors of the rainbow, some trick of the painted glass. A half-moon rose above the soaring spires, taking on the golden hue of the edifice. Even the moon was jealous of this place and tried to imitate its beauty. The courtyards about the palace proper were thick with trees, a miniature forest rising above the spiked walls. Guards walked the ramparts in pairs, and such a pair on the street hailed Olthacus as he rode toward the barred entry.

"No sightseeing after dark," said the guard, a phrase he was evidently accustomed to repeating. "Come back tomorrow."

The Stone brought his horse to a halt, and D'zan followed his example.

"Olthacus, General of Yaskatha, Right Hand of King Trimesqua, seeks audience with His Majesty Emperor Dairon."

Both guards perked up, eyeing Olthacus from beneath the rims of their helmets, then scanning over D'zan. "You carry the seal of Trimesqua?"

Olthacus showed the man his ring. The guards bowed, then opened the gate. An attendant came forth to guide them through the splendid courtyard. The scents here were overpowering, ripe fruit and flowery nectar, all the finest shrubs, hedges, and trees meticulously arranged for maximum aesthetic value. D'zan wished it were daylight so he might better appreciate the renowned gardens. Perhaps there would be time for that, if he found the sanctuary he sought in this place.

The horses were led off to the stables, and the attendant conducted them through a columned portico into an outer hall of the palace. Statues of marble and granite lined the walls, and servants brought them wine in jeweled cups. The vintage was of the finest quality, and a deep drink made D'zan's head spin. Olthacus quaffed it like water. Eventually they were shown to a smallish chamber furnished with velvet couches, beaded tapestries, and a table of polished black wood. At the head of the table stood a young man dressed in the gold and green of the royal family, a necklace of opals on his chest, a coronet of silver and ruby about his forehead. His thick hair was black and curly, falling to his shoulders, and his face clean-shaven. His arms were brawny, and he radiated the demeanor of a soldier. A short-bladed sword hung from his wide belt in a scabbard crusted with gems.

"Olthacus of Yaskatha?" asked the soldier.

The Stone nodded and dropped to one knee. D'zan was unsure of what to do, so he stood quietly and observed. Surely this youth was not the Emperor of Uurz.

"I am Prince Tyro, son of Emperor Dairon. My father regrets that he cannot greet you in person."

"When last I saw you, Majesty," said the Stone, "you were a babe in your mother's arms."

"So they tell me," said Tyro, smiling. His sharp eyes turned to D'zan, who felt suddenly dirty and disheveled. He hardly looked the part of a Prince today, caked with mud and sweat, smelling of horseflesh.

The Stone introduced him. "May I present to you Prince D'zan, Son of Trimesqua. Heir of Yaskatha."

Tyro's eyes narrowed. He bowed to D'zan, who returned the courtesy. "I am honored to welcome you to Uurz. Please sit. There is food and drink."

Servants appeared from behind the tapestries and laid out a feast. D'zan found himself entirely without appetite. He had many questions, but he did not know what to say. So his eyes turned to Olthacus.

"We thank you for your hospitality, Majesty," said the Stone. "Too long it has been since I've tasted the fare of your house."

Tyro waved the servants away. He seemed uninterested in food or drink.

"Traders brought news of Trimesqua's fall only days ago," said Tyro, addressing D'zan now. "The Emperor mourns your loss."

"I . . . thank you, Prince," said D'zan.

"You have traveled far and your journey must have been taxing. You will find safety and comfort within these walls. These are the Emperor's own words."

D'zan thanked him again, somewhat awkwardly.

"Please . . . eat, drink," said Tyro. "There will be plenty of time to talk when you have bathed and rested. My father will see you on the morrow. Tonight he is otherwise engaged."

Olthacus attacked the delicious fare, and D'zan found his own appetite. Tyro ate little, and was polite enough not to stare as the two hungry riders sated their appetites. A second princely figure glided into the room. His broad face resembled Tyro's, but he was skinny, his nose a tad longer, and a coronet supported a trio of emeralds above his eyes. He carried in his arms a great book bound in worn leather.

"Ah, my brother Lyrilan joins us," said Tyro, "having found his way out of the musty depths of the library. A rare occurrence, Prince D'zan. You are met with interest."

The thin Prince smiled at D'zan and stood at the end of the table.

"He is a *scholar*, you see," explained Tyro with the faintest trace of scorn.

D'zan caught the hidden meaning of those few words: *But he ought to be a soldier.*

"Greetings to you, Prince Lyrilan," said Olthacus, wiping his mouth with a silken napkin. "May I present Prince D'zan of Yaskatha . . . "

Lyrilan smiled at D'zan, offering the briefest of bows. "Forgive my curiosity," he said. "Tyro usually handles matters of state. News of your arrival only just reached me, and I wanted to pay my respects. I've been reading, you see . . . "

Prince Tyro laughed. "When are you *not* reading?"

Prince Lyrilan ignored the question. He laid the great book on the end of the table, well away from the nearest dish. "Your father, King Trimesqua, was a great man," he said. His fingers absently traced the engraved patterns on the book's cover. "A great warrior. A hero in thought and deed. It is an honor to have you here. I have many questions about Trimesqua's life."

"Brother!" interrupted Tyro. "Our guests have only just arrived."

"No, it's all right," said D'zan. The potent wine made him feel at ease, and there was something about this skinny Prince he liked immediately. Perhaps it was simply nice to hear someone speak so highly of his father. "What is that book you're carrying?"

Lyrilan lifted the volume to display the embossed cover, its title written in the northern dialect. "*Odysseys of the Southern Kings*," he said. "It lists the entirety of your family history going back three hundred years. Did you know your father slew a sea monster that devoured a thousand ships? The Beast of Barragur, they called it. He freed the shipping lanes for a generation of trade."

D'zan smiled. Of course he knew that story. "My father told me that one several times."

Lyrilan's eyes lit up like twin candles. "Fascinating! This is why I had to meet you. There is only so much you can learn from a book. I'll bet you have hundreds of stories to tell."

"If you want to know the best stories, ask the Stone." D'zan indicated Olthacus, who was chewing on a leg of fowl. "He and my father travelled the world together . . . long before I was born."

Olthacus nodded, his mouth full of meat.

"Plenty of time for that," said Prince Tyro, rising from his chair. "Lyrilan, don't tire our guests any further."

The Uurzian Princes said goodnight, and robed attendants led the guests through a maze of sumptuous corridors to their sleeping quarters. Olthacus insisted on sharing the same room as D'zan, and the servants finally relented. They had prepared a separate room for the big warrior, but there was no changing his mind.

D'zan stripped off his soiled road-clothes and climbed into the chamber's great soft bed while Olthacus lay down on the cushions of a broad couch. The moon gleamed through a leaf-shaped window, casting its beams among miniature trees growing around the chamber. Sleep took D'zan before he could even say good night.

*

It must have been the whisper of a naked foot on the marble floor that woke him. Something dark loomed over his bed, and a cold ray of moonlight gleamed above it. The knife came flashing downward, aimed at his throat, but never reached it. Instead, a shower of warm blood splashed his face and sheets. A severed hand fell on the pillow.

A scream rose in the bleeding man's throat, but Olthacus' next sword-blow took off his head. D'zan lay paralyzed and bloody, barely conscious of what was happening.

Then the Stone's voice filled the chamber, shocking him into alertness. "Up, D'zan! Run for the hall! Call the guards!"

D'zan rolled out of bed, nearly vomiting. He landed atop the headless, leaking carcass. The clash of metal met his ears from the other side of the bed, and he glanced up to see Olthacus kill another man. Like the headless one, he wore tight-fitting garments of black silk, his face obscured by a smooth mask of ebony.

The dead man's knife lay on the floor, and D'zan grabbed it. From hilt to point it was carved of a single jade piece. The blade was smeared with purple flakes, some kind of venom. He ran for the door as Olthacus screamed.

Two spearmen rushed in to protect the bloodstained Prince. Their corselets gleamed silver-gray in the moonlight.

The Stone sank his great sword point first into the belly of a third assassin, and the man died without a sound. Three dead men lay across the chamber, and Olthacus stood near the open window, his hands now empty and dripping red.

More guards rushed through the door, but there were no more assailants. The Stone had killed them all. Someone pulled D'zan out of the room, but he pushed his way back inside. Olthacus sat on the couch where he had been sleeping. The green hilt of an assassin's knife protruded from the big man's chest just above his heart. His sword lay across the chamber, still embedded in the body of his last opponent. The Stone's mouth was open, and he gasped for air like a landed fish.

D'zan shoved his way through the guards. The Stone's eyes focused on the ceiling, ignoring the poisoned blade protruding from his chest.

"Olthacus!" D'zan cried, but the Stone remained silent. His eyes fixed on the patterns of the ceiling, swirling traceries in the shape of grape vines spreading from wall to wall. D'zan grabbed the jade hilt and pulled the dagger free. Someone announced that the royal physician was on his way.

D'zan shook the Stone by his shoulders. The veins in the warrior's neck and face stood out starkly purple. His eyes were orbs of cloudy glass.

D'zan shouted his name again, but the Stone never moved. He sat as still as his namesake on the blood-spattered couch in the blood-drenched chamber.

Even when the physician arrived with bandage, elixir, and stitching, the Stone's wide eyes remained fixed on the golden grape-leaf ceiling.

They stayed that way until the physician's gentle fingertips pulled them shut.

4

Evening in Udurum

Thousands of books lined the shelves of King Vod's library, and hundreds of scrolls from every kingdom known to man. The pelts of wild beasts hung between the towering bookshelves, and the fanged skull of a great Serpent lay on a central pedestal beneath a dome of transparent quartz. A dozen torches flickered in sconces like the yawning mouths of gargoyles. The room was spacious enough for a Giant to comfortably peruse the shelves, but Giants did not read. Only their shamans knew the magic of capturing ideas into runes, and all their shamans were dead for two decades now. Sharadza sat in her father's reading chair and pored over tome after tome, finding only frustration in the musty pages.

She sighed as she closed the most recent volume, re-clasping its lock of bronze and staring at its embossed cover. If *The Codex of Ancient Knowledge* did not contain the secrets for which she searched, what hope did she have of finding it anywhere else? She had read at least a hundred such works in the month since her father went marching westward to give himself to the Sea Queen. Her mother made daily offerings to the Four Gods, Earth, Sky, Sea, and Sun, but Sharadza held little faith in her mother's religion. Queen Shaira had learned her faith during a childhood in distant Shar Dni. Sharadza could never admit it to her mother, but she did not believe at all in those faceless Gods.

Unseen powers of earth and air would not help her father, any more than his army of men and giants could. This was a matter of deepest sorcery, a curse that haunted Vod from before the birth of his children. The only way to fight it was through sorcery. In all the tales she'd ever read in the history texts, in all the legends told her by Fellow, even in the tales of traveling singers who visited Udurum, there was never any story of a sorcerer defeated by anything less than a more powerful sorcery. Her father was a sorcerer of legendary reputation – he rebuilt the crumbled city, slew the Lord of Serpents, and brought green life to the Old Desert – but he had given himself over to this curse and would not fight it. He was a man of honor, and that she understood. But *she* was not bound by the curse. If she could only learn sorcery, she might aid him in his time of need. She might defy the vengeance of the Sea Queen.

Had Vod reached the ocean shore yet? She checked the date on a nearby calendar. Any day now Vod's chariot would come upon the Cryptic Sea, and he would cast himself into the lightless depths. Time was running out. Unless . . . unless his magic prevented him from drowning. Would he walk the sea bottom for leagues until he reached the Sea Queen's aqueous palace? If the sea itself did not rob his life instantly, there might still be time for her to learn. Time to call up some dark power and send it to redeem her father.

She lowered her head to the dusty cover of the book, and tears welled in her eyes. She was tired of weeping; she felt dried up inside. But there was nothing in this damnable library to tell her, nothing that opened her mind to the secrets of sorcery. Why did her father keep all these books if they had nothing to do with his sorcery? Her grief turned suddenly to anger. She tossed the heavy book to the floor and kicked over her chair as she stood and wiped at her cheeks. This place was useless. Her brothers might accept that their father was doomed, but she would never believe it.

Damn them for being so chained to his will! Their sense of honor prevents them from defying him, even to save his life . . .

She called for a servant to darken the library, gathered up her cloak of purple wool, and stalked into the hallway. Tadarus and her mother were in the council chambers meeting with members of the giant and human populations, discussing taxes, tariffs, and other meaningless minutiae. Let them waste their time with such trivial notions; she would not sit and pretend that her father was not approaching death at this very moment. Signaling her personal escort, two soldiers by the names of Dorus and Mitri, she exited the palace through the lesser gate. The two men gathered up their shields and followed, but knew she was in no mood to wait so left behind their winged helms. She could not enter the city proper without their presence, or a single Giant guard. But the Giants drew far too much attention. She preferred these man-sized guardians; the fact that they were dumber than giants was a plus.

Evening in the City of Men and Giants was pleasant. Orange sunlight warmed the black stone of the towers. The lanes were dry today, and the sky was blue, filled with scattered cotton clouds. Since Vod had departed, there was hardly any rain, and no storms at all. It appeared that an age of warmth and sunlight had fallen on New Udurum, but Sharadza knew it for what it was: a drought caused by her father's absence. The weather of Vod's kingdom had always reflected his moods. Now an *absence* boiled in the azure sky, a smothering *lack* that nobody seemed to feel but her. Laughter boomed from open doors, and the drinking songs of Giants rang inside vast taverns as she walked the Street of

Grains. Such jollity only made her more angry. The entire city should be in mourning, but life seemed to go on as if Vod had never gone off to die.

"Majesty, would you rather we call up a coach for you?" asked Mitri, clomping along beside her in bronze-plated boots.

She shook her head. She didn't feel like reminding him that he wasn't supposed to talk to her. Or that doing so while she was in this mood was even less of a good idea. She did not want to say anything cruel, so she remained silent. They turned onto the Avenue of Legends, where the crowds were thicker. Along this wide thoroughfare the number of taverns, wine shops, and entertainment venues increased dramatically. Several Giant-sized drinking houses rumbled with mirth, although some of the human taverns grew even louder. Jugglers, musicians, and street performers lined the avenue. Peddlers pushed carts full of sweetmeats, apparel, or souvenirs in the form of figurines shaped like Giants. Ladies of the evening stood in doorways or windows, flaunting their fleshy wares. When visitors came from the southern lands, as they often did, they flocked to this wanton part of the city. Sharadza did not like it here, but it was the one place where she was sure to find Fellow.

She entered a plaza hemmed by enormous bronze statues of heroes (Giants) lifting spear, axe, and shield to the sky. This was the Square of Storytellers. A dozen groups of men, women, and children, and even a few Giants, gathered around the various talespinners here. Most of the orators stood on low wooden platforms, some on the bases of the great statues themselves, telling the stories of whichever hero loomed above.

Fellow sat on the rim of a marble fountain at the center of the square, beneath the pinions of a winged horse bubbling water from its muzzle. Fellow's gaudy robes set him apart from the general crowd. Those gathered about him wore the simple garb of farmhands, laborers, artisans, and craftsmen. A handful of foreigners bore the sand-yellow garb and jeweled turbans of Shar Dni. This was a good crowd for Fellow. His upturned hat was full of bronze and silver coins, and even a sealed bottle of southern vintage. Sharadza bade her guards stay back as she crept to join Fellow's audience – she did not wish to disturb his story or those enraptured by it. Nevertheless, the old man's eyes turned to meet hers immediately. He always knew when she came into his plaza, as if he had a sixth sense for comely Princesses. She forced a wan smile at him as he continued telling his story.

"So the Men of Diiranor came to the lost city of Maethos, and since they had lost their King, they were determined to avenge him. A great battle began as a horde of Ancient Terrors crawled up from below the broken walls. It is said this battle lasted for three days, and its heroes were young Tagyl and his cousin Gyrid, whose swords spilled the blood of a thousand Terrors. So I will tell you of these two heroes and how they liberated the lost city from evil . . . if you return here tomorrow when the sun sets."

The crowd moaned and pleaded for more while Sharadza grinned at their backs. Fellow always did this; in fact, every storyteller did. It seemed the audience forgot every single time and always tried to cajole or bribe the teller into continuing the tale. But Fellow waved them away with smiles and yawns, saying he was an old man and could only tell one bit of a saga per evening. "Besides," he told some of the younger listeners, "if you are respectful to the Gods, the rest of the story might come to you in your dreams tonight." Sharadza doubted if this ever actually happened, but it soothed the passions of disappointed children.

The crowd dispersed, and Sharadza approached Fellow. He emptied the jingling contents of his hat into a shoulder pouch. The bottle of wine he kept in hand . . . It would not last long. "Princess!" he greeted her with a slight bow. "Our next meeting was to be tomorrow at midday . . . or did I forget?"

"You never forget, I'd bet on it," Sharadza said. "I wish to speak in private. Is there some place?"

Fellow motioned toward Dorus and Mitri. "What about the royal goons?" he asked.

"I am forced to endure their protection," she said. "But I can order them to sit away from us that we may talk."

Fellow nodded, sat his patchwork hat atop his white head, and led her across the way toward a small tavern. Above the door hung the image of a silver bird perched on a burning branch. "I have a standing table in the Molten Sparrow," he said. They walked down a set of narrow stairs into a small deserted common room. Certainly no Giant could fit in here, and any other day she would have laughed at Dorus and Mitri as they struggled to squeeze themselves through the narrow entrance. She handed Mitri a gold coin and ordered them to drink on the other side of the room. They knew well enough her temper not to argue with her.

Fellow and she sat at a curtained booth in the back. "Best leave the curtain open so they can see me," she advised. Fellow ordered two clean cups for the wine he'd just earned. He studied the bottle, popped the cork and sniffed the vintage. "Aaaahhh . . . this one is from Yaskatha," he said. "Someone was feeling generous today."

Sharadza did not wait for the wine to be poured. She had waited long enough.

"Fellow, you are known to tell stories about sorcerers."

Fellow poured them both a generous portion of the deep red vintage. The cups were bronze, but Sharadza's was studded with imitation garnets. The innkeeper knew he had special company and this was the best he could do on short notice. He came forward to offer more services, but Fellow waved him away.

"You have heard a few such tales from me," he said before

taking his first sip of the Yaskathan wine. He closed his eyes a moment, savoring the flavor. Sharadza ignored her own cup.

"Have you any stories – any at all – about how these sorcerers gained their terrible powers?"

Fellow pondered the question, swirling the wine, inhaling its bouquet. "How does a Giant become a Giant? Or a man become a man? Why ask such an obscure question?"

Sharadza sighed and tasted the drink. It was biting, but excellent. The sunlight of a distant land had worked its magic on these grapes and cast a delicious spell. She licked her lips.

"I have been over and over the texts in my father's collection," she said. "There is nothing there that gives me any clue to his learning magic. Are you implying that he was . . . *born* a sorcerer?"

Fellow drank again, slowly, transfixed by the sun magic. "He was born a Giant, and Giants have sorcery in their very bones. It swims in their blood. Some say it was sorcery that created them."

"Not the Gods, then?" she said.

"Who says the Gods created Giants? Or Men, for that matter?"

"My mother."

Fellow smiled. "The Gods of Shar Dni are credited with mighty works, as are all the Gods of Men. The truth might be more evasive than priests and sages suspect. The world is a series of stories, Princess, and the tellers are often forgotten."

"Do you know how my father learned sorcery?"

The old man stared at her, dark pupils fixed on her green ones. One hand stroked his pale mustache. Cheap rings of bronze and glass lined his bony fingers.

"He made a bargain," Fellow whispered, "with someone who knew far more than he did. It was a bargain he regretted even to this day, I'm told."

"Who was it?" she asked. "I want to make such a bargain."

"No," he said, drinking deeper now. "You do not."

"You said Giants were created from sorcery. Well, my father was a Giant, and my father created me."

"He and your mother," Fellow corrected.

"Some say my mother is a sorceress. But I don't believe it."

"Nor should you," said Fellow. "Your mother is a fine woman, a brave Queen, a heroine to her people. Now she bears the burden of rulership like a bronze yoke on her shoulders. It is no easy task to rule a kingdom."

"Answer my question," Sharadza said. "I love my mother, but I'm not made in her image. There is more of my father in me." She picked up the bronze cup and squeezed it hard. The metal crumpled like paper in her fist. Wine ran across the table, dripping onto the floor like dark blood. "I have his strength . . . or some of it. Like Tadarus and Vireon."

"You believe that you might possess some of his sorcery."

"I know I do," she said. "And if I am right I can save him, Fellow! I can deliver him from the Sea Queen's curse!"

Fellow said nothing.

"Can you help me? *Will* you?"

Fellow drank deep, emptying his cup, then wiped his stained lip with a sleeve of triple colors. "You cannot learn sorcery from a book," he said. "No more than you can learn strength from a book. Or compassion. Or love."

She stared at him. She sensed it now . . . this storyteller knew the path she must walk.

"You already have strength, compassion, and love," said Fellow. "To master sorcery you must *live* it, as you live these other things. Because you have the first three, I think you may be able to gain the fourth."

She smiled. Here was what she had been searching for in all those moth-eaten old books. She was at the threshold of a new existence. Her skin tingled.

"Are you willing to accept the pain of Knowledge?" he asked. "For there will be pain."

"For my father's sake, I am ready."

"You may not save your father, even if you master the arts of which we speak. The Sea Queen is ancient and powerful."

"And my father may already be dead," she whispered. "I know this."

"Are you willing not only to succeed . . . but to fail?" he asked.

"If I never try, then failure is certain."

Fellow poured himself more Yaskathan wine. "Another cup?" he asked. She shook her head. He drained the cup in a single draft, then sighed and leaned his head back against the wall.

"First you must leave the city," he said. "And none can see you go. They will search for you, and your mother's heart will break."

"I will leave her a letter," said Sharadza. "She will understand."

"She will *not*," said Fellow, shaking his head. "Never."

"Where must I go?"

"North," he said. "Into the woods."

She could hardly believe the hot spark of hope that burned inside her where cold gloom had lingered for weeks. She trusted Fellow, and she would follow him *anywhere* for a chance to save her father.

"Alone," said Fellow.

The Queen of New Udurum received her brother's son not in the grand throne room, but in a smaller and more intimate hall. Tapestries of velvet covered the walls with scenes of Giants battling leviathans and toppling mountains. Fangodrel found the Uduru's ancestor worship boring and offensive. How many of these Giant heroes truly existed, and how many were the figments of dim imaginations? The Giants were dying off anyway, so it made sense they would look backward instead of forward.

They had a history but no real future. The dumb brutes were being replaced in their own kingdom and they did not even realize it.

The King of Shar Dni was Ammon, brother to Shaira, and therefore Fangodrel's uncle. That made this pompous blowhard, Prince Andoses, his cousin. Fangodrel had little appetite for the feast his mother had laid out for her nephew. Tadarus ate heartily, as always, stuffing his beefy frame with roast piglet, potatoes, and baked confections. Vireon was thankfully nowhere to be seen, and Sharadza was at her studies.

Andoses came seeking favor all the way from Shar Dni with a retinue of two hundred warriors, only to discover the Giant-King had abandoned his throne and left it to his forlorn Queen. Fangodrel held a goblet of wine before his face and listened to Andoses' obsequious rhetoric. He wanted something from Shaira, that much was certain.

"Father wishes he could come himself to visit his beloved sister," said Andoses, "but these troubled times demand his constant attention."

Queen Shaira nodded. She had fallen into a deep gloom after Vod's departure, but she looked genuinely pleased to see her nephew after so many years. She kept to her chambers most days, unless some demanding matter of state called her down. The rest of the time it fell to Tadarus to wrangle with counselors, advisors, and viziers. She had even given Fangodrel some minor responsibilities, just enough to appear kindly. Shaira was too lost in her own sorrow to rule Udurum effectively, and by rights the throne should be his. But Tadarus was the favored one, confirmed by her choice of delegation. Fangodrel avoided looking at his brother across the table. He kept his eyes on Prince Andoses, the cousin who was three years younger than him, yet commanded a cohort of warriors.

"I understand," said the Queen. "A season of strife falls upon us all. But no matter the cause, it is good to see you again. How are my sisters?"

"Fine, one and all," said Andoses. His face was dusky, his eyes green like Shaira's. A single emerald sat in the center of his turban, and his robes of yellow silk were strung with teardrops of silver. Servants had carried away his fine scimitar and war helm.

"Dara speaks of you often," said Andoses, referring to Shaira's youngest sister. "She expects her first child next season."

Shaira smiled, a brief ray of light in a cloudy sky. "I miss my sisters most of all," she said. "But what news of my brothers?"

Andoses set down his cup. "Bad news, I'm afraid. Omirus thrives as commander of father's fleet . . . but Vidictus was murdered."

Shaira caught her breath. Tadarus ceased his incessant chewing. Fangodrel listened closely, still hiding behind his goblet.

Tears escaped the Queen's eyes as Andoses explained. "He was killed at sea, leading an attack against southern pirates. They have plagued our shipping lanes for years. The Golden Sea is no longer a safe crossing for any ship. Twenty galleons lost in the last year alone. Agents bring us news that these pirate ships belong to the Empress of Khyrei. None can deny that war will soon be upon us."

Shaira spoke, dabbing her eyes with a silken napkin: "Vod nearly slew Ianthe the Claw twenty-five years ago. Later we learned she survived to rule Khyrei."

"The sorceress girds her jungle empire for war. Father will stand her nautical predations no more. That is why he sent me to call upon King Vod and his alliance with Shar Dni. If we are to stand against Khyrei, we will need the support of Udurum."

So there it was. The real reason for this family reunion. Shar Dni seeks the aid of Giants so it can march off to war against the south. Fangodrel sipped his yellow wine.

"Of course we had no news of Vod's leaving," said Andoses.

Tadarus spoke up. "My father left mother in charge of men *and* giants. We, her eldest sons . . . " He glanced briefly at Fangodrel, who said nothing. " . . . will command her armies in your service, if she so wills it."

All eyes turned to the somber Queen. She stared at her golden plate, where the viands lay untouched and cold. "War," she whispered. "What has Vod left me to?"

Fangodrel cleared his throat. A gentle prod in the right direction might make all the difference here. "Mother, if I may speak." He waited for the Queen's gentle nod. "Father long ago secured alliance with Uurz, did he not? Emperor Dairon will respond if you call upon him to aid your brother's kingdom. Surely between the armies of Udurum, Uurz, and Shar Dni, Khyrei cannot stand. I have read much about that kingdom . . . the land is fertile and rich in precious stones. There is much to gain from such a conquest."

"Wars should not be fought for wealth," said Tadarus, "but for honor. These Khyrein predators have none. But you speak truly. Their false empire cannot stand against our righteous alliance."

"Both of my sons speak wisdom," said Shaira. "I will send an emissary to Uurz, to hear the thoughts of my old friend Dairon. And I must think upon this . . . and pray."

Fangodrel stiffened in his chair. *Why must you pray?* he wanted to shout, but held his tongue. *Your Gods care nothing for war. War is the enterprise of men, and women should have no voice in it.* If the fool Tadarus agreed with him, his mother would likely endorse the war. *Perhaps I will command a legion if I speak in bold support for this conflict.*

"War means death and suffering for the innocent as well as those who fight," said Shaira. "It must be carefully considered . . . avoided whenever possible."

Andoses slammed his goblet against the table. "Six hundred men have died already, Queen. The crews of those twenty ships had families, some of them onboard at the time of the raids. The Khyreins show no mercy. More will die in the coming months, as more battles are fought at sea. And how long until the Empress sends her armies north to take Shar Dni itself?"

Silence filled the chamber for a long moment. Shaira looked at her nephew, unoffended by his bluntness. "I am aware that more than poor Vidictus have died. I will not let my grief intrude upon my judgment. Thousands upon thousands of lives hang in the balance, Andoses."

"There is something else," said Andoses, tugging at his short, oiled beard. "Yaskatha has fallen to a usurper – another sorcerer if the tales are true. They say his powers are terrible, that he cannot die."

"Superstition and poets' lies," said Tadarus, quaffing wine. "Every man can die."

"It matters not," said Andoses. "For this new Yaskathan King has allied himself with Khyrei. The Yaskathans are mighty on both land and sea."

"That does complicate matters," said Fangodrel. "If they win Mumbaza to their cause as well, the entire south will stand united. What word on Mumbaza's loyalties?"

Andoses grimaced. "The Boy-King Undutu is but twelve years old. His mother, Umbrala, rules from behind the Opal Throne. She denies our ambassadors, as well as those from Khyrei and Yaskatha."

Fangodrel grinned. "Without Mumbaza's interference we stand a much better chance at victory."

Shaira stood up. "You speak as if we have already committed our legions to war. We have not," she said. "*I* have not."

Fangodrel seethed in his chair. Tadarus remained silent as well;

as great and terrible as he was, his mother's disfavor was the only thing he truly feared. Fangodrel hated that about him.

"Since Mumbaza refuses alliance with the southern kingdoms, perhaps she will respond to the generosity and grace of Udurum." Shaira sat herself back down and dismissed the servants who were bringing in a fruit flambeau. "If we sway Queen Umbrala to join us, we will be four nations against two."

Andoses nodded agreement. He had carefully led her to this line of thinking. Fangodrel saw it, even if his mother did not.

"I cannot ignore my brother's plea for help," said the Queen, "or the suffering of my homeland. But I cannot commit the Uduru to war unless they agree. I am their Queen, but only at their sufferance. It was Vod they followed. He was one of their own."

"Let me speak with them, Mother," said Tadarus. "Let me speak to Fangodrim."

"I will speak with them myself, Tadarus. You – and Fangodrel – must go to Uurz and speak with Emperor Dairon. You will have a sizable retinue. Once you have secured Dairon's blessing, go on to Mumbaza. You will take gold, silver, and other treasures of the north to lay at the feet of the Boy-King and his mother."

Her eyes met those of Tadarus. *She never looks me in the eye*, thought Fangodrel.

"You *must* gain the alliance of Mumbaza. Only then will I commit to war with Khyrei."

Tadarus stood. "I will do this, Mother. Have no doubt." He clapped Fangodrel on the shoulder. "My elder brother and I will do this!"

Fangodrel wrinkled his nose. He disliked being touched, especially by Tadarus.

"I will keep Vireon near at hand," said Shaira. "And you,

Andoses, will stay as our guest until they return. Then if the Gods will it and the Uduru support us, we will march east to Shar Dni . . . and south to Khyrei."

Andoses stood and bowed to his aunt. "This journey will take many weeks. I beg you: let me accompany my cousins on this errand. I cannot bear to sit here while others speak on behalf of my father and our kingdom."

Shaira placed her small hand on his shoulder, stared at his face. "You are so like my brothers . . . so like poor Vidictus . . . so like your father. Very well. Go then, you three Princes together. But Vireon stays here."

Tadarus huffed. "He will not like that, Mother."

"He is off on one of his hunts," said the Queen. "By the time he returns, you will be long gone."

Back in his private chamber, Fangodrel's mind swam, and his body twitched.

Where is that cretin Rathwol? He should be waiting at my door. I'll flay his hide.

The Prince stripped off his fine raiment and stood naked to the waist before his mirror. A figure of palest marble, lean as a hungry wolf. The fire in his hearth blazed. This was the moment he had been waiting for. A trip into the Stormlands, and beyond that to Mumbaza. Certainly she was only sending him along with Tadarus to get him out of the way, but he did not care. There were many terrible things that might happen to a lumbering dullard like Tadarus on a long and perilous journey.

He pulled from a drawer his unfinished poem. The scrawled words haunted him. He read again what had taken him so much effort to create. He knew he would never finish it. His life was an unfinished story so how could this piece of verse be complete? How could a living artist ever truly represent life when caught in the middle of its tumult and fury? His poems were lies, futile yammerings unworthy of the ink in which they were scribbled. But this . . . this one should have been his redemption. It should have been the summit of achievement that validated his long climb up the mountain of suffering.

It was imperfect . . . worthless. He was a fraud.

Cursing himself for a misguided fool, he crumpled the parchment and tossed it into the blazing brazier. He watched it curl and blacken, and turn to ash. Tears stung his eyes, but he wiped them away before they could fall.

A knock at the door interrupted his reverie, and he opened it to admit the lanky servant. Rathwol smelled as foul as ever, yet his threadbare tunic had been replaced by a gray satin shirt and cloak of lavender wool, marking him as an official of the court. Fangodrel's personal attendant.

"Where have you been, sluggard?" Fangodrel asked, shutting the door and bolting it.

Rathwol winked, then wiped his dripping nose. The man was a walking sickness. But useful. "Obtaining what you desire, My Lord . . . as always."

"Enough," said the Prince. "Give it here."

Rathwol presented a small coffer of jade and crystal. Fangodrel retrieved a hidden key from his boot and opened the tiny lock. Inside sat five splendid crimson flower-tops pruned from their black stems in some apothecary's shop. He no longer asked or cared where Rathwol bought the bloodflower.

"A nice batch, Lord," said the little man. "Imported straight from the poison jungles of Khyrei – so the man tells me."

Fangodrel pulled off a single soft petal and stuffed it into the bowl of his Serpent pipe. Firing it with a brand from the hearth, he inhaled the sweet smoke and fell into the fat cushions of his divan. Rathwol was a forgotten thing now, as irrelevant as his chamber pot. The Prince's eyes clouded as the bloodflower's magic infused his body.

"Sire, I was wondering," said Rathwol. "Might I try some this time?"

Fangodrel laughed. Filled with a sudden energy, he stood and slapped the little man across his stubbly cheek. "I could sell your whole family and still not afford a single bloom," he said. "So why would I give you a single petal when I could just as easily give you the point of my dagger?"

Rathwol cowered in mock fear.

"Here," said Fangodrel, handing him a large sapphire. "Take this and get me three more coffers. No, as much as you can secure."

"My Lord?"

"I am traveling south, Rathwol," said the Prince. "I'll need enough of this to make the trip pleasant. Oh, and take the remainder to buy yourself a decent horse, and a sword. You're coming with me, as my personal groom. You do know how to groom a steed, don't you?"

"Oh yes, Lord," stammered Rathwol. "I was practically reared in the stables, I was." There was more than enough worth in that single jewel to buy more bloodflower, secure Rathwol's needs, and keep Fangodrel's clandestine activities secret. Rathwol would endure any abuse, as long as he continued getting paid. He was the most trustworthy type of man. The kind you can buy. Or sell, if need be.

"Stop yammering and go find me a girl," said Fangodrel. "I need a diversion. Be quick about it."

Rathwol slunk out of the chamber. Fangodrel opened his window casement to stare at the rising moon and the twinkling lights of the City of Men and Giants. He smoked another petal of the bloodflower . . . then another.

Soon the chamber disappeared, and he floated in the warm crimson fog where he felt most at home. He lay at the center of a blood-colored cloud, stars dancing in his veins and his eyes. The hidden thunder of his pulse filled the vermilion sky, and he cast flames from his eyes, bolts of malevolent desire. His enemies appeared like columns of white marble in the scarlet mist, and his flaming eyes destroyed them all, one by one. First Tadarus, the hulking buffoon, reduced to black ashes like the paper of his burned poem. Then Vireon, a lesser Tadarus, burned to a swirling dust. Then his mother, Queen Shaira, burning and screaming in the lightning cast from the eyes of her unloved son.

On the couch Fangodrel writhed in pleasure, laughing at his private victories, roaming the confines of the Red Dream, where he and he alone ruled men and giants, where he distributed life and death as his whims demanded.

A black palace reared above the flames now, but it was not the palace of Udurum. It was a mass of thorny spires and pointed domes, rising over a red steaming jungle. Fangodrel moaned and floated nearer, for he had never before seen this vision. He floated between the iron faces of demons that were the palace's outer gates.

A white panther came stalking toward him. It stood as large as an ox, and its eyes were red as the petals of the bloodflower. It bared golden fangs at him, and he shot flames from his eyes, but the beast did not singe. It stared at him . . . It flowed like red wine and became a stunningly beautiful woman.

Jewels hung like wisps of starlight across her body, and a twist of silk barely obscured her breasts. Black diamonds were the soul of her eyes, and they dripped cold flames. She wore a spiked crown of onyx set with topaz. Her hair was a mane of milk-white silk, and her slim fingers ended in feline claws.

She smiled at him.

You are not the son of Vod, she said. Her voice was dark honey. *Haven't you always known this?*

Who . . . who am I?

She flowed to him like water.

You are the Son of Gammir . . .

Who is Gammir?

She stood before him now, the tips of her claws gently stroking his chin.

My son. My beautiful dead son.

Who are you?

Ianthe, she whispered. The flames burst and rose about her lithe body.

Fangodrel stared at her, lust and fear mingled into some unnamable emotion.

You are the son of my son . . . my grandson . . .

He woke sweating near the fireplace, a cold draft blowing through the open window.

Shutting the panes, he pulled a blanket around his shoulders and puffed gently at his Serpent pipe. Her face swam in the eye of his memory, surrounded by red flames. Such a strange dream it was.

He had forgotten all about the girl for which he'd asked, until Rathwol arrived with her.

Soon after, wrapped in the excess of his violent pleasure, he almost forgot the panther-woman's face. But her name rang in his head like a distant bell.

Ianthe . . .

Ianthe the Claw.

Empress of Khyrei.

5

Hunters

The forest smelled like a woman. Vireon inhaled its heady blend of fragrances: the perfume of hanging blossoms, the clean musk of pine and naked earth. In his twenty-four years he had known many women in every shade of beauty. None claimed his heart as fully as the wild lands of Uduria, or stayed as constant in his thoughts. The forest was his love and it satisfied him in ways no woman ever had. Her mysteries were manifold, her secrets well hidden, yet he understood her better than any other man. Only the Uduru, his Giant relatives, knew the northern woodlands as well as Vireon, but they did not love her as he did. They had walked her depths for two thousand years, carving paths and scars along her surface, but Vireon loved her verdant soul.

Now on the edge of winter, before she donned her veil of virginal white, the forest wore a gown of myriad colors. Her leaves fell like teardrops of gold, saffron, orange, and scarlet. The moss on the boles of the mighty Uyga trees faded from green to pale indigo and mottled ochre. Still she wore a crown of late-blooming flowers, the Otha, the Narill, and the colossal Aduri, filling her windblown hair with sweetness. She was quiet mostly, demure in her vibrant garb, though she spoke in breathy whispers to those who knew how to listen. Vireon had learned to speak her language, to hear that faint voice, and to read the patterns of her silence.

He knelt between the massive curling roots of an Uyga and listened to her now. She sang to him sadly of the coming frost, yet there was a hopeful melody woven into those windy tones, a dream of spring's promise that would sustain her through months of snow and ice. Today would be the last great hunt before the weather turned and the forest settled to sleep beneath a blanket of snows. He leaped atop the tallest root, which was solid as an oblong slab of granite, and sniffed the cool air. An acrid tang of animal spoor broke the forest's spell.

He whistled, imitating the call of the arrowbeak, and the forest rumbled behind him. Fangodrim lumbered between the great trunks of the Uyga, trying his best to make no sound and failing miserably. Uduru could never travel with the silence and grace of human hunters, and Vireon did not expect them to. The Giants were not stealthy creatures, but this was their ancestral hunting ground. They had mastered the game here through other means than stalking. The Long Wait was their traditional method of hunting. Sitting like stones curled between the Uyga, they simply waited for bucks, boars, or bears to wander by, and they rose up to cast spears that rarely missed. The hunt of the Uduru was a hunt of patience. Patience and skill. They knew the paths game took toward watering holes, the routes from lair to hunting grounds, and they haunted these animal thoroughfares like towering specters . . . until they struck and carried home their kill. They were the masters of the northern forests, even if the towering Uyga trees dwarfed them.

Vireon had learned all the hunting tricks of the Uduru from Fangodrim, his great uncle. The Gray One, they called him at court, First Among Giants. Not only did he serve as the King's personal counselor, but he was the oldest and wisest of the surviving Giants. Fangodrim's brother was Vod's father, Fangodrel the First, who died in the fall of Old Udurum. Fangodrim had been Vod's closest friend, man or Giant.

The graybeard sank to one knee, bringing his great eyes level with Vireon's own. His pupils were discs of sharpest blue, and the eyeballs sat in beds of leathery wrinkles. Now the smoky odor of his uncle's beard filled Vireon's nostrils. Using the head of his spear, the Prince pointed in a northwesterly direction.

Fangodrim grunted his assent, hefted his own spear across his left shoulder, and followed Vireon as he leapt from root to ground and sprinted ahead. The Giant's steps were great strides, the typical Uduru manner of walking which ate up the miles quickly. Vireon could outrun any Giant, but a light sprint let him match his uncle's huge gait. For days now he had led Fangodrim on the search for an unspoiled herd of Welka, the Giant deer that roamed Uduria. Usually they were too fast for Uduru hunters, so if the Giants missed the Welka migrations, entire populations of the animals would thrive unculled in the upper ranges. Vireon had talked them into tracking the Welka to their distant haunts years back, and every year since he managed to find a valley full of the prized game. Now the scent of the Welka wafted strong. He found evidence of their passing, piles of dung left carelessly among the glades between Uygas and smaller trees.

Vireon raced ahead, topping a low ridge scattered with tonguegrass and spittleweed. Like a squirrel he clambered up the creviced bark of an Uyga. Looking down from his lofty perch, still far below the spreading branches, he saw into the valley beyond. An oval lake gleamed silver beyond the foliage of intervening trees, and a herd of Welka gathered to drink. The creatures' pelts glimmered black as jet in the mottled sunlight reflecting off the water. Antlers stood white and deadly sharp from narrow heads, and their eyes gleamed like onyx. Each one stood twice the size of a healthy ox, some of the bucks even larger. There must be at least three hundred in the herd; a fourth were immature younglings the size of horses with pale gray coats and no antlers. Vireon was glad he had brought only Fangodrim along, for the approach of even a few more Uduru would have shaken the ground enough to startle and scatter the beasts.

Fangodrim knelt atop the ridge now, his shaggy head directly below where Vireon had climbed. He leaped down to stand at his uncle's side.

"A fine herd," Fangodrim whispered. He smiled at his nephew, which made him look much like Vireon's father. They had the same broad-set lips. "I'm hurling for that tall buck, the one at the near bank."

"A good choice," whispered Vireon. "But I see a more impressive display of antlers there . . . near the Yagga bush."

Fangodrim nodded. Uncle and nephew took up their spears and crept over the ridge's spine. In a fluid motion they stood and tossed their twin spears simultaneously. The weapons soared through the air, turning at the apex of their arcs and plunging toward their chosen Welka. Fangodrim's shaft hit its mark a half-second before Vireon's, impaling the great buck through the spine and pinning it to the ground. Before the death of their herd-lord could spread a ripple of fear among the herd, Vireon's weapon took its target in the left side. The steel head and two feet of the Uyga-wood shaft exited from the right flank with a splash of hot blood. Vireon's kill hit the ground and the herd broke in every possible direction, powerful legs beating silver hooves against the sward, carrying them toward the high ground with a sound like rolling thunder.

"Hah!" Fangodrim shouted. He clapped Vireon on the back, and Vireon could only smile. It was Fangodrim who had taught him the spear and the ways of the hunt. Vod had rarely hunted, and when he did it was in the company of other Men, not Giants. The wilderness had not been Vod's home. The Uduru hunting ritual was alien to him, raised as he was in the Old Desert by humans. Once Vod had told Vireon, "Son, you are far more an Uduru than I ever was." Vireon never forgot those words. He carried them next to his heart like precious jewels no one else could see.

As Fangodrim and Vireon walked down the slope, galloping Welka turned aside, speeding away from them with the natural instinct of prey avoiding predators. The beasts could probably trample Vireon, but never Fangodrim. Vireon wondered if he could outrace a charging mass of them. But they fled like frightened squirrels now, up the slopes and out of the valley.

The hunters approached their kills. Vireon's buck had some twitching life left in it, so he drew his long knife and finished it with a clean slice across the throat.

By the time they finished draining the carcasses and roping the legs together for carrying, the sun reached its zenith and the lake lit up like a shield of diamonds. They reclined in the shade of a twisting Uyga, taking rest before the long trek home. As always Fangodrim offered to carry Vireon's carcass for him, and Vireon refused. Often it seemed, perhaps too often, the Uduru, even Fangodrim, forgot his great strength and that of his brother. It seemed impossible for most Giants to grasp the fact that both brothers, although standing barely higher than a Giant's knees, possessed all the strength of a true Uduru, with twice the endurance and speed. As if two Uduru spirits had inhabited human bodies.

Vireon stared at the brilliant lake, lost in thoughts of spirits and flesh. There were none in the world like Tadarus and himself. Never before had a human woman and an Uduru man produced offspring. Never before had an Uduru possessed the sorcery to take on the form of a man to make this possible. In many ways Tadarus and he were as much children of sorcery as they were of Vod and Shaira. His father had never spoken much of his magic, but Vireon wished he knew more about it. He supposed he never would, now that his father had given himself to the mercy of the Sea Queen.

"You miss him," said Fangodrim, his voice like the rumbling of distant storm.

Vireon watched clouds move across the water. "My brother?" He smiled.

"Your father," said Fangodrim.

Vireon shrugged. "You know me too well, Uncle."

"There is no shame in it," said the Giant. "A boy may cry, but a man bears his sorrow in silence, and that you have done."

"My mother weeps enough for all of us," said Vireon. Hardly a day went by without his mother's tears glistening like palace opals.

"She loved him," said Fangodrim. "*Loves* him. As you do. As you always will."

"What use to love a dead man?" Vireon sighed.

Fangodrim grunted. "You are too young to be so grim, boy. Do you think death is an end of things? Death is only a door, and those who die await us on the other side. They are never truly gone as long as our memory keeps that door open."

Vireon said nothing.

"Do you understand?" Fangodrim asked, looking into his eyes.

Vireon nodded. "Tell me about my grandfather."

Fangodrim looked upward, into the sun-speckled mass of Uyga leaves. His back leaned against the wide trunk. Vireon lay atop a nearby root on a bed of lavender moss.

"My brother, your grandfather . . . Fangodrel the Bold," he said wistfully. "You know his story already."

"I know only what you've told me," said Vireon. "How baby Vod was stolen by a black eagle. How Fangodrel searched for years to find him and returned to the city empty-handed. He died in the fall of Old Udurum, trying to slay the Serpent-Father."

"See? You already know your grandfather. Great deeds live on, even after Giants and Men die."

"What was he like?" Vireon persisted. "Did he laugh? Or was he dour like you?"

Fangodrim considered the question. "He . . . did laugh. When he was with your grandmother. She made him very happy. I never . . . I never understood it. To me, one woman is as good as the next. But Fangodrel had eyes only for Oidah. When your father was born, it was the happiest day of his life. He laughed and held the baby high so the sun would kiss him. Those were peaceful days. Our city was strong and our numbers were great. Now . . . now we dwindle."

Vireon shifted his weight to lie on his side and look into his uncle's gnarled face. "Is it true that my father was the last baby born to the Uduru?"

Fangodrim nodded. A cold wind blew through the valley and yellow Uyga leaves fell about the glade, one of them landing across the Giant's outstretched leg. He took the leaf in his great hand, cradling it gingerly. "Now our people fade. Like this tree shedding its leaves, the earth sheds Uduru. There are so few of us left, and we grow old." He crumpled the leaf to saffron dust in his hand. "It is the autumn of our kind, and winter will be upon us before we realize it."

"Still I wonder why," Vireon said. "Why can't the Uduri bear children anymore?"

Fangodrim opened his hand. The wind caught his leaf dust, spilling it across the ground.

"It is the Curse of Omagh."

"The Serpent-Father?"

"Your father slew him and rebuilt Udurum, but he could not destroy the evil spirit that dwelled within the beast. It is this power that keeps our women barren."

"Another curse?" Vireon frowned. "Father said the Mer-Queen cursed him. Is there no end to curses? Nothing that can be done?"

The corners of Fangodrim's mouth rose to wrinkle his eyes. "*You* are the end to Omagh's Curse . . . you and Tadarus."

"I don't understand."

"You and Tadarus . . . you are the link between Uduru and Men. You are something entirely new. Something great. A new breed for this world. Your children will be mighty one day, a new race that will spread across the kingdoms of the earth. It all begins anew with you."

Vireon never thought of having children. He had lain with many girls, many women, but his seed had never taken. If his uncle spoke truly, then the responsibility to have many children lay upon his shoulders, and that of his brother.

A new scent, moist and green, came to his nose. His true love, the forest, once again seducing him. It was the smell of rain. A gentle shower began to fall and the sun fell behind a bank of gray clouds. Vireon studied the bowl of the sky. This would not be a great storm, only a passing wash. The lake danced with ripples, its silver mirror illusion broken. He stood upon the Uyga root and dove into the chill waters.

Gliding through the murky depths, he passed shoals of rainbow-scaled fish and skimmed a forest of dark waterweed, an aqueous wonderland that mimicked the wood outside the lake. What secrets lay buried in the sediment among those drowned roots? That was the world, he supposed. Secrets within secrets within secrets.

He emerged on the far side of the lake, stepping out to sun himself on the green bank. Looking back, he saw Fangodrim dozing now under the Uyga's rustling canopy. The rain shower had already faded to a drizzle, and the sun hurled a rainbow across the eastern sky. Vireon watched it in quiet wonder, airy strings of jewels like a new crown for his love, arcing gracefully over the gigantic trees. The air, stunned by the wet glow of the sun, took on a golden quality, and nature shimmered like a glassy vision.

Suddenly a flash of purest white caught Vireon's eye. He turned his head and found himself staring at a curious creature. Some distance away from the lake a pale-furred thing crouched atop a green boulder, staring at him with narrow black eyes. It blinked once, and he realized it was a fox. Twice as large as a normal fox, larger than a wolf, with a regal tail swishing low behind its lean body. He stared, and the white fox did not move.

"Vireon?" Fangodrim's voice rolled across the water. A second time he called out, but Vireon did not answer. He was staring at the fox, unable to turn away, knowing it would disappear like a dissolving dream if he did so.

A third time and Fangodrim's voice broke his reverie. He turned and shouted across the lake. "Uncle! I see a white fox!"

Fangodrim rose to his feet and his voice boomed. "It is only a dream," he yelled. "Many of us have seen it. We call it the Wyrial, the ghost dancer. You must ignore it! Swim back to this side."

Vireon looked back and the fox was gone. The flip of a white tail dove into the shadows of the trees. He ran after it.

Fangodrim shouted after him. "Vireon, no! Do not chase the Wyrial! It's only a vision! Come back!"

The Giant's voice echoed across the valley, but Vireon was gone.

"Vireon!" he shouted, standing between the carcasses of the two cleaned Welka bucks. Their dead eyes stared blankly at nothing. "Vireon, come back!"

It was too late. The chase had begun.

*

Vireon ran, and the forest became a blur of green, brown, and gold. He leaped over narrow ravines, fallen branches big as logs, and piles of mossy boulders. The white fox glided between the trees like a low-flying bird, a pale shadow with the speed of a winter wind. Hours he ran after it without tiring, until the sun sank low in the sky and darkness flooded the forest. Now the fox gleamed silver in the moonlight, sometimes stopping to look back at him with its dark, almond-shaped eyes, pink tongue lolling. Then it was running again, a gleam of white threading the hem of night's dense cloak.

The sinking of the sun on his left told Vireon the fox was heading north, probably well beyond the realm of the Giants' hunting ground. How far north did the great forest extend? He had no idea. It might stretch all the way into the frozen wastes at the top of the world. He put such matters aside, reveling in the joy of the run, the thrill of the chase. His spear had been left behind with his uncle, but he had his knife of Uduru steel. All he would need to skin the fox's pearly coat when he caught it. Such a fine pelt it would be, a raiment fit for any Prince.

The last of the day's lingering warmth faded from the forest, and his breaths came in gusts of white fog. He lost sight of the running fox every now and then, but he already had caught its smell. It was unlike any animal odor. A cloying mix of jasmine, rose petals, and raw green earth. More like a woman's smell than a beast's. It incensed him in some primal way, and he pushed himself faster, running on across moonlit valleys, splashing through creeks foamy with whitewater, launching himself up the sides of fallen Uyga trunks and leaping wolf-like to the earth on the other side. The ground grew rougher and a range of wooded hills rose about him. Still the white fox led him on by sight and smell and sheer audacity. His hunter's pride hung in the balance. No beast could escape a Prince of Udurum.

He ran on through the depths of night, along pitch-dark hollows where moonlight could not reach, across bony hilltops bright with legions of spreading moonflowers. He barely noticed when the rain returned, this time falling hard and cold against his skin. He ran through the rising wind and the whirling storm; the damp only made the fox's scent stronger. Just before dawn the rain turned to sleet, and the ground became slick with gray slush. He fell once, sliding down a hill on his backside and slamming into a tree bole, but he was up and running again even before catching his breath. The icy rain washed him clean as he ran.

In the cold glare of sunrise, he saw the fox mount a hill no more than a spear's cast away. He stopped dead in his tracks, blinking at it. Atop the rise now stood a gorgeous young woman, barefoot on the frosty ground. Long hair fell bright as sunlight about her naked body, and she glowered at him down the hillside. Vireon held his breath. Her narrow eyes were dark as night, just like the fox. Her flesh was pale, the alabaster of a nocturnal being, the inhuman beauty of an airy spirit. The falling sleet turned to snow in that instant, and black clouds swallowed the early sun. The white fox raced down the hill's far side.

Vireon followed, snowflakes steaming against his hot skin. He ran through the frosty morning, ignorant of the cold. Shirtless he had come into the forest, and his buckskin leggings and boots were soaked with the night's rain. His slick black mane swirled behind his head as he crowned the hill and sprinted down its back. The white fox already mounted another hill up ahead. A thin layer of snow had covered the autumn colors of the forest floor. The Uyga still grew here, but there were many other, smaller varieties of tree. The undergrowth was thicker here, and often he jumped a cluster of white-leaf fern or a knot of tall skyweed. He ran north, into the cold lands where summer only ever visited briefly before fleeing southward.

The second day of running brought him deep into the snow-bound clime of northern Uduria. The ground was lost beneath ankle-deep snow, icicles hung from the branches of trees, and he leaped across frozen streams. Ice crystals hung in his hair and on the fringes of his boot-tops. The cold was a constant companion. He felt no pain, only a distant sense of discomfort. What would have frozen a human man to death in hours was harmless as a toothache to the son of Vod and Shaira. He would not let small things like ice and snow keep him from the white fox.

It was no animal, he knew that now. He no longer wanted to skin it. He did not know what he would do with it, but he would capture it. Time later to decide its fate.

The white forest turned to scarlet as the sun sank into the western hills. Once again he saw the pale girl, closer this time. She squatted on a low crag of icy granite, her blonde tresses mingling with the icicles along its summit. Again he stopped, a steaming icon among the wintery landscape. Her feet were bare upon the ice, and her black eyes met his own. Her lips were soft pink, the color of the fox's tongue. She watched him watching her, and she smiled. He walked closer, snow crackling beneath his boots. She raised a lithe, colorless arm and pointed southward, the way he had come.

Her eyes said, *Go back.*

Vireon shook his head, shedding bits of frost from his hair. His heavy breaths filled the space between them like a warm mist.

Without warning he bounded toward the crag, but she was gone. He climbed its face and saw the white fox leaping through the snow.

North . . . always north. Who is she?

He looked southward for an instant. Hunger gnawed inside his belly. The cold wrapped his skin like a rough fabric. She was the most stunning girl he had ever seen. If he turned back now, as she seemed to want him to, he may never see her again.

He scanned the white hills ahead; they stretched like a pallid blanket across the northern world. Who knew what lay among that white waste? What secrets did the frozen north keep to itself?

He had seen one of them.

Jumping from the crag into a snowdrift, he ran toward the fox-woman's delicious scent. Now that snow and ice muted the forest, her fragrance was easier to follow than ever. He sped through the winterland like a wild buck fleeing invisible predators. But *he* was the predator. He would catch this gorgeous treasure and hold her in his arms and . . . at least he would know her name. He would caress her marble flesh, swim the intimate depth of her eyes . . . taste those ripe lips.

All that day and into a frozen night he ran. Snow fell again, and he ignored it. He delved deep into the winterlands, far from any recognizable landmarks save the frosted Uyga trees, which grew sporadically from the snowy ground. A range of white-capped mountains stood on the horizon, rising over walls of eternal fog. He had no name for those peaks, nor had any Uduru every spoken of them. The snow was knee-deep here, and far deeper in places. Several times he fell into fissures and had to claw his way out with knife and bare fingers. When he emerged from these white caverns the fox stood nearby as if waiting . . . but it fled again at first sight of him.

On the third day a pack of wolves ran beside him, snarling with hunger. He ran faster, hoping to outdistance them, but they matched his speed. The reek of their carnivore breath and matted pelts obscured the fox's scent, and this irritated him. He turned on the pack's frothing leader, grabbing it around the neck. Locked together they rolled down a frozen slope, the other wolves loping behind, eager for a kill.

Vireon's knife slit the big wolf's throat as they tumbled, and at the bottom of the slope he left it bleeding into the whiteness. The wolves had their feast. The sound of their gnashing and chewing receded as he raced northward. The scent of the fox-woman was faint, but he caught it on the frigid wind and ran faster, the knife clutched in his fist and smoking with wolf's blood. It finally went cold and red crystals froze along the blade.

On the fourth day the icy mountains loomed closer, and Vireon's weariness caught up with him. He stopped in a deep ravine, standing up to his waist in snow, and sniffed the air for the fox-woman's scent. She was near, but he could not pinpoint her direction anymore. His vision blurred. He was tired, at last, after days of running. His limbs ached with cold, or fatigue, he could not tell. He was beginning to know his limits, something entirely new to him. But still he would not give up.

The world turned to shades of gray about him as he followed his nose and trudged up the ravine. On either side the walls rose thousands of feet, and Uyga trees topped them like snow-crowned sentinels. He stared up at the trees, seeing for a moment the image of his Uduru cousins garbed in white, looking down as if to cheer him on. Or warning him to go back. *Go. Return to the land of sun and warmth*, they whispered.

No, he breathed. His face had begun to sprout a shallow beard, frosted to the color of snow.

Then he smelled the sour stench of unwashed Uduru, and thought somehow his cousins had actually followed him. The walls of the ravine shook about him, shards of ice and shale sliding into the gorge. Six great figures rose before him, blue-skinned giants draped in reeking pelts of bear and mountain tiger. He stopped, blinking exhausted eyes. His cousins could not be here . . . This was a trick of the mind. Was the fox-woman a sorceress, and this some final trick to elude pursuit?

Vireon squinted, looking up into the face of the nearest blue-skin. A necklace of bones, fangs, and claws hung about the great neck. The face above it was heavy-browed, flat-nosed, with a jutting chin and a beard entirely frozen into jagged icicles. The wild mane of hair was snow-pale. The eyes, however, were crimson. Pupils as red as fresh-flowing blood, a marked contrast to the indigo skin. A ring of bronze hung from the broad nostrils, two more from the big flat earlobes. Vireon's head spun.

Are they ghosts? he wondered. *Spirits of frozen Uduru who wandered too far north in some ancient age?*

They barked at him, a few guttural syllables in tones of primordial contempt.

Surrounded by the stink of their moldy furs and sweat-caked bodies, he had lost the scent of the fox-woman entirely. He moaned.

The blue-skin before him raised a tree above its shaggy head. Not a tree, a mace of black iron. He realized this too late as the blue-skin brought the weapon crashing against his bare skull.

Thunder and sparks.

The snow rose up to greet him like a feather bed, and at last Vireon slept.

A ribbon of crimson flowed from his scalp, melting a tiny rivulet into the snow.

6

In the Palace of Sacred Waters

The Royal Gardens of Uurz encircled the soaring walls of the palace proper like a swathe of preserved wilderness. In the works of sages and poets they stood alongside such wonders as the Forest of Jewels in Mumbaza, the Great Earth Wall that divided the continent into Low and High Realms, and the Giant-City of New Udurum. Every known species of plant, tree, and fruit grew in Emperor Dairon's circular courtyard, a treasury of botanical imports from across the world. Rare birds from Khyrei, Yaskatha and the Southern Isles filled the green canopies with melodious warbling; blue-furred monkeys built tiny huts in the tops of the trees; feline predators, great cats in shades of gold, alabaster, and amber, walked between the walls of sunken enclosures. A popular saying held that there were more blossoms in the Emperor's Garden than living souls in the six kingdoms.

To walk the winding ways of the Royal Gardens was to visit aspects of every forest and glade, every lush jungle and valley, inhaling the redolence of the entire world's foliage with every breath. The intoxicating air made women swoon and filled men's heads with fancies, dreams, and holy visions. Yet to Prince D'zan, sitting by himself on a stone bench beneath a Yaskathan fig tree, the garden's delights were only shadows . . . dim, powerless shades existing at the edge of his dulled senses.

He did not touch the plate of fruit and cheese brought by servants for his morning meal, or the cup of spiced wine from his homeland. He stared into the green depths of the garden but saw none of its gaudy birds, hanging vines, or blooming colors. The birdsong and the distant songs of minstrels were sluggish winds in his ears. He wrapped himself in his own arms. In the humid heat of this man-made paradise he sat shivering and chewing on his lip. Beside him on the bench lay the jade dagger that had taken the Stone's life instead of his own.

The Emperor had been kind to him on the morning after the assassins struck.

"I regret that we must meet under a cloud of sorrow," said Emperor Dairon, looking upon D'zan from his throne of opal and sandstone at the very heart of the Palace of Sacred Waters. The citadel's name came from the underground river beneath its walls. Legends said the river was a gift from the God of Waters, the foundation on which the desert capital was built. A quarter-century ago Vod's sorcery had turned the Old Desert into the Stormlands, but the Sacred River still flowed beneath Uurz, unchanged and eternal.

Emperor Dairon's hands were gnarled with the calluses of a warrior but disguised by a host of sparkling rings. They lay upon the heads of eagles carved into the arms of his chair. The Princes Tyro and Lyrilan stood on either side of the throne, one a detached image of strength, the other wearing an expression of honest grief. A crowd of courtiers, advisors, and chancellors stood about the royal dais, strutting peacocks in green and yellow satin.

D'zan bowed before the ruler of Uurz. "Thank you for granting me refuge here, Lord of Waters." He wore a tunic of green and gold, the colors of Uurz, since his Yaskathan garments were stained with blood.

Dairon grunted. "You are unnecessarily polite under the circumstances, Prince D'zan. Olthacus the Stone was a friend to this court – a friend to *me* – as was your father. I mourn them both deeply."

D'zan could say nothing, so he swallowed the lump in his throat and held back tears.

"The security of this palace has not been compromised in twenty-five years," said the Emperor, his kohl-rimmed eyes still set on D'zan. "Not since the Uduru conquered this city and put the Old Emperor to death. This is a shameful day for all of us. Know that my ministers will soon discover who aided these Khyreins. I can never repay the loss of your guardian. But I swear to you I will bring justice upon the heads of any who are implicated in his murder. I only wish I knew why the Khyreins wish you harm."

"Khyrei is the enemy of my ancestors," said D'zan. "I believe the assassins were sent by its Empress, who aligns herself with the usurper Elhathym. Now I have no choice but to ask your royal protection while I gather an army to reclaim my kingdom."

Dairon frowned. "You have the protection of my house as long as you wish it. However, I cannot allow you to recruit my soldiers and citizenry for your campaign. You may contract any number of mercenaries who roam the Stormlands. They are hearty warriors who sell their sword arms to the highest bidder."

D'zan stared at the lowest step of the dais. He fought back the anger growing in his chest, mixing with the bile of his grief.

"Thank you, Lord of Waters," he said with forced calm.

He could not tell the Emperor that he had no money to hire an army. He could not beg for assistance in front of the entire Uurzian court. He could not speak the eloquent words that would bend Dairon's armies to his cause. The Stone was supposed to help him win the support of Uurz. How could he do it himself? How could he possibly do it *alone*?

"If what you say is true," said the Emperor, after some thought, "and Khyrei now stands allied with this sorcerer Elhathym . . . then the south may become a fearsome power. I will send agents to both realms to gather news. But we cannot take action against the usurper until we know the true state of southern politics, and also where Mumbaza's loyalties lie. Do you understand, Prince D'zan?"

D'zan nodded, then looked up and met the Emperor's eyes with his own. The glare of sunlight from Dairon's tall crown almost blinded him. "What of the Giant-King?" he asked.

"You speak of Vod, Lord of Udurum. What of him?"

"I have heard that he once feuded with the Empress of Khyrei, that he cast down her palace before he went north to rebuild Udurum."

Dairon smiled. "You know your history well. This is all true."

"Then perhaps he will support my claim. Will Your Majesty grant me an escort beyond the mountains to the City of Men and Giants?"

Dairon stroked his braided beard. His eyes turned to those of his warrior-son, Tyro. The young man leaned in close to his father, and the two spoke in whispers. Then the Empreror turned to his other son, scholarly Lyrilan, and those two exchanged words.

The Emperor turned back to D'zan. "You are truly the son of Great Trimesqua to ask such a favor. I salute your courage. You will have a cohort of my finest warriors as escort to Udurum. But there is something you should know . . ."

D'zan stood a bit taller. There was some glimmer of hope here. "Your Majesty?"

"We have received word recently that King Vod has abdicated his throne and gone off to the Cryptic Sea. Men say he spoke of answering a curse. His wife, Queen Shaira, rules Udurum in his stead."

D'zan blinked. "Will the Giant-King return?"

Dairon looked grim. "None can say but Vod," he replied. "And he speaks to no one."

D'zan felt his glimmer of hope fade and grow cold, like the dying embers of a fire. Suddenly he thought of nights on the Stormland plain, sleeping about the embers with the Stone snoring nearby, his big sword laid across his chest. His eyes welled.

"Then I will appeal to Queen Shaira," he said.

He no longer cared that his tears flowed freely. Let the nobles of Uurz see his pain. Let it flow like their Sacred River, down his cheeks and onto the smooth marble of their palace floor.

Let them see the cruelty of the world on his face.

Dairon's head seemed to bow under the weight of his jeweled crown. "Shaira is a great woman, Prince. She will hear your plea. And know this: if Udurum stands behind your claim, then so shall Uurz, with all its power."

A collective gasp sounded among the crowd of courtiers and spectators. The Emperor must have been moved by D'zan's tears. D'zan faced him, eyes gleaming with pride and shame.

"Your kindness honors the memory of my father," said D'zan, "and my uncle."

They gave a banquet in his honor that night, dancing girls and musicians filling the Hall of Waters, and great tables heaped with roasted fowl, barbecued pork, and braised fish. The wine flowed heavily among the revelers, but D'zan ate very little. Prince Lyrilan sat beside him and asked for tales of Trimesqua's adventures, but D'zan was too wrapped up in thoughts of the future to dwell on the past. He excused himself early and went to sleep in the new and heavily guarded chamber assigned to him. Sleep came in fits and starts. He tossed and turned and battled nightmares wrapped in black silk.

The next morning he walked into the palace grounds and lost himself in the depths of the Royal Gardens. Tomorrow would be the funeral of Olthacus, followed by another banquet to honor his memory. But today D'zan sat among the splendor of foliage wrestling with his own self-doubt.

Who was he to defy the necromancer Elhathym? A man who could call the dead up from their graves to obey his will. What other terrible powers did he possess?

D'zan was only sixteen, little more than a boy. His father had not prepared him to rule Yaskatha, let alone to assemble an army and lead it to reclaim the throne. Olthacus was the hero, the man of wisdom whose worldly influence would guide the Prince back to his people. D'zan was nothing, merely a name, and the last living specimen of a bloodline being forced into extinction. Would the Queen of Udurum help him? Would it even matter?

He considered death and weighed it against his continued living. He knew what his father would say: "If you find a thing difficult, then all the more reason to do it!" Sometimes his father's love had been disguised as cruelty. For two years Olthacus had taught him the discipline of swordplay, but he was nowhere near ready for a *real* fight. He had neither the strength nor the speed a true warrior needed. He had been pampered and made weak by a life spent under the royal roof. What could he know about being a man . . . being a King?

He contemplated the Khyrein dagger lying next to him. There would be more of these killers stalking him. Elhathym was not the type of man to let a single threat to his rule go on living. At any moment D'zan expected a troop of walking corpses to shamble upon him, eager to tear out his life with bony claws. Death hung in the sky above him like a circling hawk, waiting for the right moment to swoop and strike. And the Stone was no longer here to shield him.

D'zan wrapped his arms about his knees and rocked himself back and forth on the stone seat. The lush vegetation was a scintillating jungle where deadly things stalked unseen. Yet instead of some deadly predator it was only Prince Lyrilan who emerged from the green shadows. The scholar wore a yellow tunic, his thin waist supporting a belt of golden leaves studded with emeralds. Green hose covered his skinny legs, and his boots of dark leather seemed a tad too large for his feet. He sat on the bench near D'zan, brushing a swathe of black curls from his eyes and crossing his legs. By his very manner, D'zan could tell the Prince was several years older than himself, though his aspect was that of a young man. Lyrilan had all the height of his brother Tyro, but none of the brawn. D'zan realized for the first time exactly how similar their faces were. They must be twins.

"Do you miss Yaskatha?" asked Lyrilan.

"Is it so obvious?"

Lyrilan looked up at the branches of the fig tree. "You choose a tree from your homeland as shade."

D'zan shrugged.

"Do you wish to talk?" Lyrilan asked.

"What good will talking do?" said D'zan. "I have a kingdom to win back. I have no army. No sorcery. No gold. Talking will not change these things."

Lyrilan smiled. "Oh, will it not? The trick is to talk with the right person."

D'zan turned to meet his dark, mischievous eyes. "Can you give me these things then, Prince Lyrilan?"

Lyrilan tossed his head, his tongue emerging to moisten his

lips. "I can give you something far more precious than all of these, my friend."

D'zan stared at him, unmoved. Was the scholar truly a jester in Prince's clothing? He was in no mood to be fooled and saw no humor in Lyrilan's friendly smile.

"What might that be?" he asked, when he realized Lyrilan was waiting for the question.

"Wisdom," said Lyrilan. "Knowledge."

D'zan picked up the assassin's dagger and held it in his fist. A sudden rage filled him. "What good is wisdom against this? What knowledge can strike men down like the poison on this blade?"

Lyrilan's face lost its smile. "Wisdom and knowledge can do far more than that," he said. "Without them there would exist neither the blade or the poison. Knowledge is the root of all things both earthly and spiritual. Wisdom is the understanding and application of this concept."

D'zan threw the dagger point first into the dirt of the garden, where it stuck upright with a sound like a hiss. "I have never been fond of riddles. Speak plainly or leave me be."

Lyrilan sighed. "I know your soul aches for what you have lost. I know you carry pain like an iron cloak about your shoulders. You may think you have lost your last friend in this world. But if you will allow me . . . *I* will be your friend."

D'zan stared into the green depths of the garden. He did need a friend. But could he trust an Uurzian? The son of the man who would send him north to beg at the feet of the Giant-Queen?

"Why?" asked D'zan. "Why befriend me? I am nothing to you."

Lyrilan pushed his palms together, lowered his face. "Nothing? You are the living heir of a bloodline that stretches back into the Age of Heroes. Farther even – to the Age of Serpents. You carry the currents of history in your veins, D'zan. To me you are everything I have spent my life studying. To be your friend . . . your ally . . . is to enter the great story that began with your ancestors. You have the task of a hero before you, and every hero needs a guide . . . an advisor. Someone to read the movements of the sun and stars, interpret the deeper meanings of everyday phenomena."

"Are you a sorcerer, Lyrilan?"

"No."

"Then what power have you to offer? Other than friendship."

"Let me show you." Lyrilan stood and motioned for him to follow.

D'zan tucked the jade dagger into his belt and plodded behind the Uurzian Prince. It took some time to find egress from the sprawling gardens, and there were strange birds, beasts, and plants to marvel at with every turn of the marble path, although D'zan paid little attention to these things.

Eventually they came to a great fountain carved from white stone: a trio of winged tigers spewing water from roaring mouths. Here the winding paths of the Royal Gardens converged, meeting the wider expanse of the Main Way, which led to the steps of the palace proper. Palace servants, noble personages, and visiting potentates meandered the vaulted passageways, their bodies wrapped in myriad hues of silk and clouds of perfume. The glitter of jewels on their fingers, necks, and arms made D'zan feel like a beggar sneaking into some place he had no business being.

Lyrilan brought him at last to a tall set of double doors set with bronze plates. These were engraved with celestial insignia, swirling glyphs, and a central sun radiating beams of jewels. The doors swung soundlessly open on oiled hinges, and the rich smell of ancient parchment filled D'zan's nostrils. Here was the Royal Library of Uurz, a vast repository of books and scrolls in a huge circular chamber. Clear panes of glass lined the dome of the ceiling, and brilliant sunlight lit the room. Motes of dust danced in the shimmering beams.

Lyrilan walked inside, hands clasped at his back, and D'zan followed. His eyes scanned shelves twice the height of his head. Volume upon volume of leather-bound tomes, more than he had ever seen gathered in one place, lined the curving walls. A few bronze statues of legendary scribes, scholars, and heroes stood beneath the dome like burnished pillars. The floor was a collection of wooden tables, padded chairs, smaller shelves for special collections, and stores of ink and quills. D'zan spotted two bald scribes at work, painstakingly creating copies of some elder text, filling the pristine pages with ancient knowledge.

Lyrilan stopped at the very center of the chamber, where the floor tiles were arranged in the image of a great open book, its pages inscribed with holy passages. He turned to look at D'zan, whose eyes were still sweeping over the book-lined walls.

"What do you see?" Lyrilan asked.

"Books . . . "

"Is that all? Look closer. This is the greatest library in all the Stormlands, possibly in all the world. What do you see?"

D'zan turned his eyes from the books to look at Lyrilan, who stood now with his hands spread like a street magician about to perform a trick. Was this another riddle?

"Knowledge?" he guessed.

Lyrilan clapped his hands together. "Yes, knowledge. Here is knowledge, that's to be sure. What else?"

D'zan sighed. He should have stayed under the fig tree. Why didn't these Uurzians speak plainly like good Yaskathans? Everything here was all innuendo and court etiquette. His father had been a warrior first, a King second, and parent third. He had no time for tricky wordplay or men who did not say what they meant openly and clearly. Suddenly he remembered that his father was gone, as if he'd somehow forgotten it. His heart became a lead weight in his chest. He remembered Lyrilan asking about his father.

"History?" D'zan said.

"Indeed," said Lyrilan. "Knowledge, history . . . wisdom. The thoughts of the greatest minds of all the ages. The struggles and triumphs, the failures and tragedies, of all the men who walked this earth for eons . . . they are all here, D'zan, on the pages of these books."

D'zan watched one of the scribes working carefully with his trembling quill, squinted eyes focused on the patterns of ink he scrawled across the page. The man was oblivious to all else but the page upon which he worked.

"The tales of dead men," D'zan said. "Of kingdoms fallen to dust . . . ages that are no more than dreams to us now."

Lyrilan laughed. "Are they?" he said. "Let me ask you this: how else can a man communicate his hopes, his dreams, his thoughts across the eternal ages? How else can a *mind* reach through the veil of millennia and *touch* another mind with understanding? How else but through this glorious invention that we call the written word? It began on stone tablets, then scrolls of papyrus and myra, and finally it takes the form of these wonders . . . these *books*. This is the greatest magic of all magics, D'zan. This is immortality."

"Immortality?" D'zan said. "Only the Gods are immortal."

Lyrilan slapped him on the shoulder. "Ha! The Gods do not write books, D'zan. *Men* write books about the Gods! What does this tell you?"

"That Gods are not scribes."

"The Gods write upon the face of the world itself. They have no need of books. As the Gods write our lives into the world, so we write our lives into these books. We can invent whole new worlds in these books if we wish. Some have . . . "

"What do you mean?"

"Men whose words and thoughts live through the ages are never truly gone from us," Lyrilan said. "Their spirits are preserved on these pages. They are as immortal as the Gods themselves."

"Do you suggest that writing is a form of sorcery?"

Lyrilan smiled. "A brilliant question. What is sorcery, really? Who knows? Why do sorcerers write more books than anyone? There are hundreds of books here written by those called 'sorcerer.' But I believe that writing – the written expression of wisdom and knowledge – is something far *greater* then sorcery."

"Ah, you are a philosopher," said D'zan. What was the point of all this nonsense? Why couldn't the Warrior-Prince have asked to be his friend? The other brother could gather men and arms to D'zan's cause. What could this Lyrilan hope to give him besides pretty words?

"Not exactly," said Lyrilan. "I am a scholar. Do you know the difference?"

"No," said D'zan.

"A philosopher thinks. A scholar thinks and *writes*."

D'zan stood quiet for a moment. This was a pretty place, to be sure. But he saw little to gain from it. He needed the promise of the Uduru Queen and her Giants; he needed the pledge of Uurz's Emperor and his legions. He needed sorcery to rival that of Elhathym.

He needed hope and he had none.

"Lyrilan," he said, "why do you show me these things? Why distract me with such thoughts? Why ask to befriend an outcast with little chance of redemption?"

Lyrilan sat at a broad table and motioned for D'zan to join him. He called for an attendant to bring them wine and spoke some words to the man before he departed. Then he turned to D'zan with the most serious expression he had yet worn.

"You stand at the beginning of a great journey. An adventure to rival any of those in these books around us. You ride upon the tide of history . . . you are a legend in the making. You face an evil the likes of which you or I can scarcely comprehend, and you face it alone. Yet I see in your eyes the fire of your father, and your father's father. Warriors. Heroes."

The servant gave them each a cup of yellow wine. It sparkled in the sunlight. D'zan drank deeply. His head spun pleasantly.

"I know that you would give your very life to liberate Yaskatha," said Lyrilan. "You must walk a thousand leagues, and your first step is right here before you. You will gather about you those who can aid your cause, and you will never abandon your people. I know all this about you, D'zan."

He looked into Lyrilan's dark eyes. A sudden rush of warmth filled his limbs. Perhaps it was only the wine.

"*That* is why I want to be your friend," said Lyrilan. "That is why I want to help you. That is why I want to write the story of your life."

D'zan hiccupped. "My life?"

"The saga of your exile, your wandering, and your eventual return to power."

"What if . . . " D'zan hesitated. "What if I should die?"

Lyrilan smiled and took a drink of his wine. "All heroes, all Kings, all Men must die eventually."

D'zan grinned. "My father used to say it matters not *when* a man dies, only *how* he dies."

"Your father was a wise man."

"I accept your offer, Lyrilan," said D'zan. "You may chronicle my life as you will. Only speak the truth – that is all I ask."

"I can do more than that, brave Prince," said Lyrilan. "I can help you *find* the truth."

"Will the truth restore me to my father's throne?"

"A famous sage once wrote, 'Truth will set the world aright.'"

"Pericles of Yaskatha," said D'zan. "I've read him."

Lyrilan nodded, smiling.

"Am I to understand that you will be coming with me to Udurum?" D'zan asked.

"Of course," said Lyrilan. "What sort of scholar would I be if I did not?"

D'zan offered his hand, and Lyrilan squeezed it.

"I appreciate your confidence in me," said D'zan. "It may be more than I have in myself. But I will try to give you a good story."

"I have no doubt of that."

Footsteps interrupted their conversation, and D'zan watched two lovely courtesans enter the library. The voluptuous girls looked entirely out of place here, their spreading gowns and glinting jewelry at odds with the rather plain decor of the place. Both smiled at Lyrilan, their mouths painted ruby, eyes lined in kohl. Their brown skins spoke of days in the sunsplashed garden, and their fragrance overpowered the reek of ancient books.

"Ah! Sweet Moryia and Juniel! Come here, my darlings," Lyrilan called to them, raising his cup.

The girls approached the table, and Lyrilan introduced D'zan. He stood and kissed the hand of each maiden. Both women eyed him with sly grins, as a hungry man might eye a steak.

"Come, D'zan," said Lyrilan. "Enough of our heavy talk for the day. It is time for you to experience our Uurzian hospitality."

D'zan looked at Lyrilan, who stood with his arm around Moryia. Juniel had already taken D'zan's hand in her own. "I'd be delighted," he said, quaffing the last of his wine.

Lyrilan smiled as Moryia kissed his cheek. "I may be a scholar," he said, "but I'm still a Prince."

The girls led them into private chambers, and D'zan soon

forgot all about the long road ahead and the terrible evil he was to fight.

At least for a little while.

Prince Tyro met his father on the great veranda overlooking the green and gold city. Stormclouds rolled on the horizon, lightning danced, and the smell of coming rain filled the air. A flock of ravens flew above the domes of the Grand Temple in the distance, and a thousand thousand smokes rose into the blue afternoon sky. This was always the weather in Uurz: brief periods of brilliant sunlight between thundering squalls that came three or four times a day.

Emperor Dairon sat on a cushioned divan at the veranda's center, where he could look over his realm and see into the gray skies of the north. The Grim Mountains were barely visible along the purple horizon, hovering like smoke at the edge of the Emperor's vision. A pair of guards stood nearby, and servants prepared a tray of wine and fruits for Dairon's pleasure.

Tyro's green tunic was tied with a belt of silver and onyx. A bronze kilt left his strong legs bare in the manner of an Uurzian footsoldier. The short sword at his side had been a gift from the Emperor on Tyro's thirteenth birthday. A single emerald set into the pommel was the only extravagance in its design. Tyro had mastered the longblade, the scimitar, the dagger, the spear, and even the war axe, but always he wore this modest blade, his first weapon.

The son stood beside his father and looked beyond the city walls into the rising storm.

"What word of these assassins?" asked Dairon.

"None," said Tyro. "They may as well have sprung from evening mist. They left no trace entering the city or the palace."

The Emperor frowned. "Then they were truly the Death-Bringers of Khyrei," he said. "Ghosts of the Jungle . . . "

Tyro sat beside his father on the royal divan. Dairon had not touched the platter of black grapes or the sparkling wine.

"What does it mean, Father?" asked Tyro.

"It means that Khyrei and Yaskatha are allied," said the Emperor, "and they both want Trimesqua's son dead."

Tyro plucked a grape from the bunch and popped it into his mouth. He savored the tartness of its taste for a quiet moment.

"Surely these are evil kingdoms," said Tyro, "ruled by wicked powers. This Elhathym is some new terror unleashed. Ianthe the Claw we already know. Why not support Prince D'zan's claim for the throne?"

The Emperor smiled at Tyro. "Are you so eager for war, son? You think of the glory, yes. But what of the blood . . . the innocent lives . . . the destruction, the mayhem? What of the terror and disgrace that war brings? These things always outweigh the glory. Always."

Tyro could say nothing. His father had fought in a war; he had not. There were few among the legions who could best Tyro in the dueling pits, but that was not the same as leading men into battle. Thousands of men tramping forth to slaughter thousands more. Still . . . how could evil be defeated if not through battle and blood? Should they simply wait for the legions of Khyrei and Yaskatha to come marching north, bringing flame and death upon the Stormlands?

"Olthacus the Stone," said Tyro, "was your friend."

Dairon nodded, and the long braids of his beard shook. "As was Trimesqua . . . "

"You taught me that a wrong must be avenged," said Tyro. "That justice can sometimes only be found at the end of a sword. The world is cruel and dangerous, so we cultivate strength to preserve the innocent. Must we not do that now?"

"You are young, Tyro," said Dairon. "You understand the

subtleties of combat, the rules of the blade. But you know little of diplomacy, statecraft, strategy. These are the things that matter most. It is not enough to be strong. You must be wise in your strength."

Tyro drank his father's untouched wine. Thunder rolled in the north. The storm moved closer, threatening the blue sky with looming shadows.

"Listen to me," said the Emperor. "Never, *never*, begin a war without a strategic advantage. Preparation is everything. Alliances must be made, declarations issued. No nation can stand alone. Udurum and Shar Dni are our brother-cities. We will not fight without them."

"Then send me to Shar Dni to make alliance with King Ammon," said Tyro. "He has no love for the Khyreins – they raid his ships on the Golden Sea. He must be hungry for justice."

"Perhaps," said Dairon. "But Shar Dni does not have a quarter the military might of Uurz. They have warships, yes, but on the land their numbers are small. Ammon has already been appealing to Uurz for assistance against these pirates."

"There you have it," said Tyro. "An alliance is inevitable."

Dairon turned his squinted eyes to Tyro. This was the look his father always gave him when he was about to make an obvious point that Tyro had somehow missed.

"Tyro, why do you think I am sending D'zan to Queen Shaira? Why grant him a company of legionnaires for the journey?"

Tyro thought a moment, casting his gaze across the city. In the noble quarters servants were running through gardens as the first cold drops of rain fell. In the streets beyond, tiny figures rushed for shelter.

"Because you pity him . . . because Trimesqua and Olthacus were your friends."

"No, son. I do pity poor D'zan. But this is not the reason. An Emperor does not rule only with his heart, but with his mind."

Tyro stroked the light stubble on his chin. "You send him because you believe he will gain Shaira's sympathy."

Dairon smiled. "Now you begin to use that head of yours."

"If Udurum stands with us, and Shar Dni, will we be prepared for war?"

Dairon leaned back in his cushions. Black clouds had swallowed the sun, and a curtain of cold rain fell beyond the veranda roof. A slight spray of mist cooled Tyro's skin. The city now lay in the shadow of the booming clouds. Lightning kissed the distant fields, turning black to emerald for a brief moment.

"War is a test for which no nation can ever be fully prepared," said the Emperor. "But I have seen the Uduru on the march. I have seen the spectacle of a thousand Giants striding across the desert, heard the thunder of their feet and the clashing of their steel. They nearly brought down the walls of Uurz before you were born. As it was, they conquered the city in three days. Only Vod's intervention saved my life and thousands more who would have been crushed into dust."

"I've read the stories, Father," said Tyro. "I know the tale of your rise to power."

"It was Vod who made me Emperor," said Dairon. "He had the city in the palm of his great hand, Tyro. He could have kept it, smashed it, or ruled it forever. But he gave it to me. Someday I will give it to you."

"But Vod is gone."

"So they say. But men have said such things before."

"Men say the Giants are a dying race."

"That may be . . . but they are long-lived. No longer do they breed, it's true."

Thunder roared above the palace, and Dairon rose stiffly, walking back into his chambers. Servants rushed to prepare a fresh seat for him, and Tyro followed him. He smelled the water of a scented bath, saw the steam of hot water.

Dairon placed a hand on his son's broad shoulder.

"I know you wish to prove your manhood on the field of battle. But trust an old warrior who loves you. The Uduru are essential. We cannot face the combined might of Khyrei and Yaskatha without them. There is also the question of Mumbaza . . . but we'll discuss this later."

Tyro nodded his understanding, and Dairon embraced him, slapping his back. He turned away and servants came to remove his royal vestments.

"Let me lead the cohort, Father," Tyro said. "Let me accompany D'zan to the Giant-City."

The Emperor raised his gray-flecked eyebrows. "Why?"

"Because we could not protect him under this roof. We owe him."

Dairon sighed. His bare sunken chest was bronzed by the suns of many desert treks. Tyro glanced at the familiar scars along his father's ribs and stomach – reminders of old wounds, mementos of battles won with no small cost. Once Dairon had been a huge well-muscled man. In his old age those wounds still troubled him, but Tyro never heard him complain.

"Go then," Dairon said. "Speak with Captain Jyfard. Keep D'zan safe . . . and your brother."

"Lyrilan?" asked Tyro. "Why does Lyrilan go to Udurum?"

"Why else?" answered Dairon. "He's writing a *book*."

Tyro laughed. Dairon joined him.

Before servants led him off to the bathing chamber, Dairon's face grew serious once again.

"Watch over them, Tyro."

Tyro bowed before his father.

When he looked up, the opulent chamber was empty but for

servants darting about the pillars and preparing the Emperor's dinner raiment.

Tyro walked back to the veranda, letting the cool air and rainmist wash his face. It was too long since he'd last seen the City of Men and Giants. Six years at least. He remembered the Uduru in their armor of black and violet. Their greatswords and axes. Their hammers of stone and steel, their laughter like the very thunder that shook the earth. He had seen a hundred of them at most during that trip. He tried to imagine a thousand of them marching into battle.

He smiled, watching the storm.

If there must be war, let it come, he thought. *I will lead these Giants into the south, and all the glory of myth will flow in our sweat and our blood. We will crush the Usurper of Yaskatha and the Bitch of Khyrei. Lyrilan will set it all down on the pages of history.*

He closed his eyes and listened to the sweet song of thunder.

7

Lessons

Sharadza found the cave just before sunrise. The night was still cold and full of glittering stars. She wore a cloak of sable fur and clothes made for riding, though she went on foot. A warm fire flickered in the depths of the dark cleft. Halfway up the side of an overgrown hill the cave sat trimmed in vines and hanging blossoms. Her breath puffed out in clouds of white fog as she crushed briar and bramble beneath her boots. The moon was only half full, and she'd nearly lost her way among the twisted rootscapes of the Uyga trees. But it seemed Fellow's directions had served her well after all.

Slipping out the window of her palace room that night had been easy. Her guards had no reason to believe she was not still inside and sleeping fitfully. They had not seen the rope she smuggled from the stables, or how she shimmied down its length onto a parapet leading to the palace's outer wall. Clinging from the top of that wall by her fingers, she dropped twenty feet to land gracefully on the thick grass of an exterior garden. She kept her face hidden in the folds of her cloak as she crept through the sleeping city. The booming voices of Giants in distant taverns were the only sounds except the barking of stray dogs. At Udurum's main gate two gold coins in the gatemaster's hand kept him from asking questions. Then she was out of the city and heading north into the woods, the opposite direction of the wide Southern Road.

In the morning Mitri and Dorus would enter her chambers with a bevy of serving girls and discover the rolled parchment upon her empty pillow. One of them would read it before it made its way into her mother's hands, even though it was addressed to Queen Shaira. Her mother would be furious. The note was brief:

Dear Mother,
I've gone to rescue Father. I have help and wisdom to guide me. Do not worry, for the blood of the Uduru runs in my veins. The journey may be long, but I will return. Please do not punish the guards or servants; they had no part in my leaving.
Your Loving Daughter,
Sharadza

Already she regretted not writing more. But what was there to say? She could not speak of her plan to seek sorcery; her mother would call her foolish and naïve. She already called Fellow a contemptible fool. Shaira never had a taste for adventure; she was born and bred in a gentler, more civilized land. But Sharadza was her father's daughter. She thrilled to stories of his youthful exploits, when she had been able to pry them from his lips. She read the sagas of Kings and heroes and wizards in the royal library. She practiced riding and archery, disdaining the feminine arts her mother impressed upon her. Shaira had nicknamed her "Little Uduri" – tiny Giantess. Giant women were hardly any different from their male counterparts, excepting their physiques. The Uduri were as wild and foolhardy, as mirthful and stubborn, as quick to wrath and prone to violence as any of their menfolk. They too had fought against the Serpent-Father when Old Udurum fell, and their boldness inspired Sharadza.

Morning sunlight limned the hilltop with orange flame, and the frosted slope twinkled as Sharadza approached the cave. Behind her the forest stretched in all directions, a mix of Uyga and lesser trees extending to the horizon. She had walked all night to find this grotto, but she was not tired. The thrill of the unknown sparkled along her scalp. She climbed the last few spans, her heart beating wildly. Beneath the cloak, her hand closed about the hilt of a long dagger.

A shadow darkened the cave mouth, silhouetted by the fire's glow. A figure stood there, hulking and dark of aspect . . . a great bear rearing on its haunches or a Giant waking to greet the morning. She could not tell. Sunlight broke over the hill's summit, blinding her.

"Come, child," said an ancient voice. "This is the place you seek."

Sharadza stepped upon a rocky lip to stand directly before the cave mouth. An old woman stood before her, a withered crone. Her frail limbs were wrapped in a bearskin tunic and her white hair was tied into long braids. Feathers and the skulls of tiny animals hung from her pale locks. Her face was a wrinkled mass, toothless with wide cheekbones. Her eyes gleamed bright as the morning.

She raised a bony hand toward Sharadza, who had not moved. She took the Princess's hand gently and drew her into the cavern. A small fire was the only source of light, so Sharadza could not see how deep the crone's domain went into the hill. Bronze talismans and woven rugs hung from the walls, along with copper pots, knives, and various implements of survival.

"Sit," said the crone, and she motioned toward the fire. A pot of steaming liquid hung from a spit over the flame. Sharadza did as she was bid, and the crone poured steaming tea into a wooden cup for her. The Princess bowed, and blew on the cup, hesitating to drink.

"Fellow sent me," Sharadza said. She felt utterly foolish. The crone knew this already, for had she not greeted her upon sight? What else should she say? Who was this hermitess?

"I know who you are and why you have come," said the crone. "There is no need to explain. Drink . . . "

Sharadza drank the hot tea and a pleasant warmth spread throughout her body.

"Who are you?" she asked.

"I am who you need me to be," said the crone. Her eyes glimmered like fire opals.

Sharadza drank again, and a blanket of calm settled over her.

"You seek sorcery," said the crone.

Sharadza nodded.

"This journey changes forever the one who takes it," said the crone. "Are you prepared to become someone new? Will you accept the death of your old self, so that your new self may be born?"

Sharadza thought of her father, walking alone across the bottom of the sea, wearing the chains of the Sea Queen or languishing in some deep coral dungeon.

"Yes," she said.

"Then finish the cup," said the crone.

Sharadza drank and asked another question. "How is it that a human woman lives so deep in the woods of Uduria?"

"Am I human?" asked the crone. "Or Giantess?" She stood up from the fire and now her height filled the entire cavern. Her wizened head bobbed alongside a gray stalactite. Her shadow blotted out the cave mouth. Sharadza blinked.

"Perhaps I am an old she-bear that you have awakened," said

the crone. Now she was a black bear, dropping to her four claws and opening a fanged maw to growl in Sharadza's face.

The Princess spilled tea across her leggings as she scooted across the floor in panic, but when she looked back the little old woman sat again where the bear had stood.

"Or am I a stone sitting alone in this cave that you have stumbled into?" said the crone.

Now she was an odd-shaped boulder sitting before the fire, nothing but a worn slab of gray granite that vaguely resembled a woman.

Sharadza looked into her cup. The tea must be affecting her perception. She had drunk wine before, but this was no drunkenness. This was something altogether different.

"Drink," said the slab of granite, and again it was an old crone sitting near the fire. "And ask yourself . . . What are *you*?"

A Serpent of steel, bronze, and gold wound its way between the black mountains. The wind howled along the twisting pass and cold sunlight glinted from the tips of spears, spiked helms, and gilded shields. The Serpent was in truth a company of men garbed in the metals of war. Three riders comprised the Serpent's triangular head, the three Princes Tadarus, Fangodrel, and Andoses. At their backs flew the twin flags of Udurum and Shar Dni, a spiny crest blooming from the Serpent's skull. Two hundred mounted Udurum elite mingled with a hundred cavalrymen of Shar Dni, whose blue shields bore the cloud insignia of the Sky God.

Tadarus rode a black charger at the head of the company, a broad blade of Udurum steel across his back. At his right rode his cousin Andoses, whose great scimitar hung from the saddle of his spotted stallion. Fangodrel the Pale rode behind them, brooding and silent as the mountain wind whipped at his crimson cloak. This troubled Tadarus. He was used to Fangodrel striving to take the lead in all things, pressing the seniority of his birth. He should be riding at the head of the column on his own insistence. Yet Fangodrel had said hardly a word to him or anyone else for the first three days of their journey. Did he know what Mother had instructed Tadarus to say and do? Perhaps she had spoken to Fangodrel in private, letting him know that Tadarus was in charge. Or perhaps the eldest brother was only sulking. Tadarus would never understand the moodiness of poets.

The roar of a mountain cat rang along the ravine, and Prince Andoses turned his green eyes toward the high escarpments on either side.

"Do not worry, cousin," said Tadarus. "No tiger will dare approach a force of men this size."

Andoses' eyes searched the frosted peaks. "It is not in my nature to know fear," he said. "But these mountains are an uncomfortable place for my men. The sun's warmth cannot reach us here, and the wind never ceases to blow."

Tadarus laughed without humor. "Before my father carved this pass, there was no getting over these mountains at all. You are too used to the green valleys and gentle beaches of your homeland." The Prince of Shar Dni had sailed north from his city into the Far Sea, coming to ground on the eastern shore of Uduria. This was his first time traveling Vod's Pass. Tadarus felt his cousin's tension and respected his bravery.

Andoses lowered his gaze to the bracken and rubble along the walls of the pass. "I admit I prefer the pitch and roll of the open sea to this burrowing through the earth," he said. "I'd like to see *you* upon the deck of a ship, Tadarus. Then I'd have cause to laugh at your nerves."

Tadarus smiled. "True, cousin, true," he said. "If our errand is successful and there is war against Khyrei, you will have your chance to laugh at me."

"They say the Old Wyrms still haunt these mountains," said Andoses. "Is it true?"

Tadarus shrugged. He glanced back at Fangodrel, riding a black mare in solemn thought, his personal servant Rathwol following directly behind on a horse whose flanks were piled with bundles, coffers, and flasks. Fangodrel would not relinquish his luxuries, even on a trek such as this. Tadarus did not judge him too harshly. Fangodrel did not have the constitution of his younger brothers. Why Vod's great strength had skipped over his firstborn son only the Gods knew. Even Sharadza, the baby of the family, had more strength in her narrow limbs than Fangodrel. Yet Fangodrel was intelligent, and that counted for much. He was a prolific writer despite his dark sensibilities.

"Tadarus?" asked Andoses. "Did you hear me?"

Tadarus turned his head. "Forgive me," he said. "I worry about my brother."

Andoses glanced backward, shifting in his saddle. "He seems fine."

"Yes," said Tadarus. "He always seems fine. But never so quiet."

"Perhaps it's the mountainous gloom," said Andoses. "It penetrates the soul."

Tadarus chuckled. "You haven't even scaled the cold heights yet."

Andoses shivered, pulling his yellow cloak tighter about his shoulders. "What about the Wyrms?"

"There are a few of the old beasts left," said Tadarus. "But they delve deep into the earth and rarely emerge. At times a quake will disturb their slumber and one will rise up storming through the pass, spitting fire and hatred."

Andoses' eyes grew large, but only for a moment. "Have you seen one?"

"Never," said Tadarus. "The Giants of Steephold keep the pass secure. They deal with any Serpents that crawl from their holes. I've seen *bones*, mind you. The Giants make armor and helmets from them sometimes. Spear-tips from their fangs."

Andoses was quiet for a moment, his voice replaced by the sound of clattering hooves and the clamor of mail, shield, and spear. Someone back in the line was singing an old war song of Uurz, a deep voice half obscured by the wind. Tadarus knew that Andoses was imagining a reptile whose teeth were as large as spear heads. He thought of his father, who killed the Lord of Serpents and tamed these mountains. His heart felt heavy beneath the crest of New Udurum, the silver hammer engraved on his breastplate.

Earlier he went to an oracle in the city, an old seer whose powers were rumored to be great, and he gave her more gold than she had seen in her seventy years. She burned the sacred herbs and sacrificed lambs to the Gods of Sea and Sky. But still she had failed to answer the questions *Is my father alive?* and *Will Vod return to his kingdom?* She had only one bit of wisdom for him after all her spells and divinations: "The sea holds many mysteries, and none know what secrets dwell in its depths save the Sea God and his finny peoples." She gave back most of his gold, shamed by the failure of her own magic, and Tadarus never spoke of the attempt to the rest of his family. They must learn to accept that Vod of the Storms, father, King, hero, legend . . . was gone. Tadarus was the first to admit this, for he knew the court now looked to him as its next sovereign. Even if Fangodrel was the eldest, it was tall Tadarus that everyone approached for strength and guidance. So he bore his sadness in silence and tried his best to replace his father.

Now this campaign to unite four kingdoms in a war the likes of which had never been seen in modern history. He was glad for the chance to remove himself from court, to dwell upon the journey, the diplomacy, and the warfare that would follow. By distracting himself with bold endeavors, he might forget the pain of his loss. He must forge a new set of legends and stories to rival those of Vod. He must *become* his father by doing great things, by shaking the world into new forms and shapes.

Vireon was different. He held no ambition, and he lost his pain by losing himself in the glory of nature, the thrill of the Long Hunt. Tadarus envied him. In many ways, Vireon was still only a boy. He knew the throne would never be his, so he was free to be a child of the forest. There was little responsibility on Vireon's shoulders, though they were as wide and strong as Tadarus' own. Tadarus loved his younger brother and missed him even now, but the throne rooms and battlefields of distant lands were no place for Vireon. Besides, Tadarus did not know when he would return to Udurum, so Vireon had best keep their mother safe.

"How far until Steephold?" asked Andoses. It was only the company's first day in the mountains, but for him the journey could not pass quickly enough.

"Two days at this speed," said Tadarus. "If the weather holds."

They would find warm fires, fresh bread, and good meat at the citadel. Fifty Uduru were stationed there to watch over the pass from its mid-point. Andoses would see the Serpent bones Tadarus had mentioned. And friends were there whom Tadarus had not seen in five years, since his trip to visit Uurz with his father and brothers. He was barely twenty at the time, and it seemed Vod would live and rule forever. Perhaps it was thoughts of their father that now plagued Fangodrel?

Tadarus let his steed drop back and drew up alongside his brother. Fangodrel looked at him with piercing eyes, his face a white wedge of calm. Tadarus rode near him in silence awhile. He never knew how to approach Fangodrel without sparking an argument, so he usually avoided him. Which, given Fangodrel's introverted pursuits, was not hard to do. He rarely entered the training yard, the wrestling pit, or the stables. More likely he'd be in the library learning some esoteric history or holed up in his room writing verse . . . or cavorting with some courtesan. His appetites were notorious, but then Tadarus and Vireon also had their fair share of lovers. Fangodrel kept his affairs as secret as possible, yet there was only so much secrecy to be had in a palace. Tadarus knew how cruel Fangodrel was to his wenches, how he beat the servants and maidens who displeased him. Perhaps he thought a Prince should behave in such a way. Such behavior bred little love among the court.

"*You* must lead the diplomacy," Queen Shaira had told Tadarus. "You will be the one who convinces Dairon to support Shar Dni . . . not Fangodrel."

"Then why send him at all, Mother?" Tadarus had asked.

"He is the eldest," she replied. "To not send him would be an insult. But we both know he is no sweet-tongued ambassador."

"Nor am I," said Tadarus.

"You do not have to be," said Shaira. "You are the son of a Hero-King, and you wear Vod's image on your face. Fangodrel . . . Fangodrel is different. You know this."

"Yes," said Tadarus. "He is more like you than father."

Shaira stared at him then, as if he'd said something odd. Then she only smiled and reminded him of his duty.

"Remember that you speak for New Udurum," she said. "If Fangodrel fails to realize this you must . . . remind him."

Tadarus reassured her: he knew his role and that of his brother.

"And when you get to Mumbaza this will be even more important," said the Queen. "Fangodrel is a figurehead only. You, Tadarus, are my voice and mind. If we are to aid my brother's people, it falls upon you to secure these alliances."

"Do not forget," said Tadarus. "Andoses will be with us."

"Yes, of course. But a Prince of Shar Dni is not a Prince of Udurum. You are also the voice of the Giants. The world respects this, fears it even. It is what separates us from all other kingdoms."

"Mother . . . " Tadarus hesitated. "What if we gain the alliance of Uurz and Mumbaza, but the Giants decide not to fight? What then?"

Shaira smiled at her son, kissed him on the forehead. "Son, when have you ever known an Uduru *not* to want to fight?"

Now Tadarus rode beside the brooding Fangodrel and searched for words. The shadows of the peaks fell over them and the light of the sun was lost. A new chill crept along the pass like invisible fog. The horses breathed out white vapor.

"What do you want, Tadarus?" Fangodrel finally asked.

"You seem troubled, brother," said Tadarus. "Do you think of our father?"

Fangodrel started to laugh, but checked himself. He turned his lean face again to Tadarus.

"No," was all he said.

"You do not seem your usual self," said Tadarus.

"You hardly know me, *brother*," said Fangodrel.

"True," said Tadarus. "But this must change. We have a long journey ahead of us. Why must we stay at such lengths from each other? We are the same blood. Things should be different between us."

Fangodrel mused on his brother's words awhile. He tilted his head. "Tell me," he said. "Why do you wait until now to make this offer? You have spurned me all your life. You are favored by Mother and Father. I am at best tolerated. Now you find yourself forced to endure my presence, and you wish to make a peace?"

Tadarus pursed his lips. He would not let his brother anger him, as he was so skilled at doing. He must see past the harsh words, the mistrust. This man was his brother, and however different they were, there should be love between them. *Should* be.

"We've had our differences," said Tadarus. "But Father is gone; our family is changed. Soon the world will change too. By the things we go to do now, we will change it. Let us join together and write a new story. We are no longer children, Fangodrel. We must act like Men."

Fangodrel guffawed. "You, who are younger, lecture me on maturity? Your ego knows no bounds, Prince."

Tadarus ignored the pressure rising in his chest. "You are but a year my elder," he said.

"Still . . . I am your elder," said Fangodrel.

"What of it?" said Tadarus, a sliver of anger slipping into his words.

"The throne will be mine when Mother dies," said Fangodrel. "You cannot accept this fact. It eats at you like a disease. I see your envy dripping like poison from your eyes."

"The throne will *never* be yours," said Tadarus. Rage stole his words and ran away with them. His face flushed bright red. "You are too weak, and you are too cruel! Men will not follow you, nor Giants. What little wisdom you do have you waste on stale rhymes and cheap whores. That is why I lead this company – not you. Do not forget it."

Fangodrel rode on unmoved by his brother's anger. He blinked as the sun appeared above a ridgeline. "This is how you make peace," he said. "Well done, my loving brother."

Tadarus groaned, cursed between his teeth. His brother had done it again. Made him lose his temper. Gods be damned, he wouldn't make the mistake of reaching out to this wretch again. He leaned over in the saddle, bringing his face close to that of Fangodrel.

"Just you mind your place in my company, *brother*," Tadarus said, teeth gritted.

"Or what?" said Fangodrel. "You'll kill me? You'd be a kinslayer, a cursed criminal."

"If I wanted to kill you I'd have done it years ago."

"You haven't the stomach for it," said Fangodrel. "You'll always be Mother's little boy. Play at war if you like, throw your stones and wrestle your Giants . . . but that's all you are. You hate me because I know this better than anyone."

Tadarus refused to follow the conversation any further.

"Mind your place," he said again, and spurred his horse back to the front of the line. Once more he rode alongside Andoses.

"How fares my cousin?" asked the Prince of Shar Dni.

Tadarus breathed deeply, calming himself the way a warrior prepares for battle. "Always the same," he said. "Miserable, offensive, and insufferable."

"Good thing he's riding back there then, eh?" said Andoses.

Tadarus looked at his cousin and laughed. Andoses caught the laughter and returned it.

Fangodrel rode grim and silent behind them.

In the narrow belt of sky above the ravine, stormclouds scudded and rumbled.

Tadarus and Andoses were still laughing when the first of the cold drops fell.

The cave was a tunnel leading deep into the bowels of the hill. The darkness lived there, seething and flowing and breathing like some ancient beast. Sharadza walked into the depths of the earth, the dark flowing thick about her like honey. She smelled damp granite and the spoor of little blind creatures. She heard her own footfalls, clattering and booming in the lightless regions, and the crone's voice called her deeper and deeper into the subterranean void.

"The five senses are lies," said the crone's voice. She was

somewhere nearby, hovering in the darkness. "Down here, without light, you will see more clearly."

Stumbling, groping, crawling through the dark. Echoes of her own movements dancing across the walls, the invisible ceiling.

"The first step in learning sorcery," said the crone's voice, "is to look beyond the lies of the world. To see the invisible that dwells behind and beneath the visible. The world you know up there does not exist. Down here you are a newborn, and you must relearn. So you will come to understand the world in a new way. Eat this . . . "

Sharadza's head swam, and she felt the crone's hand against hers. She closed her fingers over some kind of root like a gnarled carrot. It smelled of dirt. "Eat," said the crone's voice.

Crunching molars, bitter taste vibrating on her tongue. The aftertaste of the sweet tea mingling with the earthy flavor of the root. Then a lightness, a dizzy flow, the pounding of blood in her ears.

The rough ground at her feet glowed now, a phosphorescence she had not noticed. A hue of nameless color. She raised her head. A vast cavern opened before her, a forest of stalactites and stalagmites stretching into the darkness. Some of them had melded into magnificent pillars, glowing with that same colorless color, glinting with crystalline deposits like skeins of diamond. The roof of the vault was too far overhead to see, as were the walls. Here was another world altogether. Now white mushrooms tall as Giants grew in the murk, with lesser fungi sprouting beneath them in masses of shifting, pulsing colors. How had she not seen all this a moment before? Where was the source of light? There was no light. She was seeing the darkness. No . . . seeing *through* the darkness.

The crone stood near a tall stalagmite, supporting her bent back with a wooden staff. She glowed like a rainbow, translucent and glimmering in wondrous shades that had no names.

"Who are you?" asked the crone.

"You know who I am," said Sharadza, the non-lights dazzling her eyes.

"Who are you?"

"Sharadza."

"Who is Sharadza?" asked the crone.

"The daughter of Vod and Shaira."

"Who are you?"

The crone was gone. Tiny beings moved among the wilderness of fungi, glowing with life. Now the fungi sprouted above her like the forest of Uduria, and she walked – no scuttled – among the blossoming foliage. She sniffed, smelling color and sound and a dozen mysteries. Her hands and arms were gone. She had four clawed appendages now, and a proboscis nose, snuffling along the ground. The cave creatures greeted her with subsonic noises and bursts of scent. She responded by instinct. She roamed the fungi world for a time without measure, sometimes alone, sometimes with her pale-furred companions, dragging a long tail that switched and slapped the ground. She nibbled at the choicest of fungi, savoring its taste, going on to sample more. She ate, defecated, and moved on. She screeched, and fought, and fed again, and sang with her sightless brethren in the swirling fungus groves.

"Who are you?" came the crone's voice.

It took her a moment to answer. "Sharadza," she chirped as best she could.

Now she came to a dark underground lake lying serene beneath a vast dome of granite. Ripples moved across its surface now and then, and she saw the glow of life drifting in its depths. The crone said something, and Sharadza *slithered* forward, letting the frigid waters envelope her. She swam the black currents, moving her lithe body, flexing flipper-like appendages, sensing the movements of subaqueous creatures by their vibrations. She swallowed blind cave fish, swirled her serpentine self over slime-encrusted boulders, and flowed into a subterranean river that fed the lake. She avoided the lunging maw of something much larger than herself. She was not ready to be devoured. She followed the swift current like an eel. After an eternity, she sensed sunlight above, and rose to find the river flowing through the forested wilderness. The brilliance of the sun made her spasm and twist in the rushing waters.

"Who are you?" came the crone's voice.

She slithered up onto the riverbank and opened her fanged mouth. With difficulty she said, "Sharadza."

Now she ran through the forest as a great black wolf. She hurdled the swollen roots of the Uyga, reveling in the speed of her limbs, the keenness of her scent. She smelled game, the magnetic call of prey, and chased a buck for leagues through the leafy landscape. The sun was a ball of fire rolling across the sky, and the forest opened its secrets to her. They poured in through her black nostrils, and her thick fur stood on end. She drank from forest pools and chased another deer, bringing it down with fang and claw. She lapped up the hot blood, tore at the fresh meat, devoured the carcass until her belly was full. Her four-legged brothers and sisters came to share her kill, and she yowled her pleasure at the rising moon.

"Who are you?"

She howled into the twilight sky, "Sharadza . . . "

Now she became that howl, and the moon grew larger, a golden orb bearing down upon her. She flapped her wings and turned from its radiance. The northern forest spread like a purple carpet below. Mountains ruled the southern and northern horizons; to east and west gleamed the oceans whose names she could not remember. She whirled and spun in the night winds, exulting in the perfection of flight. She soared above the forest among hundreds of other wind-riders above and below her, all pursuing nocturnal hunts. She flew toward the dawn as the sun rose, an infinite well of crimson, gold, and white flame. She turned back and flew westward until it stood high in the blue sky.

"Who are you?" came the crone's voice.

She hardly heard the question. She soared downward now, toward that sea of fall colors, entering the forest through its whispering roof, gliding along its cool corridors until she found the hill. She flew toward the cave mouth where the crone stood, one wrinkled hand held up to the sky. She landed on the crone's forearm, sinking her talons into a leather sleeve.

"Who are you?"

Sharadza stood now before the crone, looking down at her two hands, her two legs and her cumbersome feet. She flexed her arms, her clumsy arms that would not lift her into the skies. She smelled the forest smells, a symphony of aromas rising from the wild, as if she had never before been here. It smelled of earth, of freedom, and of power.

"*Who are you?*" demanded the crone.

"I . . . I . . . don't know," said Sharadza. Tears brimmed in her green eyes.

"*What* are you?" asked the crone.

Sharadza blinked, weeping, smiling. "I don't know."

The crone huffed. "Now we can begin," she said.

Sharadza followed her down the hillside into the depths of the autumn forest.

From the summit of the pass rose the colossal bulk of Steephold, a citadel of black rock nearly as large as Vod's palace. The sinking sun cast orange light across its dark walls as the Princes halted their company. At Tadarus' command, a sergeant blew three notes on a horn of gold and bronze, and a deeper horn sounded its answer inside the fortress walls.

The Giants were slow opening the gate, so Fangodrel stared impatiently at its embossed surface. A scene of Uduru in battle against fire-belching Serpents ornamented the black iron. The artistry was excellent, far too complex and well constructed to have been done by a Giant's hands. Fangodrel smirked at its absurdity: the great deeds of the Uduru preserved by skill of a mere human.

The saddle chafed his thighs, and his back ached from days of riding. How long would it take those lumbering morons to open the gates? Five days they had ridden from Udurum, the last three in the frigid shadow of the peaks. Sheer idiocy to send an escort of three hundred men on this mission. A company of four or five could travel at double the speed. Still, his mother had her way, as always.

Steephold would offer at least one night of warm beds and passable food. More importantly, Fangodrel would have a private chamber here, a place to lock himself away and smoke the bloodflower. In his frail tent the past few nights, he dared not indulge in the Red Dream for fear of being discovered by his brother or cousin. He drank plenty of wine in the camps, but tonight he would taste the smoke.

Ianthe would come to him again.

When she first appeared to him in the Red Dream, he thought it only the drug's illusion. But the following night he spoke with her again, and a third time on the morning before the journey began. Somewhere in the distant south, in her jungle palace filled with slaves and riches, she too dreamed the Red Dream. But she knew it better than he . . . she knew how to reach out to him across a continent.

She told him splendid things that he only half dared believe.

He wanted them to be true so very much. She was his grandmother . . . a sorceress . . . an Empress. Vod was not his father, although Shaira did give him birth. His true father was Gammir, Prince of Khyrei, who died at Vod's hand. She showed him this in a vision summoned from the past and played out in the swirling depths of the Red Dream. Vod in his Giant form, storming the Khyrein palace, calling down thunder and lightning with his cries of rage and hate. The onyx palace crumbling into shards, handsome Gammir lost beneath a heaving wall of rock, his bones crushed to powder along with his father the Emperor. Only Ianthe escaped the destruction, a white panther crawling along the blood-slick rubble.

Now Fangodrel understood why he inherited none of Vod's strength, why his skin was so pale. Like Gammir's . . . like Ianthe's. He had none of Vod's blood in him, no Uduru blood at all. Shaira had been a Princess of Shar Dni when she wed Gammir. Vod stole her away and murdered Gammir that same year. He knew now why his mother never truly loved him. Why she favored his brothers. He only reminded her of Gammir, whom she hated. Shaira had plotted her escape with Vod even before the marriage. She was a traitor and a whore. His adoptive father was a liar, may his bones rot beneath the Cryptic Sea.

Ianthe told him the truth in the ecstatic depths of the bloodflower trance. In that heaven of red shadows, he embraced her and she kissed his forehead.

"You must find your way back to me," she told him. "To your inheritance. You will be Emperor of Khyrei. All of my kingdom, my wealth, my great knowledge is yours."

"I will steal away this very night," Fangodrel swore. "I'll travel in disguise and take passage from Shar Dni."

"No," said Ianthe. "The danger is too great. The Golden Sea is full of death and pirates. War is brewing."

"But Grandmother . . . " he protested, crying tears of flame. "I want my true family . . . I want—"

"You want *power*," said Ianthe, soothing him with her gentle touch. How old was she? She seemed as young as he, her skin so white and unblemished, her body firm and perfectly sculpted. It seemed impossible that she could be two generations removed from his own, yet he believed her. He felt it in his very soul. Saw it in the visions poured like dark wine from her mind into his.

"Power you shall have, darling boy," she told him. "It is yours by right of your bloodline. That power will grow within you and bring you to me. The kyreas, which you call the bloodflower, will be your guide. Here in the Red Dream I will teach you the power and glory of blood, red and hot on your tongue. You will call upon the Dwellers in Shadow . . . The blood will liberate you; the blood will bring you to me."

"What blood?" he asked, ashamed of his own ignorance.

Ianthe smiled, and again she was the white panther, her claws and fangs stained with fresh crimson.

"The blood that you *spill*," she said. "The blood of your enemies."

At last the great valves opened and the Giants of Steephold welcomed the three Princes into the vast courtyard with rumbling laughter. A sliver of moon rose just above the central tower, and lowering clouds promised more storms.

The keep and its environs had been built exclusively to accommodate the Uduru, so every hall, chamber, corridor, and passage was three times larger than any human would need. The royal quarters were built with a few man-sized accommodations, but the bulk of the soldiers from Udurum and Shar Dni would bunk in the massive barracks meant for Giant troops in times of war. Those chambers had never been used because the citadel, like New Udurum, was only a quarter-century old. Steephold was built over the ruins of a much older fortress, one built by Giants a thousand years ago. It had fallen into ruin centuries past, but the caverns it had guarded still remained, a series of tunnels running deep beneath the mountains. In the old days, Serpents often crawled up from those depths, and Giants marched into the subterranean realms to hunt them. Now they were paved over and corked shut with great stones.

Fangodrel doubted there were still any Serpents living beneath the range, but many of their skeletons hung upon walls inside the citadel. These were the relics of ancient hunts, fleshless bodies longer than the Giants were tall, with a dozen clawed legs and a mouth full of ivory fangs. If not for the bones of these creatures kept as trophies, he never would have believed that such creatures existed. But then he was learning much these days that he might not have believed until now.

Tallim the Rockjaw served as Lord of Steephold, appointed by Vod himself when Fangodrel was an infant. Rockjaw greeted the Princes in his main hall, rising from his great chair and stalking toward them like some beefy monster. His laughter rumbled toward the high ceiling, rattling the bones of the trophy Wyrms along the walls. The furs of a dozen bears composed his great cloak, and the teeth of those same bears hung about his trunk-like neck. The hall was filled with all fifty of his Giants, standing at attention with hammers and axes in their gnarled fists.

"Young Princes!" bellowed Rockjaw. "You do us honor! How many seasons has it been? Ten? Fifteen?"

Fangodrel wished to avoid ceremony and go directly to his chamber, but Tadarus jumped at any chance to indulge in royal etiquette. He loved these vicious brutes and their savage manner. *I will not play their games of mock respect. Let Rockjaw fawn and pretend to be civilized with Tadarus. They are two of a kind.*

"Tallim!" yelled Tadarus, matching the Giant's volume. "Good to see your beard is still thick and your hands still strong."

The Giant bent to embrace Tadarus as best he could, but he did not lift him. Tadarus was, after all, a Prince, and that would not be appropriate. *At least not until they are both drunk and sprawling about the hall an hour from now.*

To Fangodrel, Rockjaw offered a stiff bow, and when Tadarus introduced Prince Andoses, the Giant repeated this motion. "My heart has been heavy since I heard of your father's fate," said Rockjaw. "There has never been a King like Vod of the Storms. He made a better world."

Tadarus nodded, accepting the sycophantic words. Fangodrel said nothing. A moment of awkward silence filled the hall, but for the crackling of the fire bowls.

"We received no word of your coming, Prince," said Rockjaw. "Was there no advance rider?"

Tadarus shook his head, removing his purple cloak. "There was no time," he said. "Our errand is urgent. We go to Uurz and on to Mumbaza, to make a case for war."

Rockjaw's huge eyebrows rose, and his great fingers plucked at his beard with interest. Several Giants grunted their approval.

"Come!" said Rockjaw. "We will feast and we will drink, and I will listen to you speak of war."

"And later," said Tadarus, a stupid grin on his face, "perhaps we'll wrestle."

The Giant laughed and clapped Tadarus on the back, a gesture that would have knocked Fangodrel or Andoses to their knees.

"I am ill," Fangodrel announced. "No drink for me this night. I'll take to my quarters immediately. My servant will return for food and necessaries later this evening."

"Yes, Prince," said Rockjaw. He assigned a Giant to escort Fangodrel to his apartments, although Fangodrel could have made the walk by himself easily enough. Three times before, he had stayed here, the last time five years ago when his father – no his false father – had dragged him to Uurz for some diplomatic assembly.

Rathwol, sneezing and huffing under the weight of the bundles lifted off his steed, followed Fangodrel. As they paced a vaulted corridor, a trio of spotted hounds barked and ran up to sniff them and gnaw at their boots. The Giant growled a command and the dogs fell back, following along now like Rathwol himself. In truth, there was very little difference between Rathwol and the canines. Except that Rathwol could speak as well as follow simple commands.

Fangodrel demanded the King's Chamber for his own, and the Giant had no choice but to give it him. "King Vod is dead," Fangodrel reminded him. "I am his eldest son. Where else should I sleep?" The Giant bowed and took up his post at the end of the hall. Fangodrel entered the drafty quarters, Rathwol struggling in behind him. Shucking his bundles, the little man closed the chamber door, shooing off the trio of yapping dogs.

The apartment was dull, hardly fit for a King, but it would serve. A great bed sat untouched for years, probably rife with dust. Rathwol would attend to it. A single Serpent skull hung on the wall, alongside a tall standard bearing the silver hammer of Vod's house. There were rugs about the floor to stave off the cold, crude pelts torn from mountain animals. Someone had at least enough sense to set a fire in the great bronze bowl at the chamber's center. A few couches and tables, and a bathing tub, completed the furnishings. There was far too much space in this room, as in all the rooms of Steephold, but Fangodrel was simply glad to be out of the cold and away from his brother and cousin.

"The coffer," he said.

Rathwol immediately opened one carefully tied bundle and

removed the small box of jade and crystal. From a sturdy wooden case he took the Serpent-carved pipe, and a packet of tinder sticks. Fangodrel shed his outer cloak and sank into a cushioned chair by the fire bowl. He opened with his secret key the coffer's lid and looked upon the twelve scarlet blossoms stuffed inside.

"Prepare my bed and heat some water," he told Rathwol.

"Master, I am hungry," said the rat-faced one.

Fangodrel glared at him. "Then do what I have told you, and you may join the feast a while. Bring back food for me as well."

"Yes, Prince," said Rathwol, hurrying to dust off the bed.

Fangodrel filled the bowl of his pipe with three delicate petals. He touched a lit tinder stick to it and inhaled the sweetness he had anticipated for days. His head fell back on the cushions, and the Red Dream enfolded him.

Flying, floating, swimming, he moved through the crimson fog. Somewhere far away, his hands moved again to lift the pipe to his lips, and his faraway lungs inhaled once more.

A spark of brilliant white in the red universe.

She was there before him, a gorgeous panther, then a gorgeous woman. Her beauty stunned him as it always did. For a moment he wished they were flesh in this place, so he might take her in the manner of a whore. Then he remembered who she was, and brushed away a pang of guilt.

"Ianthe." He smiled.

"My darling boy," she said, floating closer. "It has been many days and nights."

"Duties at court," he said. "Now I have privacy again."

"Tonight I will give you your true name. That false name we must burn away."

"Yes, Grandmother."

Flames swirled about them, driven by invisible winds.

"Your name will be that of your father, so that you may fulfill his legacy. You are Gammir, Son of Gammir." She placed her phantom hands on his cheeks.

"I am Gammir," he said. Waves of radiant bliss washed over him.

"Your throne awaits, Gammir." She kissed him.

Sitting in the chair, in some other dimension, his true body writhed with delight.

"But first you must learn the Ways of the Blood," she whispered.

"I am ready . . . "

"You will need something to kill," she said. "Something warm-blooded. An animal or a slave."

Fangodrel considered this. Rathwol would certainly not be missed. His death could easily be explained as an accident. Nobody in Tadarus' or Andoses' companies would even blink. But Rathwol was useful . . . and loyal.

"There are no slaves here," he said. "There are hounds . . . "

"Yes." His grandmother nodded. "Turn away from me now and take up a sharp dagger. Slit the dog's throat over a burning flame. Be sure it still lives when you do this."

"Yes, Grandmother. What then?"

"Give some of the blood to the fire, and drain the rest into a cup or chalice. Mix with it a single petal from the bloodflower. Then you must drink it, all of it, but not before you say these words . . . "

She whispered in his ear the strange syllables of a language that was not a language. They rang somehow with an odd familiarity in his skull. She repeated them twice more, until he could say them back. Then he shook himself, rose from the cushions, and pulled his long dagger from its sheathe. He stared at it as if he had never seen it before, red vapors swimming through his vision. The pommel was carved into the head of a snarling wolf, with tiny rubies for eyes. The blade was straight and of one piece with the hilt, forged of silvery Uduru steel. Rathwol had kept it sharp for him. It glittered in the light of the fire, anticipating the blood it was to spill.

The little man was pouring a bucket of steaming water into the bathtub when Fangodrel called his name.

"Lord?" asked Rathwol, wiping his nose with the back of a gloved hand. His watery eyes were small and hungry.

"Bring me one of those hounds."

8

In the Kingdom of Ice

Cold was his first sensation. It wrapped him like a second skin, a blanket of glittering diamond frost. Pain, formerly a stranger to him, now bent low and kissed his lips, his forehead, his chest, smothering him in its frozen lust. Then hunger, gnawing at his guts like a trapped bear cub, tearing its way from the inside out. He had never been truly hungry – or cold – before now. So many new discoveries . . . so many ways to suffer. He opened his eyes, spikes of fresh agony grinding into his skull.

Light, aquamarine and without a trace of warmth, momentarily blinded him. Emerald-indigo brilliance . . . was he underwater? No, he could breathe, though the air raked his lungs with iron claws. The numbness in his shoulders and wrists suddenly made sense – he hung suspended from his arms, fists bound together with iron chains. His feet dangled in the same loop of chain, thick black links gone white with rime. Squinting, he peered at the sheer walls of blue-green ice rising to left and right. Above, some rafter or stalactite of ice held the end of the chain. He thought of slaughtered cattle hanging in Udurum smokehouses, sides of skinned beef awaiting the butchers' cleavers.

Below him yawned a pit of sullen darkness. If not for the chain, he would fall and be lost forever in that glacial crevasse. The cavern was carved of raw ice, or ice had frozen over its every earthen surface. He saw no bare rock behind the filmy crystal; it seemed the ice was solid as granite. The watery light filtering through was refracted sunlight. Now fully awake, he realized what he had first taken for brilliance was in fact dimness.

His stomach growled, and he coughed. Something moved in the cavern behind him. A grunt, a shifting of great bulk, heavy footfalls. Something grabbed the chains above his fists and slung him to the ground. He almost lost consciousness beneath the waves of pain washing through his body, beginning from the top of his skull and raging through his limbs – all agony but for his numb shoulders and wrists. He remembered a great iron mace . . .

Two blue-skinned Giants stood over him, staring him down with blood-red pupils. Their beards were tangles of icicles, their white manes heavy with frost. Their stinking carnivore breath was colder than the wind in the cavern. They grinned at his helplessness. They boomed with laughter as he strove against the chains, gritting his teeth and pulling tighter the links of metal. Exhaustion and hunger had taken their toll. On any normal day he might tear these chains from his limbs like silken cloth. Now, fearing that his head would split open under such effort, he ceased and lay back, sucking chill air into his lungs.

One of the blue-skins grabbed the chain and dragged him along the floor like the carcass of some forest kill. The other followed with that same iron mace slung across his shoulder. Another swing of that weapon would crush Vireon's skull to pulp. But he was too worn out to continue his struggles. He lay still and let himself be dragged along a carpet of frost.

The ice cavern gave way to others, larger and wider, and carved into Giant stairwells at intervals. They dragged him through vaulted galleries grown or hewn from the endless ice. A world of frozen crystal, steeped in the turquoise glow of filtered sunshine. Walls sparkled like miniature glaciers. Icy pillars thick as Uyga trees bore spiral designs depicting tribal warfare in a style reminiscent of the ancient Uduru. His captors dragged him through a domed plaza that must have been the very heart of the palatial glacier. There hundreds of blue-skins went about the common tasks of their daily lives, oblivious to the tiny captive hauled through their midst. Gravelly voices babbled in a melange of half-familiar syllables, some ancient dialect of Uduru speech.

They wore the furs of mammoth, bear, tiger, and wolf, white as snow or dyed to shades of crimson and black. Rusted spikes adorned the iron helms of male and female warriors. Their spears were taller than their heads, and tipped with frozen blades. Enormous broadswords hung on wide belts of sealskin. Ice and frost hung in the mens' beards, in the braided tresses of the women, and their breath did not turn to vapor when they exhaled, for their bodies were as cold as the ice itself. Some stood around gouts of writhing blue flame that gave no warmth. None spared him a glance as the guards dragged him past, though in his wake he often heard avalanches of laughter.

At the top of a great pile of crystalline stairs, his captors flung open a gleaming gate and pulled him into a massive hall set with sparkling pillars of turquoise immensity. The booming of drums filled his ears, mixed with a chorus of eerie voices, low and rolling like thunder across the cold spaces. This must be the loftiest hall, the royal chamber. Blue-skin warriors lined the viridian walls. Now his jailers picked him up, only to throw him down again like a stolen treasure at the feet of their King. The savage drumming hammered against his skull.

Vireon stared up from the slick floor, blinking stars from his eyes, and inhaled a musky animal scent. The King of the blue-skins reclined on a throne built of tarnished mammoth tusks. On his left, a harem of nude Giantesses danced for his pleasure around a fountain of cold blue fire; at his right, a band of blue-skin drummers sang their primal cadences. A trio of white tigers sat at the King's feet, chained by iron collars to the base of his throne. The felines stared hungrily at Vireon, who lay merely fingerspans from their fangs; they licked their chops with ruddy tongues.

Chained like me. But still deadly.

The blue-skin King wore a crown of black metal set with sapphires. It gleamed in the icy light, like the weird fires of his domain. The ice in his beard crackled as he shifted in his great chair to stare at the prisoner. A huge axe lay at his side, its double blade of iron glittering with a sheen of frost.

The Ice King raised his hand. The drums stopped, the dancers fell upon their furs, and silence reigned in the hall. Vireon ignored the pain in his skull and limbs . . . his shoulders were coming back to life now. He forced himself onto his knees, then to his feet. They hadn't bothered to give him cloak or blanket, but at least they had let him keep boots and leggings. There was a terrible absence at his waist where his long knife should be. He stared into the blood-bright eyes of the Ice King.

The monarch spoke, and Vireon strained to understand his words. It was the speech of the Uduru – surely these people were Uduru, or had been in some remote age. But the accent was guttural and hard to grasp. He snatched what meaning he could from them.

"Little human . . . son of the South . . . You are far from home. No human . . . may come here. These are the hunting grounds . . . of the Udvorg . . . the Ice Clans. Are there more . . . humans like you . . . in our mountains?"

Vireon chose his words carefully. "I am no Southborn, no human," he said, though it pained him to speak. His teeth chattered. His stomach growled and the white tigers looked at him hungrily. "I am the Prince of Udurum . . . My father is Vod of the Storms . . . Uduru King."

The Ice King laughed, a sound like grinding glaciers.

"You . . . are a tiny human . . . nothing like the Uduru. Unless . . . they have shrunk."

The guards laughed at their King's jest. Vireon coughed.

"My father was Vod, King of Udurum . . . " he said. "But my mother was a human woman, Shaira of Shar Dni."

The Ice King raised his frosted brows. "How . . . can this be?"

"My father was a sorcerer," said Vireon. "He chose a human woman because he loved her. He has three sons. I am the youngest son . . . Vireon."

The blue-skin monarch looked about his chamber, as if gauging the reactions of his subjects, but Vireon could not tell if any communication passed between them. It was all he could do to stay balanced on his unsteady feet.

"My name . . . " said the King, "is Angrid the Long-Arm. I am King here. Long ago . . . we and the Uduru . . . were one people. That is no more . . . the truth. Once we warred on the humans together . . . We drove them past the Mountains of the South . . . into the great wasteland of Serpents."

"The wasteland is no more," said Vireon. "My father turned it into a fertile realm, a land of thunder and rain. They call it the Stormlands. There, as in Udurum, the Men and Giants live in peace."

"Lies," said the Ice King, his crimson eyes narrowing. He leaned forward in his great chair, cracking his knuckles. "You . . . are a Southborn . . . a human . . . and you invade our hunting grounds."

"No," said Vireon, and his coughing cut off his next words.

"Tell me!" growled the Ice King. "Tell me . . . where are the rest of your human tribe? Where are the invaders? Tell me . . . or you will suffer!"

"I am alone," said Vireon. "I am no human! I carry the blood of Uduru in my veins! Only give me food and rest, and I will prove it to you."

The Ice King waved a hand at his guards. "Tell me . . . and you will eat. Until then you starve." The jailers grabbed him by the arms and carried him from the hall. Vireon would have screamed, but his voice broke in his throat. Outside the great doors, they tossed him to the frozen ground again, and he lost consciousness. When he awoke, he hung once more by his wrists over the crevasse.

How long would they keep him here before dragging him to the Ice King again? How long until the King tired of him and sliced him in two with that great axe? Or would he die of hunger first? These thoughts rang through his head as he dangled there, his two guards sitting against the ice walls. Eventually they fell asleep, and he joined them in the bliss of slumber. He woke frequently, his body racked with fresh agonies. Now the cavern lay in total darkness. The moon's weak glow could not penetrate the depths of the ice here.

Vireon dreamed of his father standing on the sea shore, wrapped in a cloak of black fur, wearing his crown of gold and opals. Vod, standing proudly at his full Uduru height, stared at the rushing waves, listening to the voice of silence. The wind moaned and sighed across the strand. The sky was gray and the sun a leaden ball between roiling thunderheads.

Vod cast off his cloak, his sword and crown, and walked into the surf. Wavelets pounded his knees, and he walked on. Blue lightning flared in the dark sky. The water covered his waist and chest, and still he walked. Thunder shook the world. His crownless head bobbed above the waves, and the sun peeked out for a moment from behind the clouds.

Now Vod was gone, marching beneath the sea toward some mysterious grave.

Vireon woke with a start. A light shape was moving in the darkness. He heard the soft padding of feet and smelled a pleasant scent that had stolen his sanity days ago. Now the sound of a blade being drawn across flesh, quickly and deeply, slicing through cartilage and bone. The same sound repeated. He smelled blood, coppery and strange.

A light flared in the darkness. She stood before him: a radiant Goddess with a white flame dancing in her palm. Her other hand was a fist clenched about the hilt of his long knife. The blade dripped purple gore. The two blue-skins lay with their slit throats gushing cold, dark blood. She stared up at him with night-black eyes.

Vireon laughed as best he could. It sounded more like choking.

The fox-woman dropped his knife and used her feet to slide the blue-skin corpses over the edge of the crevasse one by one. They tumbled soundlessly into the dark pit. She turned back to Vireon and raised a key of red iron in her free hand.

Reaching out to grab his legs, she pulled hard at his ankles, and the chain above snapped through the ice. He fell, almost into the pit, but she had the lower chain wrapped about her forearm and dragged him to safety, all under the light of her blazing palm.

She used the key to unlock the chain and carefully unwound it from his body. His shoulders and wrists ached unbearably, and his stomach growled. She smothered him with her body, transmitting warmth across his chest and limbs. He reveled in the sheer ecstasy of warmth, blessed warmth . . . for now he understood what cold truly was. The flame in her hand faded, and she rubbed his arms, fingers, wrists, sending heat throughout his body. In the dark, as his senses came back to life and the pain receded to a dull roar in his ears, her lips brushed his and lingered. He wrapped his arms about her gently . . . more gently than he had ever touched a woman. The surge of his great strength had always made him a careless lover, but he did not have that strength now. They kissed tenderly and urgently, until suddenly she moved away from him.

She helped him to his feet and conjured the white flame back into her palm. He picked up the stained knife and stared into the deep wells of her eyes. How could he thank her with mere words? She pressed into his hand a piece of dried meat, and he ate it voraciously. It did not even begin to quell his hunger, but it aroused his metabolism and sharpened his senses. He could not place the flavor of it, but he did not care. It was delicious.

"What is your name?" he asked, his voice a hoarse whisper.

She looked at him curiously, tilting her head. He asked again in the southern dialect of Uurz, again in the tongue of Shar Dni. She blinked at him, wordless, and kissed his neck lightly. She spoke neither Giant nor man language. Perhaps she spoke only the language of foxes. What was she? He grabbed her, more urgently this time, but she slipped out of his grasp, motioning toward the end of the cavern. She wanted to escape now. He nodded. There was no time for romance.

They ran by the light of her palm-flame through glistening halls of chilly gloom. She seemed to know the way as he did not, so he followed her. He was used to that, having chased her for days into the frozen north. They came at last into the great plaza of the blue-skins, where the light of cold azure flames flickered on the ice. She snuffed her flame, and they peered into the plaza, across a landscape of sleeping blue-skins wrapped in furs and blankets.

Looking at him now, she placed two fingers against her lips.

Yes, we must be quiet.

They crept through the sleeping plaza, stepping between the snoring bodies of blue Giants. She was silent as a fox, even in her girl form, but he was less so. At the crunch of every icy pebble he halted, holding his breath. But these Giants slept deeply. They made it to the center of the plaza without waking a single one.

She led him toward a great open corridor at the far side. He trusted her implicitly – that must be the way out of this glacier-fortress. He stalked past a slumbering Giantess, her arm wrapped about a snoozing infant half as large as a full-grown man. Never had he seen an infant Giant, and it struck him as odd. Then he remembered the Uduru could no longer have children. This is why they were dying out. He stopped, glancing about the chamber. Two more blue-skinned babies lay swaddled in furs and masses of pillows. There, a half-grown boy . . . there a young girl. There were more Ice Clan children than he could count. And this was only *one* chamber. How many existed in other clans outside the King's roof?

The fox-woman grabbed his elbow, pulling him toward the corridor. They moved swiftly now, more sure of their invisibility. Crossing the threshold, they ran along a wide passage. She led him through a series of twists and turns, arched tunnels of solid ice, and came at last to a great wide stair. At its top they emerged into the open freedom of a starry night. Behind soared a sheer wall of emerald and indigo, the cold moon reflected on its lucid surface. There were no guards stationed at this outward gate, or she had already slain them and hidden their bodies.

She grabbed his hand, and they ran. He could only move so fast, but she slowed herself to stay with him. Into a frozen landscape they plunged, knee-deep in crisp snow. Scattered Uygas rose about them, branches dripping with millions of icicles. After a while Vireon looked back and caught his breath. She leaned into him as he enjoyed a full view of the Ice King's palace, a mountain of crystal and sapphire looming against the stars. Towers, domes, and battlements of living ice. Ultramarine walls bathed in starlight. Its size was not quite that of Vod's palace, but the nature of its glimmering substance was infinitely more impressive. It was a marvel of audacious, impossible beauty.

Then they ran again, until the Ice King's domain was lost among the frosted peaks. The golden glow of dawn lit up the pristine mountainsides. Vireon and the fox-woman fell into a bank of soft snow. The sun warmed their skins, and they made fierce love beneath the beaming sky. She gave herself to him with an animal urgency; he took her as a parched man takes cool water. A rush of mad sensations staggered him with pleasure, erasing all his agonies. Afterward they slept for a while on a carpet of green grass beneath melted snow.

Before midday she woke him, and they drank fresh snow turned to water in her cupped palms. Hunger still gnawed at him, but he ignored it. There would be game when they reached the lower climes of these mountains.

"What is your name?" he asked her again.

She gave no response.

They ran down the mountainside, toward green woodlands that still held sway below the white snows. Eventually, coming into a warm and verdant valley, he found roots and walnuts to eat. She wandered off and came back with a fresh-killed hare. She ate it raw, but he declined. He would have to teach her the art of cooking meat.

He set up a pile of tinder and motioned for her to call up the white flame. She did, and he guided her hand to the woodpile, setting it alight slowly but steadily. She marveled at this, laughing like a child. She must have never done this with her flame. Then he built a spit and cooked the rest of the hare over it. She sniffed at the smell, and he grabbed her about the slim waist. They made love again, this time on a bed of leaves the color of her golden hair, and when they were done he taught her how to eat cooked game.

She looked at him strangely but indulged his request. She enjoyed it no more or less than she had raw. He laughed.

They rested in the valley until the sun sank behind the white-capped mountains. The Ice King's mountains . . . realm of the Ice Clans.

"Long ago . . . we and the Uduru . . . were one people."

Did Fangodrim know about these *Udvorg*? Did any other Uduru know? Did they remember at all their lost cousins in the north?

Vireon thought of the blue-skin babies, the Udvorg children sleeping in their icy home.

He thought of his uncle and all his Giant cousins, aging and resigned to extinction. He thought of the Uduri, barren of womb and empty of hope. Did the Uduru really have to die out?

Could this mean hope for Vod's people?

My people.

He stroked a hand across his lover's cheek, pulling her close.

"I have to go back," he told her. "I have to make peace with the Ice King."

She blinked at him, pink lips forming a half-smile.

He kissed her again and pondered his impossible task.

9

In the Shadow, in the Sun

The sky was an inverted landscape, rolling hills of gray and black, an upside-down world given form by continental stormclouds. Every now and then a ravine opened in the cloud-scape, a fissure of blue sky, or a crevice pouring rays of sunlight onto the green fields. Rain fell in unbroken sheets, at times hard and angry, at others calm and gentle. Thunder moaned from one flat horizon to the other, occasionally clapping terribly, but usually distant and wreathed in echoes. Flares of lightning turned the gloom of a Stormlands day into whitewashed noon for seconds at a time, then disappeared only to spring up in some distant corner of the cloud kingdom. The wind blew meek or fierce, depending on its mood, but always wet, cool, and haunted by creeping fogs.

For days the jagged silhouettes of the Grim Mountains grew taller on the northern horizon. Now their immensity blotted out half the sky, a wall that separated two worlds, the ramparts guarding the Giantlands. The cohort of mounted Uurzians followed the Northern Road alongside the Uduru River, all the way from Vod's Lake. The farther north they went, the fewer villages they passed. Tonight the company camped in the shadow of the peaks, where no settlements had dared take root. The northern winds blew stronger where the land rose into a swathe of grassy foothills divided by the silvery ribbon of river.

D'zan had grown used to the perpetual damp, the cold winds, and the biting rain. This was the land of storms after all. It was the colossal darkness of the mountains that worried him.

All the way from Uurz, ten days at the front of these four hundred warriors, the Stone's greatsword hung heavily between his shoulders. It was the physical embodiment of his challenge. Dairon had given it to him after Olthacus' funeral, thinking he actually wanted it. D'zan would rather have seen the blade interred with the Stone's body; he had never seen Olthacus without it. It seemed a part of him. What's more, it was too large and heavy for D'zan to wield. All his training had been with Yaskathan longblades, lighter and quicker weapons of bronze half as tall as himself. The Stone's two-handed broadsword nearly matched D'zan's height. Its iron blade was twice as wide as a longblade at the hilt, though it tapered gradually toward its point. D'zan could lift it using both hands, but swinging it effectively was another matter, one in which he displayed little grace. To fight with the greatsword required an entirely different technique, and more raw power than he could muster.

So he carried it on his back in the way the Stone had done, but it was only a symbol of his legacy. Another, slimmer blade hung at his waist, one he could use with some basic skill if pressed. The jade dagger that had killed Olthacus he kept shoved into his boot, its blade scoured clean of poison. It was a constant reminder that he could never be truly at ease, never take for granted his safety no matter where he lay his head. It reminded him also of Khyrei, a nation of enemies. He thought of pacts, infernal and political, that must have sealed the Empress of Khyrei to the service of Elhathym the Usurper. Another twist in the long road he must follow back to the rule of his own people. Another evil to burn from the world, when the time came. Or another source of death that might be winging its way toward him even now.

Prince Tyro led the cohort. He professed friendship and dedication to D'zan and his cause. Prince Lyrilan had become D'zan's shadow, riding next to him through the rain, pitching a pavilion next to his own at every dusk, and peppering him with endless questions. Questions about D'zan's upbringing and his life in the royal courts of Yaskatha. Questions about his father and the conquests he made before and after D'zan's birth. Questions about his mother, whose face he could not remember. These and more questions, to the point of triviality. Lyrilan took mental notes during the days of riding, and each night scribbled his musings into a leather-bound tome carried in a waterproof bladder. He was wholly dedicated to chronicling the life of D'zan, and at times his attention was wearisome. But it kept D'zan from dwelling on the futility of his own task, or from brooding too deeply on his losses. He found that he enjoyed Lyrilan's company, if not his queries.

Tyro rode always at the head of the cohort, next to the standard-bearer with the gold-and-green banner. D'zan spoke with him only at the evening meal, where they drank wine – Tyro in great quantities. He told second-hand tales of the Old Desert and the Ancient North. Every night was the same: Lyrilan's pavilion on one side of D'zan's and Tyro's on the other. Tyro displayed a protectiveness for him, and D'zan saw him as a smaller, if no less martial, version of the Stone.

"Now that is a fine weapon," Tyro told him on the first day of their journey. "Takes a powerful arm to swing that blade."

D'zan sat glumly in his saddle, soft rain pelting his hood as Tyro and Lyrilan rode on either side. "More power than I have," he admitted.

"Is that so?" said Tyro. "You have skill with smaller blades?"

"Some," said D'zan. "Olthacus trained me . . . I have three years."

Tyro chuckled. "Three years! You should be a master of the longblade by now."

Lyrilan jumped to his defense. "Not everyone is as single-minded as you, Brother."

Tyro glanced at the scholar, not quite sure if he had just been insulted. He turned back to D'zan as his horse tramped through a mud hole. Behind them the cohort wound across the green-gray plain in four parallel columns of a hundred riders each. In their midst rolled a trio of canopied wagons carrying servants and supplies.

"Lyrilan has never cared for weapons," said Tyro. "Such is the privilege of a high-born lad – nobody forces you to fight and bleed. He chooses books over blades . . . as if *they* could fortify the walls of our kingdom."

"They do," said Lyrilan.

Tyro ignored the comment. "D'zan, I can teach you how to use that greatsword. It will be the icon of your birthright. Troops will rally around it during battle. The merest glimpse or mention of it will invoke your quest and inspire men to die for you. If you learn to carry it proudly. If it only hangs upon your back, I am afraid it will do you no good at all."

"You'd school me as Olthacus did?" D'zan asked.

"Tonight, when we pavilion," said Tyro, "we'll begin. First we'll build strength in your arms using rods of bronze instead of blades. After a few weeks of swinging metal, the Stone's blade will feel as light as a rose in your grasp."

Lyrilan huffed. "A gross exaggeration."

D'zan smiled. "Thank you, Tyro."

Tyro ran a gauntlet across his stallion's sodden mane. "I'll teach you technique as well. If you have the willpower, you will learn."

Every night after a crude supper, D'zan joined Tyro in his wide pavilion, where the tables and braziers were cleared to form a practice space. He sparred there with Tyro using span-length cylinders of bronze. When they clashed metal against metal, D'zan's bones trembled. The bronze was among other commodities to be traded on the streets of Udurum. The bronze of Uurz could in no way match Uduru steel, or southern iron, but it was the best bronze smelted anywhere in the north. The folk of Udurum used it for armor and implements, but not for weapons. Fighting with the bronze bars served D'zan well, sharpening his swordcraft, building his muscles, leaving his arms sore and aching every morning. After seven days he already felt stronger. Not strong enough to wield the greatsword – not even close – but enough to consider it more than some impossible dream.

Now the smokes of a hundred campfires rose into the damp night air at the very foot of the Grim Mountains, directly east of the river. This would be their last pavilion before they entered the mountain pass. The Uurzians camped in concentric circles, with the three Princes and their servants nestled in the center. Tarps propped upon cedar poles sheltered the fires, and soldiers gathered in units of four or five about the warm flames. Shifts of night guards patrolled the perimeter of the camp in pairs. D'zan felt safer in the midst of all these spear-bearing warriors than he had in the depths of Dairon's palace. And with good reason, for hadn't the Death-Bringers of Khyrei found him there?

He sat on a folding chair in his pavilion, listening to the patter of rain on the canvas roof. Scattered rugs comprised a makeshift floor, providing relief from the constant mud of the fields. Except for one night spent in Lakehold, a fortress manned by the men of Uurz on the edge of Vod's Lake, every evening was spent in such tents. Servants built them up and tore them down in minutes, and despite their mobile nature the pavilions gave him a measure of dry comfort.

A single brazier lit the tent, fuming with sweet incense, and D'zan sat with the Stone's blade lying across his knees. His eyes ran from the rounded pommel with its spherical amethyst to the two-handed grip, wrapped tight in oiled leather, to the flaring black quillions of the guard, spreading wing-like to either side of the blade. At the blade's base were set a trio of fire opals, scintillating red in the light of the brazier. In the exact center of those gems he noticed an insignia or sigil of some sort. A circular impression radiating spokes like a sun, centered within a trio of inverted, overlapping triangles forming a nine-pointed star. D'zan ran his index finger over the engraving. Among the tiny arabesques and details of the hiltwork, he had overlooked this symbol until now.

The guard outside his pavilion called out to him: "Prince Lyrilan approaches!" A dark shape stood before the tent's entrance, and he recognized the tall, slim frame. The guard had no need to shout; who else could that shadow belong to?

"Enter," said D'zan, his eyes lingering on the trio of jewels and the mysterious character at their center. Lyrilan spread the canvas flap and walked inside. He carried the working tome under his cloak, safe from the rain, a white quill stuck into its pages like a feathery bookmark. A bottle of ink bulged in the pocket of his flared trousers; his muddy boots contrasted greatly with the fine silks that draped his legs, arms and middle. His long hair was an oiled mass of curls that fell free as he tossed back his hood.

"Evenbliss," Lyrilan greeted him.

D'zan looked up for a moment. "Have a seat," he said. "You have more questions for me, I suppose?"

Lyrilan smiled, dropping into a pile of cushions. "An infinite number, Majesty . . . "

D'zan nodded. "I have one for *you* actually," he said. He motioned for Lyrilan to come closer. After spreading out his book, quill, and ink bottle on a well-placed rug, Lyrilan drew near to him. His eyes followed D'zan's to the base of the heavy blade, into the triangle of crimson opals, and the sigil where Dzan's fingertip pointed. "What do you make of this?"

Lyrilan craned his neck, squinting his eyes, lowering them close to the blade. "It's a rune," he said. "Much like the Sun God's symbol, but markedly different. Older, perhaps."

"A rune?" said D'zan.

"Yes, I've seen this sigil before," said Lyrilan. He snapped his fingers. "In *The Codex of Ancient Icons*. It's a *ward*, I'm sure of it."

"What does that mean?"

"A ward is a rune that protects its bearer from evil spirits."

"Evil spirits."

"Yes, some orders of the Sun God carve a ward like this on their talismans. Sometimes the priests inscribe them on the shields of warriors bound to a holy cause. The Sun is the eternal enemy of darkness, where evil dwells."

"So . . . some Sun Priest placed a ward on the Stone's blade?"

"Most likely . . . or it was engraved during the forging of the sword. Based on the pattern of these gems, I'd say that is most likely."

D'zan thought of the Stone carrying this sword across a blood-soaked battlefield, smiting terrible monsters and living men, wading through a swamp of black gore. If only it could have protected him from the assassins who finally took his life. But they had been living men, not spirits. Evil, yes, but flesh and blood.

"This is a priceless treasure," said Lyrilan. "My brother was right: it should be your standard . . . the icon of your cause. Guard it carefully."

D'zan nodded. He flexed his sore arms, more determined than ever to master the wielding of this weapon. Until then it would ride upon his back, symbol of all he strove to accomplish.

Lyrilan shifted back to his cushions and took the book up onto his knees. He dipped his quill in the open ink bottle and looked up at D'zan. "So . . . where were we?" His eyes scanned the last paragraph he had written. "Ah, yes . . . You were six years old when your father returned from the Battle of Teryllope. What do you remember from that day?"

D'zan slid the greatsword back into its scabbard and laid it down beside his cot. He poured black brandy from a bottle into two cups and handed one to Lyrilan.

"I remember . . . the smell of my father's cloak. Seawater, smoke . . . and blood. He gave me a little jeweled sea-beast, a trinket from the southern isles. A *seahorse*, he called it. I remember that he hugged me, and I cried when he put me down. Then he was off to matters of state. There was a victory feast . . . My cousins were there . . . I don't remember much of it."

The night drew on with D'zan searching his memories and Lyrilan transcribing them, until the brazier guttered low and D'zan began to yawn. Lyrilan took his cue and departed for his own tent. "My brother's training is wearing you out," he said. "Don't let him push you too hard."

D'zan smiled, giving birth to another yawn. "He pushes me less than I should be. Good night, Lyrilan."

"Sleep well, Prince." And Lyrilan was gone.

D'zan fell to sleep on a pile of blankets that turned the thin cot into a pleasant bed.

He dreamed of the sable mountains towering over the encampment, ripe with boiling darkness and terrible groaning thunders. He soared above the frosty peaks, in the realm of moon and stars. He looked down across ravines and gorges, where sometimes blood-colored fires danced, then faded into the dark.

A swirling shadow came up from the depths between the black mountainsides. It had waited there for him, at the edge of the range looking across the plains, inhumanly patient. A dark smoke in the shape of a winged thing . . . a great bat with the body of a bloated eel. Its eyes were shards of gleaming amber . . . the fires of wicked desire . . . the naked hunger of a thing damned and roaming. The moon was lost behind the soaring pinnacles, and the eel-bat-shadow descended toward the concentric circles of mens' fires beside the river.

D'zan shifted restlessly on his cot, sweating, freezing, and could not wake up. He moaned, and the guard outside his tent looked in at him, shrugged, and returned to his post. D'zan saw all of this in his disembodied state, and he saw the dark smoke writhing through the rain above the scattered tents. Along the edges of the camp, the night guards stood oblivious to the terror that floated into their midst, dropping like a black fog from the clouds. D'zan tried to call out, but he was bodiless in the dream, and made no sound.

He saw the black fog fall upon the guard outside his tent, soundless, covering his mouth and eyes with ebony coils. The wings flapped over him, and the guard struggled, convulsed, as the eel-thing tightened about his body. A peal of thunder drowned out the cracking of bones as the eel squeezed the life from him and dropped his pulped organs into the mud. It hungered terribly, but its feeding would have to wait. Now it flowed into the pavilion, and D'zan floated above his sleeping body, watched it crawl across his feet, wrap itself about his legs.

Cold . . . the chill of the lightless void.

His body moaned and shook, but did not wake.

The black wings spread over him, and his face was lost in their shadow. The creature wound itself about his entire body, then his neck and mouth. Its triangular head rose at last to stare him in the face. Its eyes burned yellow, slits of smoldering flame, and it opened a mouth of purest darkness, hissing something unintelligible. Suddenly, as if fallen from a great height, D'zan was back in his body, dying in the grip of the eel-thing. His eyes opened and stared into its flaming pits.

Somewhere, in some incorporeal netherworld or in the depths of night, he heard the laughter of Elhathym. The same wicked mirth he heard when dream-lost in the royal crypts of Yaskatha. Those flaming eyes, they were the eyes of the usurper. D'zan knew this as he knew he was going to die. The black coils squeezed him tighter, glistening like onyx.

His right arm, which had fallen over the cot's edge during his delirium, was free of the coils only from elbow to fingers. His fist closed and opened on empty air as the beast constricted.

D'zan gagged, spit, vomited, but could not scream for lack of air. Soon his ribs would splinter, and his legs and arms, and he would be like the guard outside, a mass of torn flesh and shattered bone. Then the beast would devour his steaming remains.

His grasping right hand brushed against something cool, knocking it from his reach.

The faint glimmer of amethyst caught his eye.

The blade . . . the ward . . .

Impossible to break the grip of those black coils, but he shifted the bulk of his and the beast's body. The cot fell over. His hand closed about the grip of the greatsword. In his mind the Sun God's sigil gleamed as the world faded.

Thunder seemed to break *inside* the tent . . . The black fog exploded from his skin. The creature hissed like water thrown on coals, coalescing almost instantly back into its eel-bat shape, wings tearing at the canvas. D'zan gasped air into his lungs, wrapping both his hands about the grip. He pulled the blade from its scabbard, lifting it with terrific effort to the level of his waist.

The shadow-thing flapped its wings and his brazier toppled, spilling coals and flame across the rugs. The beast lunged at him, but refused to touch him again while he held the blade. It was the sigil – the ward – that it detested. But it would not leave the tent. It hissed, spitting black smoke like poison.

D'zan lifted the blade high above his head like an axe. He brought it down with no finesse, like chopping firewood, yet it clove the smoky beast in two and sliced deep into the rugs. The creature screeched and faded, now only a black fog again. A vicious hissing grew fainter as the black smoke dispersed.

Soldiers ran into the flaming pavilion now, gathering about D'zan and rushing to put out the fire. A babble of voices that meant nothing to his ears. He struggled for an easy breath. They led him outside into the rain. He refused to let go of the blade, so he dragged it behind him. The cold rain on his face was bracing, and he breathed easier as it rushed into his gaping mouth.

They led him into the pavilion of Tyro, who stood bare-chested, sword in hand, surrounded by a cadre of swordsmen. Tyro grabbed D'zan's shoulders and shouted into his face. D'zan heard him, but the words made no sense. He swooned, and they set him on Tyro's bed. Someone tried to take the blade from his hand, but his fingers were locked in a death grip about the hilt.

So he lay there, one fist gripping the sword, the other hand lying numb beside him, and they forced him to drink hot brandy. At some point he became aware of Lyrilan and Tyro watching over him. Eventually he slept. His dreams were of a pale sun igniting the darkness, and ice-crowned mountains springing into orange life in the glow of dawn.

When D'zan awoke it was truly dawn. He still lay in Tyro's grand pavilion, and Lyrilan sat in a chair at his bedside. The sound of pouring rain was conspicuously absent, which made the morning strangely quiet. Tyro was out there somewhere in the early sunlight, giving orders. He heard the Prince's voice ringing through the crisp air.

D'zan tried to rise, but pain prevented him. He looked down

to see his shirt gone and white bandages wrapped about his ribs.

Lyrilan rose quickly. "Don't try to move just yet," he said. "You may have a fractured rib or two. Bruised at best. Be still . . . "

D'zan asked for water, and Lyrilan brought him a cup.

"The rain . . . it stopped," said D'zan.

Lyrilan waved his hands. "The Sun God smiles on us this day."

D'zan grunted.

"He does indeed."

10

A Storm of Blood and Darkness

Tadarus called across the courtyard to Captain Jyfard, "Have you seen Prince Fangodrel this morning?"

The captain took off his winged helm as he approached, tucking it under his arm. Tadarus' sweat stood in glittering droplets on his forehead, arms, and chest. A few spans away, Andoses stood with hands on knees, catching his breath. The two had been sparring all morning, and Tadarus had gained a new appreciation for his cousin's skill with the scimitar. Though he could never match Tadarus' giant strength, Andoses had matched his longblade skills every step of the way. Once the Sharrian even managed to disarm him. Tadarus redeemed himself by later knocking the scimitar from Andoses' grip a total of three times. A ring of soldiers watched their swordplay, and the yard rang with the metallic songs of a hundred other sparring matches. Jyfard broke through the gawkers and stepped near.

"None have seen him since our arrival," Jyfard said. "According to the Uduru sentinel, he has locked himself in the King's Room. His body servant – that smelly Rathwol – attends to all his needs."

Tadarus frowned. "Does he know about the rider?"

Jyfard shrugged. "Failing to reach the Prince himself, I gave his servant your message, Lord."

"What are you not telling me, Jyfard?"

The captain looked about at the faces of the men. Andoses drew in closer. Jyfard lowered his voice. "The sentinel spoke of strange smells . . . and sounds . . . like the singing of a dirge in Prince Fangodrel's chamber."

Tadarus turned his eyes past the towers of Steephold to the frosted peaks surrounding the fortress. "My brother has always indulged in strange proclivities," he said. "There is nothing to be done about it." He wiped the sweat from his breast with a soft towel. The morning air was chill and the promise of snow hung in the air. "Send another message. Tell Fangodrel he must attend tonight's dinner to discuss our embassy. Tell him if he does not attend, I will send him back to Udurum."

Jyfard paled. "I will tell the servant."

"No," said Tadarus. "Have the sentinel unlock Fangodrel's door if you must. But deliver the message to him in person."

Jyfard nodded. "Yes, Lord." He marched away toward the tower where Fangodrel had hidden himself away.

During yesterday's feast celebrating their arrival, Rockjaw had informed Tadarus of an advance rider from Uurz come and gone three days earlier. The herald brought news of Emperor Dairon's twin sons, the Princes Tyro and Lyrilan. They traveled the Northern Road, escorting the deposed Prince of Yaskatha to seek an audience with Shaira.

Tadarus had discussed this with Andoses over roast mutton and dark ale.

Andoses tugged on the triple braid of his beard. "Three Princes going south, and three Princes going north. It must be an omen."

Tadarus blinked. "Perhaps . . . but an omen of good or ill?"

Andoses' eyes twinkled, darker twins of the blue jewel upon his turban. "There can be only one reason for this audience. The surviving son of Trimesqua – his *only* son – seeks support to reclaim his throne."

Tadarus looked at Rockjaw, whose colossal eyes narrowed. Along the great table sat a dozen Giants and fifty Men from the Udurum and Shar Dni contingents. The Giants kept no servants here, so low-ranking Uduru cooked and served the hearty fare. It was not a graceful affair, but the atmosphere was pleasant and the food pleasing to a man's appetite. A dozen roaring braziers turned the chill of night into a pleasant warmth. The dining hall was lined with tapestries depicting the heroes of Ancient Udurum smiting Serpents and sea-monsters. Centrally positioned among the hangings was a great black drapery showing Vod's battle against the Serpent-Father. Tadarus' father stood tall as a mountain, stitched in silver on the face of the fabric, and he smote the Lord of Serpents with his great axe. That same axe, forged by Vod's dead father, lay even now in a vault beneath the Palace of Udurum, surrounded by the treasures of the realm.

"We know that the Khyrein jackals are allied with this Yaskathan usurper," said Tadarus, turning his attention from the tapestry to Andoses. "But what does this fugitive Prince's presence mean for us?"

Andoses smiled. "Think, Cousin! He comes to seek our aid in reclaiming his throne. He may have no army of his own, but the people of Yaskatha who groan under the tyranny of this sorcerer, they will rally behind the last son of their true royal lineage. This boy may be our greatest weapon. To support his cause will cost us little besides a legion or two from each of our nations. We can use him to rally a rebellion among the Yaskathans, weakening any military support they have pledged to Khyrei . . . "

"So we pledge ourselves to restoring the rightful monarch of

Yaskatha," said Tadarus "and keep the usurper busy quelling internal strife."

"Leaving Khyrei vulnerable to the assault of our three armies."

"Four," said Tadarus. "Mumbaza must join us or my mother will not endorse this war."

"Even better! Four united armies – plus the power of the Uduru – against two. And one of those distracted by rebellion . . ."

"What if this Prince proves false?" asked Rockjaw. "What if the usurper crushes his rebellion?"

"It matters not to us," said Andoses. "We will time our invasion of Khyrei so that the Yaskathan rebellion removes its ally. Whether this rebellion dies or succeeds, it draws the usurper's attention and the bulk of his forces."

"A diversion," said Tadarus.

"If the young Prince reclaims his throne, then we'll have a solid ally," said Andoses. "If he fails . . . the usurper's rule will have been weakened. He will either sue for peace, or we will march in and take his weary realm when we are done with Khyrei."

Rockjaw grinned, baring his stone-like teeth. "Men plan for war in ways we Uduru would scarcely dream," said the Giant. "All we crave is the joy of battle, the rushing of red blood, and the sweetness of victory."

"Oh, it will be sweet, Rockjaw," said Andoses. "And the world will be set right."

"We will stay here at Steephold then," said Tadarus. "Long enough to greet the Uurzian delegation and this Yaskathan Prince. Uurz must already support his claim or Dairon would not give him escort. So it falls to my mother."

"Must we return to the Giant-city, then?" asked Andoses.

"No," said Tadarus. "Her command was clear enough. We are to ally Uurz and Mumbaza with our cause. Only then will she send Men and Uduru to reinforce Shar Dni. I myself will pledge Vod's House to the Prince's cause. We will confirm this with Dairon when we pass through Uurz."

"Then on to Mumbaza." Andoses grinned.

"The final link in our chain of war," said Tadarus.

"These are great days," said Andoses. He raised a cup of red wine.

Rockjaw bellowed his mirth. He clanked his great goblet together with the cups of Tadarus and Andoses. "Let wine and blood flow," said the Giant. "It has been too long."

Tadarus turned then to Andoses. "To Mumbaza."

"To Mumbaza," said Andoses. The two Princes clinked cups and drained them dry.

Today Tadarus awaited with patience the arrival of the Uurzians. Sparring and martial training would fill the intervening days. Rockjaw suggested a tiger hunt for tomorrow, and Tadarus liked the idea. Andoses would find it exhilarating, and it would occupy their minds while the Uurzians climbed up Vod's Pass. A week at Steephold would be a pleasant diversion from the monotony of days in the saddle. Time enough later for the road and its wearisome routines.

Still, it bothered him that Fangodrel stayed sequestered in the central tower. Tadarus contemplated sending his brother home in chains then thought of making another attempt at peace. His brother must have a beating heart somewhere beneath the venomous armor he wore. Surely his own flesh and blood could not truly hate him. *Do I hate Fangodrel?* he asked himself. No, of course he didn't. *I love my brothers*, he told himself. *Both of them.*

He wished his mother had sent Vireon in place of Fangodrel. He wondered if his younger brother had returned yet from the Long Hunt. Would Vireon feel he had missed the chance to do something great? But there was still time . . . Mumbaza must be won first. Then Vireon would lead the forces of Udurum to Shar Dni. If all went as planned, the brothers would meet there in less than a year. Together they would command the united armies of men and giants, lead them south to crush wicked Khyrei. Time later for Vireon to play a role. Now was the time for diplomacy, and Tadarus was far better at it than his younger brother. Let Vireon stay and enjoy the winter. Tadarus would march into the balmy kingdoms of the south and pave the way for a glorious war.

"Shall we go again?" Tadarus asked, pointing his longblade at Andoses.

Andoses shook his head, toweling his curly mane. "I have only a fraction of your strength, Cousin. There is no Uduru blood in these veins." He called loudly for wine.

Tadarus laughed. "Enough swordplay then," he said. He was not tired at all. "Which among you gaping Uduru will match arms with me?"

The men of Udurum howled and cheered as a bulky Giant stamped forward to wrestle their Prince. Giants gathered to watch the contest. Andoses stood with the Men, staring in awe as Tadarus locked sinews with an opponent three times his size. The yard shook with the impact of the Giant's stamping; he could not catch Tadarus in his massive hands; Tadarus moved too quickly.

In the end, after an hour of rolling and slamming about the practice yard, Tadarus wrapped his legs about the Giant's neck and stole the wind from his lungs. As the Uduru fell, Tadarus jumped from his massive shoulders to land on his feet like a cat. The applause of Men and Giants rose about him like the roar of a sudden squall.

"Who's next?" Tadarus shouted, smiling at the crowd of warriors he would lead into battle in a few months. There would be glory enough for all of them.

These are great days.

Rockjaw's words echoed in his ears, riding the current of his swift-flowing blood.

The Red Dream lasted all night and well into the morning. The hound's blood ignited the fires of his mind, opening realms undiscovered. Fangodrel lay upon the bed built years ago for Vod, his arms and legs akimbo, his mind soaring above the jagged peaks outside the palace. In a haze of crimson he saw the black towers, climbing stairwells, and soaring battlements of the keep. He flew, disembodied and bloated with power, and the dog's blood turned to sweetness in his mouth.

He looked down on the feasting Men and Giants in the great hall; he saw the tired soldiers quartering themselves in the oversized barracks, their horses lining the stables on the stronghold's eastern side. He rose higher and flew across the dark mountains, skirting their ice-crowned summits. He observed stalking nocturnal beasts, tigers and stranger creatures roaming the wild slopes. He felt, rather than saw, open fissures like gaping wounds in the sides of the mountains, the openings to ancient warrens where the Old Wyrms dwelled in ages past. He sensed the lurking presence of entities that dwelled there still – shadow-things without name or purpose, lurking in the sunless depths.

The birds of night soared about the peaks, but he was invisible to them. Darker presences lingered here and there in the husks of abandoned towers and castles, the bones of forgotten kingdoms. He sensed now the incredible array of spectral life that inhabited these mountains. Ghosts and wraiths roamed here like tattered memories . . . Often they gazed up at his immaterial presence, some crawling after him as he passed. Dark and pulsing they gleamed through the scarlet film of his vision.

He flew back to Steephold and stood like a ghost himself atop the central tower's roof. She stood there, flickering like a pale torch . . . Ianthe the Claw . . . Ianthe the Sorceress . . . Ianthe the Lovely, who had opened his mind to the true power of the blood-flower and a world of immortal shadows.

"Now you see?" she said, smiling her pantherish smile at him. Was she truly here? Or a manifestation of his elevated consciousness? He saw the rim of the battements through her gossamer frame. This was her soul, speaking to him as it had in the Red Dream, but this was *more* than the Red Dream. It was his first lesson in her familial college of sorcery.

Blood magic.

"I see," he said "all the things that were unseen . . . I see them now, Grandmother."

"Yes, my Gammir. You begin to perceive, but there is much more."

"What must I do?" He lusted for more of this power, more of this invincible freedom.

"Blood is the source of all life, all power," she told him, stroking his phantom chest with her clawed fingers. Her eyes of black diamond sparkled close to him. He longed to kiss her, but there was no flesh here . . . only naked spirit . . . naked power. "From the lifeblood of a tiny mammal you have gained all this. How does it make you feel?"

"Like a God," he said.

She laughed. "You have barely entered the gates of sorcery. But you learn quickly. Soon you will be ready to come to me. Now you must learn to call upon the Dwellers in Shadow – they will be your escort."

"How?" he asked.

She whispered more impossible words into his ears, and made him repeat them.

"The blood of a living man will be required," she said.

"My servant?" he asked.

"Whoever you wish," she breathed. "Only do not hesitate. The Shadow Dwellers in this place have noticed your presence. You must call them together soon . . ."

He awoke in the King's Room, his vision still wrapped in vermilion gauze. Rathwol lay on a nearby rug, snoring horribly.

Fangodrel who was now Gammir rose to his feet, reveling in a fresh and heady vitality. He still tasted the sweetness of the animal's blood on his tongue. How much sweeter must be the blood of a man? Even a poor wretch like Rathwol . . .

The body of the slain hound lay spitted and roasted over the hearth fire. Rathwol was not one to waste edible meat.

Fangodrel/Gammir smoked five petals of the bloodflower from his jade coffer, then took up his dagger, whose blade he had licked clean. Midday sun limned the curtains drawn over the windows, and it pained his eyes. He ignored the discomfort and approached the sleeping form of Rathwol, the dagger clenched in his fist. A stray sunbeam sent a spark of fire leaping from the blade as it hovered above the sleeper's throat.

Fangodrel/Gammir paused. He weighed the value of Rathwol's continued service against the value of the potent blood flowing in his veins. Against the power that blood would bring him. In the corners of the room, shadows shifted and flowed, watching him with expectant non-eyes. A trail of spittle drooled from the sleeping man's lips.

A heavy knocking at the chamber door disturbed Rathwol's slumber. He rolled over onto his stomach, still snoring.

Fangodrel/Gammir kicked him awake.

"Ah! Master! What is it?"

"Get the door."

"Aye, My Lord." Rathwol crept across the chamber. His blearing eyes lingered on the dagger in his master's hand.

Fangodrel/Gammir placed himself to the left of the entrance, well out of sight.

"Prince Fangodrel!" came a commanding voice from the other side of the door, followed by more knocking. "I bring a message from your brother!"

"Yes, yes," said Rathwol, unchaining the door and sliding back an iron bolt. He opened the door enough to poke his head out. "Good morning, Captain Jyfard."

"*Afternoon*," corrected the captain. "I must speak with your master. Immediately."

"I shall relay the message," said Rathwol.

"No," said Jyfard, pressing his way into the chamber. His mailed chest bumped Rathwol, knocking him on his rump. Rathwol cursed. Jyfard stepped over him. "Where is —"

Fangodrel/Gammir brought the dagger down swiftly, sinking it into the captain's neck while his free hand went round to muffle the man's mouth. Jyfard struggled, twitched, and finally shoved himself free of Fangodrel/Gammir's grip. He fell to the floor in a gush of blood.

Rathwol, needing no prompt, sped to close and latch the door. When he turned around, his master knelt over the dying man as if to kiss his lips.

Fangodrel/Gammir pressed his lips against the seeping wound and sucked, drawing the captain's lifeblood into his mouth, swallowing in thirsty gulps. The blow had been fatal, severing the jugular, and Jyfard was already dead. Rathwol hesitated, watching the grisly feast. His master continued slurping, licking, and drinking. Fangodrel/Gammir paid him no mind. He squeezed the neck and pressed on the torso, as he had often squeezed the juice from a ripe pomegranate.

"Prince Fangodrel?" Rathwol asked, when he was sure the captain was dead.

Fangodrel/Gammir lifted his face, red-stained and dripping.

"My name is Gammir," he said. "Call me Prince Gammir." Drops of blood flew from his smacking lips as he spoke.

Rathwol nodded, his terror obvious.

"Help me lift him," said Prince Gammir. "Hold his neck over the fire."

As he had done with the dog last night, Gammir held his victim over the bowl of blazing coals and the last of Jyfard's blood smoked and steamed into the brazier. At last he tossed the body to the blood-drenched floor and sang a terrible song above the scarlet flames.

The shadows in the corners of the chamber crept closer, and Gammir raised his arms, his eyes, to the ceiling. His spirit soared once again into the sky, a flaming eagle defying the light of the sun. Dark clouds gathered above the keep, and he entered them, broke through on the other side, and soared over the mountain-scape once more.

Dark things climbed up from the deep ravines and the cellars of ancient ruins, straining toward the sky. A storm broke over the mountains, and Gammir flew unhindered through the roaring center of its wrath. Thunder sang in his veins. Lightning bolts played about his ethereal presence.

He felt them all now, down there below him in the lost and forgotten places . . .the Dwellers in Shadow . . . and he called them toward him.

Come, he told them. *Your Lord has arrived.*

Come. There is blood for all of you.

Come . . .

Atop the tallest tower of Steephold, the shade of Ianthe laughed into the raging storm.

"Your time is almost here, sweet Gammir," she whispered.

Far away, he heard her words.

Heedless of the howling wind and rain, a horde of shadows crawled toward Steephold.

The storm broke suddenly and without warning, spoiling an otherwise pleasant day in the yards. Tadarus and the Men rushed for cover as the downpour began. Thunder rolled like an earthquake across the citadel. The Giants laughed, fearing no storm, and walked leisurely toward the tall archways. They took great amusement from the sight of Men scurrying like rats, running from a bit of rain. Tadarus considered for a moment staying out in the tempest. He loved a good storm as much as any Uduru. But here was chance to come inside and prepare for the evening's activities. In his spacious chamber he bathed, then dressed himself in a sable tunic and purple cloak as the storm raged against the castle walls.

He thought of the Yaskathan Prince on his way to plead for alliance. How terrible it must be to lose a throne and a father at the same time. At least Tadarus had kept his kingdom. Offering help to the Yaskathan heir, though serving his own interests, was the right thing to do in any case. If someone stole the throne of Udurum, he would do anything to regain it. So he would give whatever honest help he could to this desperate Princeling. Besides, if the boy were intelligent at all, he would understand how he fit into the existing war plans. There was no need to disguise the reason for Udurum's support.

He pondered the skeleton of an Old Wyrm mounted along the eastern wall, held together with clever wires. It was at least four horse-lengths, with a dozen clawed legs digging into the stone wall. The triangular skull bore fangs large enough to impale a man. Living, it might have swallowed men whole between those snapping jaws. If it didn't singe them to ash first with flaming breath. Near to the Wyrm's bones hung an Uduru sword, a Giant's blade of antique steel. He studied its length, the polished metal, the murky gems set in pommel and hilt. The weapon stood a head taller than Tadarus, but he lifted it off the wall easily, brandishing it in his right fist.

There was time before dinner, so he practiced wielding the Uduru sword. He carved figure eights, ellipses, and spherical patterns in the air, thrust it like a spear. This was the blade that killed this Wyrm. Somehow he knew it. How long ago was this beast slain? The blade was centuries older than the keep. These relics must have been stored in the vaults of the castle that stood here before the building of Steephold. He marveled at the perfect balance of the big blade. It felt good in his hands. Often the swords forged by Men seemed little more than sticks to him. Perhaps he would keep this Giant-blade. It would serve him well on the field of battle. His men would stand in awe of its size. When the melee began they would not lose sight of him with this great steel thing in his grasp.

Thunder rolled as rain pelted the thick glass of arched windows.

Yes, he decided. *This blade comes with me to Mumbaza.* Then to Shar Dni. Then to sweltering Khyrei, where the song of battle would break loose and shake the sky. He studied the shallow runes along the spine of the metal . . . Perhaps there was some lingering enchantment in the sword as well.

A commotion rose outside his door, and he heard the booming voice of the sentinel at the head of the corridor. Someone had escaped his grasp and was running toward Tadarus' chamber. Whoever it was, he wept and grunted with panic. Now came a pounding against the door, followed by the plodding of the sentinel's huge feet.

Tadarus opened the door with the Giant-blade in hand. A bloody figure stumbled upon him, grasping at his chest, smearing it with red. A small man dressed in servant's livery, stained to black by the gore splattered across arms and chest. He recognized the bleating, weeping figure: Rathwol, his elder brother's servant. He reeked of dog flesh, filth, and fear.

"Majesty!" screamed Rathwol, clutching at Tadarus' belt. "Majesty! The darkness! The blood! Majesty!"

Tadarus pushed him back into the corridor, lowering the great blade. The giant sentinel seethed with embarrassed anger.

"He slipped through my legs like a . . . " the Giant growled.

"A rat?" said Tadarus, staring down at the mess Rathwol had made of his fine raiment.

"Majesty!" howled Rathwol, mouth drooling, eyes flooding. He trembled violently. "Save me, save me! Oh, I'll serve you faithfully – not *him*, never him anymore!"

"Bring Captain Jyfard to my quarters," Tadarus told the sentinel. The Giant tramped down the corridor.

"The shadows!" squealed Rathwol, grasping now at the Prince's boots.

Tadarus pushed him firmly against the corridor wall and slapped his face. "Calm yourself, man. What's the matter? Whose blood is this? Yours?" He kicked away Rathwol's filthy hands as gently as he could.

Thunder rumbled, and the stones of the keep trembled as if mimicking Rathwol's terror.

"Oh, so much blood . . . " Rathwol cried. "All spilled and burned . . . Now the *shadows* drink it. Save me!"

Tadarus shook him. "Where is your master? Where is Prince Fangodrel?"

The name cast a weird calm over Rathwol. He looked into Tadarus' face, silent for the space of three heartbeats. The storm beat against the windows.

"Gone . . . " whispered Rathwol, eyes staring at nothing. "Gone into the shadows . . . into the blood!" Now he keened and wailed like a woman. "Keep him from me, Master! Keep him away! I'll serve you, not him! Only save me!"

A great wind gusted along the corridor, like a hurricane suddenly unbottled. It swept Tadarus off his feet. A flying, howling blackness tore Rathwol away in a blind instant. Now his cries of terror rang in some other corridor, echoing from the darkness. All the torches in their sconces were blown out by the terrible wind. Tadarus crouched in the darkness, the Giant-blade ready in his hand. The only light came from the partially open door of his chamber, where the fire bowl still blazed.

Something moved, crackled, shifted in the dark at the end of the corridor, in the direction the sentinel had gone. Tadarus stared into the gloom. Could it be Uduru making that rumbling sound, or was it only thunder? Had some window been smashed, letting winds howl into the keep? From the infinite darkness at his back came a long, thin scream of agony. Rathwol. Darkness claimed the citadel in both directions; winds shrieked like ghosts through the distant hallways. Tadarus wanted to run inside his chamber and bolt the door, hide himself from this plague of darkness.

The thing at the end of the corridor pulsed, and something came flying through the air. It hit the floor several spans before Tadarus and rolled like a small boulder, a trail of black blood in its wake. It stopped at his feet. He looked down and caught his breath. Two bulging, fist-sized eyeballs glared at him, dead and sightless. It was the head of the Giant sentinel, severed at the neck by some jagged instrument . . . or a vast set of claws.

Now anger overcame Tadarus' fear. He yelled along the corridor. "Come forth! Face me! What are you?" He thought of the Wyrm skeleton on the wall of his room. Surely there could not be—

"I called you brother . . . "

The voice drifted from the pulsing mass of shadows. That darkness moved closer now, drinking up the dull glow from the chamber fire.

"Fangodrel?" he called. Was this some jest? Had his brother gone mad? In the back of his mind a voice whispered, *This was always meant to happen. Fangodrel was never right. What did you expect of him but murder and disaster? Blood and doom?* Now, at last, the wait was over.

" . . . but you are no brother to me."

The voice was Fangodrel's, but obscured in echoes and amplified by thunder. Tadarus could see nothing in the darkness but the writhing darkness itself.

"Show yourself!" he yelled. "Let us spill familial blood if we must. Come!" He raised the Giant-blade high above his head.

"Steel? This is your answer for every problem, Tadarus. There are things in this world stronger than metal."

Tadarus could take no more baiting. He rushed headlong into the darkness, swinging his great blade, slicing only emptiness. Something grabbed him up in formless claws, biting into his thick skin with unseen fangs. He swung the blade about him, back and forth like a reaper's scythe. Nothingness . . . he hovered in the grip of nothingness and now he could not see at all.

Suddenly Fangodrel was there, lit by the red glow of his own flaring eyes. Naked, emaciated, his skin wrapped in skeins of running crimson. The blood danced across his chest, ran along his arms and legs, defying gravity with its slick flow. Or was it shadows that danced across that pale skin? Some mixture of scarlet and ebony, living, sliding, throbbing . . .

"My name is Gammir," said Fangodrel, lips dripping with blood, teeth stained black by it. "Gammir, Son of Gammir. Prince of Khyrei."

Tadarus heard the shrieks and wails of dying warriors,

bellowing Giants, throughout the castle. The storm assaulted the exterior walls, while a storm of blood and darkness assaulted the interior. This was the heart of the bloody storm right here. This thing before him was not his brother. It had never been his brother. How could he not have known this?

The greatsword fell from his hand. No, his hand was sheered away from his wrist. Sword and hand fell clanging into the dark. The pain washed over him a second later, a burning wave to drown his senses. His warm blood squirted into the shadows. It did not reach the floor. He screamed now, for that was all he could do, held tight in the grip of some amorphous, unseen, *vast* thing . . .

Fangodrel – no, *Gammir* – crouched below the fresh stump of Tadarus' wrist, blood pouring into his open mouth. A flood of screams and blood gushed from Tadarus. He saw the face of Vireon, his sister Sharadza, and his weeping mother. His father's face was a gray blur, like an underwater vision.

"Your blood was never my blood," said Gammir, lips running with crimson. "But it is sweet . . . Uduru and man, a potent blend . . . " Gammir raised his mouth to kiss Tadarus' throbbing neck. "Sweet and potent . . . "

Darkness stole the breath from Tadarus' lungs. His final sensation was that of a ravenous beast tearing at his throat. Mercifully, he heard no more of the terrible screams that filled the halls of Steephold.

11

People of the Cold Flame

He decided to call her Alua, the name of a splendid white flower that bloomed among the Uyga vines in winter. Although she did not speak, she understood immediately that this was now her name. She knew his moods and his thoughts before he spoke them. A simple glance into her onyx eyes, or the slightest caress of her hand, these were their sublime modes of communication. So when he set about putting his plan to work, she went along in her wordless way and was eager to help.

After three days of bliss in the valley where the last days of autumn held sway, Vireon and Alua ran north again into the cold mountains. She took her fox form and he ran beside her. She guided him along the safest ravines and kindest escarpments, going ever higher into the realm of wind, snow, and ice. He found the spoor of a tiger, and they tracked it along a pale ridge. The white fox ran ahead of him, following the tracks of the beast to a shallow cave lair. Vireon climbed to a high ledge above a great precipice, and the fox pranced before the cave mouth.

The tiger sprang from its den. Its pristine hide gleamed white as the breath that billowed between its fangs. It stood larger than a stallion, a mass of rippling muscles, black claws, and yellow fangs. It roared, and across the divide an avalanche fell into the gorge. Now the great cat chased the fox. Alua ran ahead of its snapping fangs along the mountainside. It swiped a massive paw at her, claws raking through her bushy tail. She pounced forward and the chase resumed. When the tiger was almost upon her, she turned back, baring tiny fangs. The cat lunged for the kill, so focused on the fox that it failed to sense Vireon crouching on the high ledge.

Vireon sprang boots first into the tiger's skull. Its head smashed into the ice and rock, and he fell back against the wall of the mountain. The feline head rose and turned on him. The maw could tear off both legs in a single snap, but it was too late. The force of his two-legged kick sent it spinning toward the precipice. Scrambling, it slid over the edge into nothingness. It struck out with both front claws, digging into the ice. Now it hung there above the black depths of the gorge, struggling to pull itself back up onto the path. Its yellow-green eyes burned into Vireon's as it pulled itself forward and upward, bit by bit. Its massive shoulders had cleared the edge when Vireon took up a boulder and hurled it against the feline head. With a final roar of defiance, tiger and stone plummeted into the icy gulf.

Alua approached Vireon in her girl form, wrapping her warm arms about his shoulders. She kissed him, and her quiet eyes said, *I knew you would let no harm come to me.*

They hurried down the mountain and found the body of the tiger on a bed of icy rocks. Vireon skinned the carcass methodically with his long knife. Before the sun had set, he wore its white hide for a cloak, tied about his neck by its front legs. Twin claws dangled upon his chest, and the hollow shape of its furred skull rode atop his own as a crude but beautiful helmet. He gave thanks to the Sky God and buried the beast's remains under a cairn of rocks that were soon covered with a mound of fresh snow.

"Now I look the part of a proper ambassador," he told Alua. "And this skin will keep me warm should I enter that cold palace again."

Alua ran her delicate fingers along the fur, and her eyes said, *You look like a King.*

Back in the foothills, where snow was light and the wind hardly blew at all, he found a thin, straight tree and sliced its trunk clear from the roots. He pared off the bark and limbs, carving it into a perfectly round pole. He tested its strength against boulders and larger trees, wielding it like a staff against imagined enemies. She watched him with infinite curiosity, tilting her head this way or that. Finally, he took the ropes of tendon he had cut from the tiger's body and used them to secure his knife, point forward, to the end of the staff. Now he had a great spear worthy of an Uduru. He was ready.

Vireon told her with his eyes, *Do not follow me. You are my secret. If they capture me again, you may need to free me again.*

Her eyes responded, *What if they kill you?*

His eyes laughed, and he kissed her pink lips, ran his hands through her saffron hair.

"Stay here," he said aloud. "I will return soon."

He stalked alone into the highlands. Despite his plea, she would follow him in her fox form, but stay well back from the domain of the Udvorg. She was clever and elusive, his Alua. She was much more that he did not know, but hoped to learn eventually. He turned his thoughts forward, and they carried him into the mountain depths.

A day of following the scattered and obvious tracks of Udvorg hunting parties, and he found the great plateau that was the center of their territories. He climbed the wide trails, avoiding now and then a group of hunters coming or going. Wrapped in his white tiger-cloak it was easy to hide himself among the snowdrifts. One group of hunters lumbered right past him without ever noticing. They were six blue-skins carrying the immense carcass of a shaggy mammoth. He recognized its great tusks as the substance from which the throne of Angrid the Long-Arm was built. There must be vast plains to the north where such behemoths grazed.

At last he topped an escarpment and saw the blue-green spires of the ice palace. He crossed the naked plateau during a snowstorm, the glacial towers growing larger with every step. A ring of frozen peaks hemmed the Udvorg tableland. The sky was a sliding mass of gray and black cloud, an aerial sea pouring tempests upon the world.

When the vast open gates stood before Vireon like the maw of some gargantuan beast, the guards first caught sight of him. There were only two at ground level, though he supposed more must be stationed along the battlements of the outer wall. Eight guard towers lined its forward expanse. He walked unhurriedly through the flying snow toward the sentinels at the gate.

Both blue-skins took up their spears. One hefted a great axe in his second hand, while his companion held a war hammer of stone and iron. One yelled something at Vireon, raising his spear in an unmistakable command. Vireon did not catch the words, but the gesture was obvious.

His own voice pierced the wind. He spoke loudly and slowly, so they could understand every word through his accent. "I am Vireon of Udurum! Son of Vod, King of Uduru! I escaped your dungeons days ago! I come to surrender myself to King Angrid!"

The Giants blinked, exchanged a fierce glance, and lumbered toward him.

"But only to King Angrid!" shouted Vireon. "Only to the King himself!"

The blue-skins rushed at him, grinning, their crimson-dyed

furs swirling in the wind. He vaulted above the thrust of the first spear, coming down to catch its haft under his boots. The blue-skin's spear snapped in half. The second guard tried to impale him as well, but Vireon's own spear came up in a blur and turned it aside.

He rolled between their legs and swept the blade of his spear across the back of a Giant ankle. The guard howled and fell to one knee, while the other swung the big hammer. Vireon avoided the blow – Uduru, blue-skinned or not, were powerful but slow. He was the wind and they were clumsy trees. The hammer cracked open the ice-floor of the plateau and Vireon sliced at the wrist that held it. The Udvorg leaped back, dropping the spear in an attempt to staunch his bleeding. Both sentinels kneeled in the snow, dripping ichor. Vireon tore the battle axe away from the one whose leg was useless. He stood before them now, far enough away to avoid their grasp. They stared at him with red eyes more fierce than any tiger's.

"I surrender myself only to the King!" he yelled again, loud enough so those in the guard towers might hear him. Blue-skins moved along the battlements now, and someone blew a note on a great horn. The two wounded guards yelled up to their fellows.

"A little demon has come among us!" they bellowed. "Come, brothers, squash this insect! He bleeds us with his sting!"

The wind howled as the bleeding Giants crawled and stumbled back to their post. A moment later, a dozen blue-skins filled the gateway. They marched into the storm bearing axes, swords, hammers, and maces. Some of them grinned, others grunted, some looked at Vireon with eyes colder than the ice itself.

"I wish to surrender to King Angrid!" Vireon shouted at them. "Send for the King!"

They seemed unsurprised that he held up a Giant's axe with one hand, a weapon as large as his whole body. Perhaps they thought he could not wield it effectively. He disabused them of this notion when the first of the twelve came at him swinging a broadsword. Vireon ducked beneath the blade and his axe lopped off the swordsman's arm just below the elbow. As the Giant fell screaming, Vireon sprang atop his broad shoulders and shoved a spear into the eye of the next Udvorg. This one's writhing broke the wooden haft in two, but Vireon spun and picked up the fallen broadsword. He faced ten more blue-skins with an axe and a sword of their own making.

Now I am no exhausted fool, famished and chilled from days of running.

Now I am the Son of Vod at my full strength.

Let them see this and understand.

How many will have to die?

He was too fast for their weapons. They were like Men trying to swat a wasp with iron bars. These Udvorg moved even slower than the Giants of Udurum – perhaps it was their cold blood. Vireon pounced from shoulder to shoulder and cleaved skulls, darted between legs and severed tendons or entire limbs. He left the axe buried in a Giant's skull and began fighting with only the sword, which doubled his speed. Once an iron spearhead plunged toward his heart, but his dense skin turned the blade aside. It left a shallow gash from nipple to ribs. They never touched him again. He whirled and struck, darted and punished, vaulted and thrust, ran and hacked. After some time he stood alone amid twelve fallen blue-skins. They moaned, dead, or dying, and his cloak of white fur was drenched in their violet blood.

A host of Udvorg lined the walls now; faces looked out from the oval windows of towers or stood on balconies watching the slaughter.

"I surrender myself!" he shouted so that all might hear him. "But only to the King! Angrid come forth! No more will die!"

He expected more blue-skinned warriors to come howling at him, but they did not. The two at the gate had gone within, and four more took up the post, keeping their distance. A few of the beaten Giants crawled back toward the gate, though most lay unmoving in the snow. Some few would never move again. The storm wailed in Vireon's ears. He stuck the Giant-blade into the ground before him and pulled the bloody cloak tight about his shoulders.

Twice more he shouted his message, and the roof of clouds turned to the infinite dark of night. Cold azure flames danced along the walls at intervals, and the blue-skins stared at him, whispering among themselves and passing orders to and fro. Would they leave him standing here all night? Would they ignore him until he went away? If so, he would have to brave the depths of the palace himself to find Angrid. He pondered his chances of surviving such an incursion alone. The gigantic palace glittered before him, a masterwork of sapphire and emerald bathed in starlight. He waited, and snow obscured the bodies of the fallen Giants.

A great cold-fire glow lit up the gateway. Another horn blew somewhere inside, and dark shapes moved within. They emerged as a procession of warriors in oval formation about a central figure. Angrid the Long-Arm walked amid his armed escort, twenty Udvorg sentinels bearing spear and sword. The King carried his great axe casually at his side. A shaman, robed and hooded in a cloak of black wolfskin, walked behind him with a tall staff. The tip of the staff burned with a blue flame that did not consume its wood. The King's tigers accompanied him too, twins to the wild one Vireon had slain. A sentinel on the King's right held the leashes of these beasts as they strained forward. If he let go, they would pounce upon Vireon in an instant.

The forward sentinels moved apart, and King Angrid strode to the head of the column, shaman and tiger guard behind him at either side. Vireon stood his ground, arms crossed, the stolen sword planted before him. The wind whipped at his cloak, which had gathered a mantle of snow on its shoulders.

Angrid spoke first in his antiquated dialect. "Little One," he said, voice like grinding icebergs, "you already escaped my grasp. Now you give yourself to me?"

"I do," said Vireon, raising his voice above the shrieking wind. "On one condition!"

Angrid the Long-Arm lifted his axe and rested it on his brawny shoulder. His tigers growled and strained at their chains. The shaman stared from the black depths of his hood.

"What do you ask, killer of Udvorg?"

"These deaths are regrettable," said Vireon. "They sadden my heart. Here is my condition. Fight me, Angrid! I make the Challenge of Hreeg. We face each other as Uduru – arm to arm, chest to chest . . . no metal in our way. If I win, you must declare me of Uduru blood – your cousin – and accept my offer of peace."

The Ice King glared at him with ruby eyes. The gems in his crown cast a blue gleam across the snow.

"What if you lose?"

"If you best me, my life is yours. I will not protest. I will slay no more of your people."

A moment of silence fell thick as the snow between Vireon and Angrid. Then the Ice King threw back his head and laughed. His chest rumbled, and he bent over to smack his knee. His tigers writhed in their collars, sniffing and gnawing at his iron-shod boots. Shards of ice fell from his beard as he chuckled. When he looked back into Vireon's face, his thick blue lips were split in a wide smile. His teeth were the saffron color of the tigers' fangs.

"There is no need," he said. "Only a true Uduru . . . would make such a challenge. For surely I would . . . grind you beneath my heel. You face death like . . . a proud Udvorg. You use the ancient name of Hreeg, first King of Uduru. Only an Uduru raised by Uduru . . . would know of this tradition. You come back . . . to the lands of the Ice Clans . . . walking without fear to the Palace of Blue Flame. I do not *need* to fight you, Little One . . . Only an Uduru would do these things. I call you . . . *cousin*!"

Vireon stood speechless as the King's escort and the crowds along the wall cheered Angrid's announcement. He had not expected this: he had expected to fight, and possibly to die, in order to prove his blood. These Udvorg were not as savage as he presumed. Their King was wise.

Angrid dropped his axe and came forward with open arms. He offered his great hand to Vireon, who took it in both of his own. Then the King bowed to embrace him.

"Tell me again . . . the name your father gave you," said the Ice King.

"Vireon."

"Come, Vireon," said the King. "We will feast, and you will tell me of the southlands."

That was all the apology the King would offer. Likewise, Vireon would never again need to apologize for the warriors he'd slain. The ways of Uduru and Udvorg were not so dissimilar.

These were, after all, his cousins.

Drums throbbed between the blue-green pillars of the King's dining hall. A chorus of Udvorg sang low-pitched hymns to the Gods of Night and Cold. The great ice table lay heavy with mammoth beef, thawed fruits from deep cellars, gelatins of bear fat, and spiced ale from palace breweries. All the fare was served cold and raw. A hundred soldiers sat along the King's table, most of them male. Not all of the folk of the Ice Clans were warriors, or were expected to be. This society offered far more variety than the

Uduru. Of course, most of the Uduru were dead. The survivors of Old Udurum were the most hearty and warlike of the Giant folk; the rest had perished a quarter-century ago. Vireon's people may have been more like the Udvorg before the Serpent-Father destroyed their ancient city.

The Ice King peppered him with questions. Vireon sat at his right elbow; at his left sat the shaman, who pulled back the hood to reveal the face of a handsome Giantess. She wore a bronze hoop through her nose, six more through each ear, and the marks of ritual scarring ran along her high-boned cheeks. Her hair was black, unlike most of the Udvorg, whose hair was the color of snow. He noticed a few other blue-skins with black hair. Either white or black; there were no in-between shades. All their eyes were crimson, all their skin blue, so this duality of hair color was interesting. The shamaness – whose name he learned was Varda the Keen Eyes – said little as Vireon spoke with the King, but she eyed him curiously. If she harbored feelings good or ill toward him, he could not tell.

"Your mother rules the Uduru since Vod has give himself to the Great Water?" asked Angrid. Vireon followed the Udvorg accent easier now, but some words still took a moment.

"Queen Shaira," Vireon said, "rules the City of Men and Giants."

"She is . . . human?"

"She is," said Vireon. "Yet the Uduru love her. They respect her wisdom. Fangodrim the Gray, my father's brother, is First Among Giants."

"Why does your uncle not take the throne?" asked Angrid.

Vireon shrugged. "He loves my mother, too. And I think he does not want the weight of the crown. The Uduru do not care. They . . . they are dying."

Angrid put down the joint of mammoth meat upon which he

gnawed. His frosty brows furrowed. "What do you mean dying?"

"I told you how my father killed the Lord of Serpents," said Vireon. He drank a gulp of the bitter black ale. It was not bad, and it was the only thing in this feasting hall that warmed his bones. These Udvorg had become one with the cold over the centuries – they were as comfortable in frigid conditions as he would be on a sunny spring morning. He was glad of his tiger cloak. "When the beast died, he put a curse on Vod's people. The women are barren. No child has been born to the Uduri since that day."

The shamaness Varda whispered something in the Ice King's ear, and the monarch turned back to Vireon. "How many of our cousins still stand?"

"More than a thousand," Vireon replied. "Perhaps twelve hundred."

The King did not understand his Uduru numbers, so Vireon rephrased his answer. "Only a fraction of your people. Perhaps ten times more than are in this room. No young ones at all."

Angrid and Varda conversed in low tones, and Angrid nodded. Varda gave orders to a nearby sentinel, who marched off on some mission.

"This is why our people must reunite," said Vireon. "It is why I risked my life to win your favor, King of the North."

Angrid nodded, chewing his meat. A trio of male shamans entered the room, each bearing a staff lit with the blue flame. Udvorg shamans were the guardians of the cold fire; they conjured it and spread it among their people as needed. Angrid told Vireon it came from the Night God. The God visited them ages ago, when they first entered the frozen north. He taught the secret of the cold flame to spare them from the God of Darkness. It was their own hereditary magic.

Twelve clans dwelled in these mountains. Angrid the Long-Arm ruled over them all, and they rarely warred against one another. They thrived in the land of ice and snow, meeting once a year at Spring Thaw to trade wives and barter other precious things. The women of the Udvorg were not hard-bitten she-wolves like those of the Uduru; they were more like human women, despite their great size. Vireon watched them move about the chamber and found them comely, beautiful even, possessed of their own savage grace. The Uduru would find them irresistible.

"Tell me, Great King," said Vireon, accepting more of the ale. "Why did our people divide? My cousins have never spoken of the Ice Clans. Could they have forgotten?"

Angrid grunted, washing down a mouthful of mammoth flesh with a great horn of foamy ale. That which he spilled froze immediately on the rim of his beard. "It happened long ago . . . after Hreeg the First led the Stoneborn against the Serpents and brought them north across the Black Mountains."

The Grim Mountains, Vireon understood.

"Hreeg's brother, Udvorg the Dreamer, wished to go farther north. But Hreeg saw a great stone city in his mind and set to building it near those mountains in the Southern Forest. Udvorg challenged Hreeg, and they fought for three days. In the end neither could prevail. Both were mighty warriors. So Hreeg called his cousins about him and said, 'Who will go north with me to find the White Mountains of my dreams?' There was much arguing, and not a little fighting. After a day, the tribe of Uduru split, and Udvorg's followers took his name. This was in the days when our skins were all the same color.

"Udvorg led his people into these mountains, for he knew they were the ones in his dream. Here he found the ancient temple of the Night God, and became the first shaman. He called up the first of the blue flames, and it is from that light all our fires are lit. You have seen this in the chamber of my throne. This palace Udvorg's people built on the very spot of the ancient temple, so that our home is a holy dwelling.

"When Udvorg the Dreamer finished this shrine, the Cold God came on a great wind and gave his people the blue skin and purple blood that makes us strong. Over the ages, we have honored these Gods and kept the holy ways. Our shamans keep alive the blue flames, which are the heart of our kingdom."

Vireon considered the tale and found himself drowsy as the drummers kept at their mesmerizing beat. "Then truly we are of one people," he said. "Uduru and Udvorg – two races that are one, like Udvorg and Hreeg, brothers of equal might."

The Ice King smiled. "Not so equal if what you say is true," he said. "It saddens my heart that our cousins bear this curse."

"Perhaps there is a way— " began Vireon, but the King cut off his words.

"Ah, here they are!" He waved his great arms about the table, and Vireon watched a line of lovely Udvorg Giantesses line up directly across the table. All were of the white-haired variety with skins the shade of a cloudless sky, eyes sparkling vermillion. Some wept gently as they looked upon him. There were six altogether, and behind them stood eight or nine sullen blue-skin children with their heads lowered. The eldest of these young ones stood a bit taller than Vireon.

For a moment, he expected some kind of performance. He had no idea what the King meant by this until Varda the Keen Eyes spoke.

"These are your wives, Vireon the Small," said Varda, her voice icy yet feminine. "And your children . . . "

Vireon sat his goblet of ale down hard on the table, spilling it. A few of the warriors laughed, while others scowled jealously at him.

"I do not understand . . ." he said.

The Ice King spoke now. "You killed five sentinels today . . . The rest will live and have learned a painful lesson. But of those five, three had wives. Some had more than one. All these wives had children, as you can see."

Vireon stared at the King.

"It is our custom," explained Angrid, "that a man's slayer be given his wives and children. They are yours now. Treat them well."

Vireon had no words. The Udvorg laughed at his uncomfortable silence. A few rose from the table and stomped away, unhappy with his newfound wealth.

"Forgive me, Majesty," said Vireon. He stood and bowed to his new wives and their brood. "This is not the custom of my own people. I was unprepared—"

"It does not matter," said Varda. "The King has declared you one of us. So our customs are now yours."

"Sit, Vireon, sit," said the Ice King. He waved a hand, and Vireon's adopted family went back to their individual chambers. "I think you begin to understand us well, Cousin."

"Better than I ever thought to," said Vireon.

"These women are your property . . . as ill-fitted to their frames as you may be. Still you must serve as master and husband."

"He cannot handle an Udvorg woman!" shouted a warrior. The table roared. Another spouted something about a "tiny sword," and more mirth ensued.

Vireon smiled, recognizing the good nature of their ribbing. This, too, was common among the Uduru. He must laugh at himself or be ill-mannered. He laughed and drank more ale. Much more.

"The customs of my cousins are *my* customs," he said. Glances of approval told him he spoke well.

"Hear me, Cousin," said the Ice King. "Did you not say your cousins to the south are in need of child-bearing brides?"

"I did," said Vireon. "Most urgently."

"Then understand . . . There are *other* ways to win the women of Udvorg," said the King. "A warrior can gain the heart of a free woman by words and deeds. This is how most wives are taken – by mutual agreement. Only one who is shaman cannot be wived. These are married to the Gods, or to other shamans. Also wives may be *given* . . . the most precious of all gifts."

Vireon nodded, understanding. "Tell me, Great King, what happens to the children of a woman who is a gift-wife?"

Angrid smiled. "The children follow the mother, of course. None can separate the she-tiger from her cubs. This is our law."

Vireon laughed. "You have made me wealthy and happy this night."

He thought of Fangodrim . . . of Danthus the Sharp-Toothed, Ohlung the Bear-Slayer, Dabruz the Flame-Heart, and even old Rockjaw in lonely Steephold. All his cousins, lonely and in need of female companions . . . many who lost their families to flame and chaos when the Old City crumbled. These Udvorg brides and their strong broods would be fine gifts indeed.

But there would need to be more, far more, if the Uduru race were to preserve itself. Every willing male giant must couple with the unwed daughters of the thriving Udvorg. Otherwise, the pale-skinned Giants would fade from the earth. In these cold halls he had found salvation for his people. Now he must seal the compact that would make that salvation complete.

"Great Ice King!" he announced, standing tall upon his seat of iron and stone. The ale sang in his veins. "I will take my wives and children south and reunite our peoples. The descendants of Hreeg and Udvorg will drink together again. This I have seen in my dreams!"

He raised his cup, and the Giants roared their approval.

"But more than that!" said Vireon. "Let our kingdoms of north and south become one united realm. Let all the land between the Black and White Mountains rejoice at this historic unification! Let our children, blue-skins and pale-skins, sing together of the heroes and battles that make us strong! Let us come together!"

A round of cheering broke like thunder inside the feasting hall. Only the shamaness Varda did not cheer. She retained her frosty composure. Vireon could not tell if she disapproved of this unification. But King Angrid rejoiced and led his warriors in an ancient anthem. After three rounds of listening, Vireon was able to join them. His dancing feet upon the table rivaled the pounding of the drummers.

The next morning he awoke on a pile of furs. Watery sunlight filtered through the viridian walls. Someone had carried him to this chamber, though too much of the black ale had stolen the memory of everything after his unity speech. He remembered his six wives and nine children. He smiled, imagining his uncle's face when he returned to Udurum.

He stood and made himself ready for a morning audience with the King, but a great sadness fell upon him like a cloud before the sun, robbing the earth of its golden glow. He sat down upon the furs, listening to the silent creep of the ice all about him. A pain in his heart grew from a dull ache to a stabbing sensation, and he lost his breath. He lay back, gasping, a fish suddenly cast out of water.

Tadarus . . .

He moaned his brother's name. Tears flowed from his eyes. An emptiness filled the hollows of his chest and stomach. He knew, somehow, with a certainty he had never felt before. His brother was gone.

He closed his eyes. The handsome face of Tadarus swam into his vision, conjured from memory. Then other visions: Tadarus picking him off the floor when he fell as a waddling infant; Tadarus showing him how to swim in a cold lake within sight of the palace towers; Tadarus guiding his hand to perfection with sword, spear, and axe. Wrestling him, laughing with him, running at his side, embracing him. Their father's hands sitting on both their shoulders, standing side by side before the cheering city . . . Men and Giants shouting his name, and that of Tadarus. His mother hugging both brothers at the same time. Even young Fangodrel, smiling slyly at one of Tadarus' jests.

His brother was dead.

How could he know?

Yet he did.

As he pulled on the tiger-cloak, one of his wives came into the chamber. She gave him meat and a slab of green cheese. "I am Trylla," she told him. "I was the wife of Dolgir the Stoneheart."

She stood three times his height, but she kneeled so that her face was even with his. He took her great head in his hands, and kissed her forehead gently.

"Trylla, I am sorry for the loss of your husband."

She stared at him, masking her emotion as the shamaness had done.

"Gather all my wives and children together," he told her. "Prepare for a journey. We leave this very day."

Trylla had a single child, a young boy of five,who was nearly as tall as Vireon. His name was Dolmun, and he responded eagerly when Vireon asked him to lead him to the King's hall. In the throne room Vireon explained his vision to Angrid, that his brother was in jeopardy or had already died, though he knew secretly that the latter was the truth.

"Go then," said the Ice King. "Let our cousins know that our gates are open to them . . . and our hearts. Let them come, Vireon. Let them find happiness with the Udvorg."

Vireon bowed low before the King. "It shall be so," he promised.

"But remember," said the Ice King. "No humans will be welcome here. Let them stay in Vod's city."

Vireon agreed. This was no land for frail humans. Once again there would be a realm exclusive to Giants. In truth, there always had been. It had been rediscovered. He thanked the Ice King again and vowed to return.

At midday they set out across the plateau: Vireon, his six wives, and his nine children. Wrapped in furs dyed to shades of ebony, snow, and scarlet, they marched down the slopes in quiet resignation. The day was storm free and well made for travel.

Alua came to him at dusk, when they stopped at the rim of the snow-dusted foothills. She came as a white fox, gliding up a hill on four paws, but when she reached him she stood on two legs. Her arms wrapped about him, and his blue-skin wives turned away. The children stared in wonder at this transformed creature.

"I told you I would return," he said. She saw the distance in his eyes now. The sadness and the ache. He did not try to hide it from her.

To his wonderment, she spoke. "Where do you lead them?" she asked in the Uduru tongue.

He blinked, and might have laughed if his heart was not so heavy.

"South," he said. "To my people . . . "

"You are troubled," she said.

"How d-did you . . . " he stammered. "You speak?"

The tip of her pale nose touched his, and her blonde mane fell loose down her back. "Each night as we slept side by side," she said, "I took a bit of your language from your dreaming mind. Now I speak it. Does this please you, Vireon?"

To hear her say his name was a thrill he could not express. He smiled and held her close. Their hearts beat like the Udvorg drums, thrumming in perfect unison.

"Yes," he told her. "You please me. Only you, Alua."

He fought back the tears that slipped like traitors from his eyelids.

"What troubles you?" she asked.

He shook his head. He could not speak of his brother. Not now. Not in front of his Udvorg wives. He kissed her neck, soft as silk, fragrant as a blossom.

"What . . . what are you, Alua?"

She smiled, tilted her head in that endearing way.

"I am what I must be."

He laughed. It spilled from his mouth like blood from a puncture wound.

"Will you come with me?" he whispered.

She nodded, a silent affirmation. Her eyes were locked on his.

"It will be strange to you," he warned.

Now it was her turn to laugh. "You are strange to me," she said.

She conjured the white flame and built a warm fire a small distance from the Udvorg, who needed no warmth. So they all spent the night on the hilltop in comfort, the two pale-skins wrapped in each other's arms, the blue-skins lying on furs in the snow. There was no need to explain to the Udvorg that Alua was Vireon's First Wife. This they all understood.

In the morning they marched down into the lands of running water, a world of green and brown and yellow leaves, where winter was still a whispered promise.

It will be strange for us all.

12

Patterns

First came the denial of self, the surrender of ego, the death of certainty.

Sharadza ate nothing for days, drinking only the water given by the crone. Outside the mouth of the cave, sun and moon came and went, stars and clouds danced across the sky. Winds blew and rain fell.

Patterns.

The hunger gnawing in her gut eventually gave way to the comfort of emptiness. Her body accepted, as her mind already had, that nourishment was not to come. She was no longer hungry at all. How many days had it taken? Time was lost to her. Day and night were opposite sides of a coin, flipped into the air. She strove to catch it in her hand.

She meditated, sitting on the hard stone of the cave floor, in the dark, in the light, in the purple shades of twilight, the golden glow of morning. She repeated the first of many mantras, aloud at first, then quietly in her mind, revolving like celestial orbs in her consciousness.

All is One . . . There are no distinctions.

At last the crone came to her in the timeless dark, giving her a fruit like a silver-skinned pear. "The pome of Oridnis the Cloud City," said the crone, "grown by a race of ancient savants. This is mokkra, the Fruit of Enlightenment. Eat all of it, even the seeds."

Delicious, it tasted of starlight, rain, and wisdom.

The Great Oneness blossomed like the petals of a rose at the zenith of her understanding. The physical world spread about her like a spider's glittering web. It ran through her body, through her veins, through her thoughts like silver mercury.

All is One . . . There are no distinctions.

She knew . . . And awareness flowered beyond her skull, beyond the walls of the cave, through the porous rock, into the rushing sky, through the continents of cloud shifting above the fluid play of earth, sea, wind, and fire.

"The part is the whole."

The crone placed a small stone into her palm.

"This is a mountain."

She spilled a single drop of water into her other palm.

"This is the sea."

All is one . . . There are no distinctions.

A flaring ember from the coals of the fire hovered between her eyes.

"This is all fire, everywhere."

She blew into Sharadza's face, breath redolent with the strange tea.

"This is the measureless sky."

She took Sharadza's hands into her own, squeezing them together.

"This is life."

All is One . . . There are no distinctions.

Sharadza swam the sea of clouds, but she also sat in the cave. She plunged into the green depths of the ocean, but she also sat in the cave. She burned in the fires at the heart of the earth, but she also sat in the cave, an earthen womb at the center of the Living World.

Next came the unity of thought and action.

She sipped a warm vegetable broth brewed by the crone, and drank wine from a stone goblet.

"All that lives, and all that has ever lived," said the crone. "All that will ever live. All are fractions of the great spirit, the unified consciousness of Being."

Sharadza blinked, and stars swirled in her eyes. She was still in the cave, but also in the sky . . . in the earth . . . in the ocean . . . in the fire.

"The part is the whole. There can be no separation. Separation is only illusion. Do you understand?"

"Yes."

"Then show me."

Sharadza stood before the crone and squeezed the small stone in her fist. The cavern rumbled, tremors running beneath her feet. A small stalactite fell to the floor, smashed into a cloud of dust. Sharadza grabbed the dust in her hand and blew on it. Outside, a great wind rushed across the forest. She sat down. The cave grew still.

"Good," said the crone. "The infinite can be found in the smallest of fragments. The web of life invests our world with diversity. We are the sparks that move within the greater flame, which is also ourselves."

"Material and immaterial," said Sharadza. "There is no difference but that which we believe."

"Whatever we believe," said the crone, "is our reality."

Sharadza meditated again, this time repeating the second mantra.

Thought is Action . . . Non-thought is Being.

She sat on one side of the fire, the crone on the other. Days and nights flashed by, but the cave remained unchanged.

"As all things are one, so are the Mind and Body," said the crone. "Your highest self is that which determines form and motion. This invisible essence is what you seek, for it is the source of all power."

Thought is Action . . . Non-thought is Being.

"The world of flesh is a river. You have been a fish swimming in that river. But now you see that you are the river itself, and that the river is also one of spirit. Flesh and spirit, body and mind, form and formlessness. These are your tools. Seek the highest self and find there only Truth."

Sharadza was a ray of light, gleaming across the universe. That light gave birth to a flower, which also was her. The flower fed an insect, and she was that insect. The insect was devoured by a frog, which was her as well. Something ate the frog, and something devoured that, and she passed on through the chain of devouring . . . transforming, always transforming, never destroyed, never ending. She passed through a hundred lives, and then sat again in the cave with the crone and the flame.

Thought is Action . . . Non-thought is Being.

She sprouted from the earth as a newborn bud, grew into a sapling, sprouted leaves like dreams into the air. She rose toward the warm sun for a thousand years, feet planted in the earth, and stood tall as a mighty Uyga ruling over the forest of Uduria.

The crone brought her back into the cave with a whispered question.

"Which is more important? Thought . . . or Being?"

Sharadza blinked and felt the sun moving across the sky.

"There is no difference," she answered.

"Good," said the crone. "Now sleep."

*

Third came the mastery of patterns.

She studied the hidden patterns of nature, the expanding and repeating of organic forms. Infinite forms serving infinite purpose, and all those serving the ultimate Truth. She dwelled inside that inner sun of blazing, absolute Truth. From there, all things were possible.

Even the mantras were patterns – that was all.

She sat in the cave, on a mountaintop, on a cloud, on the endless seascape, in the branches of trees . . . and repeated the mantras whispered in her ear by the crone.

"These spoken things are not the patterns themselves," said the old one, "but merely the representation of the patterns. And yet, all is one, so they are the same. The part is the whole."

The universe was the cave in which they sat, day after day, night after night. The cave was a part of the universe, so it was the universe. From any point in its depths, all other points were within reach.

She saw the patterns of endless repetition in the surface of leaves as she walked the forest groves . . . in the heaving patterns of the foothills . . . in the swirling clouds and eddying pools. She saw the patterns in the births, lives, and deaths of Men and Giants. Men, Giants – they were the same. As were tigers and fawns, hawks and mice, beetles and fish, spiders and wolves. All life was composed of the same Infinite Intelligence, expressed in patterns. And every pattern composed part of a greater pattern, which led to a greater pattern, and so on into Eternity.

But why did these patterns exist? What caused the unified consciousness, Eternal Being itself, to fragment into its individual forms? Ah, the question was a lie. There are no individual forms. All is One, and yet . . . there were the patterns.

"Who set the patterns in motion?" she asked the crone. "Who set the Great Wheel of Life spinning?"

The crone cackled.

"Men blame the Gods for this," she answered. "But the Gods are only patterns as well."

"Then why the patterns?"

The crone shrugged. "It is the Way of Things."

"But if everything is illusion . . . separateness . . . diversity . . . patterns . . . all that constitutes reality, then what lies behind it? What is the Truth?"

The crone answered with a question of her own: "Which holds more power? Truth or Illusion?"

Sharadza thought first, then rose above her thoughts. They were only patterns.

"There is no difference," she answered. "All is One."

The crone cackled again. "Excellent," she said. "Now rest."

Next came the secrets of history.

"In the formless Before," said the crone, "the idea of Form was born, and so the patterns began."

The cave faded away and they stood in a black void pregnant with glittering stars. A vast blue-green globe floated in the darkness, reflecting the light of a flaming sphere that hovered beyond. Sharadza watched the patterns of white clouds move across the globe.

"The first patterns gave birth to the Old Breed, who moved across the world, shaping it to their whims. They floated in from the void, raising mountain ranges and carving oceans. They manifested Truth and Illusion together, and their patterns gave birth to more patterns, manifesting the infinitude of Nature.

"They created life from fragments of their own celestial bodies, to thrive and struggle and die and be reborn across the world that was their playground. Man was not the first. Nor Giants. Many were the shapes and forms that rose from the muck and spread their patterns across the continents. They built bright, shining cities which crumbled in an eon or two."

Sharadza saw the masses of antique races moving across the primeval world, taming swamps, slaying beasts, discovering fire, mastering the arts of agriculture, construction, the written word. Empire after empire, they crumbled to dust, each succeeding race building its monuments and walls on the bones of the last, ignorant of those that came before. In the depths of the seas amphibious cities sent coral towers into the world above, until tidal waves shattered and pulled them under. The cycles were the same – birth, progress, culmination, extinction. An endless repetition of life forms and civilizations.

Patterns.

"Ages passed, and the Old Breed grew tired of this play," said the crone. "They went back into the void, seeking distant horizons. Others grew weary and slept, and are sleeping still in the bones of the world. Still others wove themselves into the patterns below and became part of the world they had created. Some were called Gods . . . others Demons . . . others went unknown and lost even the memory of themselves. They lost themselves inside the perpetuating life cycles they themselves had set in motion, becoming what they had guided into being and observed for so long. They forsook the illusion of separateness and joined the world, but in so doing they fell into the trap of separateness. Some were reborn as new races . . . "

She saw the birth of the Uduru race, bursting full grown from the sides of mountains. The Stoneborn, they were still called by some. A race of amphibians crawled out of the sea, changed by the sun and the descending spirits of the Old Breed into the ancestors of men. Some of the falling powers took their forms in deep earth-fires, coalescing into the race of Serpents, spilling flame from their great maws. These were the three races that had shaped the modern world: Giant, Man, and Serpent. Far stranger races thrived in the far and hidden places.

She saw, from her place among the sun-gilded clouds, the Age of Serpents, when Men were devoured in thousands, until the Giants came forth to battle the Wyrms. She saw the Uduru cross the blackened mountains and built their first great city, while the Five Tribes of Man split across the continent and formed the kingdoms she knew. So fast the whole of history had passed before her eyes. But then time itself was an illusion as well.

"There are those of the Old Breed who still remember what they used to be," said the crone. "Men and Uduru call them sorcerers. Yet they do not know that many of these sorcerers live among them wrapped in coats of flesh and ignorance, limited by their own conceptions of reality. To learn the arts of sorcery is to relearn what you have forgotten.

"All Giants, and those born of Giants, carry the seeds of Old Breed power in their blood. You are of this breed, Sharadza. As was your father. As are all who walk the path of sorcery."

"Yet men can learn sorcery as well," said Sharadza. "Can they not?"

"For those descended of the Old Breed, as the Giants are, it comes as naturally as it has for you. As for the rest . . . they mumble incantations and invoke forces beyond their understanding. They think themselves true sorcerers, but such men only skirt the edges of Truth. Children playing with fire."

"So then every Uduru, once aware of his heritage, can wield true sorcery?"

"Child, the Uduru *are* sorcery."

"You yourself must be one of the Old Breed."

The crone gave her a toothless grin, and they were sitting in the cave again.

"I am one who has never forgotten," said the crone.

"And are there others who remember?"

"Oh, yes," said the crone. "A few . . . They seek to shape the world still. They weave secret patterns that bring change to the world. Theirs is an ancient struggle, a disagreement played out through a billion billion lives and numberless kingdoms living and dead."

Suddenly Sharadza knew. The crone was not a crone at all. "Who *are* you?" she asked.

"I am many beings," said the crone. "Whatever or whoever I choose to be. As are you."

Next, the awareness of other worlds.

"The Living World is composed of four elements," said the crone. "Fire, Earth, Air, and Water. These are the substance of the patterns in which we live, breathe, and work our wills. To see the unity of these four is the first step to mastering them all. Yet each is its own domain. Each requires dedication and study. But these are only the elements of the Living World. There are many others."

The World of the Dead was a cipher, an illusion that existed alongside the illusion of the Living World. They were united, yet separate. To master one was not to master the other, but to master them both would be to master the Whole. Truth lay where the two met and one became the other. Neither was eternal.

The World of Spirit was a realm beyond the reach of physical forces. Only by realizing its crucial relation to the solid world could one master its patterns. Spirits often manifest in the physical world, but physical things cannot manifest in the Spirit World. An accomplished sorcerer must belong to both worlds. This might take a lifetime.

The Worlds of Past and Future were also illusions. But since all things were equally Truth and Illusion, they might be used by a sorcerer to influence and alter the patterns of the Living World. However, becoming lost in Past or Future were terrible dangers, so these worlds could only be manipulated by the greatest of mages.

The Outer Worlds were without number. Some were formless, some contained form, and others were mixtures of both traits. These were the most dangerous of realms for the sorcerer to contemplate or to meddle in. Realities wavered, shifted, and patterns could not be counted as stable or even patterns at all. Great intelligences, and great hungers, dwelled in the Outer Worlds, some benign, some malevolent. To open the way into such worlds was to risk torment, annihilation, and madness. The absence of patterns was also a pattern: the void.

The gates of these worlds were best left alone.

Now choices must be made.

"There is much to learn, Princess," said the crone-who-was-not-a-crone. "Your inner eye has opened. Now you must decide where to begin."

Sharadza stood on the hilltop, watching the sun sink into a fog of scarlet and purple.

"My father," she said. "Do you see him alive or dead?"

The crone looked west toward the Cryptic Sea, somewhere beyond the woodland horizon.

"Look for yourself . . . "

Sharadza sent her mind into those faraway waters, gliding like a silver fish through the depths. A great ravine in the sea bed called out to her, glowing with a weird phosphorescence. She floated over the edge and saw the spires of a splendid city carved from coral. In shades of amber, scarlet, saffron, and azure it rose from the depths, and glistening sea-things darted about its towers like birds. It was not so unlike a city of the dry world, with its ramparts, gardens, bridges, colonnades, and domes. Amid the winding streets swam crowds of glittering mer-folk, busy as the citizens of Uurz or Udurum, yet wrapped in the bubbling peace of the marine world.

A great palace stood amid the city, and she knew it must belong to the Mer-Queen. A black-skinned leviathan circled it like a sentinel, and fishy guards with trident and spear manned its battlements. The scene wavered in the aqueous light, and her gaze could not penetrate those high walls; the palace was guarded somehow against her vision. Neither could she feel her father's presence, there or anywhere in the sea.

She opened her eyes and was back atop the hill with the crone. The sun had gone and stars gleamed above the roof of the forest. Winter winds blew from the north.

"The Mer-Queen is of the Old Breed," Sharadza said.

The crone nodded. "She is."

"I cannot see into her palace."

"Nor can I. It is her will."

"My father could be dead."

"Yes," said the crone.

"Then teach me about the World of the Dead," she said.

"This can be easily done," said the crone. "If you are sure."

"I am," said Sharadza. She turned to meet the old one's eyes. "Teach me when I return."

The crone narrowed her old eyes. "Return? You are leaving?"

"Yes," said Sharadza. "I will take what I have learned and go seek my father, living or dead."

"But you have learned almost nothing," said the crone.

Sharadza's eyes caught the moonlight, and suddenly she was a bear . . . a wolf . . . a stone . . . an eagle . . . then herself again.

"I have *remembered* everything," she said.

The crone smiled. "Yes, you are descended of the Old Breed.

But that is not enough . . . A child learns to walk before she can run."

"Enough, Fellow," she said, looking away from him, into the depths of the forest night.

Now it was the old storyteller who stood next to her on the hilltop. The crone was gone, if she ever had been there. The night wind whipped through Fellow's gaudy robes.

"You know?" he asked, shocked yet amused.

"How could I not? Is that even your real name?"

"It is one of my many names. Most call me Iardu the Shaper."

"Tell me, Iardu," she said. "How long have I been here, learning from you how to remember?"

"Not long, Princess," he said. "Not nearly long enough."

"Then I will return. When I have done what I set out to do."

"The Mer-Queen is no fool," said the Shaper. "Stay a while longer and learn all you can."

"If I stay, I may never go," she said.

He nodded. "Your father did the same thing. He learned the smallest thing from me and hurried on his way. The rest he discovered through trial, pain, and strife. As you will do."

"The part is the whole," she reminded him.

"It is," he agreed. "But I would spare you that pain. There are easy lessons, and hard."

"Yet these things are the same," she said.

He smiled.

"I will return," she said. "What I have not learned by then, you may teach me."

"Look for me in the city," he said.

"Come with me!" She turned to grab his shoulders. "Together we can—"

His hands waved her away. "I cannot, or I would have gone already."

She crossed her arms. "You fear the Mer-Queen?"

"No," he said. "I *love* her. I betrayed her."

She was silent for a moment. Then it burst from her like tears: "And my father? Did you betray him too?"

Iardu said nothing. He became the wrinkled crone again and stared up at the stars.

Now Sharadza was a black owl, and she flew into the westward night.

Already she had wasted too much time.

13

Flame and Fang

The Grim Mountains were well named. Four days riding up Vod's Pass and the sun had broken the gloom only once. Each day there was rain, and as the cohort rose higher into the range, rain turned to sleet. The deep ravines and twisting gorges shared a roof of leaden clouds. At times it seemed the company traveled through some gray, subterranean realm. Small, hardy trees stood along slopes every now and then, and often green valleys stretched away to east or west like hidden oases. Ripe fruits plucked from highland glades enhanced the company's rations. Hawks and eagles soared above the ranks of cavalry, arcing from peak to peak in search of prey. The roars of prowling tigers were common, but the predators never showed themselves. D'zan was glad of his well-armed escort, but the shadows of the great peaks weighed on his heart like chains of iron.

The pass had followed the Uduru River into the uplands until it reached the Great Falls. There a torrent of whitewater roared over a precipice, feeding the river from its source somewhere beneath the mountains. Clouds of mist cast tiny diamonds across the cloaks, armor, and helms of the Uurzian legionnaires. D'zan had found it refreshing, standing near to that raging cataract, the mist cool on his skin. The stop at the falls was a brief one, for they had lost too much time already. The company had lingered for two days at the foot of the mountains, waiting until D'zan's bruised ribs could stand the bucking and swaying of a horse. Each night he clutched the Stone's blade to his chest as he slept, fearing the return of the beast, or something worse. He knew Elhathym had set the demon to watch for him at the edge of the mountains, so could he not set more watchers along those heights? But no more evil spirits came. Perhaps they lay waiting for him somewhere along the pass.

The bandages tight around his midsection helped, but still he rode in discomfort. He claimed to be free of pain, but Lyrilan could tell by his eternal grimace that D'zan lied. Tyro, riding at the head of the gold-and-green column, took D'zan at his word. D'zan decided to bear the pain – he could not lie beneath those dark peaks any longer. Now, after four days of crawling up the pass, the cold numbed his pain. Despite his heavy cloak of fur and gloves of scaled lizardskin, he could barely feel his fingers and toes. The complaint of his aching ribs was a distant thing, hidden under the frigid air like grass beneath snow. He had been raised in the heated southlands, where cold came only at night and never with such violence. He marveled at the frozen peaks with their ice-clad summits, shivering in the white gleam of their glory. The wind tore at his face and cloak, a wailing ghost of winter.

Lyrilan drew his mount closer. "Yonder obelisk marks the summit of Vod's Pass," he told D'zan. "We should see the towers of Steephold rising directly ahead, as I remember."

"How long?" D'zan said into a gust of wind.

"What's that?" yelled Lyrilan.

"How long since you've traveled this way?"

"Three years . . . Tyro and I visited Udurum to represent our father at the Feast of Summer."

D'zan grunted. "Does summer ever come to the north?"

Lyrilan grinned. "Not the summer of your native shore, Prince! But it does get far warmer once we're down from between these dreadful peaks. We can look forward to a warm fire and dry bedding at Steephold."

Some grumbling came back to them from the head of the column, some message passed from soldier to soldier, a swirling rumor among the ranks. D'zan could barely see Tyro topping the slope ahead, reining his steed beneath the whipping sun banner.

"Something is wrong," Lyrilan said. He spoke with a sergeant, who leaned from his saddle to talk over the moaning wind. When the scholar turned back to D'zan, his face was worried. "Steephold has fallen."

D'zan blinked against the words, not the wind. "Fallen?"

"Come, let us join my brother," said Lyrilan, spurring his mount forward through the ranks. D'zan followed, a hollow sensation rising in his stomach. Their horses climbed the rocky incline until they reached the level ground. Tyro's stallion stood alongside those of his captain and two lieutenants.

A wide bowl of flat terrain spread before them, hemmed on all sides by soaring white pinnacles. The pass proper continued along the bowl's edge, dropping into a downward grade at its northern edge. In the bowl's middle lay a heaped pile of ruined stone, massive blocks of basalt and granite scattered like childrens' toys. A few walls of the toppled fortress still stood in awkward fragments. The husk of the inner keep that was the heart of Steephold lay beneath a million tons of rock – the remains of mighty towers that had crushed roof and walls. The stones were slick with mud and the purple-brown stains of dried blood. The ruins were fresh – only days old.

Tyro and his captain rode through the gaping hole where the

main gate had been, horses picking their way among the rubble-strewn courtyard. The mighty gates themselves lay splintered into fragments. Lyrilan and D'zan followed, mesmerized by the heaped mounds of devastation. If there were bodies, they had been hauled away somewhere. They found no bones until Tyro dismounted and turned over a block leaning against a pillar. In the space between lay the corpse of a human soldier in the black-and-silver livery of New Udurum. The collapsing pillar had smashed his skull to pulp, but his body bore the deep marks of claws. Whoever dragged the dead from this spot had missed this fellow.

"An officer of the Udurum legions," Tyro said. "Dead now four, maybe five days."

Lyrilan looked about at the silent mountainsides, as if the very stones might rise up and continue the assault. "Fifty Uduru guarded this place," he said. "Fifty Giants, seasoned warriors . . . What could have done this?"

D'zan's mind raced back to the demon in his tent, squeezing the life from him, breathing death into his face. He reached behind his shoulder and grasped the hilt of the Stone's blade. The Sun God's ward had saved him from death, there could be no doubt. Lyrilan had agreed, when D'zan told him the whole story. The Giants of Steephold – and the Men who were also here – they had no wards.

"Something terrible," said Tyro, remounting his horse. "We'd best not camp near these ruins. Bad luck . . . and scavengers probably roam here after dark. The scent of blood is still strong."

"There must be more bodies beneath these walls," said Lyrilan.

"The castle has fallen before," said the Uurzian captain. "The Uduru rebuilt it at Vod's command. They'll rebuild it again."

"Not soon enough to do us any good," said Tyro. He raised his arm to signal the standard-bearer.

The quake struck before he uttered a word. The horses reared and screeched in panic as the ground trembled. The mountains breathed an awful sigh of agony, and the earth beneath the crumbled fortress *moaned*. Men fell from their horses, and D'zan would have tumbled if Lyrilan had not reached out to grab his hand, their mounts swirling in a dance of fear. Rocks and gravel jumped, and the great stones shook, the rubble shifting and sliding as if something beneath were tearing its way through toward daylight.

"Below the fortress!" yelled Lyrilan in the roar of earth and wind. "The Giants had sealed a cavern leading to—"

Fragments of towers and walls erupted toward the ashen clouds with the sound of a splitting continent. A black whirlwind rose from the wreckage, taller than any Uduru, shedding a blanket of rock and dust from its scaly back. Clouds of dust and pulped stone rolled across the legionnaires, filling nostrils, mouths, and eyes. A bememoth pulled its body free of some deep cavern, crawling through the ruins in a blast of heat and smoke. Now its ear-splitting roar filled earth and sky. Somewhere beneath that ultimate sound, the cries of terrified men and horses rang as well. An appalling reek filled the air – burning feces, rotted flesh. The ancient stench of Serpents.

D'zan lost hold of Lyrilan's arm and fell from his saddle. His back met the stony ground, and consciousness fled for a moment. Then he blinked in the dust and saw the vast creature crawling spans away from him, spitting a gout of flame into a mass of howling soldiers. A massive wall of scales like black iron. He caught a glimpse of its eyes, flame-red orbs of primeval hate. One of its dozen legs, six on each side, came down upon a fleeing horse. Ebony claws sank like spear blades into the steed's round belly.

D'zan scrambled to his knees. Where was Lyrilan? Tyro? The captain? He pulled the greatsword from its scabbard and ran for cover. The beast – it was a Serpent, an Old Wyrm, he knew that – seemed intent on the mass of Uurzians. It had lain beneath the ruins, waiting for them. *No . . . waiting for me.* Could it sense him now, crouching like a coward behind a pile of broken stones?

Brave Uurzians rushed past their charred and screaming comrades, a forest of eager spears. The beast bellowed again, and avalanches of snow fell from nearby peaks. Men died squirming between its gnashing teeth, or pulped beneath its stamping claws. The front of its body rose high, six front-legs hanging in the air, dripping with bones and blood. It vomited burning pitch among the Uurzians, who ran or ducked behind oval shields. Most were caught in the flame and burned to death in an instant.

A thicket of spears protruded from the Wyrm's pale underbelly as it dropped back to the ground, snapping with its terrible jaws. Some men scrambled toward its back end, where its tail lashed like a massive whip, sending men through the air, braining them against piles of jagged masonry. D'zan saw a beefy Uurzian hacking at its rearmost leg with an axe. The man severed a single claw before the great head turned around and snapped him up.

Lyrilan lay senseless where his fear-stricken horse had bucked him. Any second now the Serpent's legs would trample the unconscious Prince to death. Dragging the great blade behind him, D'zan ran with head down toward Lyrilan's body. As the Serpent reared up again, spewing another gout of flame into a fresh rank of screaming Uurzians, he wondered if Lyrilan was already dead. If so, he might die trying to rescue a corpse. The heat from the sides of the beast's blast-furnace mouth swelled over him, the biting chill of winter vanished. This warmth gave him a strange courage. He grabbed Lyrilan with his free arm, dragging him back along a cloven wall to the shadow of the fallen stones. Now the beast moved forward into the ranks that assailed it, legs tromping the burned carcasses of men and horses. It ignored the spears and the bites of tiny blades as it gnashed, tore, and ripped through the legionnaires.

Lyrilan was breathing. *Thank you, Gods of Earth and Sky.* Some blood in his hair – his head must have struck a stone. Where had his horse gone? Was it burned to a crisp with all the gentle Prince's papers and quills? Enough time for that later . . . if they survived. D'zan peeked over the pile of stones, looking for Tyro.

The Serpent's thrashing limbs knocked down the remains of an outer wall. It writhed and roared its hot thunder, and more men threw themselves into the death of its claws and teeth. Tyro's commanding voice, a tiny sound, rang across the fray. The beast raised up its head and forelegs again, and the Prince called, "Run! Run!"

D'zan saw the pattern of its breathing now, the rearing that was a precursor to flaming breath, and the soldiers scattered before the rush of its flame. When the last of the gout spilled from its tongue, a volley of arrows peppered its snout. A unit of archers had fallen into place along the pass. Now the cavalrymen ran back toward the beast, stabbing at its exposed belly, Tyro at the vanguard. D'zan knew himself a coward then. How could Tyro face such a monstrosity? How could any man? They must have already given themselves over to death. Why be afraid if you welcomed death?

D'zan raised the big blade. *I, too, will die like a man.* He could not wield the weapon with much skill, but his target was so huge it would not matter. This great length of iron would sink deep into that thing's belly. He left Lyrilan lying hidden behind the rubble and crept forward toward the Serpent's right flank. He forced himself not to look away when its claws and fangs tore the guts from men, red and streaming across the ground.

Soon it would lift its head again, and D'zan would charge, strike for its damned heart.

Tyro ran from its snapping fangs, having left his spear embedded between two scales along its neck. So far it had ignored every single wound inflicted upon it. They might have been buzzing gnats against a stampeding ox. But they were Men, and they knew how to die with honor.

D'zan crouched, ready to spring and run when the serpentine head came up. Closer to it now, he heard the clang and clatter of blades against its scales. It must be the belly . . . There was no other way to pierce its ancient hide. Now the steaming snout drew back. It would raise up. D'zan would run. Any second now . . .

The earth trembled again, and he feared a second Wyrm might rise from the ruins. A chorus of war-cries rose above the howls of dying men. From behind the mound of ruins a cloud of dust rose, and the shouts rang from its direction. Booming shadows rushed across the rubble, raising mighty axes, hammers, and blades. A troop of Uduru warriors swarmed across the ruins toward the Wyrm.

Giants! Never had D'zan seen them in the flesh until now. He could not imagine a sweeter sight than those twenty-three Giants leaping upon the tail, hindquarters, and backbone of the Serpent. The Uurzians saw their rescuers and howled at the sky. The Serpent's head turned toward its rear quarters. A Giant hacked off its tail, and black gore spurted from the stump to steam like oil upon the rocks. Another Giant took a leg from the beast's body easily as chopping firewood – one, two strokes of his axe and the limb was a jerking, lifeless thing. The axeman kicked it away.

The Giants wore the purple and black of Udurum, their mail and cloaks torn and crudely patched. They had survived some recent battle, probably the one that brought down their fortress. They must have hidden in the mountains nearby waiting for . . . what? For the Uurzians? For the Wyrm? For D'zan?

The beast reared up, switching itself toward the Uduru. The stub of its tail knocked a Giant off his feet. It rose, ready to belch flame . . . and now D'zan faced it from the wrong angle. He could run to join the Uduru, but by the time he faced its belly again it would be down and snapping with its teeth. Maybe he did not have to die today after all. Maybe no more Uurzians would die today. Tyro yelled commands at his men, and now they attacked the wounded beast's backside.

The monster unleashed its breath. Fire belched forth and scattered the Giants. One of their number went down beneath the full might of the blast, the rest of them singed but unharmed.

"Now!" bellowed an Uduru gray-beard, and the Giants sprang toward the Wyrm's belly. A pair of axes cleaved it open while a half-dozen spears drove in deeper than the height of a tall man. The beast roared, gushing hot, black blood.

The gray-beard took out one of the beast's great eyes, sinking a greatsword into the red orb, which broke like glass and splattered his mail with steaming fluid. Giants hacked and pulled legs from the beast, some with their very hands, ripping tendon and bone from the Serpent's sides.

One last time it reared up to breathe, but no flame came from its torn throat. Instead, the gray-beard Uduru sheared off its head with a sweep of his axe.

Headless it writhed and flailed.The Giants continued pulling off its legs one by one. The Uduru cheered, raising stained blades toward the sky, and the surviving Uurzians joined them. The mountain bowl lay strewn with the corpses of men torn, shattered, and smoldering. But here was victory, all the more sweet when snatched from the jaws of defeat.

D'zan raised his blade and walked among the milling men. His eyes were on the Giants, who slapped one another's backs and started laying claim to fangs, bones, or scales from the dead beast. It stank more heavily now than it did while alive, crimson innards exposed and flopping among the broken stones.

Tyro hailed the Uduru with gratitude and recognition in his eyes.

"Tallim the Rockjaw!" the Prince of Uurz shouted. "Never have I been more glad to see you and your brothers!"

The gray-beard Uduru laughed, dark gore dripping from his gauntlets. "Prince Tyro? Is the Emperor with you?"

Tyro shook his head and offered his hand to the Giant. Rockjaw removed his metal glove and carefully grasped Tyro's forearm in his fist.

"My brother Lyrilan and I—" Tyro stopped. "My brother!" He only now remembered Lyrilan, and his face was grave.

D'zan yelled to him, "Prince Lyrilan lies behind those rocks. His horse bolted and he fell. I believe he lives, so I kept him out of the way."

Tyro spared him an approving glance and went to find his brother.

"That is a fine blade," said Rockjaw.

D'zan realized he was still holding the greatsword. "Thank you. It was my inheritance."

The Giant grunted. "Well now, you are not Uurzian . . . you have southern skin. You must be the Yaskathan Prince."

D'zan blinked. "I am," he said.

Rockjaw nodded, black gore dripping from his beard. "I have another Prince in my care. One who is most eager to meet you."

D'zan sheathed his blade. It must be a Prince of Udurum. This boded well for the success of his journey. But he could not think on that while Lyrilan lay helpless and the corpse of a mythical monstrosity lay before him, being stripped of its treasures like a dog's carcass devoured by ants.

"I look forward to meeting your Prince," said D'zan to the Giant. "And I thank you for my life."

The Giant bowed, then turned back to stripping the carcass with his brethren. "We've not seen his like since the Fall of Old Udurum . . . " he heard Rockjaw say.

The Uurzian captain had survived, though his cloak was burned and his cheek blistered. Still he gave orders in Tyro's name while the Prince tended to his brother with water from a canteen. D'zan went to join Tyro. Lyrilan was coming around as his brother wrapped a white cloth about the scholar's skull.

"What was it?" Lyrilan asked, his voice weak.

"A Serpent," said Tyro. "It's dead now. Rest . . . I will tell you all later."

Lyrilan nodded. A field physician tended to the worst of the wounded men while soldiers helped their fellows as best they could.

"How bad is he?" asked D'zan.

"Not bad," said Tyro without looking at D'zan. "He'll be all right when he gets some rest and some hot food in his belly. He is tougher than he looks."

Lyrilan laughed, then groaned.

Tyro stood and looked at D'zan. "I should be condemning you as a coward," he said. "But it appears you may have saved my brother's life. So I will forgive your absence in this battle."

Tyro's eyes were dark steel. D'zan could not meet them, so he looked at the charred ground instead.

"I . . . I don't know what to say," he muttered.

"Say nothing to me," said Tyro. "But thank the Gods that all these men were here to die so that you may live."

D'zan turned his eyes to the clouded sky. If the Giants had not come, they would all be dead. But if the Men had not held off the beast as long as they did, the Giants would have come too late.

"Your training resumes tomorrow night," said Tyro. "Pain or no pain."

D'zan nodded.

"It is easy to be a Prince," said Tyro. "But far harder to be a man."

He clapped D'zan roughly on the shoulder and marched off toward his men.

D'zan knelt before Lyrilan.

"What did he say?" asked the scholar.

"Only the truth," said D'zan.

"You saved my life?"

D'zan shrugged. "*Someone* has to write my life story."

Lyrilan smiled.

Giants and Men stripped the beast of every last fang, claw, and scale. Such tokens would bring high prices in the markets of Uurz or Udurum. A detail of Uurzians set about burying their fallen men under cairns of rock. All told, Tyro had lost forty-six good men, and more than a hundred endured wounds of various severity. The beast had only slain one Uduru this night, but half the number of Steephold's inhabitants had died five days previous.

D'zan overheard Tyro and Rockjaw talking as the first torches of evening were lit. There would be no camping or eating until all the dead were buried. Men worked hurriedly among the cold shadows, and the moon lost itself behind the clouds.

"Oh, it was no Wyrm that destroyed Steephold," said Rockjaw. "That devil must have crawled up out of the caverns after the fortress fell. My guess is the collapsing floors dislodged the cap we put on the old warrens. Who knows how long this thing slumbered down there in the dark until the citadel's fall woke him to rage and hunger?"

D'zan squeezed his hands until his knuckles went white. He knew the Wyrm had awakened for one reason only . . . because *he* had come into the mountains. How could this not be the work of Elhathym and his sorcery? How many had died for D'zan thus far, starting with the guard crushed by a shadow outside his tent, ending in today's massacre? How many more would die before he regained his father's throne or perished himself? He must get used to death. It was part of the world to which he now belonged. But he did not know if he truly could. He must try. He had no choice.

"Then . . . if not the Serpent," asked Tyro, "what was it that destroyed the castle?"

Rockjaw ran a hand through his unkempt beard, and his big eyes were troubled. He looked at Tyro, his craggy face gilded by flickering torch light.

"Best to let the Prince himself answer that," said the Giant.

The cohort followed the twenty-two Giants up the side of a mountain, picking their way along an ancient track wide enough for three horses to walk abreast. The few wounded who could not ride lay in the bed of a supply wagon. More men had died than mounts, but it took a while to gather the scattered horses. Lyrilan's horse was among those retrieved; D'zan's mare had been burned to death. Tyro gave him a fallen soldier's stallion to ride. Lyrilan insisted on riding his own horse, despite Tyro's objections. The Uduru marched with claws, whole legs, and fangs carried on their shoulders. Rockjaw carried the body of their single casualty, the Giant who had burned to death, wrapped in a shroud made from a furred cloak. For their own reasons, the Uduru would not bury him near the ruins with the Men of Uurz.

The line of Giants, Men, and horses wound its way up and around the mountain. A layer of snow coated the precarious heights. D'zan glanced over the trail's edge when the moon sailed free of the clouds, shedding golden light across the world. He saw the ruined fortress far below, and the legless, skinned corpse of the Serpent. The stink of burned flesh still lingered in his nostrils, and he realized it had seeped into his clothes. He nearly retched, but fear of slipping over the side of the path and falling to his death pulled his stomach back down from his throat. He did not look down again.

On the western side of the mountain the Giants filed into an immense cavern where firelight danced and warm air flowed. The smell of roasting fowl replaced all others as D'zan rode into the crude sanctuary at the head of the Uurzian column. The cavern was vast enough to hold the entire cohort, not to mention its horses, wagons, and the Giants. One Uduru had stayed behind here, a Giant with his arm in a sling, tending a few injured Uduru who slept between the pointed pillars of stalagmites. There were Men here, too. At least sixty of them, a mix of black-clad soldiers from Udurum and others wearing the blue-white cloaks and turbaned helms of Shar Dni. They gathered about fires drinking wine or ale, chewing their simple dinners, or staring at nothing, lost in their own solemn thoughts.

Tyro ordered his captain to supervise the unloading of wounded men and the care of the horses. His lieutenants set about stocking and tenting the unclaimed sections of the cavern, while the men of Udurum and Shar Dni watched quietly. Many wore the bandages and slings of battle – they too had suffered. The quiet ones seemed the most damaged.

D'zan and Lyrilan dismounted, following Tyro and Rockjaw toward the back of the cavern. They passed among the silent Men and slumbering Giants, warmed by the glow of their fires. At least in here the cold was kept at bay, and the winds did not intrude. Weariness tugged at D'zan's eyelids, and his fingers tingled. His side ached worse now. It was always worse after a day of riding. Falling from his horse had not helped his bruises.

Rockjaw led them through a ring of Sharrian guards. D'zan noted their splendid curved swords, the cobalt blue of their mail shirts. These were the elite of the eastern city's royal legions. Why were they here guarding a Prince of New Udurum? Why were any Sharrians here?

The guards spread to let them pass. At their center on a bed of soft blankets, his head propped on a rolled cloak, lay a lean young man with a braided beard and a mass of curly black hair. His arms, legs, and torso were covered in bandages, some of them stained pink by leaking blood. Sweat beaded on his face, and he lay in the midst of a terrible fever. His nose was long and sharp, and a jeweled turban lay nearby, along with a scimitar with a hilt of gold, sheathed in a royal scabbard. He awoke from shallow sleep as Rockjaw kneeled at his side.

"Prince Andoses," whispered the Giant. "The Princes Tyro and Lyrilan have arrived, and his majesty Prince D'zan of Yaskatha."

D'zan looked about the cavern. Here was a Sharrian Prince. Where were the sons of New Udurum? It made no sense. But the wounded Prince turned his dark-rimmed eyes to D'zan and smiled. His expression said, *I have been expecting you.*

"Welcome, D'zan," said Andoses. His voice was weak, but steady. "I only wish I could stand up to embrace you. As it is, my open hand will have to do." He raised his hand shakily, and D'zan took it in his own.

"What happened to you?" asked D'zan. It was the only thing he could think to say.

"Treachery," said Andoses. "Darkness and treachery. But I will live."

His face turned to Tyro and Lyrilan. "Princes of Uurz . . . " he managed. "It is good to see your handsome faces again."

"And you, Andoses," said Tyro, crouching to lean over him.

"I took a knock myself," said Lyrilan, motioning to his

bandaged forehead. "We Princes are a tough breed, eh? You'll be on your feet in no time."

Tyro gave his brother a sharp glance, then turned back to Andoses. "Tell us now, Prince," he said. "What happened to Steephold? And why are you here, so far from the Valley of the Bull?"

Andoses struggled to raise himself a little, Tyro creating a makeshift pillow to prop up his shoulders. A soldier brought a stone cup filled with water, and they waited for Andoses to gulp it down.

"We rode south for Uurz," Andoses began, "a company from Udurum joining my own on behalf of Shar Dni. We were to see Dairon on an urgent matter. There is war brewing in the east. At Steephold we received word of your approach, so there we waited. The Princes . . . the Princes were with me . . . "

"Which Princes?" asked Tyro. "Tadarus and Vireon?"

Andoses shook his head. "Tadarus and . . . *Fangodrel*." Andoses coughed, choking on the second name. After a moment, he continued. "A great storm came upon us . . . a storm of shadows . . . Terrible things came through the walls . . . darkness with claws. It was *him* . . . the eldest Prince . . . "

Tyro calmed Andoses with an arm about his shoulders, cradling his head. "Easy. Tell it slowly."

Andoses took a deep breath. His eyes were bloodshot and watery.

"First we heard the horses being slaughtered in the stables . . . then thunder rolled over the walls and the shadows tore at us . . . great, unseen beasts . . . hideously strong . . . " Andoses wept as he relived the night of death. "Men died all around me . . . I saw their guts strung across the ceiling . . . Then the darkness . . . The torches faded . . . Men cried and screamed. I ran . . . I went to find Tadarus . . . I thought we could escape. Instead I found the *other* one . . . "

"Fangodrel?" asked Lyrilan.

"The sorcerer!" said Andoses. "He walked *inside* the shadow . . . drinking it in . . . There was blood across his body . . . blood running from his mouth. He . . . showed me the corpse of Tadarus, his own brother . . . drained and broken. He tossed it aside . . . a broken doll of sticks and twine . . ."

Andoses fell silent, staring into the shadows between hanging stalactites.

Tyro looked at Rockjaw, and the Giant's big head nodded slowly. Even the massive warrior could not speak of these things. D'zan thought the Giant might weep too, but he did not. Perhaps Giants did not shed tears.

"Are you saying that Fangodrel murdered Tadarus?" asked Tyro.

Andoses nodded. "Murdered him . . . and drank his blood . . . like *wine*, Tyro."

"What about the Uduru?" said Tyro. "There were fifty stationed here before."

"The sorcerer and his demons took them," said the Rockjaw. "Tore them apart. And the Cursed Prince drank their blood as well."

Andoses blinked, coming back to himself. "He rose into the storm, and his demons howled . . . They battered against the walls . . . tore the pillars loose. Bones and rock shattered in their grip. I stood before a great wall as it crumbled and thought I would die. I was grateful to die in such a clean way instead of under the claws of the shadows. But Rockjaw was there . . . He scooped me up, and the wall fell upon his back. He carried me clear of the walls as they tumbled about us . . . The demons clawed at us like raving dogs . . . but he ran into the storm . . . He saved me."

Rockjaw hung his head. "I would have stayed to fight and die," he said. "But this was a Prince, the Queen's nephew, and I . . . I knew my duty. Nearly half our number died in that dark storm, crushed by the stones of Steephold, or torn to shreds by Fangodrel's demons."

Andoses reached up to take D'zan's hand again. "Prince D'zan," he said. "We know your plight. We support your claim to the throne of Yaskatha. Shar Dni will ride with you. Udurum will ride . . . " His voice trailed off.

D'zan squeezed the Prince's hand. "I thank you. Let us talk of these things later."

"Yes," said Tyro. "We'll take you back to Udurum. The Queen must know of all this. And we must bury her son."

"What happened to Fangodrel?" asked Lyrilan.

"Gone," said Andoses. "Into the darkness with his demons. Gods curse his name."

"When the storm ceased, we survivors sought sanctuary in this cave," said Rockjaw. "Later we retrieved as many bodies as we could find . . . including that of Tadarus. For days our scouts kept a lookout for your train."

"A good thing you did," said Tyro. "A mighty good thing."

"What happened?" asked Andoses.

"Later, Prince," said Tyro. "We'll speak of it in the morning. We are weary, wounded, and hungry. Sleep now and we'll soon join you."

Andoses laid his head back. He mumbled something about Mumbaza before passing out.

"He's been like this for days," said Rockjaw. "His fever must break soon, or he will die."

Tyro went to meet with his captain while D'zan and Lyrilan lay down in Lyrilan's tent, which sat now inside the cavern. Outside the great cave-mouth, a snowstorm began, great white flakes flying across the darkness.

"What does all this mean?" D'zan said, trying to wrap his head around it.

Lyrilan sighed. "It means one Prince of Udurum is dead, killed by another. It means the Sharrian Prince may die as well." He thought for a moment. "But it also means that if he lives, you will have the backing of Shar Dni."

"What about Udurum?"

"That will depend on Queen Shaira," said Lyrilan. "Although there is one Prince left in the City of Men and Giants. If Tadarus meant to support you, perhaps Vireon will as well."

D'zan's head swam. So much was happening, and so fast. Blood pounded in his ears. He caressed his aching ribs. If Shar Dni and Udurum supported his claim, he would have the war the Stone had promised him. This was no comforting thought. War would bring only more death and destruction. How did this Fangodrel fit into the situation? He was a sorcerer, that much stood clear. Why had he murdered his brother? Was it to prevent his alliance with D'zan? If so, he would likely return to finish what the shadow-thing and the Serpent had not.

D'zan pulled the Stone's blade from its sheath, wrapped his hands about the warded hilt, and lay back against the hard floor of the cave. He knew what Andoses meant about the shadows – one of them had come for him already. How many more were there?

"D'zan?" said Lyrilan in the dark of the tent.

"Yes?"

"Thank you. For saving me from the Serpent. I won't forget it."

D'zan said nothing. He clasped the sword's hilt tightly in his fists, the blade pointing between his feet, and fell to sleep on the rugs of Lyrilan's tent. He'd grown accustomed to sleeping in that position, like a dead warrior laid to rest in his tomb.

He dreamed a rushing sea of fire.

The bones of dead men danced there, blackened and terrible.

14

Prince of Shadows

He woke shivering in the cold rain. The world was made of mud and tall green blades of grass. He lay in a sea of that grass, staring into the heaving stormclouds. The wind tore at his naked flesh as he crouched like an animal, hugging his knees for warmth. His right fist clutched something, sodden purple fabric. By its silver trim he knew it – the cloak of his non-brother Tadarus. He pulled it about his pale shoulders, pulled the hood over his head. Now he could at least stand and face the hateful wind. The brightness of the gray day troubled him.

The rain had washed all the blood from his body, although under his fingernails lingered a brown residue, and there were congealed clots in his sopping black hair. He recalled the taste of the blood on his tongue, the sweet bitterness of it, the coppery tang. The power it brought him . . . the Dwellers in Shadow flocking to his command. Where were they now, his children of the night? His army of unseen terrors?

Rain swept across the Stormlands plains in all directions. At his back rose the green foothills and beyond those the black immensity of the Grim Mountains. The storm of blood and shadows, the storm he had commanded, had carried him southward. He saw the tumbling walls of Steephold in the diamond panes of his memory . . . his amorphous children pulling them down upon the heads of Men and Giants. The screaming, the feasting . . . the blood. The delicious flowing blood. Such a tempest his brother's blood had fueled. Now he was spent. And alone.

"Ianthe," he said into the swirling clouds. "Grandmother!"

Distant thunder was the only answer. Where was his power? Where were his ghostly servants? She had given him the key to greatness and he had squandered it in a single night of destruction. His stomach growled like a famished lion, but he did not hunger. He *thirsted.*

Blood . . . he must have more of it. The source of his power. And this time he must not waste it; he must learn to savor it. Like fine wine. Not swill and spew it forth like some drunkard wandering the back alleys of Udurum. This time he would drink wisely. But he would drink deeply.

His thirst was not only physical, but spiritual, emotional, mental. He longed for the hot sticky fluid of life. He drank some cold rain from his hands and grimaced at the bitter blandness of it. He spat, trying to rid his mouth of the earthy taste. There was no satisfying his thirst that way.

He walked through the blowing storm. Far enough from the mountains he would find some village or trading post. He walked south, bare feet sinking in the mud. The day was leaden, but the sun lingered high behind those rushing slabs of cloud. Once it broke free and a golden ray fell across his face, piercing the shadows of his hood. He cried out and pulled the fabric tighter about his head, squinting. Then the golden orb hid once more behind a bank of thunderheads, and he was glad.

He walked all day, finding no signs of road, settlement, or traveler. A wild dog, lean and starving, ran howling from his gaze.

Its base ichor held no appeal for him. Now that he had sampled the blood of Men, he would not drink that of a cur again. Not even his terrible thirst would force him to that.

As the gloom fell into purple dusk, and night rose from eastern plains to crawl westward, he saw the lights of a tiny village. It lay at the end of an unpaved road, surrounded by ploughed fields. Somewhere to the west that crude track must intersect the Northern Road, which ran from the Gates of Uurz all the way to Vod's Pass. But this hamlet was far from the main way, nestled among a few scattered cedar trees. To its south a stream flowed heavily in the wash from the storm; likely some tributary feeding the waters of the Eastern Flow.

He walked toward the collection of thatched roofs and walls of baked mud. Goats and swine stared from their wooden-walled pens, moving away from him as he passed. Coils of sooty smoke rose from the chimneys. A central plaza stood empty but for a rudely sculpted statue of Vod the Giant-King.

At the nearest of the hovels he knocked on a wooden door. The smells of roasting lamb and vegetables wafted through a round window, and curtains of rainwater fell from the eaves. A face peered out the window, silhouetted by the glow of a hearthfire. Then the door opened slightly, a young girl barely visible in the crack.

"Yes?" She was no more than fourteen, a peasant, not especially lovely or comely. Brown hair in braids, small brown eyes.

"Can you help me?" he asked. His teeth chattered. "So cold . . . "

The girl turned away but did not shut the door. "It's a man," he heard her say. "A beggar. He has no shoes."

Now the jowly face of an older woman peered out at him. "What do you want?" she asked.

"I am lost," he told her, "and hungry. May I sit by your fire for a little while?"

She eyed him suspiciously but relented. “Come in,” she said. “Take off that filthy cloak.”

“I am naked underneath,” he said. The woman and her daughter exchanged a look of shock.

“Gods of Earth and Sky, you *are* a poor one,” she said. “Nellea, fetch a dry robe for this poor man.”

He trembled in the doorway until the girl returned with a simple robe of white linen. Mother and daughter turned away while he slipped off the wet cloak and pulled the smock over his thin body. His stomach growled. His lips twitched.

“Thank you for this hospitality,” he said.

The hovel featured a table, a hearth, some blankets spread on a wooden floor, and a small back room, obviously a shared bedroom.

The woman picked up the purple cloak and wrung it with her hands just outside the door. The girl scooped broth from a boiling kettle into a stone bowl and set it at the table.

“What is your name, sir?” the girl asked. She sat across the table from him, some part of her still afraid, even in the midst of her overwhelming pity. Her mother hung the cloak on a peg next to the fireplace.

“Gammir,” he said. He stared into the steaming broth.

“Well eat, Gammir,” said the mother. “You may stay with us until the rain lets up, then you must go.”

He did not touch the bowl, or the wooden spoon she gave him.

“Ah,” the mother said, as if she had forgotten something. “You’ll need some water to wash that down.” She got up to fetch her bucket.

“No, thank you,” he said.

The woman smiled, her face pink and heavy with an old sadness. “I suppose you’ve gotten enough water out there this evening . . . ”

"Call me Nellea," said the girl. "My mother is Naomi. Please eat, Gammir. It is all right."

"What is the name of this village?" he asked. Still he did not touch the broth. He stared at the fire. The warmth made his thirst grow, and the dancing flames made him think of the Red Dream. He no longer needed the bloodflower to enter that special place.

"Vod's Way," said Naomi. "You've seen the statue? They say the Giant-King once slept here, in this very spot, when this place was still a desert. That the stream sprang up to quench his thirst when he woke."

Gammir laughed. The irony was delectable.

Naomi stood behind her daughter, hands on her shoulders.

"Where do you come from, Sir Gammir?" she asked. A cooking knife lay on the shelf at her right elbow, just below the circular window.

"From the south," he said. "And the north. Do you *believe* the legend of your village?"

Naomi shrugged. "It's what they say . . ."

Gammir nodded. "Yes, they say so many things about Vod, don't they? Such a hero, such a legend . . . The truth is that Vod was a liar."

Mother and daughter looked at one another. "You'd better go, sir," said Naomi. "You are frightening my daughter . . ."

Gammir smiled. He smelled the blood pulsing in their wrists, necks, and thighs. His nostrils twitched. His stomach roared. The flames in the fireplace raged like the fire in his blood.

"I told you I was hungry," he said.

"Then eat and go!" said the mother. She grabbed the cooking knife and pointed it at him. Nellea wrapped her arms around her mother's waist, one eye still focused on Gammir, wide and white-rimmed.

Gammir nodded. "Oh, I will." He lunged across the table, a white panther in the shape of a man.

Beneath the wind, rain, and thunder rang the screams of mother and daughter. If anyone heard they chose to ignore the sounds and stay warm inside their cozy huts.

Presently the white robe was stained to brightest red. The uneaten broth grew cold in its bowl. Gammir rose from his feast, took up the cloak of Tadarus, and walked into the storm once again, following the main track out of the village, then turning back into the tall grasses.

Lightning danced in the sky and in his veins. He laughed at the chaos above. He spread his arms, and the winds swirled about him. The Red Dream rose into his eyes, and he called for his grandmother. She came to him wreathed in vines of orange flame.

"Sweet Prince," she cooed. "Now you see the truth of the blood. You know its power."

"Yes." He told her of the destruction he had wrought in the mountains, of his great triumph, and the exaltation of slaughter.

"Now you must learn not to waste your power," she told him. He already knew this, but he did not mind her guidance. She doted on him as a mother on her favorite son. "Use it as you need, call upon the shadows when you must, but do not squander the gifts of the blood. I have much more to teach you."

"I will come to you now," he said. "Across the Golden Sea . . . to your black palace and your crimson jungles . . . to your soft bosom, warm as a hearthfire."

For a timeless moment she held him in her arms, his head against her bosom.

This is what it was like to be loved.

"No," she said. "Not yet. Go first to Shar Dni."

"Why?" he asked, a petulant child.

"To spread terror and death among our enemies," she said. "To drink more royal blood and harness its power. When you come across the water, you will come to me as a true Prince of Khyrei, with a legion of shadows at your back. Then our war song can truly begin."

"I understand," he whispered into the wind, and opened his eyes.

The moon and stars were lost in the upper dark, and the night poured down upon him. He must go east now, and he must not walk. He must ride.

He spoke an incantation, eyes blazing, and shadows raced toward him from the mouth of night. Down from the mountains they flowed like floods of dark water, converging among the grasslands at his feet.

"My children ..." he said. The shapes of shifting darkness sniffed at his bare heels, wolvish, serpentine, ever-changing, and eager. They worshipped the blood in his belly, in his veins, spilled across his chest.

The shadows flowed into a shoulder-high form, an ebony stallion, snorting and stamping, digging razor hooves into the wet earth. Its mane flowed upward from its neck, like black seaweed waving in unseen waters. Wisps of dark smoke trailed from its nostrils. He pulled himself up onto its back, a saddle of shadow-stuff forming beneath him. The dark flow continued, wrapping about his body like slithering eels, shredding the stained robe. He wore a suit of darkness now, black mail like that of a Khyrein warrior, and the purple cloak of Tadarus flapped at his back. There was another non-brother to kill ... but that would come later. A pleasure rushed and not savored was a pleasure wasted.

The black steed galloped across the plains. A horde of shadows followed in its wake, dark plumes trailing after a thunderbolt. Gammir laughed, breathed in the wet freedom of night, the cold air of liberation. The scent of ancient darkness. Faster and faster the phantom horse carried him across the Stormlands.

The blood lingered on his tongue, in his throat. He would not waste this power. Not as he had done at Steephold. He would conserve it, use it sparingly to satisfy his whims and the justice of his impending throne. The power was his and no matter how much of it he drained and swallowed and poured across the earth, there would always be more.

Always more ruby liquid flowing hot and luscious in the veins of the living.

Across an interval of darkness lay Shar Dni. An entire city filled with red blood, ripe for the taking. He threw his head back, laughing with terrible joy.

The wraith-horse sprouted black wings from its sides, flapping planes of leather which beat faster than its hooves, and it carried him into the sky. The moon, full and bloated, rose above a bank of clouds. He soared beneath its golden glow, howling gleefully into the night.

A red blush smudged the horizon just before dawn. A few cold stars glittered above the clouds, and the dark expanse of the Golden Sea lay directly ahead. As the night lost its hold on the world, the winged specter slowed its flight and Gammir sank toward the rolling plain. Between himself and the sea lay the River Orra, flowing through the broad Valley of the Bull, and there stood the white towers and blue pyramids of Shar Dni. Soon the dawn would rise up, turn the sea to molten gold, and set the city ablaze with light.

The shadow-stallion lost its wings, which dissolved like morning mist, and set its hooves upon solid ground. It had brought him to a high ridge overlooking the valley. He had covered a great distance in a single night and was not tired. The swirling shadows that followed him crept away into the hollows and crevices of the land, hiding from the sun's crimson eye. The Golden Sea earned its name, reflecting the solar glow as it faded from red to orange to gold. The shadows were fled and gone from him now; only the black steed remained, stamping nervously, blood-colored eyes glaring defiantly at the sunrise.

The first rays of sunlight fell into the valley, and the river became a silver ribbon. The walls of Shar Dni were painted sky-blue, frescoed with clouds in shades of pearl and slate. A forest of ships' masts and sails grew along the wharves that straddled the mouth of the river delta. A white barge moved along the river, heading upstream for village trade. Flocks of white seabirds filled the air. Most of the galleons in the crescent harbor flew the white bull standard of the city, but a few triremes from the Jade Isles flew exotic sigils of green, scarlet, or white. A trading ship of Mumbaza had come all the way from the western side of the continent flying its Feathered Serpent banner, but there were no Khyrein vessels here. Khyreins were the enemies of Shar Dni on the open sea, so this was no surprise.

An ancient road wound from the Stormlands into the valley, skirting the outlying villages and farms. It ran directly to the river and the great stone arch of the Bridge of Clouds, which led to the city's eastern gate. This green basin of cypress, palm, orchard, and delta marsh was a place of heat and calm winds. The Stormlands lay behind Gammir now, though his coming was a kind of storm in itself, rolling quietly toward the Valley of the Bull.

The black horse snorted and Gammir grabbed its mane. Before he turned it toward the winding roadway, he noticed a glimmering in the tall grass to his right. His night servants were all hidden now, but *something* hovered there in the watery sunlight. His eyes narrowed and the figure of a tall man wavered into sight.

Brother? called a voice that was not a voice. Perhaps he only heard it in his head. Or perhaps it floated to him on the morning wind blowing off the ocean.

Gammir stared at the apparition. "I have no brother," he said.

Whose fine cloak do you wear? asked the specter. Its face was a wisp of morning mist, its body a reflection of something that was not truly there. As if sunlight struck a mirror and projected its glow onto a wall. But there was no wall. Only the vision and its non-voice.

"This purple rag?" said Gammir. "It belonged to a fool who thought himself a Prince. It is mine now."

It was the cloak of your brother, said the apparition.

"No," said Gammir, and the black horse trampled grass under its hooves.

The specter's face came into focus. Gammir gasped at the depth of its blue eyes, the blackness of its hair, the narrow cut of the beard, the sculpted cheekbones of bronze hue.

"Tadarus?" The name fell from his mouth like a stone.

You know me, Brother, said the ghost. *You wear my cloak. You carry my memory in your heart. You remember our play and our laughter . . . when we were boys.*

Now a six-year-old Tadarus stood before him, face smeared with dirt, royal clothes untidy, clotted with grass and mud. Smiling up at him with round cheeks.

"You were never my brother," Gammir told it. "Leave me. The sun is risen. You are not wanted here!"

Tadarus stood full-grown again, sunlit stalks of grass gleaming through his chest. *You called me here. Your memories have powers that you do not even suspect.*

Gammir called upon the power of the blood filling his stomach. "Go," he said, waving an arm. "Never trouble me again."

The ghost of Tadarus frowned at him.

Why did you murder me?

I tried to be your friend.

I loved you, Brother.

"You are not my brother!" screamed Gammir, but the ghost was gone. Had it ever truly been there at all? He blinked into the sun, then turned the black horse onto the road.

He passed by a peasant pulling a cartload of green vegetables up the hill. The man wore a cheap turban, loose pantaloons, and a necklace hung with copper medallions. Gammir ignored his staring eyes. Fearing the weird stallion, the man pulled his cart to the side of the road and let Gammir ride past. Farms came next, sloping green pastures where oxen and sheep grazed and trees grew heavy with pears, pomegranates, and lemons. Villagers bustling about their morning duties steered clear of this dark stranger and his ember-eyed steed. They must have taken him for some warrior of Uurz or Udurum come to join the navy and fight pirates. Gammir almost laughed at the dull lives playing out before him. These people were little better than the animals they kept in pens and corrals. He sensed the blood flowing beneath their thin brown skins. But the hunger was not upon him yet. He had been frugal with his power this time.

Well before midday he reached the great bridge. Traffic here was more dense: basket-toting laborers, wagons laden with produce, carts pulled by those who could not afford wagons, and the occasional camel-mounted nobleman. A guard at the bridge peered at Gammir, his eyes rimmed in black kohl beneath a turban-wrapped helmet. The spear of his office stood higher than the point of his helm, and a scimitar hung from his wide belt. He motioned Gammir to stop.

"What brings you to the city?" asked the guard, his voice thick with the Sharrian accent.

Gammir's eyes ached in the full light of day, so his face lay in the shadows of the purple hood. "Duty," he told the Sharrian.

"You are a soldier?" asked the guard.

Gammir laughed. "I am far more than that."

The guard frowned. "What is your business? Where do you come from?" He wanted clear answers, not riddles and bravado.

Gammir considered the question. Killing this fool would complicate his entry into the city. "Udurum," he said. "I come from the palace of Vod. My business lies with your King Ammon."

The guard blinked and studied him. Gammir's stately black mail and Udurum cloak were impressive enough to support his claim, so the man waved him onward. The black horse's hooves clacked on the stone, and a crowd of peasants parted to allow the horse a clear route. Gammir rode toward the open gates at the far end of the span. More guards stationed there would require more lies. Easy enough to lie. Lying was its own kind of sorcery.

The same story earned him passage into Shar Dni's main thoroughfare. The street was cobbled in black basalt, lined with hanging gardens, and ran directly toward the first of the temple pyramids. A flock of priests in pale robes, faces painted indigo, walked among the crowd. Dusky-skinned girls went barefoot, their faces hidden behind veils, almond eyes gleaming green like his mother. Less reputable women bared their faces and the tops of their breasts, flaunting their worldly goods in windows and along balconies. The city seemed infested with brothels. The smells of roasting meat, camel dung, rotten fruits, and a thousand spices filled the air. Sometimes a gust of salty sea wind blew all these smells to nothing, but they crept back into his nostrils as soon as the air grew still.

When Gammir was last in this city, he had been Fangodrel, and thirteen years old. His mother had brought him in a caravan to meet all her royal relatives, brothers, sisters, cousins. His grandfather, King Tadarus the First, had just died, and he remembered watching the coronation of Ammon, Shaira's eldest brother. Tadarus and Vireon beamed with pride that day as their uncle took the oath of rulership and accepted his crown from the High Priest of the Sky God. Even then, Fangodrel had known the emptiness of the ritual and the spectacle. The people had cheered for their new monarch, and since then King Ammon was a much-beloved ruler. Yet his reign was plagued by growing tensions with Khyrei, which had now broken into marine warfare.

Prince Andoses was Ammon's only son and heir to the throne. He was sent to gather support for a war against Khyrei. Gammir smiled as he circled the blue temple-pyramid. His shadow-children had slain Andoses at Steephold . . . torn him to bloody shreds. Word of his son's death had not even reached the Sharrian King yet. Gammir would bring it. As he stood over the twitching body of Ammon, his lips wet with royal blood, he would tell the King that his son was dead by the same hand that now strangled him. He anticipated the exquisite moment.

Somehow he had always known his mother's people were not his own. Shaira was his birth-mother, that much was true. But everything he was came from his father, the betrayed and murdered Prince of Khyrei. Soon this city would bow before the new Gammir. It had no inkling that a black viper crawled through its streets carrying poison toward its heart. When Ammon was dead, and all his royal family, Khyrei would sweep across the sea to take this valley and its riches. These smug, milling crowds would all be slaves and chattels.

As he rode into the Great Market between the four blue temples, he sensed a sea of blood washing about him, foaming and dark against his boots as he rode. All these dull-eyed sheep walking through a world whose truth they could hardly suspect. The first pang of thirst came upon him then, riding among the cloth merchants, jugglers, livestock sellers, and fruit vendors. He ignored it. The sounds of the living city rang in his ears like a storm, hawking voices, clanging metal, lilting music, shouting children, groaning camels, laughter, the squawking of caged parrots. This city was a rich feeding ground. It would be his.

Beyond the plaza rose the white spires of the Royal Palace. The black steed carried him across the bazaar, and he licked his lips.

A face in that milling crowd caught his attention. Blue eyes staring directly at him, as no Sharrian had dared to do. Dead Tadarus stood there, unmoving and unseen among the busy throng. No, it could not be Tadarus . . . only some passing resemblance. But then what of the ghost on the ridge top?

Perhaps it was the purple cloak that invited the dead man's shade to haunt him. He considered dropping it from his shoulders and leaving it in the dust of the plaza. But he needed it as part of his disguise to gain entry to the palace. What's more, he liked the cloak. It was the last piece of Udurum he could claim – until his Khyrein armies took the city. First Shar Dni, then Udurum. The Giants were dying; they could not defend it forever. War was coming and it flew on wings of shadow.

Tadarus stared at him from a sea of faces.

Gammir turned away. *I'll give him his damned cloak once I've entered the palace. Damn him. A nuisance in death as he was in life.*

He looked back, but Tadarus was gone.

The outer wall of the palace loomed before him.

"I am the eldest Prince of Udurum," he told the trio of guards at the gate. "I come to speak with my uncle, King Ammon."

The guards bowed and opened the gates wide for his passage. A splendid courtyard lay beyond, a forest-orchard of palms, cypress, pear trees, marble fountains, and sand gardens. The white towers and cupolas of the palace proper rose above the green fronds of the trees.

"I'll take your mount to the stables, Lord," offered a guard.

"No need," said Gammir. He slid from the black horse, and it faded to nothing like smoke dispersing in sunlight.

The guards gasped and stepped away. Their fear was perfume to him. The blood in their veins rushed with fear and awe. They knew the mark of sorcery as a hare in the forest knows the tread of a predator. One of the men made the sign of the Sky God on his breast, and Gammir smiled. The man grew even more frightened at the sight of his feral grin.

"I'll be your escort, Lord," said the ranking guard.

"Take me directly to the King," said Gammir. "I've come a long way and I am thirsty."

The guard swallowed his fear and led Gammir through the courtyard to the golden doors of Ammon's palace.

Beneath the branches of the cedars, among the hedges and roots and untrod patches of the royal gardens, a swarm of hungry shadows awaited the coming of night.

15

Court of the Sea Queen

The owl flew beyond the forests of Uduria, across the snow-capped peaks of the Grim Mountains. When walls of dark cloud rolled into its path, spitting lightning and fierce winds, it rose higher into the sky and soared above the churning storm. It winged westward across the sleeping world, seen only by the blinking stars and mute moon. When the sun rose at its back, it sailed downward through the clouds and found a soft place on the grassy plain of the Stormlands. There it became a young girl again and slept in the lee of a mossy boulder, obscured by a sea of waving green stalks.

Sharadza awoke at midday and drank rainwater from a natural depression in the crown of the boulder. She found a wild patch of cloudberries and picked them for breakfast. Before the sun climbed high enough to battle the army of clouds, she took the black owl's form again and soared westward. After a while the clouds below her beating wings grew thinner, and a cool salty air blew into her shining owl eyes. She left the Stormlands behind and the vast blue ocean lay beneath her, a shimmering blue expanse spangled with shards of sunlight. She flew south and west now, and the coastline dwindled behind her.

By sorcerous instinct she flew toward the place she had seen in her vision. It lay beneath those sparkling waves, in depths where the sun's rays could not reach. The great waters stretched in every direction, and the owl hovered between white cloud and azure sea. Its feathers flowed like smoke and Sharadza took her true form once again. She fell feet first through the air, inhaling the rush of sea air. She dropped without panic or concern, with arms outstretched, fingers pulling from the fabric of the world those things she would need.

In her right hand she grabbed a bit of wind. Her left hand grabbed a strand of sunlight, and she squeezed its warmth in her palm.

The part is the whole . . . There can be no separation.

The dancing waters rose to meet her. She pulled the wind about herself in a tight bubble, an ethereal armor, a sheathe of fresh air welded to her skin. She draped the sunlight across herself like a cloak, spreading warmth and light along her limbs. A second before she broke the surface of the sea, she became an oblong slab of granite which kept the semblance of her features.

The ocean swallowed the warm glowing stone and welcomed it with a rush of bubbles. It fell into an aquamarine realm where sunlight refracted across schools of silver fish. The stone Sharadza's weight carried it into the purple gloom of deeper waters where sharks and rays skirted its sinking form. Then it entered the darkness that cloaked the floor of the sea, where gnarled reefs and forests of seaweed hid multitudes of darting, skimming creatures.

The stone Sharadza's journey might have ended there, but it plunged into a great fissure like a meteor, shedding the golden radiance of a miniature sun. Inside the great chasm an ultramarine glow replaced the dark, and a wilderness of massive luminescent anemones waved their tentacles in silent dances. Immense squid sailed past the sinking stone, ignoring its advent, and rainbow-scaled fish parted ranks as it found the coral ridges of the chasm floor.

Some distance away, an even greater glow lit the depths in blazing hues of crimson, magenta, a dozen greens and blues, shining amber, and deep turquoise. There stood the immensity of the coral city and its palace, a citadel of spires, vaults, and terraces formed by ancient generations of polyp and shell. Giant anemones waved along its ramparts like the flags of sunken kingdoms. Subaqueous gardens enclosed its grounds for leagues, brimming with marine flora and fauna.

When the bright stone fell to rest among a forest of dancing blue-green weeds, it lay still for a while in its thin shell of air. It still emitted the glow of the upper sun, and it had left a brilliant streak across this realm of watery twilight. A group of Sea-Folk swam from the palace in search of the sun-stone, gliding toward its resting place, waving cautious tridents in its direction. Their skins were a mix of silver and turquoise scales rippling in the aquatic light. Webbed fingers and toes propelled them through the depths with great speed, and their eyes were orbs of amber brilliance. Fish-lipped mouths hung open in wonder as they surrounded the Sharadza-stone. They bubbled in their mysterious language, spiny ridges on their backs twitching with excitement.

Making some decision, they hoisted the stone in one of their great nets and pulled it through the pastel city of coral toward the gates of the palace. Hundreds of their curious brethren watched them enter and some followed in their wake, eager to know the mystery of the glowing obelisk. The retrievers gained the accompaniment of a general dressed in plates of azure shell, and he conducted them through a great scalloped hall into the presence of their Queen. They sat the sun-bright rock on the floor before her pearly dais.

The Mer-Queen reclined at the base of a great upright oyster shell upon a seat forged of dead coral the shades of bone and sapphire. Jewels torn from a thousand sunken galleons dotted the nooks and crannies of the coral throne. The scales along her shoulders and arms gleamed soft as polished silver. Her great mane of air danced about her shoulders like black eels, alive in the subtle currents. She leaned forward, amber eyes narrowed to slits, and peered at the strange rock.

The mer-warriors slid away from their catch as it melted into the shape of a land-dweller. Sharadza stood at the foot of the Mer-Queen's throne, gleaming in her golden armor of sun and air. Her dark hair danced like the Queen's own now, though its thick curls gave her a wild and savage aspect. Some of the mer-folk shouted or whispered in their incomprehensible language, and the mer-general spewed a command, drawing a sword of jeweled bone. But Sharadza stared only at the Queen.

"My people do not speak your dry language," said the Queen, her words like the notes of an underwater music. "Yet I do. What reason for this trespass?"

"Your warriors brought me here, Sea Queen," said Sharadza. "How can that be a trespass? Am I not a visitor, having been escorted with all due honor?"

The Mer-Queen smiled, revealing pearly teeth with incisors like tiny fangs. "They thought you a sacred stone sent to us by the Sea God, or his brother the Sky. So they brought you to me. This was your intention, was it not?"

Sharadza swallowed. The brine did not enter her mouth, nose, or lungs. She breathed instead the air carried in the invisible sheathe about her skin. The golden light was of no substance, not really armor, but its glow kept her comfortable in these frigid depths.

"The Queen is wise," she said. "I am Sharadza, Princess of Udurum, Daughter of Vod the Giant-King. I come for my father."

The Mer-Queen placed a slim elbow on the arm of her throne, and rested her tiny chin against her palm. "The daughter of Vod, who was once called Ordra? Stealer of the Pearl?"

"Yes," she said. Her father had admitted the crime, no use in denying it. "Where is he? I know he came here to give himself up to your curse."

The warriors and royal mer-folk weaved about the chamber like irritated fish, trying to understand what passed between the land-walker and their Queen.

"Your father was well warned," said the Mer-Queen. "When he stole Aiyaia's Stone, I told him never to enter the sea again or he would perish. Knowing this, he did return, though it was many years later. In truth, I had forgotten my vow . . . but I know all things that pass in this sea, so I knew when he returned."

"What did you do? Kill him? Enslave him? I must know."

Please tell me he lies in some dungeon. Please tell me you did not murder him. Please let me bring my father home. Gods of Sea, Sky, Earth, and Sun, grant me this.

The Mer-Queen blinked. "I did none of these things. It is true I took a legion of warriors to seize him. What we found was only a drowned Giant. His corpse floated among the seaweed, and he bore no crown or weapon."

Sharadza winced. Her stomach writhed toward her mouth. She nearly fainted. *Could the sea-bitch be lying?*

"There were no marks upon his body, no wounds," said the Mer-Queen. "His lungs were full of brine. We found him not far from the northern shore of his own kingdom. You may doubt my words, but I tell you true: Vod walked into the sea and drowned."

"I don't believe it!" Sharadza shouted. The mer-general raised his white blade but the Queen waved him away. The salt of the Princess's tears ran down her cheeks inside the layer of air. The crystal drops could not blend with the greater salty flow of the ocean because of her spell. "You *must* have killed him! You sent him the nightmares – you drove him mad!"

Again the Queen waved back her guards. She swam upward from her throne, then glided to hover above Sharadza. "I swear by the Sea God's beard, by the Sacred Pearl which Vod took, I took no vengeance on him. I sent no visions to torment him. I had all but forgotten his name until the day he re-entered my kingdom. We accepted the Great Pearl's loss long ago, and we know who truly stole it. We do not linger on such loss here. The sea lives on, and so do its people."

"What do you mean, 'who truly stole it'?" she asked. "Was it not my father?"

"It was Iardu," said the Mer-Queen, stroking Sharadza's dry shoulder with delicate webbed fingers. The scales of her knuckles glimmered in the sheath of sunlight. "The Shaper sent your father. I knew this from the day it happened. Iardu's hand shapes everyone he touches. He uses Land-Folk and Sea-Folk for his own purposes. I did not truly blame Vod, but had made my vow in anger. If I had found him alive in my realm, I would have killed or imprisoned him. But as I said, we found him dead."

Sharadza's head seemed to spin. Iardu had indeed reshaped her, opening her eyes to the heritage of her own power. How had he manipulated Vod into stealing the pearl, and for what reason? Vod had admitted the theft, but would not give the reason. Iardu had known the reason, but never mentioned it. Did Vod steal the Pearl so Iardu would teach him sorcery? Iardu said Vod had barely learned anything when he left . . . just like Sharadza. No, there had to be more to the story. Vod must have had a greater reason for doing Iardu's dirty work.

"What about my father's nightmares?" she asked the Queen.

"Why did your words weigh so heavily on him? Why did he give up his family, his kingdom, and just walk into the sea? Why did he destroy himself?"

The Mer-Queen shook her head. Her serpentine locks twisted. "I did not know him, child," she said.

Sharadza's mind raced. *What did Mother know of all this? Did she know Iardu was Fellow? That he had used Father to steal the pearl? Iardu must have the answers.* Could Iardu be the one who drove Vod to suicide? If so, she would find out, and she would make him suffer. She would find a way.

She wiped the tears from her eyes. "I came here thinking I must be strong . . . demand my father's release . . . and now I weep like a little girl."

The Mer-Queen hugged her. "You have suffered a great loss. There is no shame in tears. Did you know that the oceans are the tears of the Gods? If even Gods can cry, why should we mortals be ashamed of it?"

"Thank you, Queen," she said. "Might I know your name?"

"Indreyah," said the Mer-Queen. "Perhaps there is something that can ease your pain. We laid Vod's bones to rest in a cairn not far from here. My warriors will retrieve them, so you may bury him on land, among those he loved. Do you wish this?"

Sharadza nodded. The Mer-Queen spoke with her general, and he set off to put soldiers in charge of the exhumation.

"Swim with me in the coral gardens," said Indreyah. "We rarely get a visitor from the dry world. Tell me the news of the land-walkers and their kingdoms."

They skimmed along a great oval passage and out into the glow of rainbow anemones and groves of wafting seaweed. Fish, eels, and stranger creatures swam about the walls of living coral. Sharadza walked on the golden sand while the Mer-Queen hovered along beside her.

"Your kingdom is beautiful," she told Indreyah. "How long have you ruled the sea?"

"I am old, child," she said. "Old as selfish Iardu. Yet my memory fades. I sometimes recall being . . . someone else . . . something greater. Yet I am content here, with my people. This is the best of all worlds, among the endless bounty of the sea."

She is of the Old Breed, Sharadza realized, *but she does not remember it. She has carved her niche here in the Living World, and carved herself to fit it. Her True Self has taken root in this form in this realm. She has found herself by forgetting herself, creating the world she most desired. Perhaps this is what all living things do, sorcery or no sorcery.*

"Iardu . . . said that he loved you."

Indreyah halted, the webbed spikes along her spine shifting, the tiny gills on either side of her slim neck pulsing. The brightness of her eyes faded a moment, as a pond might darken when a cloud hides the sun.

"Long ago, I believe he did," she said. A wall of pink anemones waved their tentacles along the garden wall. "That is why he stole the Pearl."

"What do you mean?"

"Jealousy," she said. "I loved the sea . . . and Iardu loved me. For a while he was enough, but I could not stay away from my true love . . . and he would not follow me into its depths. I founded an empire here while he sat brooding on his island. At times he would come to me, always tempting me to leave my people behind and return to the sunlit world. He could never accept my marriage to the sea. My responsibilities here. He was insistent that I be his, so I banished him from the ocean . . . but he never forgot his obsession."

"Is that all love is?" asked Sharadza. "Obsession?"

Indreyah caressed the sea-plants as she moved along the coral maze. "Perhaps," she said. "You ask wise questions, Sharadza."

"What happened? With the Pearl?"

"Iardu's last desperate attempt," said the Mer-Queen. "He sent Vod to steal it, knowing it was an object of worship that my people cherished above all else. Aiyaia was the Sea God's daughter, and she made the Pearl in an age now forgotten. Iardu took the Pearl, using Vod as his hands, thinking I would come to his island and beg – or bargain – for its return."

"And did you?"

"No," said Indreyah. "I would not play his game. He might capture me forever with his magic if I left my own realm. So I let him keep the Sacred Pearl, for all the good it did him."

"He told me he betrayed you . . . "

"So he did. Wicked, selfish Iardu. He could not shape me as he shaped the rest of the world. This he could not stand."

"Perhaps he truly loved you," said Sharadza.

The Mer-Queen shook her head. "True love seeks not to possess, but only to share itself."

"What about my father? Why did he steal your Sacred Pearl for Iardu?"

"Who can say but Iardu himself? You might visit his island and ask him yourself."

Or find him in the streets of Udurum telling stories to drunken laborers.

"I *will* ask him," Sharadza told the Mer-Queen. "By the Gods of Earth and Sky, I will."

The mer-folk brought her a great chest of stone banded with rusted iron, some relic of a sunken ship. Salt-crusted emeralds decorated the lid, and inside (said the Queen) lay the giant bones of her father. She did not have the heart or stomach to look at them. She trusted the word of the Sea-Folk on the matter. The Queen granted her a cadre of warriors to carry the chest to the shore, then it would be up to Sharadza to bring it the rest of the way home.

Indreyah offered her the hospitality of the palace for as long as she wished, but already Sharadza was growing cold in the marine depths, and she craved the fresh air and open spaces of the surface world. The Queen gave her a necklace of tourmalines and opals, dazzling in all the colors of the sea. At its center hung a fish-shaped talisman of dark jade, carved with the intricate skill of the Sea-Folk.

"This amulet will keep you safe beneath the waters," said the Mer-Queen, "and grant you passage among the People of the Sea. And if you wear it while you sleep, we may speak together in dreams. Do you wish this?"

Sharadza nodded her assent and embraced the Queen.

"I can give you only my thanks," she said, "and the friendship of Udurum."

Indreyah smiled at her. "That is more than enough."

The Sea-Folk watched, astonished, as she took the form of a golden eel, and the chest-bearers swam after her toward the upper waters. For some while they glided just beneath the surface, coming at last upon the white sands of a Stormlands beach. She was not sure exactly where, but somewhere on this same coast lay the port town of Murala.

She walked from the sea in her true form, shedding seawater like liquid sorcery. The mer-folk, eight of them in all, carried the chest onto the beach and set it gently on the sand, where its great weight sank a few fingerspans deep. The lid-stones gleamed in the sunlight, reminding Sharadza of her mother's green eyes. The Sea-Folk said farewell in their bubbly language and dove beneath the waves.

She sat down on the wet sand, one hand on the lid of the chest-coffin, and wept. It was a clear day on the shore, and no boats or wandering villagers were around to witness her sorrow. It would not have mattered. She cried until she was done with crying. Then she stood, breathed in the crisp, salty air, and stared past the dunes toward the green plains.

At least there could be a funeral now. At least there could be a final acceptance of her loss. Her brothers would bear their sadness with grace. Fangodrel might not even care, or would hide his feelings in scrawled verse. Her mother had already wept enough. For her, too, this would bring a welcome closure. One final bout of grief and their lives could find a new pattern.

Why, Father? she asked the trapped bones. *Why did you march off to death, believing it was the Sea Queen who tormented you? I must know the answer.*

She laid her forehead upon the chest and reminded herself that Vod was an Uduru, a Giant. She was the daughter of an Uduru. Her heart pumped Uduru blood throughout her limbs.

The part is the whole . . .

Now she stood three times the size of a man, a full-grown Uduri Giantess. The sea wind caught up her black hair like a tangled mass of ravens' wings. Her face was hardly changed, but her Giantess feet sank to the ankles in the sand. She lifted the massive chest onto her shoulder like a sack of flour and marched northward.

A flock of white gulls flew above, an aerial procession for the dead King's homecoming.

16

The Blessings of Winter

The benevolent rains of fall gave way to the season of cruel ice-storms.The northern wind swept across the walls of New Udurum and took up residence in its frosty streets and courtyards. The branches of trees in the royal gardens were sheathed in crystal, and the brown carcasses of plants were frozen in perpetual decay. The black towers themselves took on a silvery skin, and the cobbled streets of the city became a dangerous place for men and horses to walk.

After the siege of each icy tempest, the Giants went forth along the streets breaking up the ice with bronze shovels and stamping boots. Uduru did not mind the cold of winter that kept humans huddled about the warm hearths of their houses. Even in the depths of the icy season commerce thrived, and the Central Plaza swarmed with fur-wrapped traders, vendors, and commoners. Outlying farms slept through the season, but those who stored and preserved their produce did a fine business. The smokes of the blacksmiths' stalls mingled with the effluvia of five thousand chimneys. The city steamed in its thin mantle of ice.

Shaira watched the flow of trade from the highest window of her tower. She hated the winter and its frigid onslaught. The season reared its death-colored head each year and breathed a sea of frost across the northern world. She missed the blessed heat of the desert and the gentle shade of palm trees . . . the breeze of the delta and the fragrant winds blowing through the Valley of the Bull. It seemed another world, a vision that had faded centuries ago, as if it was never real. The desert was gone now, and so was her life in sunny Shar Dni.

The Queen sat alone in a padded chair, the empty bed immaculate behind her and as cold as the ice along the window's casement. She had grown used to the absence of Vod these past months . . . the yawning void in her life that was once filled only by his presence. The touch of his rough fingers, the strength of his embrace. The end of these things she had learned to accept, and the constant ache that never truly left her heart.

As the frosted city bustled far below, her eyes were dry. She had gone beyond sorrow. She sat enthroned in the iron tomb of loneliness. Her children were gone, like her husband. They might all be dead. Vod was certainly dead, she needed no oracle or herald to tell her that. She had known when he marched off to the sea that he would never return. She might have accepted that terrible loss, but this new one was unacceptable. Her fine boys, her loving daughter . . . all fled, and some at her own request.

Tadarus, Fangodrel . . . sent south with their cousin to stir the cauldron of war. Vireon . . . lost on a hunt with his Uncle Fangodrim. Not even the First Among Giants knew where he had run off to, or could guess his fate. "North," was all he could say. "The lad ran north, fast as the wind. I searched his trail for days and lost it in the snows of the highlands." She should have forbidden him to go on the Long Hunt, but she had thought it would take his mind off the loss of his father. Vireon was supposed to be her rock, her pillar of strength now that Tadarus was gone. Where was he?

Sharadza. The deepest cut in her heart was made by her rebellious daughter. Off in the night like a guilty thief, leaving only a pitiful scrap of parchment to explain herself. Where had she gone? Whatever path she took would lead to the sea, where Vod had gone. The girl actually thought she could bring him back from the Curse of the Sea Queen. Now that curse might claim her as well. How could she be so selfish and hard-headed?

Was I that naïve and petulant when I was sixteen? No, surely not. She had been the daughter of Tadarus I, King of Shar Dni, and duty was her all. It was not until she turned nineteen that she hatched her plan with Vod . . . but that wasn't her fault. The Gods had intervened. She had never wanted to marry the decrepit Emperor of Uurz – it would have been like marrying her own grandfather. Perhaps that is what Sharadza needed to take her mind off the death of Vod. She needed a fine Prince to marry. She needs a good husband.

Gods of Earth and Sky, please let her return safely from whatever fool's journey she has taken. I'll see her married and happy before another year turns. Perhaps one of those Twin Princes of Uurz would suit her needs. Emperor Dairon would certainly not refuse Shaira's offer. His sons were young and strong . . . one a warrior, one a scholar. There was variety for her daughter, an element of choice that Shaira herself never had. Until that day she had chosen Vod and sent him on his journey . . .

Shaira came down from her tower perch only when the duties of queenhood demanded it. There was some mumbling from her human advisors, suggestions that she make herself more visible. She could not hide away forever if she hoped to keep rule over a city of Men and Giants. The Uduru she kept at court said nothing. It was not their way to intrude on a woman's grief, however long it might last. Besides, they lived far longer than Men, so they could afford to wait out the length of their little Queen's sadness.

"Isolation is not good for the soul," said Aadu, Priest of the Sky God. "You must accept the company of others."

She heard the wisdom in his words, but ignored it.

"Your daughter will return, Majesty," said Tolomon, Viceroy of Trade. "She is only a girl; she will not go far. Homesickness will bring her back before long."

Tolomon was a well-meaning fool.

"Vireon will come back to us when he is ready," said Fangodrim the Gray. "He knows the forest better than any man or Giant. My guess is he's run off to forget the city for a while. You know he loves the Wild more than any of his girls."

She wrapped a shawl of worry about herself and stayed in her private chambers most days, sleeping or staring out the southern window at the tiny folk of Udurum, the basalt ramparts, and the black mountains along the horizon. Her servants brought spiced wine, or tea steeped with calming herbs. She drank them all, tasting nothing, her eyes roaming the heavy clouds. She waited, like green stalks wait in the frozen earth. Should spring arrive, she might sprout forth again. Or shrivel in the dirt of her own despair. She did not know.

The first real snow laid a blanket of white across the black stones and high walls. The great trees became pale monoliths, the streets filled with slanting drifts, and the brilliance of morning came early. In the sparkling light of that pristine dawn, Vireon approached the city gates with a train of blue-skinned Giants at his back.

Shaira's servants washed her black locks and dressed her in a regal gown of purple and sable, her neck and wrists hung with silver. She endured their ministrations impatiently, rushing them through their duties. Not daring to smile until she set her own eyes on her youngest son. How else could she believe it was true?

An audience of Men and Uduru filled the throne room well before she entered. There, in the midst of smiles and expressions of wonder, dressed in the crude skin of some snow-beast, stood Vireon, blue eyes blazing. The crowd spread like water, and a cheer went up to the rafters, the bellows of Uduru making stone and girder tremble.

Vireon rushed toward her, and someone else rushed behind him. He held the hand of a strange woman with wild hair the color of ripe corn and even wilder eyes. She wore the mottled furs of woodland creatures, and a cloak of dark wolfskin.

Vireon let go the woman's hand and embraced his mother. She shivered at the touch of his cold skin, as if he'd not been near a fire in days. Yet beneath that chill beat the blazing heat of his heart, a sweet medicine for her injuries. She grabbed his big hands in hers, rubbing them.

"My son," she said, locking his eyes with her own. About the dais where the double throne sat empty (like the much greater single throne behind it), the eyes of her advisors grew large as they caught the rays of her smile. "You are cold." She turned to a steward. "Bring hot wine for my son and his . . . guests." The steward rushed off to rally the servants.

"Mother," said Vireon. "I missed you. I'm sorry to have left you so long."

She hugged him again. "You are back now," she said. "The Gods are good."

"Mother," he said again, taking the wild girl's hand. "This is Alua."

He said the name in a way that told her everything. This was no casual dalliance he had found in some hidden village and dragged home to please his manly hunger. He gave her name as he might give a precious jewel into his mother's hands, or a holy object from some distant temple.

The wild girl blinked her coal-black eyes. They sparkled like the morning snow. She said nothing, so Shaira spoke in her place.

"Those who are close to my son's heart are close to mine," she said. She took Alua's hand. Cold, like Vireon's skin. The girl lowered her eyes and smiled. *Demure as a Princess. Or too ignorant to behave otherwise.* "Welcome to Udurum," said the Queen.

"I have much to tell you," said Vireon. She saw a sadness swimming in his eyes, a hungry fish gliding beneath the surface of a frozen lake. "What word from Tadarus?"

"No word," she told him. "Certainly he and Fangodrel have reached Uurz by now."

Vireon's lean chin sported a half-grown beard. It made him look a bit older, more like Tadarus. Or perhaps it was the raw concern on his face. *He worries for his brother.*

"Has there been no messenger confirming his arrival?"

"No word from Uurz has come," she said. His questions brought back her cloud of worry. "What troubles you?"

"Nothing," he said, turning away. "I miss my brothers . . . that is all."

Now her eyes fell on the blue-skinned Uduru standing in the hall. Some of them were possibly human men or women, for their height was much less. They sweltered and sweated beneath cloaks of thick fur, and the Giants of Udurum stared at them in silent wonder, marveling at their indigo skin, and waiting for the Prince to explain them. That time could be postponed no longer. When Vireon spoke, she realized that the tallest blue-skins were all female.

"Cousins!" announced Vireon, stepping onto the dais. "Where is my uncle?"

Fangodrim the Gray made his way through the crowd, smiling. "Prince!" shouted the First Among Giants. "Your hunt went on far too long!" Giants rumbled with laughter as Fangodrim and

Vireon embraced. Shaira took her seat on the throne behind her son, who commanded all the eyes in the room.

"I am sorry for leaving you in the forest," Vireon said to his uncle. "But as you will see, my hunt has been a good one." Fangodrim stepped aside and Vireon addressed the crowd. The wild, silent Alua stood with her hand in his. They seemed inseparable. Shaira decided not to worry about this unless it became necessary.

"Uduru! People of New Udurum," Vireon began. "These are the women and children of the *Udvorg*!"

A wave of astonishment flowed across the hall. The city Giants, mostly sentinels and palace staff, rubbed their beards and stared at the blue-skins, who stood blinking and resigned. The smaller ones looked afraid, some clinging to the skirts of the Giantesses. Shaira did not know the word Udvorg, but it seemed some of the Uduru did. Or they half-remembered it.

"The Long Hunt took me into the far north, to the White Mountains," said Vireon. "There I discovered what has been forgotten these many centuries. Our cousins, People of Hreeg like us! The Udvorg, who went north before Old Udurum was built . . . who made their own kingdom in the land of ice and wind. You see now the descendants of our ancestors. Yes, recognize them! These are their *children*!"

He shouted *children* with an emphasis no one could mistake. These were not blue-skinned Men, they were the offspring of these white-haired beauties in their pelts of black and scarlet. These were Giants who were not living on the brink of extinction. *Children!* How long had it been since the Udurum had seen Giant children? Twenty-six years since the day the Lord of Serpents fell upon the old city and murdered most of their kind.

The curiosity of the Uduru turned to joy. Some fell to their knees and took the Udvorg children by their shoulders, hugging them, lifting them, tugging at their cheeks. The blue children laughed, exchanged grins with their mothers. The Giantesses did not lack for attention either. Some Uduru took their hands in the sign of universal greeting; some embraced them like hungry bears; others even dared to kiss their azure knuckles.

My son has brought a miracle to his people.

Vireon turned from the spectacle to look at her. She took his free hand, tears brimming in her eyes, but these were tears of gladness. Vireon stood between Shaira and Alua, both of their hands in his own.

Fangodrim came to the dais, carrying an Udvorg girl-child on his big shoulders. "You hunted beasts and found Giants!" said Vireon's uncle. His eyes also brimmed with tears of joy. "How many are there? Up there among the White Peaks?"

Vireon smiled. "*Thousands*," he said. "Entire clans, Uncle! All under the eye of the Ice King called Angrid the Long-Arm. He welcomes his lost cousins into his kingdom. Once again the Uduru will have wives and children. The Uduru will live!"

Fangodrim turned toward the excited crowd, the girl laughing on his back.

"*The Uduru will live!*" he shouted. The Giants cheered, and the palace walls shook.

Shaira rose from her throne when the tumult died down. "Let there be a feast," she ordered. "For my son has returned, and the Udvorg have come to Udurum."

Another round of cheers, and word of Vireon's miracle was spilling now into the streets of the city. Rumors began to fly, and tales would grow of how Vireon had "conquered" the northlands.

She watched him introduce Fangodrim to one of the blue-skinned Giantesses. Pots of heated wine were passed among the hall, but the blue-skins would drink only cold liquids. She directed the servants to bring such for them.

"Uncle, this is Lydrah, first among my Udvorg wives," said Vireon. "According to her own custom, I may give her to a warrior who is worthy of her. So I give her to you, Fangodrim."

Fangodrim stared at his new wife, speechless. It was Lydrah the Giantess who spoke first, though her thick accent made her words muddy. "I accept you, Fangodrim the Gray," she said, and took his hand. "Vireon has told me . . . much about you. We shall have . . . strong children."

Fangodrim, still mute, lifted Lydrah in his great arms and spun her about. The nearby children laughed and began to spin themselves. Now all the Giants were spinning, laughing, talking of this great thing that Vireon had done.

Vireon went among them, picking carefully the right husband for each blue-skin Giantess. He delivered a mate to Dabruz the Flame-Heart, Ohlung the Bear-Slayer, then Danthus the Sharp-Toothed. Each of the Uduru greeted their new wives – and the accompanying children – with respect and jubilation. Shaira watched in amazement, laughing as she had never thought to laugh again, crying and happy all at once. She barely noticed the wild girl, Alua, standing patiently at the side of her throne, where Vireon had placed her. There was no jealousy in the girl's eyes. Instead, a familiar glow beamed from her smiling face, shimmered in her black-diamond pupils. Shaira took a moment and put a name to that peculiar glow.

She loves Vireon. Truly and deeply.

Alua's eyes never left Vireon as he went about choosing husbands for the last two Udvorg ladies. Many Giants requested the honor, but it was Boroldun the Bear-Fang and Ogo the Spear who had the luck. Now there stood nine Giant couples in the room, with six children between them. The blue-skins seemed overwhelmed by the shower of love and affection.

Vireon returned to the royal dais and took Alua's hand. She

hugged him and he kissed her. "You have done a good thing," she whispered to him. Shaira heard this and silently agreed.

She wondered at the sheer delight brimming in her palace hall. Would humans have reacted differently in such a situation? She thought so, but then again humans were not facing extinction. The Uduru were, in many ways, a simpler people than Men. Their ways were not those of the Small Folk. Not even centuries of separation could sever their common spirit.

Vireon grabbed his mother's arm, bending to one knee. "Mother, where is my little sister?" In all the excitement he had forgotten about Sharadza. For a moment, so had she. A pang of guilt stabbed her chest.

"Gone," she told him. "Not long after you and Tadarus left."

"Gone where?" asked Vireon.

Shaira could not speak, so she only shook her head.

Stubborn girl, you have ruined this moment of joy!

"Vireon," she said. "Your sister has a strong will. We'll speak of her later."

Vireon embraced her again, sensing her worry.

"Now," she continued. "Tell me about this Ice King . . ."

Today would be a feast to rival all other feasts. Word of the blue-skinned Udvorg and their invitation would travel to every Giant in the city, and celebrations would be heard in every quarter. But the Honored Uduru and their new families would gather about the Queen's Table and Vireon would tell of his adventures. Shaira would ignore the empty chairs where her other three children should be sitting.

My son is returned, she told herself. *That is enough for now.*

Yet the glimmer of an unspoken sadness swam in Vireon's eyes, even in the midst of his gladness. She wondered what it was.

Vireon held Alua close to him and said nothing.

17

Six Princes

Deep snows filled the pass. A column of Giants drove through the white depths, shifting it aside with their great shields and the strength of their arms. The company of Men, a haggard mix of Uurzian, Sharrian, and Udurum, rode through the corridors cleared by the Giants' hands. Beneath the snow, often invisible, lay patches of deadly ice. Horses were sent lame when they slipped, or went sliding down treacherous slopes and broke their necks. At times riding was impossible, and the line of over three hundred men walked on foot down the northern side of Vod's Pass.

Andoses had sweated and moaned and babbled for three days until his fever finally broke. Snow had fallen all that time, and it was two more days before the Sharrian Prince regained his full strength. Soon it was decided: the blended company must make for Udurum before the fullness of winter fell upon the Grim Mountains. D'zan learned this was an early snowfall, a pale shadow of storms to come. Winter had not yet fully conquered the lands below these slopes.

"The snows come early and deeper at these heights," said Rockjaw. "Now is the season of ice-storms in Uduria. If we leave now, we may reach the city before the first snow."

Tyro and Andoses had agreed. They had gathered the reserves of their living men, bolstered their spirits with brave words and flagons of wine, and decided to set out at once. The men took heart from Andoses' recovery, which they saw as a sign from the Sky God. Andoses was on a holy mission to save Shar Dni, and there could be no denying it. Those soldiers too wounded to travel would spend the season in the cavern with a contingent of Rockjaw's sentinels; the pass must never go unguarded. Their refuge was packed with provisions and emergency supplies, so there was no danger of starvation. The men may not have liked their Princes' decision, but they would abide it. Besides, traveling through the snow-choked pass probably would have killed them.

As cold and miserable as it was along the pass, exposed to the elements and the perilous mountains, D'zan was glad to be moving north again. He walked down a precarious path, boots searching for clumps of snow and mud. He watched for those hidden traps of ice that might prove his last step in this life. The fierce wind tore at his cloak as he dragged his reluctant horse along by its reins. Far ahead and below, the Uduru gathered themselves into a dip in the pass before tackling the next wrinkle of the white landscape. Ahead walked Tyro, leading his own mount, and Andoses came between them. At D'zan's back came Lyrilan, quoting lines of verse to distract himself from the bitter cold. Behind Lyrilan came the long double line of soldiers leading their own steeds. In the midst of the warrior columns rolled the supply wagons, pulled now by straining men, since the terrain was too slick and deadly for horses. They worked in shifts, aware that the first of those wagons carried the shrouded bones of Tadarus, Prince of Udurum.

"The Prince must be taken home," Rockjaw had said. Tyro had tried to dissuade him. They could return for Tadarus' remains in the spring. But the Giant would not hear of it. "It took many days to find his body among the broken stones of Steephold. We will carry it to the Queen, or we will not go at all." So there dead Tadarus rode, wrapped in a Giant's cape and pulled by grunting, freezing men toward a tomb in the city he might one day have ruled.

Finally, after twelve days of stumbling, sliding, freezing exhaustion, the snowdrifts gave way to a frosted range of low hills. A road ran level, winding between those white lumps crowned with leafless trees. The company filed out onto the road while the Uduru rested atop the nearest knoll. When D'zan took to the saddle again, he found that his ribs were no longer sore. His legs and arms were aching, his feet and toes permanently chilled, but at least his ribs had healed. *Thank the Gods, we made it through the pass.* He sat on his horse, staring north into the Giantlands.

They had not beaten the first snow of winter after all, but down here the snows were light, perhaps a fingerspan thick. The range of hills was shallow, giving way to the broad plain a few leagues north. Groves of trees dotted the plain, and a stream only partially frozen ran down from the uplands. The trees of the plain grew thicker as the eyes traveled northward, becoming at last a mighty wall of impenetrable forest. The trees there must be incredibly tall, though at this distance D'zan was unsure. They seemed tall as the spires of cities, stretching great branches in all directions. Everywhere a white dusting of snow coated the world. Still, some green persisted in the black depths of that soaring woodland, evergreens and pine gleaming in the shadows of monolithic trunks.

"They're called Uyga," said Lyrilan, bringing his horse up beside D'zan.

"What?"

"Those great trees that tower over all the others. Uyga trees. They dwarf even the Uduru."

D'zan's perspective fell into focus, and he realized exactly how big the Giant-trees truly were.

"It's said a man can build an entire house out of a single Uyga root," said Lyrilan.

The rest of the soldiers and the grateful wagon-pullers filed out onto the level road. Soon they would be moving again, some riding alone, some sharing mounts. At the head of the column, the bannermen of Tyro and Andoses unfurled the standards of Uurz and Shar Dni. One of Rockjaw's lieutenants joined them, flying the hammer flag of New Udurum.

"How far until the city?" asked D'zan.

Lyrilan pulled back his hood and scratched his curly head. "Best ask a Giant," he said. "It's hard to tell these thing from maps."

"Have you not visited Udurum before?" asked D'zan.

"I have," said Lyrilan. "It was summer, and I rode in a coach. I remember sleeping during this part of the journey."

D'zan laughed.

"I was much younger then," Lyrilan reminded him.

They rode the rest of the day and pavilioned at the very edge of the forest. The concentric camp lines took formation to the east of the wide road that ran directly into the gargantuan wall of trees. The night was chill, but far warmer than Vod's Pass. The wind was less here, and the light snow melted about their fires. D'zan stood outside his tent and pondered the depths of those great woods. What creatures lurked in their dark underbrush? Or lived in the vast expanses of their branches? He heard tales of colossal elk, of moose large as houses, and even wolves tall enough to bite a man in half. How much of these tales were true he had no idea.

At length he went inside his tent to undress. Each Prince would have his own pavilion tonight, so D'zan would enjoy relative comfort. First he would heat a pot of water and soak his feet. Then drink some mulled wine and fall asleep under a pile of furs.

His goal was so near now . . . already he felt a lightening of spirits.

Prince Tyro came stamping into the tent. "Well, D'zan, welcome to the Giantlands. Don't take off those boots. It's time for your lessons to resume."

D'zan sighed. "I thought we'd rest first and in the morning—"

Tyro grunted. "When the sun rises we'll be marching toward Udurum. We've wasted too many good days in that pass. Pick up your blade and follow me. Quickly now, I'm tired too."

D'zan pulled on his cloak, took up the Stone's blade, and joined Tyro in the frosted shortgrass. As campfires blinked to life about them, men unloaded wagons, fed horses, and settled down for the night. D'zan ran through the warm-up exercises under Tyro's critical eye. Next came the sparring with bronze rods. D'zan performed exceptionally badly and earned several new bruises. Before the session was over, the smell of cooking meat filled the night air and the deep laughter of Uduru floated among the smoke. His arms were numb when Tyro finally dismissed him.

"Get some sleep," Tyro said. "Tomorrow, if no storm slows us, you will meet the Queen of Udurum."

D'zan went back to his tent, forgot about the hot water, drank a cup of chilled wine instead, and crawled beneath the covers of his cot. Some time during the middle of the night he woke in a panic, realizing he did not have the Stone's blade in his hand. He grabbed it up from the rugs and placed it upon his chest, pommel pointing toward his chin, fists wrapped firmly about the hilt. Sleep returned, swift as an eagle.

The colossal forest was an amazing sight, but the City of Men and Giants dwarfed it for sheer spectacle. It rose from a vast clearing in the center of the woodland, encircled by outlying farms, and its great black wall stood taller than the tremendous Uyga trees. The gates stood open as the four Princes approached, the lowering sun at their backs. They had ridden all day through the forest and were arriving as Tyro had anticipated – in the orange glow of early evening. Behind the Princes a pair of horses pulled the wagon housing Tadarus' body, and behind that came a company of twenty-two Uduru. The long train of cavalrymen followed at their heels, winding outward from the shadows of the trees.

The flames of great braziers burned at intervals atop the wall, and men tiny as ants walked the high ramparts. Here and there an Uduru strolled between battlements, but the Men far outnumbered the Giants.

An advance rider had galloped through the forest that morning, carrying word of the company's approach. Now a contingent of Uduru, led by a graybeard in sable and silver, came to greet them at the Great Gate. The Giants stood like iron statues, dressed in full armor and the purple cloaks of sentinels. Beyond, in the city proper, a crowd of humans braved the cold to catch a glimpse of the arriving Princes. Other than a few wall-guards and the contingent of royal escorts, no other Giants could be seen.

The ebony spires of Vod's Palace stood at the city's heart, each wearing a crown of pristine snow. Here was a castle that set all other castles to shame; it made the great edifice D'zan's father had kept in Yaskatha look like a pile of sticks and tinder. Here was a palace – and a whole city – built for giants. To find humans here at all was an astounding thing. It had not always been this way. Yet when Vod rebuilt the original city, he planned it to accommodate the sizes of both races. D'zan's mind boggled at the blend of great and small architectures comprising the streets, plazas, houses, shops, and taverns. Through the arching gate, he saw all these structures and more. The gray-bearded Giant raised his arm and bellowed a greeting.

"Hail, Princes of Uurz! Hail, Prince of Shar Dni and Queen's Cousin!"

Tyro spoke for all of them. "Hail, Fangodrim the Gray, First Among Giants!" As they reined their horses at the very lip of the gates, Tyro spoke again to the Giant. "Know that Prince D'zan, Heir of Yaskatha, rides with us."

Fangodrim the Gray turned his grizzled face to D'zan. His courteous bow was slight, but proper. "Hail, Prince of Yaskatha. The Queen of Udurum heeds your coming and welcomes you."

The Giants walked beside the mounted Princes as they proceeded along the broad cobbled street. The curious faces of children, laborers, soldiers, wives, and merchants looked up at them, white breath rushing from their mouths and nostrils. Behind the Princes the innocuous death wagon rolled along the street, its tragic cargo yet to be revealed. Now the twenty-two Uduru from Steephold filed through the gate. Fangodrim went back to greet them personally, and he embraced Rockjaw.

"Where are Tadarus and Fangodrel?" Fangodrim asked Rockjaw. "Your rider's message said nothing of them."

Rockjaw's response was a half-grunt, half-moan. "Best to ask the Prince Andoses," he said. "I would not speak for him."

Fangodrim turned his big face toward Andoses, but the Sharrian Prince looked straight ahead, toward the black palace in its cloak of snow. "I bring grim news," said Andoses. "It should be the Queen's ears that hear it first."

Fangodrim grunted. "She awaits you in the Great Hall with Vireon."

At the palace gates grooms took their tired horses toward the stables. A squad of men came forth to assign lodging and barracks to the warriors of Shar Dni and Uurz, while the returning Men of Udurum were greeted with smiles and handshakes. None of them spoke yet of the sad news they too carried.

Rockjaw himself took the body of Tadarus from the wagon, carrying it through the arch of the palace gate. Trailing behind the Lord of Steephold, his face dour, Fangodrim escorted the Princes through the snowy courtyard, up the marble steps, and into the massive hall. It seemed a curtain of heat hung there above the steps, and D'zan almost fainted when he entered it. He had lived with the cold for weeks now; this haven of crackling flames was like a paradise. Fires roared in huge braziers hung from iron chains. Pillars of jet streaked with gold and silver supported the enormous vault of the roof, and tapestries stitched with untold wealth sparkled along the walls.

Six armored Uduru stood on either side of the royal dais, and twelve human guards lined north and south walls. A Giant's throne sat empty in the shadows at the rear of the dais, and before it sat two normal-sized chairs, carved and jeweled to rival the glory of the Great Throne. In one of these seats reclined the Queen of Udurum, a small yet beautiful woman with long flowing hair the color of night. Jewels and gold glimmered on her fingers and at her neck; even from a distance D'zan could see the emerald green of her eyes. In the chair beside her sat not her husband, but a young man of powerful build, a narrow-faced Tadarus dressed in a tunic of purple silk and cloak of white fur. This must be Prince Vireon, brother of the dead man. At his feet on the highest step of the dais sat a gorgeous girl with flowing blonde hair, dressed in a rather simple gown the color of fresh snow.

Rockjaw walked in solemn grace, sinking to one knee before the dais and placing the enshrouded body on the marble floor. Tyro, Lyrilan, and Andoses went also to their knees, heads bowed, and D'zan knew enough court etiquette to follow their lead. He stared at the floor and did not watch Vireon come down the steps and pull back the shroud. Nor did he see the Queen rise from her throne and rush down the steps. But he heard too well her awful scream as she saw the face of her dead son. It rang through the Great Hall, a demon-struck bell reverberating among the splendor and flames.

Her scream faded to fierce sobbing. The Princes kept their eyes on the polished floor, but D'zan dared a peek in the Queen's direction. Vireon held her now, and her body writhed in the storm of her grief. Diamond tears welled in Vireon's eyes, and D'zan knew this was a man who had loved his brother greatly. He saw tears also in the eyes of the great Rockjaw, and the Giant sentinels wiped at their eyes with the hems of their cloaks. He could not see if the human soldiers along the walls cried too. He returned his gaze to the floor.

"You *knew*," the Queen said to Vireon, accusing him of prescience with her streaming eyes. "Somehow you knew, didn't you?"

Vireon nodded, holding her hands. He looked at the withered flesh that had been Tadarus. "I only felt it . . . in my bones," he said.

Fangodrim spoke gently. "The bond between brothers is a powerful thing. This is a terrible day for Uduru and men alike. Our recent bliss now turns to sorrow. Tadarus was the noblest of men."

Rockjaw spoke next. "A young King he was. All who saw him knew he would rule with honor and strength." He turned his reddened eyes to Vireon. "My Prince . . . my Queen . . . his death falls upon me. He died at Steephold, even as our walls fell about us . . ."

Vireon raised a hand. "Let my mother rest and reclaim herself," he said, "and we will hear all that is to be said."

"No!" said the Queen, breaking away from him. She knelt and put the shroud back over Tadarus' dead face. "Tell me now. Tell me everything. Where is . . . where is *Fangodrel*?"

D'zan could not tell if she spoke in fear, anger, or sorrow.

Perhaps a mix of all three. She looked not at Rockjaw, but at Prince Andoses, whose eyes were downcast.

"Andoses!" she demanded. She rose and stepped toward him. "Where is my other son?"

Andoses looked up. D'zan could not see if he wept. He spoke as if the words caused him pain. Likely, they did.

"Gone," said Andoses. He pointed at the corpse. "The Pale Prince slew his own brother . . . and escaped into the night."

The Queen gasped. Vireon's fists clenched.

"He killed many more besides," said Andoses. "And nearly myself." He threw back his cloak and opened his shirt, showing the fresh scars and bandages retained from the night of terror. "Steephold fell under his will alone. His . . . and that which he commanded."

"What did he command?" asked Vireon. His eyes simmered, pools of blue fire.

"Sorcery," said Andoses. "A host of shadows . . . demons . . . ghosts. Things that crawled out of the night to kill Men and Giants. They brought the walls of Steephold crumbling on our heads!" Now the Sharrian wept openly, and D'zan felt pity for him.

"Why?" asked the Queen, ignoring the fresh tears on her cheeks. "Why would he do this?"

Andoses shook his head and wiped at his eyes.

The Queen turned to Rockjaw. The Giant had no answer either.

Finally she embraced Tyro, then Lyrilan. "Sons of my dear friend, would that we met under less tragic circumstances. What do you know of this?"

"Nothing at all, Majesty," answered Tyro. "We arrived to find the castle broken. Rockjaw and his sentinels met us there, and we learned the fate of poor Tadarus."

"There was a Serpent," said Lyrilan. The Queen turned her face to him. "An Old Wyrm crawled up from beneath the ruins."

Rockjaw grunted. "An aged beast, stirred by the commotion. We slew it easily enough."

Tyro bristled. Only one Giant had died battling the Wyrm, but nearly fifty Men.

"Great Queen," said D'zan, "I might know something of this evil that plagues both our houses."

"May I present Prince D'zan," said Tyro. "Scion of Yaskatha. He has come a very long way to seek audience with Your Majesty."

"Prince D'zan," said the Queen, turning her green eyes on him. Their heat seemed more dangerous than the flames leaping from the braziers. "Of what evil do you speak?"

"The Sorcerer Elhathym, who slew my father, desecrated the bones of my family, and stole my ancestral throne for himself. His power is terrible, and his reach is long. Already he has allied himself with the Empress of Khyrei and sent assassins to murder me. He fears I will return to claim my throne."

The Queen thought for a moment. "What has this usurper to do with Fangodrel?"

"I know not, Majesty," said D'zan. "Yet when one speaks of sorcery, all things must be considered."

Vireon spoke up. "Could this Elhathym be responsible for Fangodrel's betrayal? Tadarus' death? Is that what you're saying?"

D'zan stared up at the half-Giant Prince who was a full head taller than him. "I-I cannot say," he stammered. "Perhaps the death . . . the demons . . . were meant for me. As was the Serpent."

"Then why are you not dead?" asked Vireon.

"I carry a ward against evil," said D'zan.

"So you bring a plague of sorcery into our land . . . " said Vireon, his voice rising. D'zan feared the man might strike him. *I must maintain courtesy and grace, or be disgraced in this court.*

Andoses stepped forward. "Cousin, calm yourself. Prince D'zan sought sanctuary in Uurz and it was granted. He has the protection of Emperor Dairon and the King of Shar Dni."

"Is this true, Tyro?" the Queen asked. "Does Dairon send you on behalf of this boy?"

"No," said Tyro. "I came of my own free will, as did my brother. But Uurz supports D'zan's right to claim his throne. If Udurum will stand with us . . ."

The Queen fell silent. Vireon looked from D'zan to Tyro to Andoses. Lyrilan stood awkwardly in the middle of them all, blinking uncomfortably.

"Sister of my father," Andoses said to the Queen, "we stand on the verge of a Great Alliance. Udurum, Shar Dni, Uurz, and now Yaskatha, whose people cry for the return of their rightful lord. This was the dream of Brave Tadarus. If there is to be war—"

"Enough!" said the Queen. "I will not speak of war while my dead son lies unburied at my feet." She wept again, and caught her breath.

A silence fell upon the chamber.

"Prince D'zan," said the Queen, "you are welcome here. I do not believe you bring madness and death in your wake. The evil that killed my son is well known to me. It was born of my own mistake, long ago."

Vireon drew in his breath, but the Queen silenced him with a wave of her hand. She turned to Tyro and Lyrilan.

"Princes of Uurz, you are always welcome in our home. Stay and be comforted."

Lastly, to Andoses: "Son of my brother," she said, placing a hand on his cheek, "we will speak of these weighty matters after the funeral. Tomorrow we honor Tadarus."

"What about Fangodrel?" asked Vireon, still seething in the thrall of his anger.

The Queen walked back to her throne. "Forget him," she said. "He is lost to us."

Vireon stalked up the steps. "No," he said. "I will *never* forget what he has done. He will die by my hand for this. I swear on Tadarus' bones—"

The Queen slapped his face.

Vireon stood stunned for a moment, all eyes avoiding him. Then he turned away, took the hand of his pretty consort, and walked into the shadows.

The Queen gathered herself, then gave out a litany of commands. Stewards and servants rushed to do her bidding. "Let the guests be housed and the returning Sons of Udurum be given all they need. Open the royal barracks and prepare a banquet for all those who crossed the mountains. Send heralds into the streets to announce the funeral pageant of Tadarus. Tomorrow at the zenith of the sun, Udurum will mourn its fallen Prince." And then, in a softer, hoarser voice: "Prepare the Royal Mausoleum."

A gracious steward led the Princes to their respective chambers. D'zan would have hot water in which to bathe, warm food to eat, and many things to occupy his mind. And tomorrow would bring the death march of the Son of Vod.

In the haze of torchlight that filled the palace corridor, Vireon walked alone. Alua slept safely in his bedchamber, guarded by a trusted Uduru. His mind churned with memories of Tadarus. Visions of childhood, fleeting glimpses of hunts and fights and the reckless laughter of youth. He had known, weeks ago in the Palace of Blue Flame . . . he had sensed the death of his brother. So why did he grieve so deeply now? Having foreknowledge of the loss did nothing to soften its blow.

At the door of the Queen's Chamber he nodded to the guard and knocked gently. A servant answered, admitting him quietly.

He knew his mother would not sleep this night. Neither would he.

"Go to her," Alua had said, stroking his chest with her pale fingers. "She needs you."

"But she is angry with me," said Vireon.

"No, you are angry with her," said Alua.

She was right. The last thing his mother needed right now was his storming temper. He had only been returned nine days, and since then had spent more time with Alua than Shaira. He must make time for his mother now that she truly needed him. Now that Tadarus was gone.

Shaira sat before a great table laid out with swords, daggers, tunics, and other items of clothing and jewelry. These were meant for Tadarus, he knew instantly, and it made him want to weep. She was choosing his death garb, and the treasures that would go with him into the tomb. She did not notice his presence, so intent was she on these objects of finality.

"Mother?" he whispered.

She turned to him with an exhausted smile. "Son," she said, and there was power and solace in the word. It gave her strength just to say it. He embraced her.

"This color will best suit him, don't you think?" she asked, running her hand along a violet shirt with silver trim. Vireon nodded, having no real idea how to dress a dead man.

"I am sorry," he said. She looked at him with her weary eyes.

"For what?" she said.

"For the oath I made . . . for my anger. I behaved foolishly."

She rose from her chair and kissed his cheek, standing on her toes to reach it.

"You only miss your brother, as I do," she said. She sat back in her chair and continued arranging the items. In the corners, patient servants waited for her choices. Down somewhere in the palace's lower chambers, priests were preparing the body of Tadarus for burial. Vireon chose not to think about that. Better to do as his mother did, fiddle with precious, comely things that would turn their mourning into a glorious and beautiful thing.

"What did you mean earlier," he asked, "about a mistake you had made? Something to do with . . . " He could not say the Kinslayer's name. He might never be able to say it again. It was a poison shame in his mouth, in his thoughts. It made him want to lash out and spread death, spill blood. It was the lust for vengeance growing like a poison blossom in his heart.

Shaira sighed and leaned back in her chair. Her shoulders slumped as if carrying a great weight. Or had decided to set one down.

"Fangodrel was not the son of Vod," she said.

Vireon did not understand at first.

"He did not carry the blood of Vod in his veins," she said. "His father was another man . . . a cruel beast . . . a monster."

Now the words took root in Vireon's mind. Of course. This too he had always known somewhere deep inside. Always known and refused to admit it.

"How?" he asked.

"When I was nineteen my father sent me across the Golden Sea to Khyrei. I was to marry Prince Gammir, son of the Khyrein Emperor and the Sorceress Ianthe." She looked into the shadows, never meeting his eyes as she told the story. He knew these memories pained her, and she had never spoken of them until now. He did not need to ask why.

"Gammir hated me," she said. "He locked me in his dungeon. He raped me. I suffered more than I have ever suffered in those months that seemed like years. I thought I would die . . . but time after time I lived through his brutality. His mother made horrible potions that dimmed my mind. I became like an animal, a thing he used for his disgusting pleasures. I knew he would eventually kill me. I came to look forward to it."

She grew silent then, and he was amazed that she did not cry.

"What happened?"

"Vod came across the sea with thunder and lightning at his back. He faced the sorcery of the Emperor and Empress. His rage shattered their palace. Everyone there died but us two . . . or so we believed.

"He took me back to the land of my father, nursed me back to health. Something magical he fed me, I never knew what it was. A strange fruit. But it restored my mind and memory. After that we were married, and we came north to rebuild Udurum. When my belly began to swell, we both thought it was Vod's child. But when he was born, pale of skin and dark of eye, we knew the truth. Vod decided to raise the child as his own, and even named him after his own father. Yet Fangodrel was truly the son of Gammir . . . a bastard. We tried to give him our love the best we could. Then Tadarus came, and you, and Sharadza. It may be that we forgot Fangodrel then. We never told him why he was different. Yet I saw it tormented him. Now he *must* know . . . he must have been told. This is why he murdered Tadarus. Out of spite."

"How can you know this?" asked Vireon.

Her green eyes bored into his. "Because word reached me years ago," she said, "that the Empress of Khyrei did not die in the destruction of her palace. Ianthe the Claw survived through her sorcery. Now this sorcerer Elhathym conquers Yaskatha. How could these two not be twined together in some conspiracy?"

Vireon considered everything he had heard. "Do you believe . . . that Gammir's son inherited the sorcery of Khyrei?"

"Did you not inherit the strength of your own father? The iron of his skin? The force of his will? Perhaps it was only a matter of time."

"How could this sorceress reach across the world to corrupt . . ." He could not say the name. It would spill from his mouth like burning magma, set his world on fire.

Shaira leaned her head back to rest a moment. "How could a Giant shrink to the size of Man and grow back into a Giant when he pleased? How did Vod slay the Lord of Serpents? There is more sorcery in this world than you can guess, Vireon."

He thought of Alua's white flame, dancing in her palm. Of her naked fox-form running across the snow. Could she be? She must be.

Sorcery.

The word tumbled through his mind, splashing into the waters of his imagination, making ripples of thought. *What is sorcery?* It had killed his brother. Yet it had saved him. It had built this city. It had flowed in the blood of his own father. *Is it in my blood too?*

"Get some sleep," said Shaira. "I am sorry I never told you these things before now. Please understand . . . I could not."

"I understand," he said. He kissed her cheek and walked toward the door.

"Vireon?" she called after him. He turned.

"Your friend Alua." Shaira smiled. "She loves you."

He nodded, returned her smile, and exited. As he walked the dim hallway, those ripples of thought pressed against the walls of his skull.

Sorcery. Love.

Love and sorcery.

Does any living Man truly understand such things?

18

War Plans

Tadarus lay upon a bier of silk, gold, and snowflowers. A shirt of silver mail hung over his fine robe of purple and sable. His gauntlets gripped the hilt of a jeweled sword upon his breast, and his face was obscured by the winged helm of an Udurum soldier. Tyro watched Vireon, dressed in armor of blackened bronze scales, place a Giant's hammer at the side of his dead brother.

"It was the last gift I ever gave him," Vireon said.

Tyro had no words for the grieving Prince. He looked instead at his own brother. Lyrilan was the only Prince who did not wear mail or plate this day. Lyrilan's robes were cloth-of-gold trimmed in green, the colors of Uurz. His black curls were oiled and held from his brow by a golden band set with emeralds. The persistent stubble that never quite became a beard was gone. Lyrilan's chin was shaved to the cleanness of boyhood, which almost made Tyro laugh. Lyrilan was his other half, the thought to his action. Each twin had mastered the skills his counterpart lacked. Together, they were body and mind. To lose Lyrilan would be to lose himself. Such thoughts kept Tyro from meeting the sad eyes of Vireon. Alua, dressed in a black gown of mourning, remained at Vireon's side, a steady presence to guide him through the service. For the first time Tyro realized how beautiful this strange girl was, despite her lack of finery and jewels. Or perhaps because of it? Her eyes gleamed, yet they were darker than her funereal silks.

Andoses stood tall in gilded mail and turban-helm, scimitar gleaming at his waist. D'zan, poorest of the Princes, had been given a shirt of bronze links and a black tabard by his Udurum hosts, and the great sword hung on his back as always. Tyro had supplied him with a new pair of spotless boots for the occasion – since he claimed the throne of Yaskatha, D'zan must look the part of a King. His cloak of fine brown fur was washed and groomed, and a circlet of fine silver held back his thick blonde mane. He looked presentable enough, if somewhat out of place this far from home.

Fangodrim and fifty Uduru sentinels in full armor formed the heart of the procession, and Queen Shaira arrived last of all. Servants had draped her in black: a flowing dress, shawl, and a cloak pinned by a silver brooch in the shape of the Udurum hammer. An elaborate headdress replaced her usual crown of slim silver. Twelve rays of a platinum sun spread outward from her brow, radiating from a faceted amethyst at the center of her forehead. Her green eyes glimmered through the delicate lace of a veil. Her feet were bare in the traditional Sharrian mode of mourning. The day was cold, so this was a bold choice. Perhaps the chill could be no worse than the pain of losing her son.

A quartet of Uduru lifted her chair onto a broad palanquin hung with black silks. Another four Giants lifted the bier of Tadarus. At noon four priests representing Earth, Sea, Sun, and Sky filed from the palace gates swinging censers full of incense. The Dead Prince came next, followed by the Living Queen, both held high on the shoulders of the solemn Giants. Next came the five Living Princes, Vireon and Alua at their head. Fangodrim and his fifty Uduru marched at Vireon's heels, then a hundred spearmen in silver helms, purple cloaks, and black mail. At the rear of the procession rode a captain on a black stallion, holding high the banner of New Udurum.

The procession went first along Giant's Way, the city's main avenue, toward the Great Gate, which stood closed for the funeral. The procession turned north and made a circuit along the Outer Ring, a road running in the shadow of the city wall about the entire city. A frigid wind blew, but the streets were largely clear of snow. A drab sky hung above, heavy with cloud, as if the sun refused to look upon the Dead Prince. No rain or snow fell, but the tears of the gathered Udurumites rained from their eyes to stain cheeks, chins, and chests. Vod's people lined the streets by the thousands, climbing onto the roofs of houses, stables, and taverns to catch a glimpse. Some wailed aloud, lamenting Tadarus the Brave, Tadarus the Strong, Tadarus the Mighty . . . Tadarus the True Son of Vod.

Mournful Giants and Giantesses gathered among the crowds. More Uduru than Tyro had ever seen – hundreds of them standing with heads bowed along the avenues. Some wore the accoutrements of war – helms, armor, and shields – while others wore the smocks of blacksmiths and builders. Obviously, plenty of the Uduru chose not to make the warrior's way their focus.

So very like humans. Like my brother and I.

Tyro had seen grand funerals in Uurz, but never one with such honesty on display. These people had loved their Prince. Some even shouted the name of Vireon – Vireon the Hunter . . . Vireon the King.They thanked the Four Gods for sparing Vireon. Some cried vengeance for Tadarus. The Uduru kept silent in a show of respect, but human men and women could not restrain their grief, their anger, or their tongues.

All afternoon the procession wound slowly about the perimeter of the city. Sentinels upon the walls looked down upon the funeral march, their sadness no less than the multitudes lining the streets. Foreign traders stood solemn among the populace, mimicking the mute Giants. At the end of the third hour, Tyro was glad to see the gates of the palace looming ahead. So much weeping and moaning could wear on a man's soul. It reminded him of his own mortality, and that everyone he knew would some day die and be mourned.

Once inside the palace courtyard, the procession wound toward the Royal Mausoleum. The Queen's tears flowed as she neared the granite tomb. Tadarus would be the first of his line to inhabit the death-house. Tyro swallowed hard to contain a surging grief that had lain dormant in his stomach until now. The royal father had built this house for himself and his Queen, but the son would lie in it before either of them. The Queen descended from her palanquin to weep over her son's body, to embrace Tadarus for the last time.

The priest of the Sky God spoke a litany over the body, then a Giant pulled open the marble door of the vault. Vireon and a crouching Fangodrim carried the dead Prince inside and lowered his body into a sarcophagus along the far wall. Other coffins lay empty and waiting. By the size of this tomb, Tyro realized that Vod had intended to be buried as a Man, not a Giant. There were no sarcophagi here large enough to house a Giant's bones. He wondered if Vod were truly dead, or if he might return some day to reclaim his throne.Yet he feared the world had seen the last of Vod. Vireon would rule the City of Men and Giants now . . . as soon as his mother relinquished the throne or joined Tadarus in the vault.

The ceremony ended with the singing of a dirge by the Uduru. It was the song of a warrior who died in battle, a plea that his soul be taken into the House of the Gods. When the last of their umbling basso voices faded, the calm of winter filled the courtyard, and the Princes gathered in the dining hall.

A banquet in Tadarus' name began without the presence of the Queen. The Princes sat about her empty chair while captains, advisors, and chancellors lined the rest of the long table. Servants brought dish after dish of steaming poultry and meats, glazed vegetables, fine cheeses, towers of skewered fruit, and carafes of blood-dark wine. None would touch the food until the Queen arrived. By that time the men had been drinking for an hour, Vireon and Fangodrim sharing their memories of Tadarus. The specter of sorrow, while not completely gone, had faded like smoke into the air, and wistful laughter began to slip across the board.

Queen Shaira emerged in a plum gown and a slim silver crown bearing diamonds. The black shawl still hung about her shoulders. Her eyes, though wiped clear of tears and lined with kohl, were red and swollen. She accepted a cup of the rich wine and drank deeply from it.

"Eat," she said in a gentle voice. "And drink to the memory of Tadarus."

"To Tadarus, Prince of Udurum, True Son of Vod!" toasted Fangodrim. Along the great table, sixty cups were raised and sixty voices joined him.

Tyro sat to the left of Vireon, who kept Alua on his right. Tyro asked why there were no other Giants present.

"This feast is for immediate family and the persons of court, those who served Tadarus," said Vireon. "Fangodrim is our uncle. Also, the Uduru usually do not eat for several days after a funeral."

Fangodrim the Gray drank deeply but touched none of the fine food. The rest of the attendees were not so shy. The day had been long and most were famished. As for the Princes who had come across the Grim Mountains, this was the best food they had eaten since leaving Uurz. Even lean Andoses ate like a starved man. His recovery from the ordeal at Steephold was nearly complete.

Alua picked at her food, eating only a little meat, despite Vireon's prompting. The girl was most strange. There must be quite a tale behind Vireon's love for her. Tyro would ask for it later.

The Queen seemed restless and barely touched her food. After a few more toasts in the name of Tadarus, she turned to quiet D'zan.

"Do you miss your homeland, Prince?" asked Shaira.

D'zan washed down a mouthful of fowl with a gulp of wine. "Very much, Majesty," he said. "I miss the sea . . . the people . . . my father and uncle."

"Tell me how you lost the throne, if you will."

D'zan described the terrible night of Elhathym's assault on the city. Those near him lost their appetites when he spoke of the dead rising from their tombs. He praised the Stone, whom he called his uncle, and described their narrow escape on a northbound vessel, their arrival in Murala, their trek across the Stormlands to Uurz. He seemed unable to stop talking, as if telling this tale was a great relief, a burden lifted from his shoulders. Finally, he told her of his first night in Uurz, when the Death-Bringers of Khyrei stole the life of Olthacus the Stone. Tyro still felt the shame of that attack burning in his own breast. It should never have happened under Dairon's roof. All the more reason to make Khyrei answer for its actions.

"You have suffered much," said the Queen. She leaned across the table and took D'zan's hand. "More than one of your age should have to bear. That you survive is a testament to your strength of mind and body."

D'zan seemed lost in his thoughts, reliving all that he had

related. Andoses spoke for him. Tyro glanced at the Sharrian, hoping he would not seem too eager. The Queen was in a fragile state now. They could not press her into war. They must be subtle and let her come to the decision on her own. He trusted that Andoses understood this.

"Prince D'zan's journey thus far is the stuff of legends," said Andoses. "Why, Lyrilan here is writing it all into his book."

The Queen looked at Lyrilan. "True," said the Scholar-Prince. "I joined D'zan because I wish to chronicle his life in as much detail as possible."

"When he regains the throne and tosses the bones of this Elhathym into the sea," said Andoses, "what a terrific ending your book will have."

"What of you, Tyro?" asked the Queen. "Your brother seeks the preservation of knowledge through art. Why do *you* join D'zan?"

Tyro considered his words carefully. "Justice," he said. "D'zan is the rightful heir to one of the world's greatest kingdoms. Yaskatha is the jewel of the south. It pains me and my Lord Father to see a crime such as this. We seek justice not only for D'zan, but for his people. Surely they suffer under this black-handed tyrant."

"A sorcerer," said Vireon. He looked across the table at D'zan, who remained quiet. "Such an enemy is to be feared. Prince D'zan, I apologize. Yesterday I spoke out of grief and rage."

D'zan grinned at Vireon. He raised his wine cup. "To new friends," said the Yaskathan. The entire table drank to his toast. Alua nestled close to Vireon's shoulder, her keen eyes smiling at D'zan.

"Shar Dni is the kingdom of my brother Ammon," said the Queen. "The Raiders of Khyrei have all but crippled their trade. The island kingdoms of the East fear to enter their waters. Many of Ammon's ships have been lost, and the Men of Shar Dni have perished in these sea battles . . . including Vidictus, another of my brothers. Khyrei is the enemy of Udurum because it is the enemy of Shar Dni."

"So Andoses has explained to me," said D'zan. "There is . . . too much death these days."

A silly thing to say, thought Tyro. *But D'zan speaks with a pure heart. The Queen likes him already.*

Andoses responded to the use of his name. "There is no doubt that some covenant exists between the Empress of Khyrei and the Usurper of Yaskatha. Why else would Khyrein assassins travel all the way to Uurz and attempt to kill D'zan? This Elhathym obviously fears the return of the rightful Prince. He knows, as any tyrant should know, that the people will stand behind their true King, no matter his age. When D'zan returns, he will foster a rebellion to end this sorcerer's rule."

"Is this your intention, D'zan?" asked the Queen.

Answer well, young Prince, thought Tyro.

D'zan sat quiet for a moment. "I must do now what my father would do," he said. "I follow a path laid for me by Olthacus the Stone. This sword I bear was his, and I will raise it as a banner to rally my countrymen. I will take back the throne that my father lost . . . or I will die in the trying. I can do no less."

"Well said, Prince," said the Queen. "You are your father's son indeed."

"He will need the backing of all our kingdoms," said Tyro, seizing the moment. "A rebellion of peasants will achieve little. The power of Uurz, Shar Dni, and Udurum must be the first to rally beneath this banner. Yours is the final word, Majesty."

"Before you answer, Shaira, consider this," said Andoses. "Fostering revolt in the name of D'zan will divide the forces of Yaskatha and distract the tyrant. During a time of insurrection Khyrei will not be able to rely on Yaskathan aid. We will be three kingdoms united against one mutual enemy."

"There remains the matter of Mumbaza," said the Queen. "They are a mighty nation. If they ally with Khyrei's Empress or the tyrant of Yaskatha, it will not go well for us."

Andoses slammed his hand against the table. "Sister of my father!" he said. "We do not need the hordes of Mumbaza! We have the *Uduru*! Three armies of men and a fourth of giants! Who could stand against that?"

"A sorcerer," answered Lyrilan, ever the voice of reason. "Or a sorceress. Do you forget that both Empress and Usurper wield the powers of darkness? You heard D'zan's tale – what other horrors might this usurper call upon to cut down an army of living men? And Ianthe the Claw . . . her wizardry is legend itself. They say she feeds on the blood of the living and consorts with demons. There is more to power than marching feet and waving spears . . . "

Tyro noticed Fangodrim glancing at Vireon, who nodded.

"I have spoken with the Uduru since Vireon's return," said Fangodrim. "We have a duty that precedes all else. We will go north into the realm of the Ice King, there to join the Udvorg and make families. If we joined this war instead, there may be no more Uduru to preserve our line. The Queen has granted us permission to go . . . and so we will."

Tyro was speechless. He turned to Andoses, who was just as surprised.

So Vireon told the tale of discovering the Udvorg. Because of his uniting this fractured people, the Uduru no longer faced extinction. Yet because of that same heroic act, this war had lost an army of Giants.

This changes everything, thought Tyro. *We do need Mumbaza. We need . . . we need . . .*

Andoses guzzled the dregs from his cup. "You mean every last Giant refuses to fight?" he asked. "I thought the Uduru relished any chance for war."

Fangodrim nodded. "Most do," he said. "But not now. Our duty is to future generations. However, there is a group of my people who refuse to make the trek northward. They would likely join your battle."

"Superb!" said Andoses. "How many will march?"

"Ninety-nine," said Fangodrim.

Andoses' jaw dropped. "There are at least twelve hundred Uduru in this city! And only ninety-nine will go to war?"

The Queen stared at Andoses. "Do you not understand, nephew? Fangodrim's people are dying. Reuniting with the Udvorg is the only chance they have. Why accept the death of their race and march off to war when the Gods have offered them life instead?"

"Ninety-nine Uduru is still a powerful force," said Tyro. He must not appear ungrateful or disrespectful. That might destroy the entire alliance. Andoses was a blood relative of the Queen, but the Uduru held no relation to him.

"*Uduri*, actually," said Fangodrim.

Tyro's brow narrowed, and Lyrilan chuckled.

"Uduri?" asked Tyro. "What does that mean?"

"Female Giants," said Lyrilan. "The ninety-nine are Giantesses."

Andoses looked from face to face, and back to Fangodrim's grim visage. "You're giving us your women?"

"No!" said Fangodrim, displeased with Andoses' manner. "Our women will not come with us. They can bear no children, and they understand this. They have chosen to stay and ordered us to go. *They* are giving *us* . . . to the fertile Udvorg women."

"Andoses, have you read the Uduru Sagas?" said Lyrilan. "The Uduri are every bit as fierce and terrible as Uduru. After all, these ninety-nine survived the death of Old Udurum, the Coming of the Serpent-Father."

"So we will have three armies of men," said Andoses, tugging at his braided beard, "and ninety-nine Uduri."

Tyro nodded. "Where the south has two armies, each led by a sorcerer. Have we any sorcerers?"

Lyrilan laughed. No one else did.

Vireon whispered something in Alua's ear. Shyly, she raised a hand over the table. A white flame sprang from her open palm, dancing and twisting with life.

The feasters leaned back in their chairs.

"Alua . . . " said Vireon. "She is a sorceress."

Andoses smiled. "Will you join our cause, Great Lady? Will you go with us to—"

"She goes with *me*, Cousin," said Vireon. "She goes wherever I go."

Andoses grew calm. "And where *do* you go, cousin?"

Vireon held back his words and turned his eyes to meet those of Alua. She closed her palm, and the flame was gone without a trace of smoke.

"You heard my vow," Vireon told the table. "I go to seek vengeance for my brother. I seek the head of the Kinslayer."

"Then you are going to Khyrei," said the Queen, her voice suddenly weak. "For that must be where Fangodrel has fled." She exchanged a mysterious look with Vireon. "I know that you are a born hunter, Vireon. I have accepted this. Go . . . and do what you must."

Andoses crossed his arms. Tyro expected him to speak, but the Sharrian said nothing.

"What of Mumbaza?" Tyro was forced to ask. "Queen Shaira, you speak wisdom. We need to win the support of Mumbaza. Now more than ever."

Now Andoses did speak. "Such was the goal of our mission, Tadarus and I," he said. "We were to see Dairon in Uurz, then on to Mumbaza to win the Boy-King's favor."

"So that mission must resume," said the Queen.

Tyro smiled grimly. "Winter has come. Vod's Pass will soon be impassable."

"Then you must go *quickly*," said the Queen. "Rockjaw has cleared the northern half of the pass."

"If there are no more early storms," said Vireon, "our passage should be smooth."

So the plans of war were drawn: Shaira's messengers would go immediately to Uurz and Shar Dni. The five Princes, with a cohort of four hundred, would go to Murala and sail south to secure Mumbaza's alliance. D'zan, Tyro, and Lyrilan would then lead half the cohort directly into Yaskatha to foster rebellion and take the throne.

When the winter broke, Shaira and her Uduri would lead the Udurum host across the pass to join Dairon's legions in Uurz. Ammon's Sharrian host would meet them at Allundra, where The Great Earth-Wall met the Golden Sea. Vireon and Andoses would guide the forces of Mumbaza to rally at Allundra, completing the Alliance of Four Armies before midsummer. Then their hosts would cross the border to Khyrei and victory.

"I do not wish to go to Mumbaza," Vireon protested, "but directly to Khyrei to find the Kinslayer."

"You are the Lord of Udurum now, son," said his mother. "You will be King soon. You must go to Mumbaza and extend the hand of our kingdom. It is your duty. Then you will on your way to Khyrei."

Vireon agreed to the Queen's plan. Tyro breathed a sigh of relief. This endeavor needed the son of Vod more than any other Prince. Here was a hero whose deeds could put fire in the hearts of a million soldiers. Tyro and Andoses were the brains of this campaign, but Vireon would be its handsome face and its strong right arm.

Weary from a long night of planning and studying maps in the

Queen's council chamber, Tyro reflected on the bitter satisfaction of getting what he had wanted all along.

There would be war.

He should feel triumphant, exhilarated, eager for the taste of battle. Yet he felt only exhausted, and he dreaded another march over Vod's Pass. The path to war was long and difficult. Patience was the armor he must wear.

Yes, there would be war. A season of death, blood, and glory.

A season that, like any other, manifested ever-so-slowly to cover the world.

All his life he had been waiting for it.

Even now it sank shallow roots into the ground, colored the dawn sky with bloody gloom, whispered its coming on the wind.

Let it come, this savage season.

I am ready.

19

Sunrise in Khyrei

The moon was a pale and scarred face haunting the night. The waters of the Golden Sea sparkled with a million reflected stars. The only sound was the rushing wind and the beating of the black horse's leathery wings. Gammir, formerly Fangodrel, sat comfortably on its back in his mail of gleaming shadow, basking in his mastery of the night-time world. A black cloud that was not a cloud at all flowed across the sea behind him, a mass of shadow-things exhumed from mountains, valleys, tombs, and graveyards. The rich blood of a King lined his throat and stomach, suffused the substance of his pale flesh, mingled with that of seven Princesses and a young Sharrian Duke.

Spots of dried brown ichor speckled his lean chin and cheeks. He should have taken that last one as well . . . There was no good reason to let him live. No good reason, only the damning visage of his own dead brother. The words that only he could hear.

Curse him! Curse his rotting bones . . . He'd best not cross this sea with the rest of the shades.

King Ammon had received Gammir with open arms, calling for a feast to honor his presence. He had even kissed his nephew on each cheek (there were no bloodstains there yet). He must have assumed that his sister in Udurum was sending her eldest to observe the Khyrein piracy problems.

"It has been too long since you visited us, Fangodrel," Ammon cooed. He stroked the braids of his black beard, the same irritating mannerism his son Andoses had adopted. Ammon's seven sisters would join them at table, and the two grown sons of his brother Omirus, who was still at sea protecting trade routes from Khyrein reavers. "Why did Andoses not come back with you?" he asked.

Gammir smiled, refusing wine. His thirst was great, but not for the blood of grapes. "Andoses and Tadarus have gone to seek the favor of Uurz," he said. The name of Tadarus was a sour taste on his tongue. Then he remembered the sweetness of his half-brother's blood and rediscovered his smile.

"This is good," said Ammon from his throne of ivory and onyx. "My sister gathers support for a war against these jungle devils." The banner of the white bull on a sky-blue field hung behind him. Servants bustled in carrying the feasting table. They placed it directly before the Sharrian throne, which sat on ground level with the rest of the chamber. Gammir found it odd that the Sharrian Kings chose not to raise themselves upon a royal dais. Some ancient tradition perhaps. Ammon was all but ruled by the Seven Priests who guided his every decision. Perhaps it was they who kept the Sharrian Kings at ground level.

"Tell me, Uncle," said Gammir. "Why do you wish to bring war upon Khyrei?"

Ammon's face grew petulant, his lips pursing. "Have you not heard my son's words? They are pirates, murderers, and thieves. They ruin trade by sacking our ships, and take our mariners as slaves. They are an unwholesome race who have long resented our prosperity."

"I have heard they are a great and noble people," said Gammir. "That they lived at peace with Shar Dni until wronged by the sorcery of Vod. Did he not steal my mother from the Prince of Khyrei? Did he not murder the Khyrein Emperor and his son?"

Ammon laid his head back against the satin lining of his throne. His eyes searched the face of the man he still thought was Fangodrel, perhaps only now realizing that this was not him. The blue jewels hanging from his turban crown trembled as his arms shook with restrained rage.

"You speak ill of your own father?" shouted Ammon. Servants withdrew, and the noble women who were gathering at the table cast their eyes downward at its mahogany surface. Children squealed and ran into adjoining corridors. "You find sympathy for the pale demons of the south? Has my sister never told you the truth of her marriage to Prince Gammir?"

Guards in blue surcoats and gilded mail moved restlessly between the pillars as the King stood up to tower over his nephew. "No! She could never tell you! Gammir was a beast. He tortured her. He kept her as a slave until Vod came. A Princess of the Sharrian House locked in a dank cell like an animal!"

The King had drunk too much wine and was obviously not used to anyone telling him what he did not want to hear. *Anyone but the Seven Priests*, thought Gammir. Those holy personages were in their great temples conducting the Rites of Twilight. Would he have raged so in their presence? Gammir doubted it. These lies about his true father must come to an end.

"He was her master," said Gammir in a quiet voice. "Was it not his right to treat her in whatever way he chose? He was a Prince; she was his property."

King Ammon beat his fist upon the table and silverware jumped among the dishes. His sisters coughed and sipped at their wine, hoping the rest of the food would arrive soon to fill both King and Prince's mouths. Now the Dukes Dutho and Pyrus, the teenage Sons of Omirus, entered the hall and came to the table.

They were dressed in the manner of warriors, though Gammir doubted if they had ever left the palace grounds.

"You are young and ignorant," said Ammon, returning to the seat of his throne. He grasped his wine goblet with an agitated hand. "There is nothing of Vod in your looks ... in your manner ... and I'll wager there is none in your veins either."

The table grew silent. Two servants carried the steaming carcass of a roast pig across the floor, placing it at the center of the board. No one dared say a word. The King gulped his wine and would not look at the nephew he had insulted.

Gammir did then what they least expected him to do. He laughed. Threw back his head and howled. The assembled Princesses, Dukes, and guards turned all eyes upon him. Still no one spoke and still Ammon ignored him.

Finally, grasping his stomach, Gammir let his mirth fade. "You are quite correct, Uncle," he announced so that all there would hear it. "I am no son of Vod. Gammir the First was my father. Vod stole me from my rightful home and murdered my sire. This was the fruit of a conspiracy hatched before I was born."

Now King Ammon did turn to face him, his face a purple mask of rage and shock. The torches in their sconces, freshly lit to ward off the growing darkness, dimmed and snuffed themselves. The flames dancing in the twin braziers at either side of the hall fell away to fading embers. A ray of silver-gold moonlight streamed through the skylight at the apex of the throne room, bathing the table in pale gloom. In this gloom, Gammir's black mail gleamed and sparkled like the midnight sea.

"Your fool of a son is dead," Gammir told Ammon. "By my own hand."

He raised that same hand like some white jewel to glimmer in the moonlight. The King's eyes, and the eyes of all those at the table, watched his writhing fingers. Gammir smiled.

The hand struck like a pallid viper and seized the throat of Ammon. The King's eyes bulged, his wine spilled across the table, and the ladies of the court screamed. A roar like that of a tiger split the air, and Gammir's teeth sank into Ammon's throat. A gout of scarlet spewed across the plates, goblets, and the steaming pig carcass.

The guards rushed forward, crying alarm, but the shadows along the walls rose up to seize them, ripping mail and flesh with phantom claws. Gammir drank deep of the blood gushing from his uncle's pierced neck vein, his merciless hand holding Ammon still against his own feasting board. The sons of Omirus rushed at him, raising jeweled scimitars. A glance from Gammir froze them in terror, and the shadows rushed forth to enshroud them, lifting them above the marble floor. They slashed futilely at the air with their weapons, bellowing hate and fear.

The seven sisters of Ammon ran, but rising walls of darkness blocked every exit. Terrible things floated out from those walls to gather them up in arms cold as death. The throne room was a vault of echoing screams, splashing blood, and death. Gammir, finished at last with the King's sharp juices, turned one by one to the other guests. He let the Dwellers in Shadow take the impotent guardsmen and the terrified servants. He heard their bones crunching and the pieces of their torn bodies slapping against the floor as he went from lady to lady . . . aunt to aunt . . . sucking at the necks of his mother's sisters. A wolf among penned sheep would have had no easier a feast.

This royal blood was saccharine, tasting of privilege, ripe fruits, good wine, and glittering ruby. It spilled across the table, the floor, stained the white-gold pillars to the red of cherries. The blood that fell across Gammir's black mail seeped into the non-metal, feeding its enchantment. Gammir saved the two young Dukes for last. They wept like infants, minds reeling in the horror of the slaughter whose every second they had witnessed.

"Cousins . . ." said Gammir, his lips and chin dripping dark fluid. He stared at them with a predator's eyes, his tongue flicking like a Serpent's. The shadows about their bodies lowered them within reach of his teeth. "You need weep no more. The end of your suffering has come. Your father will soon join you."

He sank his teeth into the neck of Dutho, tearing out the warm juice within, slurping it into his belly. Pyrus wailed beside him, and the legion of shadows swirled and feasted in their own mysterious ways among the mutilated bodies. Dutho, drained to a still whiteness, fell from Gammir's grasp and lay in a black puddle.

He looked up from the corpse and saw Tadarus standing among the shadows.

"No!" he shouted, pointing with a bloody claw that was his finger. "You cannot be here!"

Tadarus only stared at him, wordlessly accusing him of being the fiend he truly was.

Gammir tore off the purple cloak of Udurum, stained black with the blood of Ammon's court, and threw it at the ghost. "Take it!" he screeched, and the shadow-things writhed and twitched. They flowed about the ghost of Tadarus like harmless vapor. They could not touch him. He was already dead. Perhaps he was one of them.

Brother, said the wraith. It made no move to take up the cloak. The fabric lay over the corpse of a dead Princess, soaking in the bloody pool beneath her. The shadow-things seethed and snuffled between the pillars. Behind the walls of darkness that barricaded the chamber, Gammir heard the shouts and cries of soldiers and priests.

"What do you want from me?" asked Gammir. "Why torment me? Do my bidding as these other dead things do . . . or leave me be."

Why have you called me here to witness this? asked the ghost. It wept ethereal tears. *Can you not see what you have become? What you are becoming? Turn back from this path of shadows. It is not too late to redeem yourself with the edge of a clean blade.*

Gammir grabbed the throat of quivering Duke Pyrus, the only thing left living in the chamber besides himself. The tendrils of shadow moved away, and the Duke's mouth was freed. "Please . . . " he wept. "P-p-please, cousin . . . " Gammir smelled the tang of filth among the blood. The whelp had soiled himself.

"I'll ignore you, Tadarus," said Gammir. "As I ignore the bleating of these pigs."

Can you ignore yourself? You called me here, as you did before, to remind you . . .

"Remind me of what?" said Gammir, still holding Pyrus in his hands, a begging, dripping sack of meat.

That you are human, said the specter. *You are not one of these things that serve you, no more than I am. Remember, Fangodrel. Remember the warmth of sunlight, and the ink you scrawled on countless parchments. Remember who you are. This is why you called me.*

"No!" bellowed Gammir. "I did not call you . . . You haunt me! This – all this – is who I am. I've embraced my true heritage . . . a legacy of blood and power."

Tadarus was gone. Shadows swam in the empty air where the apparition had stood.

Gammir dropped the squirming Pyrus onto the floor, where the lad immediately lost consciousness. *My belly is full of royal blood*, he told himself. *I do not need this one. Let him carry the tale of what was done here. Let them know what is coming for all of them. Let them see.*

The black horse walked out from a wall of shadow, pacing toward him through spreading pools of red. Gammir leaped upon its back, leaving the cloak of Tadarus among the corpses. A pulse of shimmering sorcery ran along his limbs, and the horse sprouted its immense bat-like wings. It crashed through the skylight toward the bloated moon, leaving a shower of glass in its wake. The walls of darkness fell and the warriors of Shar Dni rushed in to view the massacre as a black cloud flowed upward through the broken ceiling and disappeared in the night.

Now, hours later, a dark coast appeared along the southern horizon. At last, the shores of Khyrei. The phantom steed's speed was terrific, fueled by the potency of the Sharrian blood. The sun would not rise for quite some while, but already the beast arced down toward the vast spread of the jungle lands. The steaming wilderness looked black beneath the stars, but its true color was that of fresh-spilled blood . . . like the petals of the bloodflower he had used as a surrogate for the liquid itself.

Ianthe's capital hugged the coast, and the jungles ran from its southernmost wall as far as the eye could see. Here was the thorny palace of onyx and jet he had seen in the depths of the Red Dream. Its spires stood sharp as barbed spears, ready to pierce the moon and drink the red rain of its death. The city's buildings, too, were of black stone, low and dull, bearing none of the glory of the splendid palace. The castle's central tower bore a crown of curving spikes, and flocks of jungle bats flew about its balconies and bridges. In the light of the sun, the dark palace would stand against the backdrop of scarlet jungle as it had stood against the flames of the Red Dream. The city cowering in the shadow of those regal towers, with its thousands upon thousands of pale slaves and bronze-masked warriors, would all be his. It was already his. This was his birthright, laid before him at last.

Somewhere within that edifice of night, long rebuilt from the days of Vod's perfidy, the pale Empress sat waiting to kiss his lips and embrace him with a passion his own mother had never shown. His gorgeous, ageless, grandmother, Ianthe the Claw. She kept a hoard of secrets hidden here, and they would open wide for him now like ruby blossoms.

The black steed flew over the black ramparts and entered the grounds of Ianthe's citadel.

She received him in the eight-sided courtyard grown thick with jungle plants, the gossamer flow of her gown disturbed by the wind of the black horse's wings. She stared at him with eyes that mirrored the pre-dawn sky, ripe with miniature constellations. The beast faded to a dark fog and wafted from his body as his booted feet met the stones of the yard. Now the simmering heat of Khyrei washed over him; in the fierce winds of the upper air he had not felt it. It crawled across his skin now, damp and thick, an invisible layer of wet silk beneath the cool exterior of his shadow-mail. He stood before her not in any dream or vision, but in the quivering, sweating flesh. He inhaled the jasmine scent of her skin, dazzled by the moonlight bright as diamonds on her skin.

The spiderweb of a crown rose from her alabaster forehead, pushing back the whiteness of her thick hair. Her lean shoulders supported a diaphanous robe, cut low below a necklace of jade, moonstones, and opals. Golden bands encircled her arms above and below the elbows, and the rings on her lithe fingers refracted the light of the stars. Her nails were the claws of a panther, hard and sharp as diamond. About her narrow waist hung a belt of silver set with lapis lazuli, sparkling above the triangular shadow of her loins. Diamonds blazed on her slim ankles, and her long feet were bare on the jet surface of the cobbles. She stood the exact height as him, and her feline face met his own with an expression of perfect grace. Her lips were the color of wet, delicious blood; her smile thrilled and frightened him.

"My Prince, my Blood, the Son of my Son," she said, her eyes locking onto his. He could never look away from those eyes unless she wished it. "Prince Gammir . . . welcome home." She wrapped her arms around him, and he melted into her. Tears ran along his cheeks, but he did not care.

"The King of Shar Dni is dead," he whispered into her ear, a pointed porcelain seashell.

She pulled away and took his face between her hands. Her smiled was unchanged.

"I see his blood swimming in your eyes," she said. "You make me proud."

She led him by the hand along the starlit glades, between a pair of guards with the masks of leering demons, their husky bodies shelled with intricate armor. The blades of their spears were hooked and curved, works of art that could only be used for murder. Once past the main gate, she conducted him down a long hallway past more of the faceless guards, through a great hall where slaves cowered like dogs to await her pleasure. She ignored them. He drank in the sights of the place, the pillars of jet and ruby, vast murals of war and ritual, demons and Serpents crawling across gilded frescoes. Witchlight filled the corridors; glowing balls of flame hung weightless in the air, shifting from red to orange to green and amber. It seemed the walls were alive with grotesque beauty. Silent as the night itself, a black panther glided from a passage and nuzzled against Ianthe's slender legs. She stopped for a moment to stroke its massive head between the ears.

"Say hello to your new Prince, Miku," she told the cat. It stared at him with yellow eyes, slit with green. Its red tongue came out and licked his hand. Pearly fangs hovered over the skin of his hand but did not threaten. The tongue was rough, yet pleasant. He smiled at the beast, smelling its raw-meat breath, and recognized a kindred spirit.

"Beautiful," he told her. Instinctively he knew the panther was female. It glided about his legs now like a playful puppy.

"Come," said Ianthe. He followed, and the panther loped behind him.

They climbed a set of black spiral stairs carved with wards and runes of an unknown language, past the arched doorways of sealed chambers. At the very top of the stairs, she opened a portal of heavy bronze with a wave of her hand. Inside lay her inner sanctum. A pointed dome rose above a hall large as a throne room, but filled with the paraphernalia of sorcery.

A desk of black wood sat piled with curling scrolls and moldering books. A collection of ancient tomes lined the shelves on the walls. The skulls of humans, beasts, and other entities also sat upon the shelves, some with burning candles perched atop their empty craniums. Artifacts from obscure ages hung upon the walls: the shields of fallen empires, jeweled blades of esoteric design, daemonic tapestries spun of gold and platinum, and many other curiosities for which he could find no name. An oval mirror taller than a man stood along the wall, its frame carved into the forms of grinning gargoyles and grasping limbs of demons. The entire room swam murkily in the depths of that glass, a distorted reflection of what was real. At the very top of its frame a fanged devil's face held a massive yellow topaz in its jaws. Of all the weird contrivances in the chamber, the cloudy mirror seemed the most strange.

Four windows rose high along the walls of the sanctum. They looked north, east, south, and west over city, ocean, and jungle. This was the summit of the great barbed tower standing above all others. Outside the sun was stirring, and the eastern horizon glowed orange and violet. The moon sank into the rolling jungle hills. Ianthe raised her hand again, and black drapes fell across the four windows, blotting out the dawn. A globe of spinning fire hovered in the center of the chamber, casting stark shadows and saffron light.

Miku the panther crawled onto a pillowed couch and licked at her paws.

"This is the heart of my wisdom, the center of my power," Ianthe said. "The seat of learning here is now yours." She motioned to the high-backed chair, much like a throne, sitting behind the cluttered desk. "Sit. Your journey was long. You must now be comforted."

She clapped her hands, for what reason he did not know, and turned to the great mirror. "This the Glass of Eternity," she said. "It will show you the past, the present, and sometimes the future."

The chamber door swung open, and a hulking guard dragged in two slaves by chains attached to neck-collars. They were two girls, young and pretty, naked and shaved bald from head to foot. The guard grunted behind his fanged mask, and Ianthe waved him away. As the door closed, the two slaves huddled together on the chamber's woven rug. They made no attempt to escape or cry out. They quivered with fear, and Gammir's lust began to rise. No, his thirst. But there was no longer any difference. He licked his lips.

Ianthe ignored the cowering girls. "Grandson," she spoke from beside the dark mirror, "what do you know of the world's history? Did your northern tutors teach you any truth?"

"I know of the Age of Serpents," he told her. "The birth of the Uduru, the Time of Flame, and the Five Tribes."

She laughed dismissively. "As I thought . . . You know nothing. This continent is far older than the six kingdoms that claim it," she said. "Older than you can imagine." She gestured to the mirror, turned her eyes upon it, and the light in the glass swam. It became a vision, moving and living inside the oval frame, like a scene outside a window.

A primal landscape of volcanoes, flame, and raging oceans took shape in the glass. Vast beasts, terrible and alien, lumbered across the steaming rocks. Blazing stars hung above the primeval world, far more than he had seen in any modern sky. Dark things moved in the starry void, sinking to earth, colossal and formless, gleaming with eyes of fire.

The creatures from the void took on terrestrial shapes . . . They became colossal obsidian gods, and lesser beings worshipped them – walked gladly into their open maws, built idols to honor them. Fantastic cities grew like fungus about their towering temples. The creatures who walked those twisting streets and gave tributes of blood and flesh were not human, but some distant ancestor of man. Apish, brutal, and filthy, they nevertheless built a crude civilization, carving it from the hot stones of the earth. Volcanoes roared and sank their cities beneath floods of magma, and the green ocean washed in to fog the world with steam.

The beings of darkness strode through the gaseous atmosphere, raising up the crawling, shuffling life-forms they found into new and more bizarre civilizations. Impossible architectures sprouted mould-like from the primordial swamps. Again the temples of the dark gods rose into the sweltering sky, and a red sun slowly burned away the continental marshes. Again the shaggy ancestors of humanity came into the vision, making war on the city-builders with stone and spear, ultimately claiming their domains. Then the pre-humans warred upon each other, and the dark gods watched in amusement, feeding on them now and then like great reptiles on tiny insects.

The sub-human empires fell, and the dark gods reveled in the tumult of the unstable earth. Millennia passed, and the pattern repeated itself. New races came and built their temples and cities . . . they fell, conquered by other races, or devoured by the whims of the dark ones . . . only to spring up again in some other corner of the continent.

The void-born ones walked upon the world, wrapped in the

celestial glory of their immensity. They began to take the forms of terrible beings, or beings of great beauty, playing always their cruel games with the lesser forms of life . . . fostering empires, then watching as they crumbled. They moved like the shadows of mountains across burgeoning forests. They raised or sank island kingdoms for their pleasure.

These patterns played out again and again on the surface of the mirror. Gammir forgot himself and the chamber in which he sat. He saw the ancient beings, the terrible gods of death and war, the blood-hungry deities of a hundred nations, the endless wars of tribe against tribe, city against city, the genocides, the slaveries, the annihilations and rebirths of a thousand peoples, all leading toward the birth of humanity and its own proud kingdoms. The patterns swirled, repeating, unchangeable. The dark gods laughed, and reveled, and toyed with empires.

Until they grew bored . . .

Some of the dark ones took to the void, losing themselves among the stars. Others dwindled to mere shadows, and took on the forms of lesser beings – men and women who ruled over the tiny kingdoms of earth. Still others faded into distant worlds, stretching their bulk into unseen dimensions, while some merely slumbered, sinking into the bones of the earth and becoming one with its stones, winds, and waters.

Yet a few of the dark ones who had fallen into fleshly shapes . . . *remembered*. They remembered the caress of the void, the taste of blood spilled on their altars, the divine power that was once theirs. They could never regain their lost forms.They were *diminished* . . . absorbed into the world they had toyed with for long eons.

Yet they *remembered*, and they drew to themselves the remnants of the great powers that once were their birthright. They saw into the stars and moaned the loss of their brothers and sisters. They belonged now to this singular world and its never-ending patterns of birth and death, night and day, creation and destruction, rising and falling through the centuries. Time itself had conquered their divinity.

Among the empires of men they were called *sorcerer*.

Or *sorceress*.

The mirror grew cloudy again, and Gammir blinked. The vision was gone. His head spun, and Ianthe sat herself upon the desk before him. She caressed his cheek like a favorite sculpture.

"We are of the Old Breed, you and I," she said, and he understood. "There is much that is forgotten and will remain so . . . yet there is still much to learn. We will play the games of conquest. We will spread blood and fire, for this world is ours."

He smiled, and she kissed his lips.

She turned away and pulled him by the hand toward the cowering girl-slaves. They would not meet his eyes or hers. Fear consumed them. His thirst raged.

"Now we drink royal wine," she said.

With a single finger, she slit the throats of both girls.

They drank deeply from the writhing bodies, drawing upon every last drop of precious fluid. Potent with the tang of youth.

They arose from the limp forms, dripping red and satisfied, and Ianthe laughed.

She is the most beautiful thing I have ever seen . . . or will ever see.

He licked the bloody residue from her chin, like a young hound feeding from its mother.

She held him then in silence. The world faded into oblivion.

"My sweet boy," she said. "My sweet Gammir."

The panther Miku lapped at the red pool beneath the dead slaves.

A subtle movement in the close air of the chamber, or perhaps a faint sound, caused Ianthe to let him go. She turned to stare at the Glass of Eternity.

A new image floated in the mirror. On a tall throne of ebony and crystal sat a man robed in darkness. A strand of blood-bright rubies hung across his chest, and a long mane of slate-gray hair swept back from his high forehead. A crown of gold and sapphire sat strangely upon his tight-fleshed skull, as if it did not belong there. His eyes gleamed, colorless fires in their deep sockets, and his fingers were long-nailed talons. He stared *through* the mirror, directly at the blood-drenched grandmother and grandson. His face was cruel and stone-like, but he smiled.

"Ianthe," his voice echoed across the chamber. The sound of bones grinding. "You enjoy yourself too much . . . "

The Empress returned his smile and licked the remaining gore from her lips.

"Gammir has returned," she said to the mirror. "As I said he would."

The mirror-King's eyes pierced Gammir through the mirror. "Never did I doubt it. All that which was lost shall be regained in time."

"Gammir," said Ianthe, her hand on his shoulder, "meet the Great Elhathym . . . Ruler of Yaskatha long before it held that name, and now returned to claim his birthright – just as *you* have this day. You shall be great allies."

Gammir stared at Elhathym through the pane of enchanted glass.

"Hail, Prince of Khyrei," said the sorcerer.

"Hail, King of Yaskatha," said Gammir, a single red droplet falling from his chin.

He knew instantly that he hated this man, and would always hate him.

Ianthe laughed and kissed his bloody cheek.

"We three have much to discuss," she said.

She burned like a pale flame between the locked eyes of Gammir and Elhathym.

20

Mother and Daughter

The great eagle fought the winds of winter, flying north into the Giantlands. When the snow and sleet grew too fierce, she rose above the winter clouds, where the air was even colder but the snow did not reach. The talons of her claws were black and shining, like her eyes, and they gripped a heavy bundle wrapped in leather, bound in sailors' rope. The pinnacles of frozen mountains pierced the cloud-roof, so she knew the Grim Mountains lay below.

Night and day she flew, all the way from Murala on the coast. Days ago she had entered that town wearing the body of a Giantess, carrying Vod's remains in a corroded iron chest. The folk there were unused to the presence of Uduru, and they had stared at her with wonder and curiosity. Three decades earlier they would have run screaming from her. That was before Vod brought Giants and Men together and changed the desert to a green and fertile plain. How could they know this weary Giant-girl carried the very bones of the hero himself . . . the Giant-King who had conquered every enemy but the sea?

With her oversized fingers she had pulled the ancient emeralds from their rust-caked holes in the surface of the chest, trading one of them to a Muralan jeweler for a bag of gold. After walking leagues along the desolate shore, yet before she took lodging and rest, she hired the town's undertaker to remove Vod's body from the trunk and restore it as best he could.

"I am sorry, Milady," he told her the next day. "The body of this poor Giant has obviously lain for months under the sea, and only his jumbled bones are left. But I have cleaned the salt encrustations from them and laid them out on my embalming table. Would you care to take a look?"

"No," she said. "Wrap them for me . . . in some expensive oilcloth. I must carry them a long way." She gave him the bag of gold and he followed her instructions to the letter. The iron chest was not only rusted and undependable, it was far too heavy. If she walked with it on her shoulder, it might take her a year to cross the Stormlands, then the mountains, and reach Udurum. She must fly instead. When she picked up Vod's remains that evening, the undertaker had wrapped each bone carefully in a velvet cloth, then stacked them inside a canvas bag and tied it at the top like a great pouch of coins. She was glad of the velvet, for it kept Vod's bones from rattling when she carried the parcel.

She walked inland from Murala, far enough that no eyes would see her. Then she took the form of the great eagle, grabbed the bone-bag in her claws and flew north toward the dark and jagged horizon.

After days of flight the mountains sank beneath an ocean of clouds flowing northward as far as her eagle eyes could see. She pulled back her pinions and arced down to break the cloud layer. The Forest of Uduria rushed beneath her, cloaked in a mantle of white snow. She skirted the heads of the mighty Uygas, speeding toward home. She was unsure how long it had been since she left Udurum. She longed to see her mother again and feel the warmth of her hugs. There would be tears, both for the end to her absence and the return of Vod's remains. No longer would the false hope of Vod's survival linger in her mother's heart. His bones would bring Shaira peace, as they had for Sharadza. Only by knowing the truth of his death could they truly let him go.

The jet walls of Udurum rose from the pale forest. The dark towers wore hoods of white, and the city steamed its warmth into the afternoon sky. There was plenty of daylight left, but the gloom of winter simulated an early darkness. The watch-fires along the city wall blazed like miniature suns. The lights of street lamps and windows created the illusion of a vast blanket scattered with twinkling jewels. She beat her tired wings toward the palace and came to ground in the snow-packed courtyard where she used to meet Fellow and hear his stories. It seemed so long ago. She still thought of Fellow and Iardu as two separate entities, even though she knew it was a lie. Iardu had lied to her for years. But perhaps *all* stories were lies, and all storytellers were liars. Perhaps what really mattered were the lessons one could learn from a well-told lie.

Of all the trees, paths, and walls in the courtyard, she saw only one walkway clear of recent snows. It led to the far precinct of the gardens and the Royal Mausoleum. A brazier burned now before its doors, turning their white marble to gold. The mausoleum itself had also been scraped clean of ice and snow. Her heart sank. There could be only one reason why servants had polished and cleared the tomb, which had never been used. She meant to inaugurate it with her father's bones. But someone else in her family had died and already been laid to rest there. A pit of emptiness yawned open inside her stomach.

Mother!

The great bag of bones sat in the snow now, and Sharadza ran toward the palace gate in her girl form. Guards stared in awe and shouted as she ran by them, leaving a trail of melting snow. She heard their commotion behind her as word spread. "The Princess has returned! Gods of Earth and Sky be praised! Send word to the captain! Send word to the Queen!"

But there was no need. Sharadza ran up the stair of the Great Tower to the oak-and-gold door of the royal apartments. For some reason, there were no Uduru sentinels in the halls today. A man stationed outside the Queen's chamber knelt as Sharadza banged on the locked door.

"Mother!" she shouted. "Mother, are you there?" Saltwater welled in her eyes, which were green now that she was a girl again.

"Her Majesty is resting," said the guard, and Sharadza sighed.

She turned to the bronze-armored man. "Then who . . . " she started. "The tomb?"

The door opened at the hands of a servant and Queen Shaira stood in the doorway, dressed in a thick gown of white wool. Her face lit up as her eyes met Sharadza's.

They fell into each other's arms, and their tears fell each upon the other's shoulders. Shaira pulled her into the room, rubbing her chilled hands, calling for mulled wine and a warm dry robe. Servants bustled in a fury of excitement and restrained joy.

They sat together on a soft divan and Shaira kissed her cheeks. Sharadza saw her mother clearly now as she wiped her sudden tears away. Shaira looked old. Lines of worry had invaded the smooth skin of her face; dark rings hung below her eyes, and crow's feet nested in their corners. The green irises floated in pools of bloodshot milk.

"Oh, Mother," she moaned and pulled her close again.

"The Gods are good," said Shaira. "You have come back to me. My selfish, foolish, stubborn little girl!" Relief, rage, and affection mingled to a dark brew in her mother's eyes.

"I am so sorry," said Sharadza. Her words were not enough. What had happened to wear down her mother so heavily? Or was she already this worn when Sharadza had stolen away?

"Why?" asked Shaira. "Tell me first why you would do such a thing."

Sharadza looked at the burgundy carpet. A servant handed her a mug of steaming spice-wine. She cradled it in her hands, unable to look now at her mother. "For Father," she said. "I thought I could help him."

"How?" asked her mother. "Where did you go? Who talked you into leaving me? Don't you know how sick with worry I was? Don't you know how I've suffered without you?"

There it was. The cold stab of guilt mixed into the warm liquid as she sipped the wine. "I left you the letter," she said, hating herself for the words. "I promised I'd be back. And here I am."

"Where did you go?" asked Shaira. "What have you done?"

"I have learned so much," she said. "*Remembered* so much. I am the daughter of Vod, and I know now what that truly means."

Shaira stared at her. That was no answer. She waited.

"Who lies in the tomb?" asked Sharadza.

Shaira's eyes brimmed again. She turned her face to the ceiling, or to the Gods, or both. "Tadarus," she sighed. "Your brother is dead, Sharadza."

Her lungs stopped working. She could neither inhale or exhale. Then she burst into weeping, and the paralysis was broken. Her mother's arms were a dim comfort around her neck.

"How?" she asked.

Shaira held her in silence for a moment, steeling herself for what must be told. Then she spoke of Fangodrel the Kinslayer . . . how he called up demons and murdered Tadarus with some vile sorcery. She went on, spilling secrets like tears. She told of Fangodrel's bastardy, of her time in the dungeons of Khyrei, slave to Gammir the Cruel, the true father of her eldest child. Of the day Vod crossed the Golden Sea, wrought vengeance on the pale devils, and carried her home.

"The evil of his true father runs in Fangodrel's veins," said Shaira. "As much as we tried, we could not keep it down. And now it has consumed him. He fled to seek refuge in Khyrei, where Ianthe keeps her wicked court."

Sharadza's wine had grown cool in the cup, but she drank the last of it anyway. Her head spun from its potency, but it made this news more bearable. She had lost not one brother, but *two*. One to death . . . and one to sorcery.

Shaira told her that Vireon had gone south with four other Princes and a mysterious girl whom he apparently loved. He had vowed to avenge the death of Tadarus.

"Mother, can you forgive me for not being here for all of this?"

Shaira nodded, kissed her forehead. What other choice had she? A child who was thought lost and then regained was a treasure, no matter how vexing that child's behavior. Sharadza's weariness crept upon her suddenly and she longed for sleep. She could not ponder Fangodrel's betrayal right now. Yet there was one thing she must do now.

"Come with me," she said. "Put on your warm clothes and come into the courtyard."

Despite her protests, Shaira did as her daughter bid. "I have much more to tell you, Sharadza," she said, pulling on a cloak of gray fur.

"Tomorrow," said Sharadza. "I am too weary. But there is something I must give you before I sleep."

Shaira ran a hand through her daughter's hair before they left the chamber. "You are taller," she said, a tinge of pride in her voice. Sharadza grinned.

They descended the tower steps and passed a pair of Giants guarding the doors of the Great Hall. Sharadza blinked. They were female Giants . . . Uduri. To her memory there had been no

Uduri on the palace staff. Another change. She saw no other Giants that night.

A trio of spear-bearing soldiers followed them into the white garden. Sharadza bade them stand some distance away as she led her mother to the great bag. She stood before it as if to perform some rite or ceremony.

"What is this?" asked the Queen.

"Father's bones," said Sharadza. "They are all that is left of him. He walked into the sea and drowned."

Shaira stared at the bulging leather canvas coated with crystals of frost. She looked at her daughter. "You . . . Where did you . . ." She was incapable of finishing the question.

"I spoke with the Mer-Queen, Mother. She did not kill him. She swore it. She let me take him home, though the waters had taken most of what we remember. Now he can lie in the tomb that he built. Next to poor Tadarus."

Shaira did not weep. Her daughter was amazed by this fact but too tired to ponder it.

"We must have a funeral," said Sharadza.

"No," said the Queen.

"What?"

"No," said Shaira. "The People of Udurum have endured too much sorrow. Too much death. There will be no march, no procession, no ceremony. We will lay Vod's bones in the tomb tomorrow, and the Sky Priest will give a blessing. No one else must know he has died."

"But . . . why?"

"As long as our people believe that Vod may return some day, they will have *hope*. If we take that away from them . . ."

Sharadza nodded. She had taken that hope from her mother. She had been wrong to do it.

"I'm sorry," she said.

The Queen kissed her cheek. "You honor your father with this act. He would be proud of you. As I am."

She insisted that Sharadza go and sleep. Sharadza could not argue.

Two of the soldiers carried the heavy bag into the palace and stored it in a secure vault for the night, completely unaware that they shouldered the very bones of their dead and beloved King.

Sharadza slept soundly in her warm and familiar bed. Her dreams were formless flowing questions. Or perhaps incomplete glimpses into the future. Or fragments of the past.

Nestled in the comfort of oblivion, she did not know or care.

During a breakfast of fresh bread, green cheese, eggs, and pomegranate juice, Sharadza learned from her mother about the Ice King and his kingdom in the White Mountains. The Uduru had marched north a month ago, only one day after the five Princes marched south. Even the Giants of Steephold had come down from the heights to join the exodus – their castle was fallen in any case. A legion of Shaira's warriors would lead architects and masons into the pass in early spring to rebuild the fortress. Now Men, not Giants, would keep the watch on Vod's Pass. There had been many a tearful farewell between the Uduru and their human compatriots in the city. Some of the departing Giants were the longtime lovers of the Uduri, who bade them go north and procreate. Such was the selfless nature of their love.

"Will they ever return?" Sharadza asked.

"Some will," Shaira said. "They will bring Udvorg wives and children south with them, and they'll pick up right where they left off. Others will grow to love the Icelands. They will enjoy the presence of a King who is truly a Giant. But even for those who return to Udurum, it will be years from now. Time passes more slowly for the Uduru."

“Was Uncle Fangodrim happy?”

Shaira smiled. “You should have seen him when Vireon gave him a wife! He danced like a schoolboy. Danthus, Dabruz, they were the first to be married to those blue-skinned Uduri. Some even gained instant children already half-grown!”

“Why did *they* go north then?” she asked. “Those to whom Vireon brought wives?”

“A show of unity,” said Shaira. “Fangodrim was First Among Giants in Udurum. He could not send his people off to the Ice King unless he went too. It was a matter of honor. The rest of them felt the same.”

“All but the Uduri.”

“Yes,” said the Queen. “Yet they supported their men. Many gave up their mates for the future of their race. Most will not get them back.”

“So your Elite Guard is now these ninety-nine Uduri . . . ”

“I could do no less than honor them in such a way,” said Shaira.

“It is good the Giants will live, and they have Vireon to thank for it. My brother the hero.”

Shaira smiled. “You should have seen the feast. They honored him for days. Already he is a legend in their tales. He did a fine thing.”

“What about this girl? Who is she? Is she beautiful?”

“She is,” said Shaira, “and a sorceress. She lived in the forest. Alone. Try as I might, I could not bring myself to disapprove of her. She seems such an honest soul. And she dotes on him. I have never seen him so attached to any girl.”

Sharadza laughed. “They say love comes to all men when they least expect it. Perhaps it is the same with women . . . ”

The Queen’s face was serious, and her eyes looked far away. “I think not. Women wait for love with the patience of buds lying beneath the snow. This always seems the way.”

"Did you wait for Father's love?" asked the Princess.

The Queen grew quiet. Sharadza chewed at a steaming hunk of bread. Warm food, such a delight. How long had it been? She could not say. Her days in the cave with the Iardu-crone remained unanswerable to time, a blur of memories.

"Yes," said Shaira. "I waited for him." She looked out the open window of the dining hall into the crystal freeze of the garden. She could not see the polished tomb from this angle, but Sharadza knew she thought of it. In a few hours, the Sky Priest would arrive, and they would quietly lay Vod's bones in the crypt alongside those of his eldest son. Snowbirds chirped and darted among the snow-laden branches.

"Mother, what do you know of . . . Iardu?"

Shaira turned to stare at her. She hesitated, obviously deciding whether to lie or admit what she knew.

The Queen sighed. "Iardu the Shaper," she said. "A sorcerer who lives on an isle in the Cryptic Sea. He is mentioned in many of the history texts, especially in the *Chronicles of Uurz*."

"What about the Pearl of Aiyaia?" said the Princess. "The stone Father stole from the Mer-Queen?"

"He called out the name of that stone in his sleep often enough," Shaira said. "Sometimes he called the name of Iardu as well. At the end, he hardly slept at all."

"The Mer-Queen told me Vod stole the Sacred Pearl at Iardu's request."

Shaira's shock seemed genuine. She had no words.

"Do you know why? Father would never tell us, but do you know why he stole the sea-stone for Iardu?"

The Queen dabbed at her eyes with a silken napkin. "I . . . I think that *now* I do."

"Now? What do you mean?"

"When I first met Ordra – Vod, your father –" Shaira

whispered, "he was a Giant. As tall and fearsome as any Uduru. Yet in his heart he was a Man. I was in a caravan traveling across the desert to Uurz. The son of the Old Emperor had come to sweep me away from Shar Dni. My father had granted him my hand in marriage. It would seal the peace between our kingdoms. Prince Aivor was young and handsome, though I barely knew him. I was glad to be his bride.

"Bandits set upon us in the desert. Aivor fought bravely with his soldiers, but he died. We all would have perished that day but for a young Giant who rushed out of the dunes and drove off the raiders. His name was Ordra, who would one day be called Vod.

"Aivor and I would have been married when we reached Uurz, but now that could never be. Ordra came with us to the city. I asked him to. Even then, I saw something in him . . . something in his eyes. The way he looked at me. I cannot explain it.

"When we reached the city, Emperor Iryllah, who was the oldest man I have ever seen in this world, declared that he would take me as his seventh wife in order to seal the peace treaty. But first would come a year of mourning for his fallen son; I must wait until then for the marriage. I was to live in the luxury of his palace all that time. Ordra became my personal guard, and my constant companion. I read to him books from the Great Library. We counted the stars, and all the court thought him a hero. But there was more between us. It grew as a plant grows, sinking its roots deep in our hearts. We fell in love.

"I had no wish to marry old Iryllah. It would be a loveless arrangement and children would be impossible. I knew it was my duty to the throne of Shar Dni . . . I had promised my father. Yet I grew selfish. Love can make you selfish, did you know that? It can do wonderful things, yes, but it can ruin you as well.

"I read about Iardu the Shaper in the Emperor's books . . . how his sorcery could change men into beasts and beasts into men. He sometimes visted Iryllah's court in the shape of kindly men or friendly animals. He was the master of shape and form. So I told Ordra about him and . . . I hatched a plan. I could say it was Ordra's idea, but it was all me. I will take the blame. I wanted to escape before the end of the mourning year and avoid marrying the codger. I wanted to be with Ordra, though it seemed impossible. So I told Ordra to seek the Shaper on his island . . . to ask a great favor.

"Ordra would ask the sorcerer to turn him from Giant into Man, so we could be together at last. We would run away. Even if my father cast us out of Shar Dni, we would find somewhere to live. You see, Ordra *hated* being a Giant, for he was raised by human parents. He thought himself a freak, that his great size was a curse . . . and I am ashamed to say that I did too. Later we learned it was not a curse at all.

"Giant Ordra went away, and months later he returned as Man. As we made ready to escape the very next day, the Uduru laid siege to Uurz. We were trapped in the city, fugitives from the palace."

The Queen paused in her story. "Ah," Sharadza said. "I have heard this part of the story. Vod challenged the King of Giants to a duel, which he won, and so lifted the siege of the city."

"No," said Shaira. "That is not how it happened at all. Men are liars and they have short memories. Ordra *lost* that challenge and was taken prisoner by the Giants. Iardu had taught him to make himself a Man whenever he chose . . . but also to become a Giant again – his true self – whenever he wished. Iardu was wiser than either of us in that matter."

Sharadza's mouth fell open. "That's it, isn't it?" she said. "Father stole the Mer-Queen's Sacred Pearl for Iardu, so the Shaper would teach him sorcery."

The Queen nodded her head, lifting the napkin to her eyes again. Her red lips trembled.

"When Vod's nightmares began . . . and when he spoke of the Pearl . . . I suspected. But I never knew until this moment. Now the pieces all fit. Ordra stole it for Iardu and learned his shape-changing magic for *me*. He did it for me, Sharadza! And earned the curse of the Sea-Folk."

Sharadza grabbed her mother's hand. "Mother, you must understand. The Mer-Queen had all but forgotten her curse. It was *not* her who called Father to his death. It was not your fault."

"Yes, it was," said the Queen. "I made him go! I looked on his Giant body as a curse and I made him go to Iardu."

"It was his choice," said Sharadza. "And he was in love. You said yourself, love changes you. You know the philosopher Therokles? He said, 'Love is the death of Wisdom.' Do not blame yourself. Father would not want you to."

The Queen regained her composure. She squeezed her daughter's hands.

"Tell me though," said Sharadza. "Why did he take the name Vod?"

"When the Giants captured him, Fangodrim the Gray recognized Ordra as the lost son of his brother Fangodrel, who died at the fangs of the Serpent-Father. When he realized this was his own nephew, he gave Ordra his true name. Fangodrel the First had named his infant son Vod. Ordra was the name Vod's human foster-parents gave him. So Ordra become Vod, and regained his people. Yet he lost me . . . I blamed him for betraying Uurz to the Giants. A year later my father sent me to Khyrei to wed Prince Gammir."

"Then Vod rescued you," said Sharadza. "And re-won your love."

Queen Shaira nodded, a mix of old emotions dancing in her

eyes. She drank a cup of the pomegranate juice. "Are all your questions answered?" she asked.

"No," said Sharadza. "One remains. The most important."

Her mother looked at her, green eyes matching green.

"What was it that tormented Father so terribly that he would gladly walk into the sea and drown?"

Shaira's eyes fell. "*Her*," she said. "It had to be her. She took Vod and now she's taken Fangodrel. One is dead and one is lost."

"Who?" asked Sharadza.

"Ianthe," said her mother. "Empress of Khyrei . . . the sorceress. I told you how Vod brought her palace down about her ears, killing her husband and son. They were evil and deserved to die. We thought she had died too, but we were wrong. Word of her survival reached us years later, when the boys were still small. We thought she would stay away from us – New Udurum had become a great power – but her sorcery knew no bounds. It must have been her taking vengeance on Vod, poisoning his mind with visions. She stole his sanity . . . and now his adopted son."

Sharadza considered the enmity of the sorceress. Ianthe had sent the nightmare madness that killed her father and blamed it on the Mer-Queen. Then she had somehow seduced her grandson away from his foster-family – driven him to murder Tadarus as she had driven Vod to murder himself.

"Sharadza?" asked her mother.

"Yes?"

"Where did you go? Tell me now."

"I went to study . . . with Iardu," she said. Her mother's face tightened as if she had been smacked. "He taught me what he taught Father. He made me remember what I truly am. He taught me sorcery."

Shaira said nothing. She looked out the window again, studying the snow. *She is truly an old woman now. The last of her youth has fled, if not her beauty.* Sharadza felt pity for her mother and wanted to cry. But there had been enough tears lately.

"Tell me of these Princes," she asked. "Why does Vireon lead them south?"

"They go to Mumbaza," said the Queen. "To gain their alliance in the coming war."

"War?" said Sharadza. "Against whom?"

"Who else?" said the Queen. "*Khyrei.*" She spoke the name like an adder spits poison. "And Yaskatha . . . to regain the usurped throne."

"You have planned a war for vengeance?"

Shaira explained the growing tensions with Shar Dni, the nautical conflicts, the onslaught of Khyrein pirates, and the sorcery that had slain the true King of Yaskatha. Two sorcerers. Shaira and Vireon gathered nations to war against two beings of immense power, each with a vast army that dwarfed the size of Udurum's human legions. Shaira explained the plan to add Mumbaza to their ranks, to foster rebellion in Yaskatha. She would lead her own legions across the peaks when spring arrived.

Sharadza sat in stunned silence. It was not her father alone who had gone mad, it was the entire world.

"Is this right?" she asked. "Is it even wise? You know the cost of war, you've read the histories. Soldiers die gladly but it is the common people who suffer most. 'War is the death of innocence.'"

"Do not quote Therokles to me!" said her mother, rising from the breakfast chair. "That bitch took your father and two of your brothers. Her malevolence is legendary. She was spilling the blood of innocents long before you or I were ever born! She will pay, Sharadza. For all that she has done."

Sharadza recoiled from her mother's sudden rage, and the gravel tone of her voice. It was the sound of unchained hate, given rein and let run free.

"How can you hope to defeat both Ianthe and this Elhathym with swords and spears?" she asked. "How many mens' lives will you throw away in your lust for vengeance? How many more families will suffer as these armies tear across their lands and trample them to bloody dirt?"

"Vireon is the Son of Vod," said Shaira. "He is mighty. If I did not agree to this war, he would have gone off alone to find and murder Fangodrel. Now he will have four armies at his back when he faces Ianthe the Claw. As for the Yaskathan tyrant . . . he will have his hands full trying to hold on to a stolen throne. Our strategy is sound, Sharadza. I would not rush into war lightly."

It was no use. She could not reach her mother. The course had been set. Vireon was the master of the great horse upon which her pain and anger rode. The wheels of war were already in motion. Summer would bring blood and death washing across the world in a smothering tide.

"Come," said Shaira. "We must go to lay your father's bones in his tomb."

"No," said Sharadza. "I have spent enough time with those bones." She stalked through the arch to the main hall, grabbing up a cloak of sable fur.

"Where are you going, Sharadza?"

She turned around, buckling the hasp of the cloak. "To see Iardu. He is here . . . in the city. He always has been."

The Queen blinked at her. "Why?"

"This will be a war of sorcerers," said the Princess. "Who else should I see?"

She stalked through the Great Hall, brushing aside the guards who offered her escort. Across the palace grounds and into the city she went, knowing she would find him at the Molten Sparrow, his white beard stained by wine and lies.

21

Wisdom of the Shaper

The streets of Udurum were lined with snowdrifts. The main thoroughfares were trampled flat by the steady traffic of boots, hooves, carts, and wagons. The roofs of houses and stables lay under blankets of white, and an unsettling quiet filled the city. The rumbling laughter of Giants was gone. The clomping of their feet on the cobbles, the deep honey of their voices, their ribald drinking songs . . . all these were missing. The towering homes of the Uduru, longhouses built of Uyga logs and basalt blocks, all stood empty, windows filled with darkness. Even in the glare of pale sunlight, Udurum wore a mantle of gloom.

Sharadza walked past a mounted guardsman on his rounds, a seller of dried fruits hauling his wares in a cart, and a group of children playing at war among mounds of snow. She skirted the Market Plaza. Business was sluggish there without the great appetites of the Uduru, who usually bought up most of the produce and livestock. A herdsman led a dozen goats from the plaza, heading back into the countryside. His face, like the rest of the men and women she passed, was solemn. The heart of their city had ceased its thumping. Without the twelve hundred or so Giants that augmented its populace, there was little to separate Udurum from any other town or village. Except its great walls, tremendous palace, and those massive, tenant-less buildings.

She wondered how the coming war would affect these people. The best and strongest would join the legions, inspired by tales of war and conquest, the "glory" that all Men worshipped, but that existed only in stories. It was lies that fueled wars. More sages than Therokles had documented the horrors of actual warfare and its terrible cost to those who had nothing to do with the fighting. Men were like those children in the street throwing snowballs – eager to rush off into the misty depths of legend because they had no real understanding of where they were going. Even her own brother Vireon was caught up in the illusion.

She remembered Tadarus and him as young boys dreaming of battles and victories . . . studying their swords and shields as she studied the books and scrolls of the world's great thinkers. Fangodrel had been more like her, interested in scholarly pursuits. They called him "book lover" and laughed at him. Another reason for him to hate his brothers. As distant and cold to her as Fangodrel was, she still had loved him. Now that she knew they shared only a mother, the loss of him felt no less painful. But what she truly feared is that Fangodrel, bolstered by the might of Khyrei, would kill Vireon as he had killed Tadarus. The two were destined to meet, and one would die. Fangodrel had murdered Tadarus, so he must pay the price. She would mourn him when that day came, as she mourned Tadarus even now. And she would aid Vireon, her true brother, if she could.

Selfish, to be thinking of my own loss at such a time. This war will destroy thousands of families – brothers, fathers, cousins – women and children. The stakes were too great to fixate on the blood feud between Vireon and Fangodrel.

The sign of the Molten Sparrow hung from its usual doorjamb, on a street of taverns quiet as a row of tombs. A stray dog rooted through garbage in the alley, the only visible client of the larger establishments, which had catered mainly to Uduru. The Sparrow might actually pick up some business; it was too small for Giant patrons anyway.

She entered the common room, where bags of onions and empty wine bottles hung from the rafters. The smell here was not as bad as she remembered . . . a hint of spilled ale, smoke, and roasted mutton. A half-dozen Men with downcast faces – likely unemployed since the Giants' exodus – sat about the scattered tables nursing mugs of brown ale. Fellow sat at his usual place, a booth in the rear corner where he could look across the room and see everyone who came and went. He drank wine from a copper goblet, a bottle sitting half-drained at his elbow. His eyes turned toward her the moment she entered the torchlight. Despite his familiar smile, he was not Fellow at all . . . but Iardu the Shaper . . . a sorcerer and a legend.

She did not return his smile.

"Arthus, bring your finest goblet for the Princess," Fellow called to the tavern keeper.

The robust host noticed for the first time that a royal personage had entered his very own house. "Right away, Majesty!" He addressed Sharadza, not Fellow, and almost cracked his skull against the bar with an awkward bow.

Sharadza held her hand in his direction. "Save it," she said, not unkindly. "I did not come here to drink." She sat herself down across the table from Fellow.

"How was your . . . expedition?" he asked.

"Fruitful," she said. "I managed to bring his bones home."

He nodded, as if confirming what he already knew. Vod was truly dead. "You know about Tadarus . . . "

"I know about *everything*," she said.

"That is quite an accomplishment." He smiled drunkenly.

"How much have you drunk, Iardu?" she asked.

"Shhhhh," he urged her. "My name is Fellow, remember?"

She ran her tongue along the front of her upper teeth. Of all the times for him to be drunk . . .

"The Giants have left us," he said, feigning heartbreak. "The grand experiment is over. They've gone to seek blue-skinned wives and have cold-blooded little babies."

"Listen to me," she said, leaning closer to him. She closed the booth's stained curtain so the owner and his meager clientele would stop staring. "I know how you used my father for your own selfish ends. I know how you betrayed Indreyah, and how it gained you nothing. I know you have tried to use me as you used Vod. But I do not condemn you for any of this."

"What else do you know, child?" he asked, pouring dark wine into his cup.

"I suspect . . ." she said, "that it was you who stole the baby Vod from his parents before the fall of Old Udurum. You who gave him to that human couple to raise."

Fellow smiled. "You have learned a few things from me . . . a few things only. Did I not ask you to stay and learn more? Did I not?"

"Focus," she told him, taking the goblet from his hand. He watched it move down the table but made no attempt to grab for it. "Listen to me. Do you know there is a war brewing? Vireon, Andoses, and three other Princes are making an alliance with Mumbaza as we speak. My mother plans to lead her legions to join Dairon's. They will march to Shar Dni, and together they will invade Khyrei. They even plot a rebellion in Yaskatha."

Fellow nodded and sighed. "War is a season like any other . . . a sad season, yes, but it has its day . . ."

"Tell me what you know of this Ianthe the Claw, and this Elhathym who commands the dead."

His wrinkled eyes narrowed, looking beyond the walls of the tavern. "She is *old* . . . " he said. "Old as I am . . . and she *remembers*. He is . . . older than either of us." Then his voice fell to a gentle whisper. "He has come back from the void . . . taken a man's form again . . . after millennia. *She* brought him back."

"They are of the Old Breed," Sharadza said. "I knew it."

"More fearsome than their considerable legions is their sorcery," he said. "Men cannot stand against such dark powers. They have traveled the Outer Worlds . . . breached the realms of Living and Dead . . . and the elements are their playthings. The Dwellers in Shadow serve them – ghosts, demons, wraiths . . . and *worse* things."

"You made my father into the Giant-King," she said. "You shaped his life so that he would be both Man and Giant. You tried to stop Ianthe, didn't you? You tried to balance the world by giving it Vod of the Storms. And for a while it worked . . . "

He stared into her face, grinning without pleasure. "Nothing lasts, child. Not in this world."

"What about you? You have lasted. You wanted Vod to do what you feared to. Now you have a second chance. *Come with me*. Help me destroy her. And him . . . both of them. Before it's too late."

His face soured. "It is already too late," he said. "You have seen the patterns. The patterns never change. Though I tried and tried . . . they never change."

"What do you mean? You have re-shaped the world again and again. You *have* changed the patterns."

"No," he said. "I've only complicated them. Added a tiny flourish here or there. The river flows on. I stand on the shore making ripples with stones."

"I don't believe you."

"Give me that wine," he said. "I'll show you."

Reluctantly she handed him the full goblet. He poured half its contents onto the oaken table. It spread into a dark puddle, the color of half-dried blood. He stirred it with his forefinger.

"Look . . . " he said, his eyes growing large.

She stared at the puddle. The light of the table's candle flickered there, danced, and begain to swirl. The reflected flame broke into a tiny flood of colors, and visions danced on the surface of the wine.

An ancient plain, dotted with the raging fires of war. Shaggy men rush upon each other with stone axes, clubs, and their own gnashing fangs. Blood spills like rain across the blackened earth. Women flee from savage oppressors, brought down like forest deer. Children perish like blossoms trampled beneath the feet of red-handed primitives. Along the horizon, strange piles of stone rise toward the moon, the early temples of some dark God.

The scene shifts to another plain, outside a walled city. Men with spears, swords, and axes, armored in leather and bone, tear each other to bits. Torn standards droop from poles driven deep into the ground. The gates of the city collapse inward and the blood-mad conquerors rush inside, spilling the guts of defenders, pulling women and children from stone huts and setting fire to gardens. The red sky mirrors the flames devouring the streets, and piles of severed heads rise in the central plaza.

The colors diverge, cascade, and blend into a new dream. Two armies clash along a river; it runs red with their blood. The men ride horses now, and wrap their bodies in plates of bronze, fantastic helms perched on their heads. They impale one another, hack off limbs, open bellies and split skulls like melons. Their flags whip furiously in the wind, and their generals watch from distant hills, ordering more men to their deaths. A village burns nearby, scattered with blackened corpses. Some are tiny.

Flames consume the vision, giving birth to a new one. A tall proud city built of marble, jade, and crystal. Along the perfection of its streets, red war flows like a tide of disease, invaders cutting down the white-robed citizens and once more bringing the scourge of fire. Groves of divine beauty become the killing grounds of a wizened people; children twitch on the end of lances; warriors toss women between them like blood-soaked trophies of silk and skin; a vast library holding the knowledge and histories of eons goes up in flames while the gauntlets of men rip the living hearts from their enemies.

"Enough!" Sharadza cried out. "Stop it!"

Iardu wiped away the wine with the edge of his sleeve, and the vision with it.

Tears ran along her numb cheeks, and she looked at him stunned and wordless.

"You see?" he said.

"Why did you show me those horrors?" She wiped at her eyes. She was tired of weeping.

"Sharadza, dear girl . . . I have spent thousands of years trying to cure men of this disease that afflicts them. This thing they call war. They worship it even above their own gods. It dwells within them, girl. It is part of their inherent nature. I have educated them . . . inspired them . . . terrified them. I have re-shaped their kingdoms and their religions. I have even re-shaped their bodies into a multitude of diverse forms. Still this pattern emerges. It is *who they are*."

"I don't believe it," she said.

"Even the blue-skinned Udvorg in their isolated kingdom engage in bloody tribal feuds. War is a part of human nature – they are made to slaughter themselves periodically. I no longer have any hope that I can prevent it. Or that I even should."

"When did you give up, Iardu? When did you stop trying to

re-shape the world? You made Vod. You shaped him so he could build the City of Men and Giants."

"I *made* giants . . . out of men long, long ago."

"And later you re-united them. You are still shaping the world. You re-shaped me."

He grunted. "You are not the world, Sharadza. You are only one lovely girl."

"*The part is the whole*," she reminded him. "*There can be no separation*."

Now he smiled at her, his eyes red and swollen. His head fell back against the booth wall.

"How can you be so blind to your own teachings?" she said. "When you change one person . . . one being . . . one life, you change everything."

"And nothing."

"*All is One . . . There can be no distinctions*. Success and failure are illusions. You taught me to reject duality. Whatever victories or defeats you have endured in the past do not matter. The only question before you now is, will you help me?"

He stared at her, a new expression in his old man's face. Or maybe one she had simply never noticed before. Was it . . . love?

He sighed and drank the last of his wine in three large gulps.

Now Fellow was gone and Iardu sat across the table. His face looked far younger than Fellow's, and his eyes were flares of prismatic light, unable to settle on a single color. His pointed beard was short and silver-gray, as was his mustache. A robe of orange-red silk hung upon his narrow frame, and on his chest a living blue flame danced without heat, strung like a burning sapphire from a silver neck-chain. He was handsome in an ageless way, his gold-brown skin inhumanly smooth. Rings of ruby and emerald lined his fingers; his nails shined white as pearls. His teeth, as he smiled, gleamed with that same whiteness.

"Because it is *you* who ask me, Sharadza, I will go south with you. Though it will make no difference in the end. You cannot cure this sickness in the souls of men."

"Perhaps not," she said, taking his hand. His skin thrummed faintly, as if lightning surged in his veins. "But if there is no Empress to lead them, the Khyreins may not fight at all. If Elhathym should lose his stolen throne, none will have to die in his name. Bring down these sorcerers and we avoid war altogether."

Iardu shook his somber head. A circlet of gold held back his hair, which fell to his shoulders. His chromatic eyes gleamed. "And if we die at the hands of these tyrants?"

"Then we'll have done no harm but to ourselves. Besides, you told me the Living World and the World of the Dead are merely twin illusions."

"Yes," said Iardu. "But there are much worse fates than death."

She leaned across the table, surprising even herself, and kissed his cheek.

He stared at her with his glimmering eyes. "I believe . . . " he said, "that it is *you* who are re-shaping *me*."

They left the tavern, which had emptied while they spoke behind the curtain. The owner had fallen asleep on one of his own stools. Sharadza left a single emerald from the sunken chest lying at his elbow. She fastened the door as they stepped into the street.

They walked toward the palace, and she sensed that everyone around her saw the old man Fellow. She saw ageless Iardu in all his splendor. Unless . . . unless Iardu's true form was only another lie. Could she trust him? But this was a question she must ask of any man, sorcerer or not.

He has agreed to face death with me.

"Is there no other sorcerer in all the world that we might win to our cause?" she asked.

The blue flame flickered on his chest. He walked in silence until the palace walls rose into the street ahead.

"There is *one* . . . who might be . . . persuaded," he said. "But he dwells far from here."

"Where?" she asked.

"Mumbaza."

Her green eyes twinkled. "Then we will fly."

"Yes." He smiled. "We will fly."

22

Three Ships

Dairon's Spear sat upon the water like a colossal swan feathered with gold and emerald. Its triple-masted bulk dwarfed all other ships moored along the docks of Murala. The yellow sun emblem of Uurz sat upon the green field of its mainsail, and its prow bore the sculpture of a gilded hawk tall as a man. The hawk's wings were spread to catch the same winds that would fill the great sails. Uurz itself was not a sea power, but Murala was its official territory, so the Emperor's ship kept a permanent berth here. Its lean yet hulking presence reminded visiting merchant vessels that the port was an outpost of the Stormlands. Piracy was rare on the Cryptic Sea, but when it did plague the shipping lanes, *Dairon's Spear* delivered the justice of Uurz.

Lyrilan had ridden on the ship when he was a boy, along with Tyro and their parents. Dairon had brought his family to Murala to celebrate the finish of the galleon's construction. What Lyrilan remembered most from that trip was his mother's nervous smile and the pressure of her hand on his own. Neither of them had sailed before, and they looked to one another for courage. Tyro had stood bravely near Dairon, either fearless or pretending to be. She had died a year later. Some southern-born fever had infested the city and struck indiscriminately at commoner and noble alike. Lyrilan and Tyro were eleven when she passed; Lyrilan and Dairon cried at the opulent funeral, while Tyro did not. Later, in the shadow of the palace gardens, Lyrilan caught Tyro weeping alone. He never told Tyro what he had seen that day.

Dairon had defied the custom of the previous Emperors of Uurz by taking Jarinha as his one and only wife. His chancellors pestered him to take two or three more wives and produce more heirs, but always he refused them. "Jarinha has given me two strong sons," the Emperor told the court. "That is enough." When she died, they expected Dairon to change his mind, but even then he would claim no one to replace her. Lyrilan hoped one day to know a love like that shared by his mother and father. It was the stuff of legends . . . and tragedies. But these two things went hand in hand. Anyone who studied the lessons of history knew that.

Today, standing in the forecastle of the great ship, Lyrilan could not help but remember his mother standing on the same deck. How her black hair danced in the sea wind, the dress of azure and carmel she wore that day, the white pearls of her smile. A mass of white clouds rolled across a sapphire sky. The blue bay glittered with refracted sunlight, scattered diamonds floating atop the brine. The masts and sails of a hundred or more ships lined the wharves, many flying the colors of distant lands. Not surprisingly, the only kingdoms not represented here were Khyrei and Yaskatha. Those ships, according to the *Spear*'s Captain Lonneus, had stopped coming earlier this year. First the Khyrein trade ceased, then the Yaskathan. There were sleek caravels from Mumbaza, the Feathered Serpent writhing on their sails, and a few exotic galleys from the Jade Isles, along with traders from Shar Dni and the Southern Isles. Above them all, like a Giant among Men, rose the shining hull and olive sails of *Dairon's Spear*.

Tyro had used the authority of his father's word to commandeer the ship for the mission to Mumbaza. Lyrilan would not have had the presence to make such a demand upon Lonneus and his crew. But Tyro was well-known as Dairon's Right Arm. Who better to grasp the Emperor's *Spear*?

Tyro and Vireon hired two Muralan merchant galleons, the *Cloud* and the *Sharkstooth*, as troop transports. Tyro and a hundred Uurzian warriors would ride the *Cloud*, while Andoses and a hundred Sharrians sailed on the *Sharkstooth*. Lyrilan and D'zan accompanied Vireon and his sorcerer-woman Alua on the *Spear* with two hundred soldiers from Uurz and Udurum. Each ship carried in its hold cavalry horses and enough food and grain for men and animals. The *Spear* carried extra provisions in the belly of its massive hull. It was a sign of respect that Tyro gave Vireon mastery of Dairon's behemoth. Lyrilan knew his brother was a strategist, and this war would hinge on the rising legends of D'zan and Vireon. Their names would stir soldier's hearts to battle and make them laugh at death. Tyro would command from Vireon's shoulder, but he would not stand in Vireon's shadow.

The second passing over the mountains had not been difficult after all. The weather was balmy those two weeks, with only light dustings of snow along the heights. However, on the southern half of the pass snowdrifts lingered. Lyrilan watched as Vireon took Alua aside and spoke with her encouragingly. She amazed the Princes by calling up a wall of flame to rush over and melt the deep drifts. So their small army rode through mud instead of snow, and came down into the Stormlands without injury. Along the way they picked up a few of the wounded men left at the Giants' cave. Some had mended and were able to ride, so Tyro accepted them back into the ranks with great praise.

It took less than a full month for the five Princes and their cohort to reach Murala. Three days were spent appropriating the ships, buying feed and rations, filling out the crews, and consulting with the captains regarding routes and sailing conditions. Lyrilan did not sit in on these meetings; he worked instead on his manuscript. The journey of Prince D'zan had grown from uncertain desperation into a life-or-death struggle upon which the fate of nations balanced. Lyrilan's responsibility as chronicler of these events had grown immensely. The tale expanded, the plot thickened, and unexpected characters arose to fill the pages. While he hoped to remain the invisible author, transcribing the noteworthy events of D'zan's odyssey, his own brother had become an essential part of the tale. If Lyrilan was not careful, the tale would pull him into itself as well. Perhaps he was already slipping into D'zan's story, even as he wrote it.

Every night along the road, despite the chill of winter or the wetness of storms, Tyro had trained D'zan in the art of the greatsword. He had become the Wise Warrior figure in D'zan's story – he was the voice of martial expertise, the one who ushered the young Prince from boyhood to manhood, transformed a soft-hearted courtier into an iron-muscled warrior. As for D'zan, he took to his martial lessons with great fervor. The boy's arms had grown solid and thick, his legs trunk-like and steady, and his belly lean and hard as a board. All the complacency of court life had drained away from D'zan. Crossing the mountains twice had burned away (or frozen away) his boyhood. He hefted the Stone's blade every evening to spar against Tyro's Uduran broadsword. As far as Lyrilan knew, D'zan had yet to beat Tyro in one of these sparring matches, and he bore a few cuts and bruises for his troubles. But he no longer feared the weight of the blade, or the swing of sharp metal in his hands, or his opponent. Tyro was making him a warrior, finishing what poor Olthacus had begun years ago.

At night Lyrilan sat in D'zan's tent, writing in his book, while the Yaskathan Prince oiled and cleaned the great blade. Lyrilan wrote all of this in the manuscript – how the sword had replaced the Prince's lost uncle . . . and perhaps his father. Sometimes, too, D'zan pondered the griffin-head dagger that he kept in his boot; it had been a gift from King Trimesqua. But the Stone's blade held far more importance for him. It represented everything he stood to gain or lose, the entirety of Yaskatha. The jeweled broadsword with its ward against evil was all the Prince still owned of his kingdom. It was the iron key that would unlock the doors of Yaskatha for him.

The last of the provisions were loaded onto the galleons. The horses and men were already set, and Lyrilan had taken a break from writing to watch the impending launch. He left the bound manuscript and his quills on the desk of the cabin assigned to D'zan and himself. Vireon shared the Captain's cabin with Alua, at the insistence of Lonneus, who seemed in awe of the Udurum Prince. In fact, all the people of Murala and the Stormlands, and especially the Uurzians, looked upon tall Vireon with amazement. This was the Son of Vod. Vod, who had made the desert a fertile kingdom, united Men and Giants, and reshaped the world. They never spoke of Vod's madness, of how he wandered off to lose himself in the sea. If they did, it was only in whispers, and they ended with the prophecy that one day Vod would return, having conquered the sea the way he once conquered the Serpent-Father. Others saw Vod's return as they looked into Vireon's blue eyes.

As the last of the crates and barrels were hoisted onto the lower deck and carried into the hold, D'zan joined Lyrilan in the forecastle and looked out across the waves. D'zan wore the black and silver livery of Udurum with the addition of the Yaskathan emblem stitched on its chest: a golden tree whose trunk was a raised sword. The Queen of Udurum had given him this uniform, a gift showing her dedication to his cause. The attached cloak was purple with a black lining. The wind whipped it about D'zan's boots as he walked.

"What? No quill and parchment, Prince?" he asked.

Lyrilan smiled. "Even scholars must rest sometimes. I wouldn't want to miss such a splendid launch. We're sailing into history today."

D'zan eyed the glittering sea, his arms crossed. "I suppose we are," he said. "A memorable day. But we've a long way to go. Twelve days to Mumbaza at least . . . if the weather holds."

"You made this same journey in reverse," said Lyrilan, "only months ago."

D'zan nodded. "It took longer since the Stone and I changed ships so many times. I was . . . terrified by all of them. It's a wonder I didn't fall overboard."

Lyrilan breathed deeply of the salt wind. "How do you feel today?"

"Ready," said D'zan. "Ready to reclaim what is mine. Like I've spent *years* here, not months."

"You are no longer afraid."

"I did not say that," said D'zan, grinning. "Fear is a constant companion in this world. Did not one of your beloved poets say that?"

"Kopicus said, 'Through the blessings of Fear and Pain we know we are alive. Let us honor them alongside Love and Laughter, which give our lives meaning.'"

D'zan studied the mass of rigging at the ship's middle. "My father would have loved this ship."

"My father does," said Lyrilan. "Although he's only ridden it once, he boasts of it to every visiting dignitary. It is the heart of his sea power, as it were."

"We should be safe enough from reavers in such a massive galleon."

"I pity the poor pirate who tries to assail us," said Lyrilan. "He'll find an entire cohort of seasoned warriors from three different nations. No, we've nothing to fear from *Men* along these coasts."

D'zan caught his meaning. "Yes," he agreed. "Nothing from Men."

Vireon, bare-chested in his white tiger-cloak and wearing a greatsword at his waist, strode up the plank beside Alua. Her face was that of a child beneath her honey-colored hair, and her black eyes were wide with wonder. She had obviously never seen a city before Udurum. To gaze upon a vast sea vessel was enough to strike her temporarily dumb. She held Vireon's hand as he guided her onto the lower deck, walking between barrels of fresh water and the shuffling porters who carried goods toward the ship's hold. She wore a snowy gown trimmed with crimson, a cloak of sable hanging from her shoulders.

"What do you make of her?" asked D'zan, his eyes upon the sorceress.

Lyrilan shrugged. "She seems a sweet and kind girl. Untutored. Yet she carries herself with a certain . . . purity."

"A sweet and kind sorceress," said D'zan. "Can there truly be such a thing?"

"You have seen her flame. What else could she be?"

"Where does she come from? Has Vireon told anyone?"

"My guess is everyone fears to ask. The Son of Vod is a God to most of these people. She is his consort. I say we're lucky to have her."

"Hmmm," said D'zan. "Still, it nags at me that someone with such power could come right out of the wilderness."

"Where does power come from?" asked Lyrilan. "Obrin says—"

"Not another quote." D'zan smiled. "Tell me later. I must speak with Vireon."

"I'll be up here until we cast off," said Lyrilan. He looked forward to the open sea. With all its perils and the inherent risks of nautical travel, there was nothing else like it. The sea would always remind him of his mother, and the way they had felt together on that grand day long ago, laughing and skimming across the waves. It was exhilarating.

D'zan made his way down the forecastle steps and greeted Vireon with a shake of his hand, Alua with a bow. She fluttered her dark eyes at him. The last of the water barrels were carried into the hold, and now four bearded Muralans carried a large crate up the ramp. Probably extra foodstuffs. With all these men and horses and perishables, the captains had no room for merchant cargo; but then they were being well-paid by the thrones of Udurum and Uurz for their troubles.

A flutter of movement caught Lyrilan's eye. One of the crate-bearers sprang toward D'zan. Something flashed in his hand. Vireon pushed the Yaskathan Prince aside. D'zan fell to the deck on his rear, but avoided a stabbing. Lyrilan gasped as Vireon grabbed the knife-wielder by the throat, his other hand on the attacker's wrist. Vireon tossed him mercilessly against the main-mast, halfway across the deck. Even in the forecastle Lyrilan heard the cracking of the man's spine.

The other three loaders dropped the crate and sprang toward D'zan before he could stand up. Their knives glimmered in the sun. Green-bladed daggers. *Jade*. The weapons of Khyrein Death-Bringers. The foremost among them shoved Alua aside – she did not matter – and sprang blade first at D'zan. The Prince's booted heel caught the assassin's sternum, and he kicked the man backward. Another assassin jabbed at him, barely missing his skull, pinning D'zan's cloak to the deck. The assailant pulled the dagger from the planks, elbow swiveling for a final strike. But D'zan struck first, jamming the dagger from his boot into the assassin's neck.

Two more killers scrambled at D'zan but faced Vireon instead. His broadsword flashed and the strength of his blow split a man in two. Alua pounced on the last Khyrein's back like a rabid hound, digging her nails into his flesh, *biting* at his throat. He stumbled forward and fell face down on the deck. Vireon's boot stamped down upon his dagger hand, crushing it. The man howled, unlike his brothers, who had died silently.

Vireon pulled Alua off the Death-Bringer's back, and D'zan ended him with a downward thrust of his greatsword. Lyrilan gasped. This was the first time D'zan had killed with that blade. The Prince pulled it from the dead man's body, staring down at the bloody corpse a moment. Lyrilan's fascination expired and he dashed down the steps toward the scene, picking his way through the wide-eyed soldiers filing out of their quarters beneath the foredeck. He saw Vireon lean down to tear a false beard from the man D'zan had killed.

"Khyreins." D'zan nodded. "Their skin has been painted brown to appear Muralan." He kicked at one of the jade knives with his boot. "These are poisoned."

Alua drew close to Vireon, and his great arm fell about her shoulders. He addressed the soldiers and sailors milling about the bloody deck.

"These men came to kill the Prince of Yaskatha!" Vireon shouted. "These are the cowards of Khyrei." He grabbed D'zan's hand and raised it high with his own. "The Prince lives!"

The soldiers cheered, and the sailors joined them. Lyrilan motioned D'zan to hold up his sword. The Prince lifted the red point of his blade toward the sky. The cheers grew louder. "Hail the Princes!" someone shouted. This burst into a general chaos of bellowing approval.

Vireon yelled an order that every soldier, crewman, and laborer be checked for painted skin before they cast off. There could be more of these assassins hiding in their midst. His words were cut off by Alua's sudden scream.

The first man to die, his spine cracked against the mast, shambled through the crowd like a drunken devil. By some prevalent instinct, some innate disgust of the supernatural, men drew back from him and he ran crookedly toward D'zan, blood leaking from his lips, eyes blank and filled with death. Vireon's head turned to the dead man just as a steely grip caught his ankle. The man he'd sliced in two had grabbed him and crawled legless toward D'zan, a green dagger still in his other hand.

The rushing dead man wrapped his fingers about D'zan's throat, squeezing with the inhuman power of death. D'zan fell backward against the railing. Vireon speared the half-man to the deck with his Uduru blade, dodging the sweep of its jade dagger. Sailors fled in terror while soldiers stepped back or fumbled for their blades. The other two dead men, one gushing red from the base of his skull, the other bleeding from his severed heart, stood and lunged gracelessly for D'zan. The Yaskathan Prince brought his greatsword down one-handed on the skull of his strangler. Brain and bone exploded, but the strangler was already dead, so did not release its grip. Lyrilan watched the dead men strive to kill the living men, feeling helpless and caught in the middle of a dreadful storm. He longed to run, but his feet would not move.

Vireon's heel crunched the skull of the dead man he had pinned to the deck. The other two swung daggers clumsily at D'zan, striking the dead strangler instead, which D'zan used as a shield. The smell of corruption, filth, and blood replaced the fresh sea air. Vireon chopped at the man he had killed; headless, its arms still grasped and writhed, and the legs twitched like blind worms. Vireon's eyes glowed with primal terror as he sliced the grasping limbs to pieces. D'zan finally cut the strangler in half with his greatsword. The legs and hips fell backward, spewing fresh gore across the deck; but the torso and arms hung from his neck now, entrails sliding like red ropes from its ribcage as it continued crushing his throat.

An Uurzian soldier came forward with a longblade and swept it across the strangler's arms, severing them from the torso. The disembodied hands now choked D'zan by themselves, and one of the dead men stabbed the Uurzian with its poisoned blade. The valiant man crumpled.

Now Alua cast a white flame at the two stalking dead men. Their garments and skins ignited. They ran crazily about the deck, flaming, jaws snapping, until a group of sailors pushed them over the railing with poles. They fell sizzling into the sea. The stench of burned flesh lingered horribly about the decks.

Lyrilan tried to tear the killing hands away from D'zan's throat. D'zan's face had gone from red to purple. He was almost unconscious when Lyrilan finally pulled one of the hands free. He tossed it, unthinking, across the deck. It rolled a bit and then scrambled like a spider until someone brought a barrel down upon it, crushing it to pulp. Vireon grabbed the other strangling hand, removing it instantly from D'zan. It writhed in his grasp. He placed it carefully into Alua's blazing palm, where it withered into black ashes.

Lyrilan helped D'zan regain his breath. Rough nails had torn the flesh of his neck. The dead soldier, whose name was Farimus, was to be honored for saving the Prince's life. His comrades carried his body away, for the southern poison had killed him instantly. A burial at sea would be most proper, they decided, for the first soldier to die in the war against Khyrei.

"Our enemy plays tricks on us with sorcery," Vireon told the warriors. "Still we stand strong! This is Alua, Sorceress of the Northlands. She sails with us. She will burn this black magic from our path with the white flame of justice!"

Again the crew and soldiers rallied, though not as fervently as before. Some eyed the water where the burning dead men sank, expecting them to crawl up and kill some more. Word soon spread through the entire ship, and across to the *Cloud* and the *Sharkstooth*, that the enemy had already struck. Non-essential personnel were carefully searched and removed from the ships. No more brown-painted Khyreins were to be found.

Tyro brought a Sky Priest onto the *Cloud* with him, and this man blessed the three ships before they cast off. He walked the planks of each ship, casting rose blossoms and burning incense. By the time he reached the *Spear*, the crew had just finished washing the blood and offal from the decks. Now only dark stains remained where the assassins had fallen, and fallen again. The priest's ceremony restored the courage and certainty of the cohort. *Tyro had known it would*, Lyrilan reflected.

Before the sun reached its zenith, *Dairon's Spear* left the dock, the two lesser ships following in its wake. A strong winter wind out of the north filled their sails. D'zan rested in his cabin, neck treated with salve and bandaged. His wounds were superficial. Lyrilan sat on the second bed, watching him. D'zan's hands were wrapped around the hilt of the greatsword, as they always were when he lay down to rest. It was, ironically, the traditional pose of a fallen warrior. Lyrilan had brought him a flask of wine, and waited for him to wake.

"It was Elhathym," said D'zan. He wasn't asleep after all.

"D'zan?" asked Lyrilan.

"I'm awake. It was Elhathym who sent those . . . things."

"But they were men from Khyrei . . . Death-Bringers, like the ones in the palace. Servants of Ianthe the Claw."

"Yes, and no," said D'zan. "While they lived, they served Ianthe. As soon as they died, they became the servants of Elhathym. Like those in the palace, they waited for *me*. Like the shadow at the edge of the mountains. The Serpent beneath the ruins of Steephold. All sent by *him*. All waiting for me."

"Fearsome things," said Lyrilan. "But here you are. You survived. Yours is the just cause. The Gods are with you. The Gods and many good Men. And at least one Man-Giant with a sorceress."

D'zan raised himself to sit on the side of his bed and looked at Lyrilan. The golden light of noon poured through a round porthole. The bandage around his neck was dotted with red spots.

"Yes," said D'zan. "All these are good. And I no longer fear this tyrant's magic."

Lyrilan poured a cup of wine for him. He handed it across the small cabin and D'zan took it gratefully, wincing as he gulped it down.

"But what other horrors are out there?" D'zan asked. "What else is waiting for me?"

Lyrilan drank his own cup of wine now, and he shivered. Not from the drink, for it was warm as seawater. He said nothing, but soon took out the manuscript. There was much updating to do.

D'zan drank another cup, then lay down again on the bed behind him. He snored gently while Lyrilan scratched his quill across the bound pages.

The floor of the deck rocked and swayed gently, creaking in a woody voice.

What else is waiting for me?

The words echoed in Lyrilan's mind.

What else is waiting for us?

It was a question that had no answer. Yet.

He ignored it, scribbling madly, enraptured by the orderly rows of black ink spreading across the parchment.

23

On the Cryptic Sea

D*airon's Spear* sliced the open water. Vireon stood behind the great hawk fronting its prow, peering past the golden wings. The sixth morning broke clear and pristine over the purple sea, and Alua lay sleeping in the cabin. He inhaled the briny wind, tasted its salt on his tongue. Tapestries of blood and saffron hung along the horizon as the sky filled with daylight. The western horizon was flat and keen as a blade, while the eastern showed a thin line of coast, yellow and brown in the light of dawn.

Vireon had never ridden the sea before. It took no time at all for his feet to grow accustomed to the ship's constant movement. He enjoyed the freedom of the waves, the ultimate rush of water toward mysterious sky. What lay beyond the endless western waters, across the unexplored realms of the Cryptic Sea? Perhaps continents and kingdoms undreamed of by Men or Giants . . . whole other worlds and civilizations. Or perhaps a vast wilderness ripe for the conquering . . . untapped reserves of game and alien creatures. For that matter, what strange lands lay *beneath* these ceaseless waves?

His mind fell into the green-black depths, and he thought of his father. Was Vod walking the bed of this very sea right now? Did he linger in some watery dungeon, chained there by the Queen of the Sea-Folk to fulfill her curse? Or did his body float among the fish and marine life that slowly picked his bones clean? Vod was likely dead. But like the rest of his people Vireon held on to the hope that his father would return from the sea eventually. Perhaps he did not truly believe it, but he kept it close to his heart anyway.

He had known Tadarus was dead the moment it happened. The bond with his brother had been forged inside their mother's womb. That bond had carried them through twenty-five years of brotherhood and friendship. It was the core of their family, especially when their father grew older and began keeping to himself. At times Vireon still found himself wondering what Tadarus was doing, where he was at . . . then came the stabbing memory that he was dead. Vireon's heart ached each time he remembered that Tadarus was forever gone.

Vireon's thoughts inevitably fell toward Fangodrel and vengeance. No matter that he sprang from the same womb as Tadarus and Vireon. Even his mother had not wanted him. He was a freak, an abomination born of lust, torture, and cruelty. Fangodrel was the spawn of a sick society, and its taint had simmered in his blood like a disease. Until it consumed him. Somehow, he had remembered who he truly was and had murdered Tadarus. Somehow he had inherited the sorcery of his immortal grandmother. Vireon would kill him and the wicked bitch who ruled the jungle kingdom. Let her walls come crashing down as they had when Vod stormed her palace. Let her jungles go up in flames. Let her bones rot in the earth alongside those of the Kinslayer. When this was done, when the south was purged of its evil infection, Vireon would come north again and sit on the throne of Udurum. But not until then.

His thumb played upon the ruby-set pommel of the greatsword at his side. It had been made by his Uncle Fangodrim from Uduru steel and was nearly as long as Vireon was tall. A relic of Old Udurum, it bore the sigils and curling symbol-work of the old language. Sharper and more durable than any blade of iron, this was the blade that would take the life of Fangodrel. It was only fitting that he die by Udurum steel. No sorcery or summoned demons would save him. Vireon no longer saw the brilliant sun or the spectacular vista of the waves. He saw only the blood-red anger burning behind his eyes while the heat of the day beat upon his bronze shoulders.

The touch of a cool hand pulled him away from those invisible flames, and he turned to face Alua. The wind danced in her light hair, and her body was cool as the snow against his hot skin. He wrapped his arms around her. Along the length of the ship, crewmen crawled through the rigging, adjusting sails and plying the exact arts of their trade. At midship a mass of soldiers had come above decks for fresh air.

Five days now on the sea and they were all a bit restless. They brought horses up in pairs when the sea was very calm. The animals were not built for confinement on a sea vessel, even one as big as *Dairon's Spear*. They were free spirits that needed to run and feel the green earth beneath them. Like Alua, his sweet snow blossom. He felt her restlessness too, in the nature of her touch and the softness of her voice.

Beyond the billowing triple sails, the lean hulls of the *Cloud* and *Sharkstooth* clove the waters behind and to either side. The standards of Uurz, Udurum, and Shar Dni flew from each of the ships. Vireon could just make out the tall figure of Tyro standing at the prow of the *Cloud*. He did not see Andoses over on the *Sharkstooth*; the Sharrian came and went, pacing the decks lower and upper. Of them all, Andoses was the most eager for war. It was the wish of his father he pursued. The livelihood of the Sharrian throne was at stake. Vireon sought vengeance; Tyro sought justice and perhaps glory; Andoses sought to secure the very future of the kingdom he would one day rule. As for young D'zan . . . the quiet boy wanted only to win back his throne. Andoses usually spoke on his behalf. And why not? The entire war, the alliance of kingdoms, was to the benefit of Shar Dni, which stood in the face of Khyrein brutality. As for Lyrilan the Scholar . . . Vireon liked the man, but did not understand him. He seemed interested only in writing everything down in that big book he carried. It reminded Vireon too much of Fangodrel and his obsession with verse. Yet jovial Lyrilan seemed nothing at all like the brooding Kinslayer.

Sharadza would understand Lyrilan, he thought. *Where is my sister?* When he had left Udurum, his mother was still worried for her. He had prayed to all four Gods that she return safely and soon. She should play no part in the bloody events to come. "When she returns, keep her safe in Udurum," he told his mother. Shaira kissed his cheek and asked him not to worry.

Alua laid her head against his chest and looked across the sea. "So beautiful," she said. "But I miss the woodlands."

"So do I," he said. He kissed the top of her head. His fox-woman, his sorceress. His strange and mysterious love. "But there are new lands to see. And after Mumbaza we will pass by the forests of the High Realms, which are deep and wild and full of hidden splendors."

She smiled at him. "How much longer on these waves?"

"Another week at most."

She leaned, quietly satisfied, into his arms.

He no longer asked her about her origins. She remembered nothing but the snowy wilderness, the wild summer hills, the flowing waters of Uduria . . . and the utter freedom of life without walls or rules. She did not recall her parents, or anything of her youth, did not even have a name until he gave her one. It seemed she had never been young at all, but always lived in ageless youth. Her companions were the foxes in the fields and sometimes the birds. She spoke their language but none other until Vireon had chased her and won her, and she had learned his tongue by sleeping next to him. What else might she be capable of? He had coaxed her to use her magical flame in the frozen mountain pass. She was learning to use it whenever necessary, as she had on the Khyreins who refused to die. She had no idea of the depths of her own powers. She only did what she needed to do, to protect herself and those she cared for . . . to invest life with those things she required for happiness and survival. He was learning to accept her for what she was, however baffling that might be, because he loved her above all other things. She was nature manifest in the body of a woman . . . as if created just for him, as no other woman ever could be. She was simply Alua, and he loved her.

When the war was done, he would marry her, and she would be Queen of Udurum. His mother would be happy. His first son would be named Vod, and his second Tadarus. He shook such thoughts from his head. In her presence, his mind often wandered to such domestic fantasies. Now he must concern himself with the war to come. His mind must be sharp and spotless, like the blade of his sword. Time enough later for the spoils of love. War did not allow for such tender things.

D'zan climbed up to join them on the foredeck. Lyrilan must still be below, scribbling in his book. D'zan greeted them with a raised arm; he still wore a bandage about his neck, but his wounds no longer bled. The poisoned daggers of his assailants had been tossed into the open sea. They were wicked and unsavory weapons. Let the ocean gnaw them slowly into sand.

"Shall we have another duel?" asked D'zan. Now that Tyro was separated from him on the other ship, he had turned to Vireon as his sparring partner. D'zan wielded his great broadsword with both hands, while Vireon used only a wooden pole, one-handed, to even the odds. D'zan fought with heart, but he had yet to avoid being disarmed by Vireon's staff.

"Later," said Vireon. "Breakfast first."

The wind blew strong and cool across the forecastle, and a sailor's song began on the rear decks.

D'zan leaned against the rail. "I tire of these sea rations," he said. "Can we not pull something fresh from the depths of the sea?"

"Perhaps a great whale?" Vireon smiled.

"Or better yet, a mermaid," said D'zan.

They laughed, Alua with them.

Thunder rose from the water. The speeding ship must have struck a reef, or some underground barrier. Soldiers went flying across the middle and rear decks; barrels crashed against the rails; a horse panicked and fell on its flank. As the deck pitched terribly upward, Vireon grabbed the railing with one hand, his other arm tight about Alua's waist. D'zan fell but managed to grab hold of Vireon's lower leg. He held on to it like a child as the deck rocked back and forth violently. The *Cloud* and *Sharkstooth* came up alongside the *Spear*, overtaking her. From their decks, the soldiers and sailors were shouting, pointing to the water at the *Spear*'s keel, screaming with terror in their eyes. In the mass of confusion aboard the *Cloud*, Tyro shouted orders at someone.

Now the *Cloud* and *Sharkstooth* raced ahead. A sound like the moaning of the earth itself bubbled up from the deeps, and a massive serpentine head rose above the prow. The sea-beast's skull was triangular, finned with bat-like flaps of translucent membrane, and vast enough to swallow a whale. Its great black orbs were focused on the forecastle of *Dairon's Spear* with a hideous intelligence. A deluge of sea-murk spewed from between its great fangs, which were white as ivory. Men screamed and called upon the Gods for help as the demonic head rose higher above the decks.

A fresh round of shrieks came now as the leviathan's spiked tail rose from the sea and curled about the ship's middle. It slid through a crowd of men with the speed of a hurricane, spearing bodies before it dove back into the water on the other side. Again it rose, and again, as more and more of its tremendous coils came rushing from the sea, encircling the galleon like rope about a toy ship. It smashed the yardarms to kindling, tore through the sails and rigging like paper. Two of the three masts broke beneath the beast's scaly mass, splintering and thundering. Its bulk was thicker than an Uduru was tall, and its scales were black emeralds gleaming with the muck of the deep sea beds. Tiny coral colonies grew along its fishy spine. It squeezed the great ship the way a constrictor squeezes a rat before swallowing it whole.

Men died beneath toppling masts, or were crushed by the scaled hide of the monster. Some even died from fear looking upon the monolithic devil. It was like a Serpent from the tales of old, but legless and of far greater weight and mass. Long enough to wrap itself several times about *Dairon's Spear*.

In the prow, watching the devastation of the ship's middle, Vireon held the rail with one hand and with the other unsheathed his great Uduru blade. Alua and D'zan hugged the rail with both arms. They could do nothing but hold on for their lives as the ship broke in two, prow and stern rising toward the sky in opposite directions.

The hull burst, spilling terrified horses and men into the ocean. Some who clung to the decks sank spears into the scaled gargantuan, but it did not seem to notice. What it *did* notice, peering and scanning with those great black eyes, slitted nostrils flaring, was D'zan. Its breath was a wind reeking of rotted sea matter. A crimson tongue darted out like a tentacle, thick as Vireon's waist. It slapped D'zan, who screamed and clung helplessly to the railing; the forked tongue wound about his body as the leviathan's coils had wound about the galleon. D'zan cried out, but his words were lost.

"Hold on!" Vireon yelled to Alua.

With one hand steady on the railing, he raised the sword in his other hand and sliced through the tongue as it lifted D'zan into the air. The Yaskathan Prince fell toward the swirling chaos below. There was no midship now, only the wreck of the triangular prow and square-shaped stern floating and sinking, heavy with clinging men.

The Serpent's head, squirting black ichor from its severed tongue, rushed past Vireon and Alua on the rail, racing toward D'zan as he fell into the floating wreckage and the deep water. Vireon did not think; he seized an advantage. The beast had ignored him in its quest to devour D'zan. His legs launched him away from the rail, out past the flaring neck-fins. For a moment, he flew downward like a hawk, falling through the air near to the Serpent's rushing neck. Then he slid along the scales of its skull on his backside, toward the jutting ridge of its forehead. A half-second before he reached the slimy snout, he took his sword in both fists and drove it home with all his strength.

The skull-bone cracked and split beneath him. The sword sank into something at once spongy and sinewy. He hung on to the embedded blade, riding the pierced skull like a great bull into the littered sea. Now the blue depths rose about him on all sides. He saw men swimming for the surface, D'zan among them. Floating barrels and casks rose quicker than men, while soldiers sank with pieces of mast stuck in their bellies, others tangled in the mutilated rigging and sails. Horses sank into the black depths, or twisted and writhed toward the air above.

Vireon twisted his blade inside the creature's brain, driving it deeper and ripping the skull wider. The beast thrashed, sending men and wreckage flying from its coils. Its great head came bursting out of the water, black blood gushing, and Vireon came with it. Men on the two undamaged ships stared, hundreds of eyes looking right at him for a moment – a bit of frozen time – then the head slammed back into the sea, carrying Vireon down again. He hung on, holding his breath, digging deeper into colossal flesh. Once more the Serpent's head came up, spewing a final roar of torment, vomiting black fluid from its snapping jaws.

The third time it went under, Vireon pulled free his sword and broke away from the skull. The orb eyes were glazed and mindless now. The bulk of its coils spread throughout the undersea, twitching and floating slowly toward the surface. He swam into a cloud of the black ichor and could see no more. But he was sure the leviathan was dead.

He burst from the water, gasping foul air into his lungs, wiping the gore from his eyes. He floated among the winding coils that stretched at least a half-league across the waves. The debris of what had once been a mighty ship drifted all about him. Horses swam past, making terrible sounds. Men wailed too, the wounded clinging to flotsam, casks, chunks of mast, each other.

"Alua!" he called. His head swiveled to survey the remains of the *Spear*. "Alua!"

She burst from the water not far away, swimming quick as an eel toward him. She wrapped slim arms about his neck and checked him for wounds. He assured her he was fine.

The massive Serpent head finally bobbed up to the surface. Its slitted eyes were gray and lifeless. Everyone on the two surviving ships, and those who clung to life in the water, could see now that he had killed it.

"Vireon!" came the cry from the *Sharkstooth*. Then the mass of soldiers on the *Cloud* took up that cry. "Vireon! Vireon!" As they lowered nets and ropes, scooping survivors out of the brine, the crews and warriors of the two ships yelled Vireon's name.

He looked about for D'zan and saw the boy climbing up a rope on the side of the *Cloud*'s hull. But what of the scholar Lyrilan? He was in a central cabin when the beast came; most likely he had gone down with most of the ship's crew.

But no . . . There he was, clinging to a barrel, his face pale and desperate. As a rope ladder fell into Vireon's hands from the *Cloud*'s railing, he yelled up at Tyro, who was scanning the wreckage.

"Your brother!" called Vireon. He pointed to hapless Lyrilan floating among the wreckage. Other men drifted around him, and a few horses.

Tyro yelled to Lyrilan, and the scholar waved his arm. His hand was red, bloodied, but he seemed intact. As Vireon followed Alua up the rope ladder and stepped onto the *Cloud*'s deck, he saw D'zan among the cheering sailors, bellowing as loudly as anyone.

"Vireon! Vireon! Vireon!" they cried.

He took Alua in his arms and the men patted his back, greeting him with smiles and handshakes. Some touched his shoulder or elbow, so they could later say they had done so.

"Save them," Vireon panted. He looked over the rail at the corpse of the monster and the spreading wreckage of the flagship. "Save as many as you can. The horses too . . . "

Both ships pulled men from the ocean first, and by then most of the surviving horses had tired and drowned. The few who were reached in time had to be coaxed into nets, and they were lifted aboard by a crew of ten men. Vireon lifted nine such horses by himself, one at a time, each one drawing a fresh round of cheers. He waved away the acclaim. Now was no time for such things. Fearing that the dead Serpent might rise up and menace them again, like the dead Khyreins had in Murala, the crews poured buckets of pitch onto the floating carcass. Alua then set it alight with a white flame dropped like a flower petal from her fingertips. The smell of the beast's cremation was a gut-wrenching foulness, yet the reek was reassuring. Better the smoke of its burning flesh than the wrath of its second life.

Lastly, they hauled aboard the floating barrels of fresh water and any unbroken crates of provisions and horse grains. Of the two hundred and twenty men aboard *Dairon's Spear*, only eighty-five survived, plus the three Princes and Alua. Of the two hundred horses, only twenty-three were saved. Most of the rations and water were recovered, but the two ships were desperately crowded now. By men, if not horses.

During the last hours of the salvage, done in the calm light of a half-moon, D'zan and Lyrilan came to the railing of the *Cloud* and stood near Vireon.

D'zan took his arm and met his eyes, a mixture of seawater and tears staining his cheeks. "Thank you, Vireon," he said. "I can never repay what you've done for me this day. You knew that thing had come for *me*, yet you—"

"I did what had to be done," said Vireon. He patted the boy's shoulder. "Repay me with your allegiance when you take back your stolen throne."

"I will," said D'zan, and Vireon knew he meant it.

Lyrilan stared over the middle rail at the spars and shards of wreckage, spread now far and wide across the sea. White flames danced along the coils of the Serpent's corpse, devouring its flesh even below the waterline. The ships had begun moving away from the blazing carcass.

Lyrilan sighed and stared at the black waters. "My book," he whispered. "My quills . . . my ink . . . all gone."

The scholar mourned the loss of these things more than all those who had died. Vireon would never understand such men. The face of Lyrilan was pale and drained of hope. A red bandage wrapped his right hand.

D'zan seemed to understand the scholar's mood better. He clapped Lyrilan on the back, and his hand lingered there.

"These are only things," he told the scholar. "You are alive, Lyrilan. Think of those who are not."

Lyrilan nodded, pulling back a mass of oily curls from his face. "Yes," he said. He looked at Vireon. His eyes glittered with moonlight. "There is only one thing to do."

"What is that?" asked Vireon.

"Start over," said the scholar.

Vireon looked at D'zan, who shrugged.

"The Mumbazans make a fine parchment," said Lyrilan, turning toward his new cabin. "There must be a single chapter all about today. 'Vireon and the Sea Monster' . . . " His voice trailed away as he lost himself among the men filling the crowded deck.

"Is the Prince all right?" Vireon asked D'zan.

"He will be," said D'zan. "As will we all, once we get off this damned ocean." The Yaskathan walked away, his head hanging low. More men had died for him today. More would die in the days to come. The bloody mantle of war would not hang easy on his young shoulders.

Vireon watched the smoking remains of the leviathan fade into the night as the ships drew southward.

"What was it?" Alua asked, stroking his chest with her cool fingers.

"Something from the deep," he said. "Some ancient cousin of the Serpents my ancestors killed. But a thing of water, not fire."

"I felt its thoughts," she told him, looking into his eyes. "They were the thoughts of a *man*, not a beast."

"What did these man-thoughts say?" asked Vireon.

"*The Heir, find the Heir*, it thought. *Swallow the Heir, chew his bones*. And when it saw D'zan, it *knew* he was the one."

The tyrant, thought Vireon. *Not the Sea Queen, but the Usurper of Yaskatha*. The northern ships sailed into the reach of Elhathym's power. He had commanded this devil of the Old World. Made it rise from the depths and kill all those men in the hope of killing just one. He would never stop until D'zan's threat to his rule was removed.

Elhathym and all his walking dead, ancient devils, and terrible sorcery.

So be it. Elhathym must die.

Before or after the Kinslayer, it made no difference.

Fangodrel, Elhathym, Ianthe . . . There was much killing to do.

Vireon had left winter sleeping in the frozen north.

This was the hot, southern Season of Blood.

It flared now in his chest like the flame from Alua's palm.

24

Land of the Feathered Serpent

They rose from Udurum as twin hawks, he crested in black feathers and she in white. Soaring above the continent of clouds, they reached Uurz at sunset. Drawing as little attention to themselves as possible, they lodged in separate rooms at a modest inn called the Raven's Perch. From her window Sharadza watched the towers of Dairon's Palace fade from gold to dark silver as night fell across the city. The songs of minstrels floated from roof gardens as she lay upon the soft bed, her mind racing with thoughts of Vireon, Fangodrel, and her cousin Andoses. Nightmares came, distorted visions of the horrors she had seen in Iardu's spilled wine. She woke to the sound of bellowing merchants and rolling thunder outside her window. She and Iardu breakfasted on dates and honeyed bread; he drank wine while she sipped water drawn from the Sacred River. In a dark alley they became hawks again and flew into the Stormlands sky, leaving Uurz to bask in its sudden showers, ephemeral rainbows, and ripe orchards.

They flew across the southern reaches of Dairon's realm, an emerald plain scattered with villages and burgeoning farmlands. When they broke through the cloud layer into a crystal blue sky, the Great Earth-Wall lay far below, running in a crooked line from east to west, dividing the continent into Low and High Realms. Sharadza's hawk-eyes studied the green roof of a vast forest beginning at the top of the mighty cliff and rolling into the southern horizon.

The colors of fall never came to the forests of the High Realms. Here the trees grew thicker than in the northern forests and were never troubled by the kiss of winter. The High Realms were a green wilderness where cities, roads, and walls did not exist. The lower world of the Stormlands lay hidden beneath a sea of rolling clouds to the north. Sharadza flew beside the black hawk, humbled by the sheer immensity of the High Forests, while Iardu's beaked head focused only on the horizon. He had flown over these lands many times, and probably knew what every part of the continent looked like from the vantage of the sky. Strange tales were told of the beings who dwelled deep in those woodlands, and she wondered how many of their secrets Iardu knew. Perhaps she would ask him, when they became man and woman again, exactly how long he had roamed the world. Since seeing his true form for the first time, she found herself increasingly curious about him.

Their wings carried them west now, as well as south, and the forests sank into deep valleys and rose across furrowed ridges. The land gradually fell back to sea level as the mass of trees grew thinner. By late afternoon they soared over the windy brown steppes of Mumbaza. Somewhere ahead, perhaps closer than she imagined, lay the capital city atop its pearly cliffs, overlooking the blue sea as it had for centuries. Mumbaza was among the world's most ancient kingdoms; despite the dangers ahead, she thrilled at the prospect of walking its ancient streets.

Iardu changed his course, and she was bound to follow. He dove toward the flat heat-browned grassland. A village of domed huts passed below, and herds of horned cattle. Dark-skinned Mumbazans walked trails among the grass with tufted spears, talismans of gold and copper gleaming on their chests. Another village nestled on the edge of a lake that glistened like a dark jewel. The swarthy villagers gathered here, some in crimson cloaks and hats of woven feathers. Dusky children gamboled between white sheep and black goats.

Eventually the Iardu-hawk alighted on the leafless branch of a twisted old tree near a cluster of round huts. Sharadza perched herself there beside him, blinking her avian eyes at the scene below. Here was the smallest of the villages yet. A single herd of goats gnawed the grass on a nearby hill. The golden steppe stretched out in all directions.

The two hawks sat on their branch and watched a few children run among the hide-walled huts, where the smoke of cookfires rose from clay chimneys. Sharadza sat patiently next to Iardu, although she longed to ask him what they were waiting for in this unlikely place. Where was the one they came to seek? This looked like no place a great sorcerer would live, but then what did the lair of a sorcerer look like? She rustled her feathers, trusting in the Shaper's guidance. The sun sank toward the flat horizon, an orange ball of flame singing the steppe.

The goats moved off the hill and came slowly toward the cluster of huts. A man walked behind them with a crooked staff, the legendary tool of the herdsman. As he drew near, he looked right at the two hawks with his keen dark eyes. His skin was ebony, shining with sweat, and his thick hair tied into a mass of braids reaching the middle of his back. A loincloth and moccasins were his only garb, apart from the golden armbands, the copper amulets about his neck, and the jade bangles hanging from his pierced ears. His forehead was tall, his muscles lean and tight under smooth skin. His nose was broad and flat above ample lips, and the marks of ritual scarring formed zig-zag patterns on his chest and shoulders.

He led the goats into a pen, his eyes ever returning to the tree.

When he closed the pen's gate, he came to stand before the tree and spoke to the hawks in the language common to all Men, accented in the lilting dialect of Mumbaza.

"Go away, hawks," he said. "Your kind bring only trouble."

Iardu melted from the branch and stood now as himself before the Mumbazan. Sharadza did the same, standing beside him in a traveling robe of green and black.

"Khama," said Iardu. "How are you, old friend?"

Khama did not return Iardu's smile. His eyes glittered like black pearls.

"Why do you come here, Shaper?" he said. "You are not welcome."

"I come only because I have to," said Iardu. "We must speak. This is Sharadza, Princess of Udurum."

Khama turned away. "I cannot welcome you here, knowing what you are. You should have stayed in your northern kingdom." He walked away toward the cluster of huts, where three curious children stared at the strangers. Iardu walked after him, and Sharadza followed.

"This is no way to greet a friend," said the Shaper. "Surely you remember the things we've shared."

Khama stopped and turned to face him. "I choose *not* to remember," he said, voice low so the children could not hear his words. "I am only a *man* now, Iardu. These are my children, my goats, my land. I have found peace here. Why must you disturb it?"

"All of these things are beautiful," said Iardu. He waved at the children, who responded with white grins. They shuffled shyly among the huts.

A voice called from one of the structures, and a lean Mumbazan woman looked out from its doorway. "My wife calls," said Khama. "You must go. Please. Leave me to this simple life I have chosen."

"You are a man of peace," said Iardu. "I respect that. We do not bring you trouble, Khama. We bring a warning. War brews in the south. All that you love is in danger. Mumbaza is the fulcrum in a struggle for power. Elhathym has returned."

Khama slammed the butt of his herding staff into the ground, raising a cloud of dust. "I do not know this name." He stared at Iardu as if he might strike him.

"You do," said Iardu. "*Remember* . . ."

A cloud fell across the glow of Khama's eyes, and he looked into the blue sky. He sighed, a long exhalation of regret, remorse, or perhaps weariness. The goats in their pen made helpless bleating noises. The children giggled and rubbed round stones across their palms.

Khama turned his eyes to Sharadza for the first time. His wife still stared from the doorway of their home. "Come and share food with us," he said, and walked toward his family.

Sharadza shared a quiet glance with Iardu. His face said, *Trust me*. She decided she would. They followed Khama through the doorway of his lodge, and the laughing children filed in behind them. The family welcomed them with smiles and bowls of cool goat's milk. Flat bread and roasted vegetables steamed on a small hearth-stove. Khama's wife was named Emi, and his three children were Tuka, Bota, and Isha, two boys and a girl. Sharadza enjoyed the warmth and joy of their round, amiable faces.

"My oldest son Kuchka is out with our second herd," said Khama. "We have forty-seven good sheep. Wool brings a high price at the capital."

They served generous portions to the visitors, and Sharadza was famished. Flying all day took as much energy as walking all day. She ate well, but not enough to embarrass herself. Iardu did the same, and she knew he would rather be drinking wine than milk. Khama's family spoke only Mumbazan, so they understood nothing of what Iardu told his old friend.

He told the herdsman of the recent events in Yaskatha, the usurping of the throne by the tyrant sorcerer, the murder of the Udurum Prince, the alliance of Ianthe and Khyrei with Elhathym and his new throne, and the war that was coming. As they spoke the sun began to set, and Kuchka returned with the sheep, herding them into a second pen near the goats. He came into the hut and ate the rest of the meal, his eyes darting back to Sharadza every few moments. A handsome lad, strong and well built like his father. If Khama was a sorcerer, then Kuchka would be too. But did he *know* anything about the ancient legacy of his father? She guessed not, since Khama lived here in the bosom of domestic bliss.

This man had found the happiness that Iardu never was able to grasp. Emi was a beautiful woman, a perfect wife and mother. Sharadza felt a pang of guilt for bringing Iardu back into Khama's life. Yet what else could they do but seek aid wherever it could be found? What history did Khama and Iardu share? There was no doubt he came of the Old Breed, yet was trying to forget it. Like the Sea Queen, who had forgotten and carved her own paradise beneath the waves. Perhaps in a few more years Khama would have forgotten his true nature as well and truly become the simple man he so wanted to be. But Iardu had done something, looked into his eyes with a certain intensity, and it had all come rushing back to him.

Khama remembered . . . but would he help?

A sliver of moon stood over the prairie and stars blazed in the black sky. They walked with Khama to stand near the old tree. Talismans of bone and wire hung from its branches. A gentle wind blew across the steppe, dispelling the heat of the day.

"If we can remove Elhathym from his Yaskathan throne," said Iardu, "there will be no chance of war with Mumbaza. Khyrei is far away. Fire and blood will not spill here."

Khama crossed his arms and leaned against the peeling bark.

"Mumbaza has known peace for a hundred years," he said. "The grandfather of our current King forged a peace treaty with Yaskatha at my urging. How do you know Elhathym intends to break the treaty?"

Iardu frowned. "Do you remember Takairo the Great? Before Elhathym left the world he shattered its opal towers and murdered or enslaved every living thing within its walls. Takairo, whose people had *never* known war. He is a predator, Khama, and worse now that he has endured the strangeness of the Outer Worlds. He raises the dead to conquer the living. He takes what he wants. It will not be long before he decides to take Mumbaza."

Khama watched the stars, keeping his thoughts to himself.

Sharadza could stay quiet no longer. "Even now a delegation of Princes from the northlands seeks alliance with your Boy-King. A choice must be made. Mumbaza will be forced to side with Yaskatha and Khyrei, or with those who oppose them. Like you I fear the coming of war. This is why I have convinced Iardu to help me prevent it. He says you can help us. If you do not, you will face the coming destruction knowing that you could have done something about it."

"I have enjoyed living as other men do these past decades," Khama said. "Yet the Great Wheel turns always, and now you remind me that men face war in their time. It has always been so. So if I am to be a man, I must face it too. Though my heart screams to run from here, to take my children where they can be safe, I know that safety is an illusion. Still . . . to leave them now, I am unwilling."

"Open your Inner Eye," said Iardu. "Look to the south. Feel the currents of shadow smothering Yaskatha."

Khama's eyes closed. A night-bird cawed somewhere over the plain. The cool wind blew, and the grasses whispered earthy secrets.

After a moment the herdsman opened his eyes. He shivered. "The Dwellers in Shadow," he whispered. "They answer his call. A great many of them . . . legions of hungry darkness . . . "

Iardu nodded. "You feel what I have felt. His power will only grow stronger until he strikes. And it may be well before the northern armies can assemble."

"Oh, it will be," said Khama, his face haunted. "Such hunger cannot be held in check for long. It could consume the world."

"Stand with us now," said Iardu. "We'll take him before he ever knows of our coming. Surprise will be a dagger that kills in our hand, Khama."

Khama shook his head, ran a hand through his braided locks. "Emi, the children . . . I must take them to the city . . . hide them behind the walls of the palace." Tears welled in his eyes but did not fall. "Understand. If I join you in striking at Elhathym, I break the treaty of my King. I must speak with him first. Only with his blessing can I do this thing."

Iardu looked at Sharadza. His eyes glowed, twin prisms brighter than the moonlight. The blue flame danced on his chest. She had grown used to this wonder and hardly noticed it now. She wondered what Khama's family saw when they looked at Iardu.

"We will accompany you to the city tomorrow," said Iardu. "Once your family is safe there, and you have spoken with the Boy-King, we will fly south together . . . to douse the fire of war before it burns across the steppes."

Khama nodded. "I must speak with my wife."

"We will sleep in the grass," said Iardu.

Khama stopped halfway to his hut and turned to look at them. His face was unreadable in the dark.

"Hawks always bring trouble," he said, and went inside to seek his wife.

*

Mumbaza sat like the King of Cities on its precipice above the turquoise sea. Its docks were vast marble quays lined with ships from every nation, a forest of multicolored sails and vessels of every size, from lean coast-huggers to round-hulled behemoths. The city kept a standing navy as well, a fleet of two hundred war galleons patrolling the coast for leagues, each flying the sign of the Feathered Serpent. Carved into the surface of the pale cliffs, the Upward Way climbed from the docks directly to the Seaward Gate in a series of terraced switchbacks. The city was unassailable from the sea thanks to its lofty position, and no nation had ever been foolish enough to assault the Upward Way.

Andoses watched from the forecastle of the *Sharkstooth* as the glittering bluffs grew larger. The pearly domes of the city could no longer be seen this near to the seawall, though from farther out Mumbaza had shone brilliant as the sun itself. Soon the eager crew would bring their ship to anchor, and the *Cloud* sailed close behind. Fifteen days from Murala to this proud capital. Of course, a day had been lost in salvaging men and provisions from *Dairon's Spear*, but the weather had favored the voyage. Andoses longed to feel solid ground beneath his feet. He had sailed the Golden Sea many times, but always for pleasure trips of a day or two. Two weeks of crowded decks, cramped quarters, and sea rations was more than enough. In the palace of the Boy-King there would be splendor and luxuries to enjoy.

After seeing the terrible thing from the depths that destroyed the *Spear*, Andoses no longer trusted the sea. What other ancient horrors slumbered down there? He thanked the Gods of Cloud and Sky when the port of Mumbaza finally came in view. He might never look upon the calm waters of the sea again without thinking of the leviathan and the splintering galleon. The men who wailed and died like helpless insects. The rotten reek of the beast on the wind. He still smelled it at times, or imagined he did.

So many deaths. But Vireon had emerged more the hero. The men worshipped him now. All to the good of Shar Dni. With Vireon at the head of the Four Nations, men would rush into battle as if the Gods themselves rode at their backs. All Andoses needed to complete this masterpiece of a plan was the allegiance of the Boy-King. Undutu and his royal mother Umbrala must join the cause. How could they refuse? Five Princes came now to their doorstep, and Vireon the Great among them. The Killer of Serpents . . . the Son of Vod. Yes, the Mumbazans turned Prince D'zan away when he sought refuge here months ago . . . but he was no longer a lone, scared boy running for his life; he was a key member of the Alliance of Nations. This was history, gathering like stormclouds about Mumbaza's wharves, brewing up a storm of glory.

Andoses left captain and crew to their duties and went to prepare himself. Soldiers lined the decks, peering upward at the cliff road. They, too, were anxious to tread the land again. Inside his cabin he donned a shirt of golden mail over a blue tunic with white trim. His leggings were white leather, and his boots black as coal. The sapphire at the forehead of his turban-helm was polished; it gleamed brightly in the small mirror he used to oil his beard and mustache. A cloak of sea-blue silk bearing the White Bull of Shar Dni completed his wardrobe, along with the jeweled scimitar on his broad belt. He marched on deck, ready to face Boy-King and the Queen Mother.

The *Cloud* moored itself alongside the *Sharkstooth*, and he saw in its forecastle the other Princes arrayed in their finery: Vireon in snow-tiger cloak and silver mail shirt over a black tunic, the sword of a Giant on his back; Tyro in the green-gold mail of Uurz, the sun emblem at his breast, a helm of gilded bronze hiding his dark curls; Lyrilan in his scholar's robes of jade silk, golden belt and bracers, and even a longblade hitched on his side; D'zan in jet with silver trim, purple-cloaked and with the golden sword and tree emblem of Yaskatha on his breast, the bright hilt of his greatsword rising above the left shoulder; and Vireon's woman, Alua the Sorceress, looking every bit a northern queen in a gown of white and gossamer, gold hoops glimmering on her neck and fingers, bright as her hair . . . a vision of frosted beauty with midnight eyes.

Tyro hailed him across the narrow interval of water, and Andoses waved. Then the gangplank was lowered and he walked onto the quay, an escort of ten hand-picked guards behind him in the silver-and-blue mail of Shar Dni. Each of the Princes would have ten such guards, representing all the colors of the Alliance. A small but effective show of unity; entering the city with any more soldiers might be considered a hostile act. So Tyro had settled on this number, and Andoses thought it good. As his boots clicked across the marble wharf, mingling with the caws of seabirds, he thought suddenly of wine – the rich dark wines of Mumbaza were highly prized in every realm. Soon he would taste of that fine vintage and feel like a Prince once again. As soon as they climbed that army of stairs. He breathed deep of the clean sea air, steeling himself for the long vertical walk.

A company of Mumbazan soldiers led by an officer in a cape of crimson feathers greeted the five Princes. There was no advance word of their coming, so messengers must be huffing up the steps even now carrying word to the palace. The officer gave a short bow, his hand resting on the hilt of his curved sword. His powerful body appeared carved from obsidian, and he went bare-chested like all the Men of Mumbaza, though his leggings were loose pantaloons tucked into tall boots. A circlet of gold, the sign of his rank, held back the mass of braids and beads that was his hair. This was the common fashion of Mumbazan men.

"I greet you, Princes, in the name of Undutu, King of Mumbaza,

Lord of the Feathered Serpent, Master of the Pearl Coast. I am Antuu, Marshall of the Port." His voice was almost musical, steeped as it was in his exotic accent.

Andoses had arranged to speak for the five. The game now began.

"Evenbliss to the King and Queen Mother," said Andoses, removing his turban and tucking it under his arm. "Greetings to you, Marshall Antuu. We are five Princes from the north, come to see the King on a matter of utmost urgency. We bring tributes of gold, jewels, and fine silk for His Majesty." He introduced each of the Princes by his respective name and nation. The Marshall bowed to each one in turn, and lastly to Alua. He kissed her hand in the manner of a suitor. *Some things remain the same, no matter where you travel*, thought Andoses. Alua smiled like a young girl, something she did quite often. Andoses had never known a sorceress before, but in all his visions and readings, he had never imagined one with such an aura of innocence. The woman was almost annoying in her girlishness.

Then the long climb began. The heat of the day was great, but strong cool winds blew off the sea. This made the great stair more dangerous, yet the heat more bearable. Andoses led the train of Princes, and each of his ten guards carried a chest of wealth for the Boy-King. Marshall Antuu and twenty of his white-cloaked spearmen led the way, and twenty more Mumbazan soldiers brought up the rear. They were both formal and careful, these Mumbazans.

Andoses looked out across the sea as the great ships grew smaller. At this pace, the embassy should reach the palace by the afternoon. The rest of the cohort, and the crews of the two galleons, would come up later to enter the city. Every man among them would enjoy the pleasures of Mumbaza. The stay here would be some recompense for the terror they had endured on the voyage.

He focused on the tall granite steps, taking them one after the other. Vireon soon overtook him, walking without a trace of effort. If he had not been with Alua, he might have ran up the great cliff-stair and waited for the entire procession. The man was truly touched by the Gods . . . or the Uduru, if truth be spoken. The blood of Vod not only flowed in his cousin's veins, but also the strength and vitality of a Giant. Perhaps even more than one. Andoses envied his stamina and power – what it must be like to be Vireon – yet he must settle for being Vireon's cousin and friend. If he lived to be a hundred years old, he would still be telling the story of Vireon and the Sea-Serpent, and there would still be wonder dancing in his eyes.

After an interminable period of mindless legwork, the company gained the top of the cliff and gathered before the massive gates of the city wall. They stood open as if to honor the new arrivals. The Feathered Serpent motif wound across the surfaces of the mighty doors, a masterwork of raised gold. How many thieves had tried to chip some of that gold away for their own pockets? How many had died trying it? The city wall was built of white stone that gleamed like mother-of-pearl. Looking over his shoulder, Andoses saw the tiny ships far below, and he turned away lest vertigo overtake him.

Now the pearly city lay before them, domed temples with roofs of milk-white chalcedony and terraces of bright malachite; slim towers of marble crowned with beryl and amethyst; hanging gardens ripe with fruit vivid as jewels; winding streets of pale stone where fresh-water fountains danced and laughed at the sea. The people in the streets were icons of dark beauty, their lean bodies glistening like statues of ebony. Women carried woven baskets on their heads, full of round fruit luscious as their ample breasts. The Mumbazans wore gold, copper, and bronze about their long necks, arms, and wrists . . . even their ankles. They laughed and sang and danced along flowery lanes as the five Princes and their retinue marched toward the palace. Children gathered on street corners in loincloths or white smocks, watching them with wide ivory eyes. Dromedaries draped in myriad colors and strings of bells carried riders and baskets of green produce. A few noblemen rode pure-breed horses of brilliant black or creamy white, caparisoned in strings of gold and gems. The buildings gleamed, dazzling as white sand.

Andoses breathed in the drifting smells of the city. The fragrance of a dozen blossoms borne on the sea wind, the scents of roasting meats and simmering garlic. At times a whiff of camel-musk distracted him from these goodly smells, but always the sweet odors returned. They mingled and merged into a delicious scent, the perfume of Mumbaza. His mouth watered, and he craved wine. After that climb it would be sweeter than water on his tongue.

The palace was a white eminence of terraced gardens, opalescent arches, sculpted cupolas, and towers of white marble glazed with beryl and topaz. Marshall Antuu gave orders in the local tongue, and the five Princes entered a vaulted corridor. Jade pillars here were carved into twisting Feathered Serpents, their heads supporting the arches of the roof. At the end of the wide hall rose the dais of the Opal Throne. A brace of soldiers lined each wall, white plumes rising from golden helms, spears hung with horsetails. The sun blazed through high windows, and the Boy-King of Mumbaza looked upon his guests.

Undutu was twelve years old, yet he sat with all the grace of a full-grown King on the throne that dwarfed him. Andoses noticed first the brown bottoms of his bare feet, which hung over the lip of the great chair. A single massive opal gleamed behind and above his tiny head, and a crown of diamond and ruby – sized perfectly – sat upon his small brow. A crimson cloak hung from his shoulders, and although his chest was bare, his kilt was cloth-of-gold. A sleepy lion yawned on either side of the Boy-King's throne, collared by gilded bronze.

At Undutu's side, in a lesser throne of silk-lined gold, sat his mother Umbrala, a woman of middle years and considerable beauty. She wore no crown, but needed none. The power of her position radiated from her sharp eyes. Her hair rose tall and sculpted behind a conical headdress of wire and jewels. Her dress was a one-shouldered affair similar to others Andoses had seen in the city, but made of costlier fabric. Jewels sparkled along her brown fingers and toes. She smiled toward the procession as it drew near, while the Boy-King stared in his best imitation of the marble statues lining his hall.

Marshall Antuu announced the Princes one by one. Andoses' men carried their ten chests to the foot of the dais, unlocking and flinging back the lids. The splendor of their jeweled contents cast brilliant hues across the hall. The queen seemed impressed, but the Boy-King held his stone face. No doubt he had been well coached and had plenty of chances to practice.

"Great King," said Andoses, speaking to the boy but addressing the mother, "we come with this tribute of wealth to show our high regard for you and your kingdom. We represent four nations allied in the cause of justice. We would speak with you of adding Mumbaza's might to our alliance."

The Boy-King nodded. "I accept your tribute," he said. His reedy voice was that of a typical boy, yet weighted with the iron of responsibility. "We hold all your nations in high esteem. We will speak of this alliance as we eat and drink together in this hall. You shall enjoy the hospitality of my roof as long as you like. Your retinues are likewise welcome here. But before we speak of alliances, there is a messenger for you, Prince Andoses."

The Queen Mother turned to a robed functionary. "Send for the

Sharrian," she said, her voice smooth and deep. Andoses thought her twice his age, but still he marveled at the smoothness of her thighs, the deep color of her cheeks, and the fullness of her hips. These Mumbazan women had splendid hips. It took a moment for him to realize what she had said.

"A Sharrian?" he asked.

"Yes," said Queen Umbrala. "A herald from your homeland arrived thirteen days past. Thus we knew of your coming. He bears a personal message from your father's court."

The Sharrian messenger entered through a far door and approached down the corridor. The Boy-King ordered wine brought for his guests. Andoses had forgotten his thirst. He recognized the man in the blue-and-white livery of Shar Dni.

"Prince Andoses!" called the Sharrian, rushing to bow before him.

"Dyartha the Swift," Andoses said. "I did not expect to see you so far from home."

Dyartha was chief herald in service to the throne of Shar Dni. He carried messages to Uurz and Udurum, but Andoses had no idea he traveled this far. He must have ridden south to Allundra at the eastern end of the Earth-Wall, then west along its fringe all the way to the steppes. Hard riding for weeks, leaving behind a string of spent horses. Only a single rider with a good supply of strong mounts could travel so fast. Only a skilled warrior could survive the dangers of such a journey.

The smile fell from Dyartha's face as he took a tube of white bone from his belt. He withdrew a curled scroll from within and handed it to Andoses. The King's Hall grew quiet as Andoses read the message on the parchment. His knees grew weak, and his legs abandoned him. Dyartha caught him as he fell, and helped him to a cushioned divan between pillars. A murmur of concern rushed like a momentary wind through the hall.

"What is it, Cousin?" asked Vireon, leaning over him. Andoses slumped on the couch, his fingers numb, his heart shattered like a glass globe. His stomach churned, and he gasped for air. Someone handed him a cup of Mumbazan wine . . . the wine he had so anticipated. He quaffed it to the dregs but tasted none of it.

"Speak, Andoses," said Tyro. "What is the message?"

"My father is dead," he said. The words sounded distant, faraway syllables spoken by someone else. "I am to come home at once . . . and be crowned King."

"What happened?" asked Lyrilan. "What else does the scroll say?"

Andoses handed it to Lyrilan. The world spun about him, and he held his head in his hands. His father could not be dead . . . not Ammon the Strong . . . he was still hearty and full of life. Tears welled, but Andoses wiped them. He would *not* blubber in the hall of the Boy-King. It was bad enough that the five Princes gathered about him now like a group of maids about a vexed housewife. He forced himself to stand.

"According to this," said Lyrilan, as the Princes' eyes fell upon him, "it was Fangodrel. He came into the palace and unleashed some kind of sorcery, killing everyone in the royal hall. Ammon, his seven sisters, and a Duke named Dutho, Son of Omirus . . ."

"My father's brother," said Andoses, regaining his composure. There would be time for grieving later. Not now. "My Uncle Omirus holds the throne as Regent until I return."

"You are King of Shar Dni," said D'zan.

"Not until the Sky Priests have performed the Rites of Coronation."

"I am sorry for the loss of your father," said Tyro, placing a hand on his shoulder.

"Not here," said Andoses in a low voice. "Remember our goal."

Vireon simmered silently. Alua whispered something in his ear, but the Prince of Udurum held murder in his eyes. Ammon had been the brother of Vireon's mother. Another victim of his mad half-brother.

Andoses swallowed his pain.

Use it, use it all. Hide the sorrow, the tears, the hate.

Use it to guide you. It is a dark power . . . See it burning in Vireon's eyes.

The Princes returned to their formation before the Boy-King.

"The tragedy of your loss is felt in our hearts also," said Queen Umbrala. "Please accept our condolences. Tonight we will feast in honor of King Ammon's memory, and you will know the comforts of our palace."

"I thank you, kind Queen . . . great King," said Andoses, bowing.

This, too, can work in your favor.

It must. Otherwise it could destroy you.

"We accept your gracious offer. There is much to discuss before I depart to claim the Sharrian throne."

The Queen Mother clapped her hands, and robed servants came to attend the Princes. The hall became a bustling scene of activity, and the guests were led to their individual chambers to prepare for the feast.

Andoses was given a vast room of hanging silks and jasper murals. A tall window overlooked the brilliant sea. When the servants left, he ordered his personal guard to stand outside the door. Then, alone at the window, caressed by a cool sea breeze, he wept.

None heard the sound of his sorrow carried away on the fragrant winds.

25

A Shadow from Zaashari

At Iardu's touch the gnarled tree became a four-wheeled wagon with a canopy of woven grass. He called two white goats from the pen and changed them into strong horses to pull the carriage. In the misty gold of morning Khama loaded his three sons, his daughter, and his wife into the wagon. He set the rest of his sheep and goats free to find their own grazing grounds, then joined his family on the conveyance. Food and clothing were bundled into burlap sacks, and five clay jars of fresh water completed the family's provisions. Iardu and Sharadza sat on the driver's bench as the horses trotted westward across the steppe. Khama wore a cloak of feathers, its colors fading from red along the shoulders to green at its middle, then blue around his ankles. Squatting at the back of the wagon, he watched his tiny farm diminish until the tall, windblown grass swallowed it.

They came to an unpaved road leading west toward the capital, and here the white horses picked up speed. Sharadza watched the villages of Mumbaza pass by, all of them similar to Khama's own. The ripe crops of farms were being harvested, and herds of livestock were tended by brawny black youths. The road crossed a bridge of arching stone above a lazy river. Mumbazans lined the riverbanks, filling ewers and jars for nearby villages. Groups of shouting children jumped into the brown water, and riverboats glided gracefully into the west. Commerce in this land ran always toward the city and its ancient wealth. The river wound like a great glistening ribbon, and from the middle of the bridge Sharadza saw a dozen villages hugging its course. Soldiers in white-plumed helmets manned a garrison at the bridge's far end, but a wave from Khama's hand brought easy passage. She did not think he worked a spell; the soldiers knew his face. Probably he passed this way several times a year going to the Great Market.

After a time the pearly spires of the capital came into view above a forest of yellow grass. Traffic on the road grew thicker now. A cadre of noblemen rode jewelled stallions, returning from a hunt with the carcasses of long-necked birds tied to their saddlehorns. Merchant carts drawn by sluggish camels blocked the road at times, but Iardu's ensorcelled goat-horses pulled the carriage effortlessly around them, veering through the high grass and back onto the thoroughfare. Ebony women carried baskets and bundles upon their heads, and a troop of white-cloaked soldiers marched eastward, helmets gleaming like the heads of golden birds.

The city walls and domes rose high above the road now. Sea winds caressed Sharadza's skin and danced in her black curls. Beyond the spires hung a great blue gulf of sky; flocks of seabirds flew between the bright towers. The road brought them through the Western Gate, iron portals graven with the coils of the Feathered Serpent. The gate stood wide open in the hour of late afternoon, and Khama hailed the guards as the wagon rolled near. Directly ahead lay the shimmering heights of the Boy-King's palace, an intricate structure that seemed carved of a single great opal, so great was its glow in the joyful heat of the sun.

In many ways the city was like Uurz. The people and their

dress were different, but the atmosphere of close-knit livelihood, the winding streets brimming with secrets, the verdant balconies and terraced gardens thick with fruiting blossoms . . . all these reminded her of Dairon's city. Yet here the sun ruled the sky, and the storms of Uurz were only rumors. The city was not so hot as the steppe had been; the ocean winds sighed through its avenues and glided over its walls like benevolent spirits.

At the palace gate Khama, who carried his herdsman's staff as if it were a soldier's spear, exchanged words with the guards. They granted him entry with a series of bows. He led his family along a marble path between terraced orchards while Iardu and Sharadza followed at their heels. The children of Khama walked in quiet awe. The city streets were familiar to them, but the palace grounds were another world entirely. Khama must have been here often, but his family had never crossed the royal threshold before today. Emi held her husband's hand as they walked an avenue of bronze statues, warriors recreated from the pages of history.

Khama brought them into a vaulted hall of twisting pillars, and at last they stood before the thrones of the Boy-King and his royal mother. Stern-faced spearmen in livery of pearl and gold lined the walls, but it was the six figures standing politely near the royal dais that drew Sharadza's attention.

Vireon . . . Andoses . . . and those must be the Twin Princes Tyro and Lyrilan of Uurz. The handsome fair-haired lad of her own age could only be D'zan, Scion of Yaskatha. A gorgeous blonde woman in milky robes stood at Vireon's elbow, the mysterious Alua. Sharadza's gaze fell upon her brother. It had been months since his blue eyes smiled back at her.

Khama bowed low before the seated Boy-King, and his family followed suit. Iardu and Sharadza sank to one knee in the manner of visiting officials. In such situations, the King or his representative must speak first.

"Wise Khama," said the Boy-King, sitting up straighter in his regal chair, "our hearts soar at your presence." Queen Umbrala stared approvingly at Khama. An old passion simmered in her dark eyes.

Khama's face rose to regard the King. "Your Majesty grows tall and mighty," he said. "Soon he will tower above the spires of his own palace."

The Boy-King laughed and turned to share his mirth with Umbrala.

Khama addressed the Queen now, his eyes still on her son. "Queen Umbrala, it has been too long since I stood in the light of your smile. Please forgive my long absence. This is my family." He introduced them by name, as well as Iardu and Sharadza.

Vireon strode forward, his white teeth gleaming, huge arms spread wide. Sharadza beamed and rushed to embrace him. "Little sister," he whispered.

"Brother . . . " she breathed at his ear.

They pulled apart, speaking in low voices.

"Where have you been, Little One?" he asked.

She took his face in her hands. "I have much to tell you. Later . . . "

Vireon explained to Undutu that his long-lost sister had arrived in the company of the esteemed Khama. Boy-King and Queen Mother were pleased.

"Family is the First Gift of the Gods," said Undutu. "Last night we mourned the death of a great King. Tonight we will celebrate the reuniting of family and friends."

Khama spoke loudly: "Great Majesty, before we sit at the feasting table, we must sit at the Council table. A dire threat grows in the south. I ask sanctuary for my family here within your impervious walls."

"You shall have it," said the Boy-King. He glanced at his

mother, who nodded. "These five Princes have come to speak of this same threat. Let us enter Council together."

Servants came to conduct Khama's family to their quarters. The herdsman hugged each of them desperately and kissed his wife. He promised her she would see him again before he went south. Then the King, Queen Mother, and the nine visitors walked a carpeted hallway leading to the airy dome of the Council Chamber. There a great oval table of polished obsidian was headed by two lesser thrones for Undutu and Umbrala.

As the guests filed into the room and seated themselves about the table, Sharadza approached Andoses, whose face was pale. She embraced her cousin, and he returned her affection with his own strong arms. Normally he would have shouted a greeting and been smiling at her by now. Something was wrong.

"Are you ill, Cousin?" she asked.

He told her of Ammon's death, and the others. She could not prevent the tears from escaping her eyes.

First Tadarus, now Ammon, my seven aunts . . . sweet Dara, silver-voiced Thoria . . . even kind Dutho. How many more would die at the hands of Fangodrel? Things were moving too fast. The storm of death had already begun. Perhaps Iardu was right . . . perhaps there was no stopping this slaughter. She hugged stiff Andoses again and consoled him as best she could, but then it was time to sit and engage the Boy-King. Servants loaded the table with cups and carafes of wine, and bowls piled high with grapes, olives, and mangos.

"The five Princes came to us only yesterday," said Queen Umbrala, her almond eyes focused on Khama. "They speak of Yaskatha and Khyrei, whose rulers are both sorcerers. They ask us to join their Alliance of Nations and oppose our fellow southern realms. Yet as the King and I have explained to them this very morning, we have a long-standing treaty of peace with Yaskatha.

When Trimesqua fell, Prince D'zan came to us seeking sanctuary, and this we could not grant by virtue of that same treaty.

"This Elhathym is called a tyrant, but he has yet honored this treaty. The Yaskathan ships of trade still flourish at our docks. We hear from traders and refugees the stories of his cruelty, but our borders are secure. If we take up arms against Yaskatha, we end the treaty and forfeit our national honor . . . and if we ally with those who strike against Yaskatha, the same will be true."

"Majesty," spoke Andoses, blinking bloodshot eyes, "we all know the King is an honorable and righteous leader, as were his fathers before him. We value treaties and diplomacy as highly as any kingdom. Yet when Elhathym murdered the father of Prince D'zan and claimed the throne through blood and terror, he invalidated any treaties made by the rightful king of Yaskatha. In order to restore that treaty which has kept your nation free and powerful for so long, you *must* act against this usurper and restore Trimesqua's rightful heir to his throne."

Sharadza listened. Andoses, the eternal diplomat, had spoken well.

"But the treaty remains in effect," said Queen Umbrala, "as long as the usurper has not violated our borders or otherwise disrupted our peace."

"How long will that be, Majesty?" asked Tyro. Sunlight streamed through a high casement and flashed upon his green-and-gold mail shirt. "Even now he plots against you with the Bitch of Khyrei at his elbow. Their sorcery is foul, and it grows in silence like a plague. I implore you not to wait for the strike that is destined to come, for it may be a fatal blow."

The Boy-King's white eyes shifted from speaker to speaker. He was clever this boy, clever enough to hear what everyone had to say before he would speak. Including his wise mother.

Khama spoke now. "I have looked southward, into the shadow

of what grows there – it is something terrible. Something from the Outer Worlds . . . Evil spirits are afoot in the night. Regardless of your decision regarding the alliance, Majesties, I ask permission to go south and confront this Elhathym. Iardu the Shaper and his protégée will accompany me. We will face the usurper before his own throne. It is our dearest hope to avoid the coming of war, whatever the cost. I give my family over to your shelter so that I may do this thing. *War* is the Great Destroyer that has been banished from our land for generations. It cannot be allowed to return."

The Queen Mother spoke in whispers with her son, while those about the table sat mute. Iardu helped himself to the wine; Lyrilan dropped a fat grape into his mouth.

"The King gives you his blessing, Khama," said Umbrala. "You are not an official servant of the court, therefore you may confront the usurper without any stain upon our honor. If you can do good in Yaskatha, then go."

Khama turned to Iardu. The pair nodded.

"Yet linger a little while," said Umbrala. "At the least you must dine with us tonight."

Khama bowed his head. "We are most honored."

Andoses spoke again. "Majesties, I beg you to hear the words of brave Prince D'zan. He has faced death and more to sit at this table."

All eyes fell to D'zan, who sat uncomfortably in his chair. Sharadza liked him instantly. His eyes were blue, like Vireon's, and his face was fair. His broad shoulders were impressive for a youth. His broad mouth was expressive, the lips of a well-spoken Prince. She found herself curious to hear what he had to say.

"I am . . . overwhelmed," said D'zan, "by the support of my friends and allies in the north. We have crossed seas and mountains together . . . endured ice and fire . . . faced the horrors of sorcery and the fangs of awful beasts. We have walked with death at our very backs, and many have perished on our journey. That I live at all is a miracle I owe to these four Princes." His eyes turned to the Boy-King. "My father cherished the long peace he held with Mumbaza, as did his father before him. He once spoke of it as the brightest jewel in his crown. There were other wars, campaigns against the southern island nations, the war with Khyrei that happened well before I was born. But never did he speak of Mumbaza with anything other than love and great respect.

"I understand why you could not offer me sanctuary months ago. I bear no ill will toward you for that decision. When the throne of my father is once again mine, I will keep Mumbaza in my heart, along with the Northern Nations. A great philosopher once said, 'War is failure.' I believe that, Majesties. War is a failure of diplomacy and compassion to conquer fear and hate. It is the failure of peace-loving peoples to act in prevention of threats that grow in the world's dark places.

"I pledge to you now that as long as I sit on the Throne of Yaskatha, there will be only peace between the five nations gathered here. Should Mumbaza refuse to join me against the usurper, that pledge of peace will still stand, both from myself and my descendants. But until Elhathym is deposed . . . until his blasphemous power is hidden from the Sun God's eyes . . . until that day . . . the specter of War hangs over this kingdom like a shroud. I speak from my heart, and for the free people of Yaskatha."

A silence fell upon the chamber. Sharadza turned to Iardu, whose smooth face was inscrutable. Vireon nodded his head in blatant approval of D'zan's words. She could tell he favored the young Prince. Andoses sat with a half-smile, his eyes on the Boy-King. Tyro's face was stone. Lyrilan ate another grape, mentally noting all the proceedings in the scholar's detached way that was his nature. Alua sat with an expression of purest innocence next to

Vireon. She looked entirely out of place here, yet completely comfortable in the presence of her lover.

"Your words are moving," said Queen Umbrala, "and the King values your friendship. Our goals are the same – eternal peace and prosperity for Mumbaza and all other nations – yet for now we can only send Wise Khama to Yaskatha . . . to do any more would violate that very peace of which you speak."

Iardu sighed. D'zan looked at the table.

"Have you any word of good will from this usurper?" asked Andoses. "Any renewal of the treaty's precepts, or even the smallest tribute to show his fidelity?"

"We have received no word from Elhathym," said the Queen Mother.

"Have you sent emissaries to him?" asked Tyro.

"One," she admitted. "He has yet to return."

"So you have nothing but silence from this bloody-handed sorcerer," said Andoses. "And you take that for peaceful intentions? Majesties, this is a gross error. The scorpion is most silent before it kills."

"Silence can also heal," said the Boy-King. All eyes turned now to his small round head with its glittering crown. "The Queen has spoken for me, and now I echo her words. We will not join this Alliance against Yaskatha unless Elhathym moves against us. Neither will we condemn or reject your offer. We will be wise and patient instead. We will *wait* . . . and we will see."

"As you wish, Majesty," said Andoses with an air of exhaustion. "I must be gone with all speed in the morning. The throne of Shar Dni sits empty until I am crowned. I regret that I cannot stay longer and attempt to sway your royal wisdom. The war against Khyrei will proceed. I hope that you will change your mind and join us before the coming of spring, when we march upon the city of Ianthe the Claw."

"I go with you, Andoses," said Vireon. "I have fulfilled my mother's wish in coming to Mumbaza. Now vengeance calls me eastward, and I would bring you safely home, Cousin."

Andoses stood and bowed. "I could never be safer than in your company, Vireon."

"In the morning you three go east while we three go south," said Khama. "What of the rest of you?"

Tyro and Lyrilan looked to D'zan.

"The time has also come for me to return to my homeland," said D'zan. "I go south."

Tyro slammed his fist against the table. "My brother and I go with you, Prince! We have a cohort of a hundred and fifty northmen to ride with us."

"Take my hundred Sharrians as well," said Andoses. "Vireon, Alua, and I require no escort. A group of three will travel much faster atop the Earth-Wall than a host of men."

"So be it," said Tyro.

"So be it," said the Boy-King. "Now let us forget the perils of war and travel. We will feast tonight in honor of these assembled families before the sun shines on their parting." His mother looked pleased at his fine words.

Sharadza would have preferred to leave immediately for Yaskatha. But Khama relished one more night with his family. *No harm in some rest now*, she decided. *We will need all our strength when we face the tyrant sorcerer.*

Already she smelled the roasting meats and sweet baked confections that would line the Boy-King's table.

A night in Mumbaza. She looked out an arched window at the crimson glow of sunset on the purple ocean. *It's like some tale of heroes and maidens . . . some exotic legend from pages in father's library.* Yet it was all too real. *Tonight will be splendor, tomorrow will be danger.*

She resolved to enjoy the splendors of Mumbaza while she could.

The feast ran late into the night, and Sharadza drank more than her share of wine. She drank with Andoses and Vireon, the first time she had done so. The Boy-King's table was covered with delicacies from the sea, great swordfish roasted whole, carmine lobsters, and tentacled things in pools of creamy butter. Dancing girls performed for Undutu and his guests, followed by a match between two hulking Mumbazan wrestlers, and a fire-eater. The young monarch was much amused by all these diversions, while his mother sat reserved and attentive. A band of royal musicians played on silver-stringed instruments, oxhide drums, and a brace of woodwinds.

Vireon told Sharadza of his adventures in the Ice King's realm, how he met Alua, and his battle against the Sea Serpent. Andoses augmented the latter tale, praising the heroic skill of his cousin and his matchless courage. Alua did not speak much, but when she did she talked of the northern forests and her travels in the land below the White Mountains. Sharadza found her sweet in the manner of a child, yet possessed of a subtle intelligence. When Vireon described her white flame, her learning of his language through sleep, and other strange things she had done, Sharadza knew Alua was far more than she appeared.

She is of the Old Breed. She has forgotten her origin, but still carries its power within her. She uses it naturally, as a child learns naturally to walk or swim. Perhaps Vireon is bringing out her true self, in the way that Iardu brought out my own . . . yet not that way at all. It could be that Alua will bring out Vireon's heritage as well. The strength of Vod already flows in his veins; what other sorceries lie inside him, waiting for expression? The same as those that lie within me. Alua was a good match for her brother. She was glad he had found someone to replace his endless trysts with nameless girls from Udurum and Uurz. She had never seen him respond to anyone this way. He held Alua's hand like his palm would ache without it. He looked into her ice-blue eyes like a man looking at the clouds and imagining his future. Their mother was correct. Vireon was in love.

Over brimming wine cups they shared memories of Tadarus and toasted his memory. And they drank to King Ammon, their lost uncle, and the rest of Andoses' family one by one. Andoses shed a few quiet tears, but he wiped them away like flies buzzing around his goblet. He was a sturdy soul . . . as indestructible as Vireon in his own way.

After Khama's family retired for the night, Khama returned alone to speak with Iardu in guarded whispers. The Shaper enjoyed the King's wine, and none there drank more than he. Not even Andoses, who drowned his grief in a purple flood.

Vireon demanded to know where Sharadza had gone and why she had left their mother in such worry. As she explained her tutelage under Iardu, Tyro and Lyrilan peppered her with questions, most of which she could not answer. Prince D'zan listened as well, though he held his tongue. When he looked her way, his eyes sparkled like gold in the candlelight.

Vireon demanded evidence of her sorcery, as if he disbelieved her tale. Tyro joined him in calling for a show of her skill. This went on until she silenced them by transforming herself into a white wolf. She crouched on her hind legs in the feasting chair, staring at them with blood-red eyes, red tongue lolling between her fangs. Vireon laughed, half-drunk on Mumbazan wine, but the rest only stared in quiet awe. The Boy-King smiled and clapped to show his appreciation of her "trick."

Iardu only frowned in her direction, and once again she became Sharadza.

"My dear sister, the sorceress!" bellowed Vireon, slapping the table. Then he grew suddenly serious and raised his cup. "You are the Daughter of Vod, and you bear his power. To Vod's Daughter!" They drank yet another toast, this time in *her* honor, while she blushed.

Several times she caught D'zan eyeing her, though he looked away every time. *How brave he must be to endure all that he has*. He was quiet and a bit mysterious. *I must speak with him.* Yet the feast ran on, and she never did get around to speaking with him. The torches guttered low on their tall mounts, and the Boy-King fell asleep in his tall chair. Servants carried him off to bed and Queen Umbrala followed, bidding good night to her guests. Soon after, Sharadza stumbled to her own quarters, realizing too late that she was not a skilled wine drinker at all. She had no time to admire the opulence of the guest chamber before she fell into slumber.

Nightmares swam up from the depths of the dreamworld to torment her. Clawed things rushed and fell, slithered past her on the waves of a dark sea. Serpentine beings slid beneath her as she walked across the glassy waves without sinking. A white hawk flew down to sit on her shoulder and whisper something in her ear. She could not understand the ancient words. The sea beneath her was not water at all, but *blood* . . . and people drowned in it . . . the black-skinned people of Mumbaza screamed and wept and sank. Dark beasts rose up from the blood-sea to rend them with claw and fang, to gnaw their bones. She screamed and tried to work sorcery, but the slaughter continued and the sea of blood refused to swallow her. At last a single massive claw rose to wrap around her waist, squeezing until her bones cracked. The talons sank into her flesh like swords. She awoke to the gentle prodding of a bald servant-girl with golden hoops in her ears.

The chamber's windows were still dark; the moon had set, but the sun had not yet risen.

"The Queen Mother summons you to Council," said the girl, her accent thick and melodic. "Right away . . ."

The servant waited for Sharadza to dress, then led her along a corridor she did not remember. *Too much wine. Never again.* As they walked, Tyro and Lyrilan joined them, also bleary-eyed. Then D'zan and Vireon, Khama and Iardu, and finally Andoses in his gleaming turban. All had been awakened. She guessed that less than an hour of night remained. It must be something urgent to summon them from their beds before even the dawn broke. Shards of nightmare swam in the back of her head like evil fish in muddy water.

Servants guided them into the Council Chamber with the long black table. Queen Umbrala sat at its head in a robe of sapphire silk. Her headdress and jewelry were absent. She, too, had awakened not long ago. The Boy-King was not present. A grimy soldier sat in the chair to the Queen's left, his hands trembling about a goblet of wine. Soot and dirt smeared his bare face and arms, and a white bandage wrapped his left shoulder. His face bore the pall of exhaustion and terror. Perhaps he had been weeping. His white cloak hung in tatters.

The five Princes, Sharadza, Iardu, and Khama took their seats. Vireon had not roused Alua.

"Majesty," said Khama. "Is the King all right?"

Umbrala nodded. "He sleeps. I am his voice until he wakes."

"What has happened?" asked Andoses.

"This is Wayudi, a captain of the garrison at Zaashari," said the Queen Mother. The haunted soldier gave a modest bow, his unsteady hands gripping the goblet like a holy talisman. "Explain to them what you have told me . . ."

Wayudi was an educated officer, schooled in the northern languages. His words were flavored with fear. "They came out of the night . . . seeking our blood." His eyes grew round, the black pupils tiny in pools of white. "*Shadows* . . . things made of shadow . . . some like tall wolves with eyes of fire . . . others slid like Serpents across the ground . . . or flew like bats . . . Some walked like twisted men. They came at dusk, when the last of the sunlight faded. There was no moon anymore . . . only the brightness of their scarlet eyes . . . the color of the blood they crave."

Wayudi paused to drink deeply from his wine cup. Iardu and Khama shared a silent glance.

"These things . . . they flowed through the streets like a flood of dark water . . . or black smoke . . . finding men, women . . . even children. They *tore* at them, lapping at their blood like hounds. It was their screams that roused the watch . . . Commander Ulih ordered us into the streets with spear and sword . . . I headed the cavalry. They ripped our horses to shreds beneath us . . . then tore into men like jackals. One leaped on my back, biting me here." He pointed to the bandage on his shoulder, spotted with seeping red. "Our metal was useless . . . Spears, swords, knives . . . we could not touch them . . . They were . . . they were ghosts . . . *muraki* . . . evil spirits." He set the goblet down and put a hand on his shoulder. "Gods, how it aches."

"You will rest soon, Wayudi," said Umbrala, her tone motherly yet firm. "Only tell the rest of it first."

Wayudi's eyes scanned the table, as if he might find some belief there, or some comfort that did not exist. He breathed deeply. "We could not count their numbers – there were far too many. The town died and the men of the fortress died . . . We died trying to protect the people. Ulih . . . they pulled off his limbs, drank his blood like all the rest. I know I am a coward, but I fled . . . I was not the only one. Five or six of us fled through the shattered gate of the garrison. We rode hard along the North Road. One by one they picked us off our horses until there was only me riding north to the capital. I don't know why the one that bit me flew away. I have a coward's luck." Wayudi bowed his head, ashamed. He gulped more wine. "Zaashari is fallen," he said, looking at Khama. "They are all dead. It belongs to the shadows . . . "

His head nodded slowly forward until it touched the table, and he grew still. Beyond the tall windows, stars glimmered against the black.

"Khama," said the Queen, "what can you tell me?"

Khama's grave face met the Queen's. "The Dwellers in Shadow, ancient things that I have seen in my visions, they gather in the south and serve the Usurper."

The Queen looked upon each face at the table, a wordless apology that her pride would not allow her to voice. She quietly ordered two servants to carry Wayudi to a bed. They lifted the soldier to his feet, his arms about their shoulders, and he stumbled away to rest.

"He *knows* we are here, Khama," said Iardu. "We have lost the element of surprise . . . if we ever truly had it."

"And so the treaty is broken," said Umbrala.

"Yes," said Khama. "Knowing we would come, Elhathym struck first. Next his shadows will come north, to the gates of Mumbaza and into its streets."

"Only the sun will stop them," said Iardu. "His living legions will ride into Zaashari at sunrise and take control of the fortress, now that all in it are dead."

The Queen turned to Andoses. "We will join your Alliance of Nations," she said, "but we cannot now send legions to Khyrei, for we must go to war against Yaskatha."

"I am sorry for this slaughter," said Andoses. "But I am glad for your allegiance. You can serve the Alliance by restoring Prince D'zan to his throne. While Mumbaza battles Elhathym, we in the east can march on Ianthe's kingdom. When the tyrant is vanquished, send your legions to join us in Khyrei."

The Queen nodded, her fine mouth set into a grim frown.

Iardu looked at Andoses. "You do not know the power of Elhathym," he said. "Or Ianthe. This will not be a war of sword and shield, but a clash of forces you can scarcely comprehend."

"We three go now to drive back the sorcerer and his demons," said Khama. He faced the Queen. "Assemble your legions to retake Zaashari and march on Yaskatha."

D'zan broke his silence. "Great Queen, I will fight with Mumbaza this day. Tyro and his warriors ride with me. The people of Zaashari will be avenged, and the usurper will pay for this peace-breaking."

The Queen's look changed from troubled to impressed as she eyed D'zan. "You will ride with my generals, Prince D'zan. And you *will* sit upon your father's throne."

Tyro gave Lyrilan a devious smile. Lyrilan licked his dry lips, coughed, pinched his nose.

"I would stand with you as well," said Andoses, "if circumstances were otherwise. I must still depart this morning."

"The King understands your need, Prince Andoses," said Umbrala. "You have his blessing and eternal friendship. Once we have smashed this usurper and his army of shadows, we will support you in Khyrei."

"Your Majesty is both wise and gracious," said Andoses with a bow.

"I must meet with the King's advisors now," said Umbrala. "My servants will see to all your needs."

The assemblage rose from their chairs, all but the Queen. A line of worried officials came through the doors to replace them. The sun was about to rise.

"Let us go at once," said Khama.

"Wait," said Iardu. "We must look in on poor Wayudi first."

"Yes," said Khama. "We must . . ."

Sharadza followed them to the room where Wayudi slept. He

lay on a bed below a window overlooking the dark sea. A cool wind blew through the casement, but Wayudi sweated and groaned as if in a fever.

"Is it poison?" asked Sharadza.

"Of the worst kind," said Iardu. "Not a physical poison, but a spiritual one."

Wayudi's spasms grew worse as the far sea warmed with pink light. The sun was coming.

Khama bent over the suffering man, mumbling a chant.

"What were those things?" Sharadza asked. "The Dwellers in Shadow you spoke of?"

"There are many kinds of shadow spirits," said Iardu, "but the Spirits of Vakai are the most deadly. When living men die, most move on to the World of the Dead, manifesting there the illusion of their own afterlife. Yet those whose souls were consumed by hatred, avarice, or cruelty often cannot find their way into the Deathlands, so they linger in the dark and forsaken corners of the world, or haunt the places where they died. When such entities spill the blood of the living, they consume its essence and gain power . . . but this power eventually forces them into the void, an Outer World called Vakai, where there is nothing more to feed on. A formless place of eternal hunger and torment."

Wayudi tossed and turned, his chest heaving, yet still unconscious. His teeth gnashed as if he were chewing a piece of leather. Khama sang and waved a hand over his shivering body. The first sparkles of sunlight danced on the ocean, and the tip of the sun-orb rose above the waves. Wayudi cried out like a dog in pain, then growled.

"These Spirits of Vakai can slip back into our world at times, or someone like Elhathym may summon them. They cannot abide the sunlight, so they roam at night. When dawn comes they sink into the depths of the earth and its very stones, where no light can penetrate. Yet at night they emerge into physical forms like wolves, reptiles, or flying beasts, to seek the blood that gives them power and substance. The *essence of blood*, torn from the living, is their only concern. Those they drain but do not kill – like Wayudi – bear their curse."

The first sunray fell through the window and Wayudi fell still. "It is too late," said Khama. "I cannot save him."

Brightness grew on the pristine walls and ceiling, and Wayudi grew dim before Sharadza's eyes. His flesh and clothing became transparent, and he flowed like water into the sheets, then into the stones of the floor. A black shadow bearing his shape lay on the floor, then that too faded.

"At nightfall he will rise and haunt the palace," said Iardu. "Unless we bind him to this room."

Khama nodded and sighed.

"You mean . . . he is . . . one of them?" Sharadza asked.

"A Vakai, yes," said Khama. "He will crave only blood."

"Why do such terrible things exist?" she asked.

Iardu looked at her as if she already knew the answer.

"Patterns," he said.

Khama instructed a servant to bring certain herbs, a strong lock for the door, and boards for the window.

"We will wait in the Lemon Garden," said Iardu, his hand on Khama's shoulder.

Sharadza had time enough to say goodbye to Vireon. She hugged him and Alua.

"Come with us to Shar Dni," said Vireon. She knew he feared for her in Yaskatha.

"I cannot," she said. "I *asked* Iardu to face Elhathym. I cannot abandon him."

Vireon seemed to understand. "We will meet in Khyrei then . . . when you are done here."

"We will," she said.

She ate a few grapes, drank some fresh milk, and joined Iardu on the terrace of a secluded garden. A ring of tall thin trees bore vivid fruits the color of topaz stones, and birds sang among the branches. The sky was blue and cloudless overhead, a hot southern sky. She had no time to visit the famous Forest of Jewels that lay somewhere in the heart of Undutu's palace. Such wonders must wait for more peaceful times.

"This is your last chance to change your mind," Iardu told her, his prismatic eyes glistening. "Once we leave here, there will be no turning back."

"What is our other choice?" she asked. "Wait for the hordes of Vakai to come raging into Mumbaza? Then Uurz? Then on to Udurum? No . . . we must do this."

"Khama and I must," he said. "But *you* do not have to. Go east with your brother and cousin. They need you in Shar Dni."

She tilted her head at him. He would go to face Elhathym without her if she asked him to. There it was again, that strange endearing look in his inhuman eyes.

"We three must go," she said, and he said no more about it.

Khama came forth in his cloak of gaudy feathers. He had finally let go of his herdsman's staff, leaving it with his wife. Without a word he sprang to the ground, balanced on his fingers, legs stretched taut behind him. The sea wind picked up and blew strong over the city as Khama's cloak lengthened and grew. Beneath its feathery folds, the man-shape blurred and was lost. The feathers multiplied in all their shades: crimson, emerald, azure. He *lengthened* impossibly, his head growing into a huge triangular shape, his body coiling and writhing among the trees of the lemon grove. Sharadza grabbed Iardu's elbow as Khama grew and swirled about them like a tri-colored wind.

A moment later his great head turned amber eyes to stare at

them. They stood now in the center space of his massive coils. Khama was the great Feathered Serpent, his neck the height of a tall horse, his body tapering in coil after coil toward the end of his pointed tail. A black stinger rose from its tip, sharp as the blade of a spear. His snout was frighteningly fanged, nostrils flaring with citrus-scented breath. She could not tell from the middle of his coiled immensity exactly how long he was.

"Climb upon my back," said the Serpent in Khama's voice, only deeper. A forked tongue long as a whip came darting from between his fangs, drawn as quickly back into the cavern of his throat. His eyes narrowed into slits as he watched them grab his plumage and lodge themselves behind his reptilian skull. Sharadza was amazed at the softness of the bright plumes.

All these wonderful feathers, and no wings . . .

Khama did not need wings. His head rose into the air and his shifting coils followed, straightening to his full length. He rose toward the clouds and flew wingless above Mumbaza, two riders on his back, the sun glistening in three colors along his feathered length.

"How can he fly without wings?" Sharadza shouted through the wind at Iardu, who rode behind her.

"He is a Creature of the Air," said Iardu. "Do you know the story of Mumbaza's founding? How the Feathered Serpent told its first king Ywatha the Spear where to build his great city?"

Sharadza nodded. The legend could be found in any proper history text. *Ywatha and the Feathered Serpent* had always been one of her favorite epics.

"That was Khama," said Iardu.

Sharadza had no words as the city dwindled below, a collection of luminescent domes and steeples gleaming like a single pearl beside the vast green sea.

26

The Game of Blood and Fire

The warships of Khyrei were black and crimson, the colors of city and jungle, night and blood. One hundred and twenty lean galleons skimmed the Golden Sea, shards of darkness escaped into the daylight. Their sails bore the white panther sigil of Ianthe on a field of black, and their prows were iron rams in the shape of horned devil-heads. Eighty slaves manned the oars of each vessel, chained and whipped, made impossibly strong by herbs and drugs that would burn away their lives in months. Upon the decks strode the demon-masked captains draped in scales of bronze, while in the holds a hundred faceless soldiers waited for the call to slay, driven to fury by the smoking bloodflower in their braziers.

Prince Gammir stood beside the Empress in the forecastle of the flagship *Talon*, scanning the northern horizon. An unnatural wind filled the black sails, and behind the ships came an invisible storm . . . a rush of forces skimming the water, darkening it from sun-gold to inky jet. The storm would rise up into a thousand deadly forms when the doors of night opened.

Gammir wore plate mail of glittering black, a longblade of sharpest obsidian sheathed at his waist. His dark hair had grown long; it writhed Serpent-like in the wind. The sunlight pained his eyes, but it would not be much longer. He squinted, searching for the first sign of the Sharrian coast. The fleet had launched in the dead of the night, powered by Ianthe's summoned wind, and it had not ceased in its headlong flight across the waters. The plan was to reach the Valley of the Bull at sunset, or soon thereafter. Two trading galleons, one from the Islands, one a Sharrian merchant, had crossed their path earlier in the day. The merciless iron rams had torn into their hulls like arrows into bales of hay, and while the main fleet gusted northward a few ships lingered to scuttle and burn the traders. Now those ships, their crews incensed by an early taste of slaughter, had rejoined the fleet. The red sun hung low in the west, and Shar Dni grew closer with every passing second.

"They plot against us," Ianthe had told him days ago. "They plan a season of war to follow their northern winter. In their ignorance, they imagine we will wait on their legions to march southward. What idiocy! They send Princes to Mumbaza to plot against our Elhathym!"

She had laughed, the sound of beautiful cruelty. Slaves cowered about her throne of ivory and jade, and the panther Miku lay sleeping at her feet. Gammir sat on a similar throne, where his grandfather the Emperor would have sat if he were still alive. If Vod had not killed him all those years ago. Gammir enjoyed the slaves of Khyrei; they served his every need, carnal and otherwise. There was none of the charade played out in his mother's court – no pretense that servants were worthy of kindness and sympathy. Ianthe's pale people – *his* people – knew their place. They lived and died to serve their Empress. And now their Prince.

Ianthe had confessed to sending the nightmares that drove Vod to madness. She sent the Red Dreams that pulled Fangodrel to her, so she might teach him the secrets of power. Now she had laid her kingdom at his feet in all its shameless splendor. Now he was truly Gammir, and Khyrei was his realm as much as hers.

"What shall we do, Grandmother?" he asked. He already knew, but it pleased her when he played the role of innocent youth. It was one of the many ways he indulged her.

Ianthe fingered the necklace of moonstones about her slender neck. Her white hair was caught up in a beehive, wrapped in strings of beryl and agate. Her smile was a splash of blood on a statue of sculpted marble. The statue of a Goddess driven by wicked whims.

"We will strike first," she said. "Elhathym has promised me half of his Vakai horde. He will send them to us through the mirror. Already he moves to take the border of Mumbaza. Soon his shadows will drink the blood of the Boy-King and his court, and we will drink that of the Sharrians. We will not bother with tiny Allundra, but make directly for Shar Dni."

"Why not take Elhathym's gift and kill him?" he asked. "Surely he holds no real interest for you."

Ianthe turned her black-diamond eyes at him. "There is much you have yet to learn," she said. "Elhathym is of the Old Breed. He ruled an empire on the southern coast before any other nations claimed this continent. He walked the Ancient World at my side and we played the games of blood and fire. The world was our toy, even after the Great Descent, when we took the shapes of mortals."

"Where has he been all these ages?" he asked. "The world has forgotten him."

A floating globe of fire above their thrones turned from orange to emerald and its light shifted the contours of her perfect face. "He grew bored and went off to explore the Outer Worlds for amusement. His earthly empire crumbled without him, and three thousand years of wandering yielded him no more pleasurable sphere than this one. Yet he stumbled, perhaps caught in his own terrible ennui, and fell into the void where the Vakai dwell. He lingered for ages among those famished spirits, observing their torments. They could not drink his blood, but they reveled in his pain for it distracted them from their own suffering, so they kept him there. In his madness he called out to me. Across a divide of centuries I heard his cry. So I pulled him from the void, sealing him to a pact that would meet my own needs.

"First he reclaimed the heart of his former kingdom. Now he has called forth the Vakai, his former tormentors, to serve him. In this world he is their master, and he assembles them now in great numbers. Together, Yaskatha and Khyrei are indomitable. As in the Ancient Times, we will stride across the world and spill its blood for our pleasure. This is our world, Gammir. You must learn to love Elhathym as you love me."

He bristled. "You love him?"

She laughed again, musical knives upon his bare skin. "He is my lover . . . but he is not my husband."

"I will never love him," said Gammir.

She smiled and reached over to caress his cheek. The fire-globe turned to deep scarlet, his favorite color. "My sweet boy," she cooed. "None will ever come between us. If you will not love Elhathym . . . then you must at least show him the respect due a fellow warlock."

He said nothing to that. He would show the necessary courtesy to the gray-haired sorcerer. Until the day came when he found the chance to destroy him. For now, let him send his shadow legions to join those of Ianthe. What could it hurt? The destruction of Shar Dni was worth even this sour alliance. Time later for his own designs.

Ianthe spoke often with Elhathym in the Glass of Eternity.

Gammir arranged to be outside the sanctum when this occurred. Let her deal with him; Gammir gave only silent consent. Three days ago, he saw Elhathym walk *through* the mirror, to stand in fleshly form inside the high tower. He had come to taste the sweet flesh of Ianthe, to ravish her and satisfy his inhuman lust. So the Prince went down into the Torture Garden alone to distract himself with blade and tongs, screams, and bits of torn flesh. He had no wish to dwell on what was happening in Ianthe's lofty sanctum. Even among the wails of the dying slaves, he heard the moans of the Empress as her ecstasy spilled like a faint stink throughout the palace halls.

Not long after this tryst, the Vakai came flowing through the mirror like a deluge of black water, flooding out the sanctum windows, into the courtyard and the city beyond. They sank into the shadows and stones until they were called forth to flock behind the war fleet.

Four admirals commanded the Khyrein navy, but Ianthe set Gammir above them all. Now the *Talon* was his own ship, and she stood at his side calm and cool as marble. His thirst was rising . . . Nearly a full day since he drank the blood of nubile slaves. Tonight, Ianthe and he, and the host of shadows that followed like a black storm, would drink Sharrian blood.

There . . . The green coast came into view at last. The Valley of the Bull with its verdant slopes, the reedy delta thick with flocks of white birds, the city of white towers and azure pyramids, the cloud-painted ramparts. The smoke of temples rose into the evening sky like futile dreams . . . Their Gods would not help them this night. The sun kissed the western horizon. The inky waters in the fleet's wake steamed now as if boiling.

Gammir saw the ghost of Tadarus standing near the rail, wrapped in his purple cloak, unstirred by the wind. Tadarus stared at him with eyes as blue as the Sharrian temples.

Brother . . .

Ianthe must have sensed something, for she turned her feline face toward the phantom. Yet it was gone. Perhaps he had only imagined it.

She leaned against him, her slim body wrapped in a crimson cloak and little else. She placed an arm about his waist and they eyed the blue-white city together. "Their King is already dead by your hand," she said. "Whoever they have placed on his seat will be fearful and inexperienced, and they have no warning of our attack. This night Shar Dni belongs to us, Gammir. We will tear it to shreds, drain it dry as sand, burn it from the earth. We will build a new city on its ashes – *your* city. Its temples will worship us with blood and pain."

She kissed his lips, stealing his senses. When she pulled away, the last rays of sunlight burned blood-bright across the Golden Sea. The Sharrian Navy rushed forward to meet the assault. A hundred gold-painted galleons flew the Sign of the Bull on their silks. The Khyrein warships crushed hapless fishing vessels caught in their path. Less than half the Sharrian ships had launched when night claimed the sky.

Now the legions of shadow rose from the waters like a wave of black clouds, roiling above the Khyrein vessels. Ianthe threw off her cloak, baring herself to the dark, and shouted into the mass of whirling shadows.

"Blood, Vakai!" She pointed her clawed finger at the Sharrian sails. "Your mistress offers the blood of all those aboard the golden ships! Take them! Feast, children of the void!"

A dark storm, lit by a mass of tiny red fires, rushed toward the Sharrian warships, which came boat after boat into the banks of howling shadow. Ianthe's sorcerous wind fell away, and the black fleet crept slowly now toward the dark fog that consumed its enemies.

As the *Talon* moved closer at the head of a triangular formation, the shrieks of dying men reached Gammir's ears. Famished Vakai swarmed the decks and rigging of his enemies, rending flesh and spilling blood. He licked his lips. Perhaps he should summon the phantom horse and join the blood-drinkers on those slippery decks.

"Be patient, Grandson," said Ianthe, stroking his chin. "In the city beyond these meager ships runs a deep red river. We will sip from it soon."

The black ships slid across the waves toward the wall of darkness. No golden galleons emerged from that writhing storm of shadows. Only the cries of dying men and the smell of steaming blood. The moon rose, a horned sickle between guttering stars.

At last the legions of Vakai rose back into the sky, leaving a hundred red-stained ships floating aimlessly with tattered sails. Their decks were littered with drained white bodies, trails of crimson spilling over the rails . . . a forest of unmanned ships waiting to be fired and scuttled.

A great war-shout went up among the Khyreins, and they sailed among the dead ships, torching and ramming them to make a path for the *Talon*. Gammir and Ianthe sailed through a corridor of burning ships, and the walls of Shar Dni loomed near. The black cloud of death hovered and writhed above the *Talon*. Clusters of flame-red eyes stared at the ripe city, thirsty for more slaughter.

Along the city wall the flames of sentinels burned bright, and legions of foot soldiers gathered to repel a siege. Gammir pictured in his mind the legions of cavalry inside the wall, forming up to ride forth and meet the invading Khyreins at the docks.

Doomed fools . . .

It mattered not whether they hunkered within those high walls or rode out to meet death like heroes. They were all going to die.

As the *Talon* left behind the forest of burning galleons, it entered the wide Sharrian bay. Trading ships and fishing vessels sat abandoned at the docks. It seemed every Sharrian citizen had fled to the Southern Gate. Now that gate opened and ranks of cavalry charged out to defend the docks. They poured forth like bronze ants, thousands of spears glittering in the glow of stars and their own blazing ships.

Gammir watched them gallop toward the wharves and form their lines of battle. They were children playing some absurd game. He laughed at them from his perch behind the devil-head on the *Talon*'s prow. His laughter spilled across the dark water like blood from rent flesh.

Ianthe raised her lithe arms toward the black cloud again, and the legions of Vakai fell like a black rain upon the legions of Shar Dni. Khyreins cheered, waving their swords and axes as their enemies were smothered by a pall of mutilating terrors. By the time the Vakai rose to hover above the heaps of slain men and horses, the *Talon* and its vanguard had seized the docks. Armored Khyreins bounded from the rails and raced among the scattered dead, falling into formation before the Southern Gate, now closed again and no doubt well barricaded.

Gammir took Ianthe's hand and escorted her along the quay. They stepped between the shredded corpses of two thousand soldiers and the remains of their hapless mounts. The smell of blood filled his nostrils, filled the night itself, drowning even the stench of the burning galleons.

Beyond those gates . . . a red river to spill at our feet and quench our thirst.

Gammir smiled as the shadow legions floated over the mighty walls and sank into the city streets beyond. He waited only a moment for the symphony of screams to begin, and then it came.

He stood there, a Prince among his warriors, listening to the sound of a city being murdered. After a while he called forth from the feeding shadow legions a band of his own Vakai. They followed his orders gladly, blood-drunk as they were.

A sound of thunder came from behind the bronze gates. And again. A third time and the portals burst open, shadows flooding outward and upward.

As the Vakai moved across the maddened city, the Prince and Empress of Khyrei entered its streets in a haze of crimson glory.

The red river was indeed sweet.

And so very deep.

27

The Laughter of Elhathym

Atop a green hill stood the walled fortress of Zaashari, built of gray granite with a central tower overlooking the sea. Between the waves and the fortress lay the town of the same name. Its roads, residences, and warehouses spread from the citadel ramparts to the white-sand beach. Outlying farms girded the settlement in fields of ripe corn and olive trees. The sun blazed high between scattered clouds, but Zaashari lay in deep shadow. Riding on the back of the Feathered Serpent, Sharadza looked down upon the unnatural gloom that smothered the town. In the midst of that eerie dark, the armor and spears of Yaskathan legions glimmered like shifting constellations.

Khama's flight from Mumbaza was shockingly fast, and only his sorcery kept her and Iardu from being swept away by the fierce winds. Along the way Iardu advised Sharadza, helping her to grab sunbeams from the sky and mold them about herself, until she wore golden armor of condensed light with a helm of dancing flame. She forged a brilliant spear from that same light and grew herself to the impressive height of an Uduri. Iardu called thunderbolts down from the clouds into his hands, stuffing them into a quiver on his back. Now white flames streamed from the Shaper's eyes as Khama's great bulk descended toward Zaashari.

Five thousand silver-mailed Yaskathans marched through the conquered town. Bodies lay mangled and drained along every street and in every house. These human warriors had lifted no finger in last night's slaughter; the Spirits of Vakai had slain Zaashari. A horde of shadows that lay sunken and dormant among the stones, alleys, and fields while the sun held the day. A dark stain on the earth itself. The grounds of the fortress proper resembled a battlefield, littered with piles of bodies and the carcasses of horses. Along the wooden docks modest fishing vessels sat still under shredded sails, some crowded with the drained corpses of townspeople who had fled too late. The Yaskathans had built huge bonfires in the early morning, and they tossed body after body into these flames. Once Zaashari was clear of decaying flesh, its occupation would be complete. Then the shadows would rise and move on toward Mumbaza for a similar yet far greater massacre. Elhathym had brought no more than five legions of men because no more than that would be needed after his blood-hungry demons were set loose.

"Look!" Sharadza shouted through the wind to Iardu. "The tyrant!"

Through an outer courtyard of the fortress Elhathym rode in a chariot of carven bone, drawn by a great black lion with gleaming eyes. It stood tall as an ox with the curving tail of a scorpion. The usurper's robe was night-black, set with a crescent of sparkling rubies. The golden crown of Yaskatha sat brazenly atop his gray head. His eyes flashed brighter than the lion-beast's when he looked to the rushing Feathered Serpent. Even from this distance, Sharadza heard his laughter like a flock of arrows winging past her ears.

Khama opened his fanged maw and roared his wrath upon

Zaashari. The sound of it was deeper than the ocean, louder than a crumbling mountain, and a terrible wind blew through the streets and over the battlements of the captured fortress. Armored men were swept across the ground like leaves, smashed to death against walls, pillars, and each other. Spears and shields flew from the Yaskathans' fists as they grabbed hold of whatever chunk of stone or supporting beam they could find. Their eardrums burst and their blood seeped into the shadow-stained ground, which drank it up greedily. Mailed horses flew through the air as well, increasing the devastation when their bulk slammed into groups of wailing soldiers. The tower of the fortress crumbled, raining deadly stones among the invaders. The battlements cracked and fell to the ground, burying warriors beneath splintered masonry. The wooden structures of the town itself exploded into kindling, clouds of flesh-piercing shards that found the exposed areas of armored bodies.

Khama the Feathered Serpent had belched a hurricane across the murdered town, and the Yaskathan legions were decimated. All save Elhathym. He stood unmoved in his bone chariot, and the lion-shaped demon that pulled it roared back at Khama. Elhathym's head was thrown back in laughter as he raced down the hillside, but Sharadza's ears still rang with the roar of the Feathered Serpent. If she had stood before that terrible gust, rather than directly behind it, she would have died along with the Yaskathans. As the roaring echoes faded, Khama floated directly above the devastation, and Iardu grabbed her hand. Together they jumped from Khama's back toward the speeding chariot below.

Giant-girl and sorcerer came down gently, guided by the currents of Iardu's power. Elhathym raised his hands and shouted at the darkness. A host of shadows, the ravenous Vakai, soared up from the bloodied earth, a torrent of inky blackness rising toward the Feathered Serpent. Khama swirled above the ruins, twisting his great coils in a spherical pattern, growing ever faster, casting brightness from his tri-toned feathers until he blazed like a second sun in the sky. The Vakai swarmed up to smother his light, a deluge of darkness brimming with ten thousand claws and fangs. Rays of illumination shot through cracks in the writhing black cocoon.

"The shadows are weakened in daylight," said Iardu, "Khama will handle them."

Now that Sharadza stood in her Giantess form, the Shaper looked so very small.

So much death in these first few seconds. We must finish this soon . . .

The black lion sped toward them, and Elhathym's grinning skull-face hovered above the chariot wall behind it. His eyes were twin voids, pathways to nothingness. Iardu tossed a bolt of lightning from his quiver. The chariot exploded into a shower of bone fragments. Now the black lion roared, and a thick tongue came spilling from its fanged maw. The tongue was a hissing cobra, spitting venom. Elhathym stood unfazed, watching the battle of light and darkness in the sky. The thunderbolt had not harmed him.

The Feathered Serpent spun faster in the sky, and its light grew hotter and brighter, until its colors merged into a single white flame round as the moon and hot as the sun. The Vakai shrieked and shriveled, and were annihilated. They dripped from the tiny sun, falling like a black rain that evaporated before it touched the earth. The sky itself turned to a blazing vault of whiteness.

The black lion shrugged off a second thunderbolt from Iardu. Sharadza grabbed its poisonous tongue in her fist, which was sheathed in a gauntlet of sunfire, and ripped it from the beast's mouth. Now the beast fell upon her with fury, stamping her to the ground and gnashing at her helm with fangs black as ebony. She kicked it off her, stabbing at it with the golden spear, but it was quick and she missed. Its scorpion tail struck forward, clanging off her fiery breastplate. She thrust the point of the sun-spear into its flank. It howled more like a wounded wolf than a lion. The great white light dimmed in the sky, and she looked up to see the last of the Vakai fading like smoke. Yet now another shadow blotted out the true sun. A far greater shadow.

Elhathym's laughter filled the vault of blue sky. He was a black mountain rising toward the clouds. One massive foot stood upon the ruins of the fortress, crushing it to dust, while the other stamped the ruined town into a flatter desolation. His mighty head wore a second crown now, a wreath of clouds, and his hands were gargantuan spiders that might tear whole islands from their homes in the sea. Khama was only a glowing ball of fire before the God-sized sorcerer.

An icy terror froze Sharadza's heart. She was so very small. Miniscule. They all were.

Iardu lay on the ground struggling against a mass of black tentacles that strangled and constricted his limbs. They rose from cracks in the earth, like living roots, but their substance was pure darkness. The Shaper screamed. His flesh withered where the dark vines curled about it.

All this Sharadza took in with a moment's glance, then the black lion clamped its jaws about her leg. The scorpion tail lunged at her again. She sliced it in two with the blade of her spear. The grip of the lion's fangs would not break. It shook her, slammed her against the ground. Its fangs sank through the solid light and pierced her skin. She grabbed a pebble from the grass and became a thing of stone. The lion-beast pulled away, growling at the granite obelisk that no longer bled or offered resistance. It turned luminous moon-eyes toward the divine bulk of Elhathym, recognizing his earth-shaking laughter.

In a flash, she became flesh again, shed of the golden armor now, and raised the sun-spear. The black lion lunged and she rammed the blade into its maw, shoving with all the strength of Uduri limbs. She forced it backward and vaulted atop it, impaling and pinning it to the earth.

Now colossal Elhathym stomped his right foot, and an earthquake struck. Sharadza fell to the ground beside the dying demon lion. Ocean waves leaped skyward along the beach. The earth cracked like green glass, and a fissure spread east and west from Elhathym's monolithic foot. She could not stand, but lay on her belly as the earth split wide, the fissure yawning, becoming a vast chasm. The scattered debris of town and castle fell into the abyss, and a cataract of seawater rushed into its steaming depths. She watched, buffeted and shaken, as Iardu wailed inside the tangle of black vines that stole his life. Elhathym reached out to grab the spinning ball of flame that was the Feathered Serpent. His hand took it as a man might grasp a firefly. Now it was the Serpent again, a squirming, burning cinder between his clawed fingers.

Elhathym raised his fist toward the clouds, then hurled Khama into the great chasm. The coastline moaned, ocean heaved, and his laughter boomed. The Feathered Serpent plummeted into the abyss like a discarded olive pit.

He is a Creature of the Air. Surely he will fly out again . . .

Elhathym clapped his hands. They sparked with dark flames and the earth-fissure groaned, closing as fast as it had opened. The walls of the crevasse collided with a bone-rattling crunch. Somewhere deep below, the Feathered Serpent was caught and crushed.

Iardu had told her in the cave that earth was the nemesis of air, as water was to fire. Of course Elhathym had known this, and used the earth itself to destroy Khama.

The world grew still for a moment, but Iardu's shout broke the stillness. The killing vines shattered like kindling about his blackened limbs. His mouth and eyes blazed with white flame, and the Shaper grew. He grew beyond the ability of her eyes to follow. Rivers of white flame danced along his carmine robes . . . and now he stood as tall as Elhathym.

The two sorcerers filled the sky.

Taller than the Gods themselves . . .

She lay there, stifling a scream, a prisoner of awe, as they wrestled above her, their feet stamping hills into prairies and hurling quakes along the coastline. The ocean crashed about their ankles. She imagined herself a gnat caught between the feet of feuding Uduru. The black lion had melted to a pitchy sludge, and she pulled loose her golden sun-spear. She stumbled toward the western hills, dragging the weapon behind her as the soil trembled and trees uprooted themselves.

Iardu spewed gouts of white fire from his mouth, but Elhathym only laughed as his face melted and reformed. His serpentine tongue wound about Iardu's neck, a flame of darkness, and his huge claws locked between Iardu's fingers. They shouted indecipherable words of power that split the earth and sky worse than any thunder. Sharadza fell among the grass of an open field, transfixed by the spectacle of warring titans.

If they should fall . . .

Instinct demanded that she run . . . flee this terrible sight before she went mad . . . or watch the sky-tall sorcerers fall into the sea and set loose typhoons to swallow half the earth. But she could not tear herself away from their struggle. Iardu did this impossible thing because of her. She witnessed the summit of his powers now, and she knew that he was not the equal of Elhathym. Not in strength, ferocity, or sorcery.

What could she do? What could a speck of dust do to aid a mountain?

She clutched her spear of sunlight and watched the wrestling of immortals.

Elhathym opened his great mouth hideously wide. Stars and nebulae swirled inside. It yawned wider and wider, beyond the confines of his godly head. The stars fell away, swallowed by a sea of infinite darkness, and the maw grew wider and taller than Iardu, who struggled to pull away from its celestial gravity. Elhathym was a vast black gullet now, large enough to swallow the ocean, sucking clouds and wind into the void at its center.

Iardu turned away, his white fires dying.

It was too late.

He fell into the cosmic orifice, shrinking as it pulled him deeper. Where Elhathym had been was now a swirling shard of the ultimate void. Iardu was a tiny speck lost in the depths of nothingness. Now rocks, trees and debris went flying into the void-mouth. It closed slowly, deliberately, until it was again the mouth of a yawning titan. Then that titan was a Giant, then the Giant was a solitary man wrapped in black silk and blood-colored jewels. He stood in triumph amid a wasteland that had once been called Zaashari.

Sharadza had crawled through the grass between mounds of rubble as he diminished. Her soundless tears spilled onto the ground like the trail a slug leaves behind as it glides.

Elhathym stood quietly in the smoking desolation. The waters of the sea had invaded the ruined cornfields, and the structures of man were obliterated. The coastline had been altered by the powers unleashed here. Perhaps he reflected on the loss of his five thousand Yaskathans or his legions of Vakai. For whatever reason, he stood silent as a statue, his silver mane waving in the wind.

Behind him Sharadza rose from a pile of pulped masonry, and she hurled the sun-spear with all her might.

It sped toward his back, and time seemed to slow. Dust-motes danced in the air . . . Brown leaves blew between her and the sorcerer, stirred by the wind of her cast.

The bright spear struck Elhathym between the shoulders and passed half its length through his body. He stood transfixed by the bolt of sunfire, his robe smoking and burning, but he did not bleed.

He turned to face her, the golden spear-blade pointing from his breastbone like an accusing finger, flaming with sorcery. His eyes met hers across the brief expanse of ruined ground, and they were lightless things . . . as empty as the void he had become.

She held her breath. Her knees trembled.

His head fell back once again, and he laughed. The crown sparkled on his brow as he wrapped a hand about the spear and yanked it from his breast. He snapped it in two and it melted into rays of sunlight that faded on the wind.

He smiled at her, and she stared at the hole burned completely through his chest. As she watched, powerless to move, unable to fall or scream or even speak, shadows bled forth to fill that gaping wound.

He has no physical body.

This is only a garment he wears to disguise his true substance.

He is not a man at all.

Elhathym reached a claw toward her, and a second claw, much larger and made of darkness, wrapped itself about her body. She reacted instinctively in the only way she could. Her flesh took on the gray pitted substance of the rocks under her feet. She became a statue of solid stone, frozen in his awful grip, but rigid and unfeeling. She could not have borne his chill touch on her soft flesh. It would have killed her.

He drew her close to study her granite features, admiring a skillful piece of sculpture.

"Princess," he said, and even with ears of stone she heard him.

Inside the stone her consciousness lived and was fully aware.

Trapped.

"You have taken a form that is pleasing to me," he whispered. "What a fine ornament you will make for my throne room."

The dark claw shrank, and the Sharadza-statue shrank with it. She was fully in his power now. She could no more regain her fleshly substance than she could speak or run. Now she dwindled to a tiny figurine, a mere trinket in the palm of Elhathym's hand.

"Perhaps in a while I'll restore your tender and lovely flesh," he said, "and you will please me in other ways."

He tucked her into a pocket of his black robe. After that she knew only darkness.

Despite all her efforts, war had come and swept over her, a tide she did not even see until it completely drowned her. Like the ocean that drank the torn fields of Zaashari, it would spill across the land and devour every living thing.

She wanted to weep for Iardu, for Khama, both of whom had died because of her.

But a stone figurine could not weep any more than the statue of a Giantess could.

Gods of Earth and Sky, forgive me.

28

Death in Victory, Victory in Death

The legions of Mumbaza moved across the plains of northern Yaskatha, a sea of white silk, bronze blades, and ebony faces. In their fists gleamed ten thousand spears, and tall plumes waved atop their masked helms. The vanguard was three legions of horsemen, their stallions caparisoned with silver and gold. At their center rode a blended cohort of warriors from Uurz, Shar Dni, and Udurum, northern banners flapping beside the flag of the Feathered Serpent. D'zan, Tyro, and Lyrilan rode in the front ranks, alongside a coal-black charger that carried the High General Tsoti. A blade of Udurum steel hung at the general's side, a golden spear in his hand.

Behind the cavalry came five thousand spearmen on foot, wrapped in ivory cloaks and corselets of boiled leather. Each man bore a curved bronze blade and dagger, but they were devotees of the spear. Their shields were pointed vertical ovals made from wood, hide, and bone reinforced with ribs of bronze. In lieu of metal helms the footmen wore headdresses of war, towering displays of plumage on frameworks of bone and wire. From afar they seemed a vast flock of predatory birds.

Two thousand archers marched behind the spearmen, their

great bows of horn and cedar hung with the pale feathers of seabirds. Quivers stuffed with barbed arrows hung on their backs and bronze blades at their belts. They were Fangs of the Sky God, elite bowmen whose skills were legend across the continent.

A train of wagons bearing servants, supplies, fletchers, armorers, and weaponsmiths rolled after the archers, pulled by two hundred oxen and three hundred dromedaries. The rearguard was another legion of mounted cavalry to protect the precious caravan.

Priests of Sky, Sun, Earth, and Sea walked among the ranks, blessing warriors and speaking ancient parables. The six Adjutant Generals rode at strategic points among the legions, each reporting twice a day to Lord Tsoti. Since passing through the remains of Zaashari, the Mumbazans had craved priestly comfort more than ever.

In three days this massive force had been assembled under Lord Tsoti's supervision. The Boy-King must remain in the city, so Tsoti was his eyes, ears, and hands in the field. D'zan learned quickly that the man was a hero to his people, a figure of nearly divine esteem. Tsoti stood taller than any man D'zan had seen, excepting the Giants of the northlands. His muscles seemed hewn from onyx, and the gray at his temples was the only sign of his age. Although Mumbaza had avoided war for a century, Tsoti had earned fame as a mercenary fighting in Trimesqua's armies during the Island Wars. They said he slew a flesh-eating monster on some deserted island where his ship had been wrecked, saving hundreds of lives. D'zan met him in the Boy-King's throne room, where he reported the readiness of his legions. He looked upon D'zan, the son of his old comrade, with fatherly eyes.

"Prince." He greeted D'zan with a bow and a voice smooth as molten iron. "I knew you only as a babe in your mother's arms. Now you are a man . . . and soon you will be a King." He embraced D'zan, and the Prince could only smile and thank him.

Tsoti asked for word of Olthacus the Stone. His wide grin turned to a frown when D'zan gave him the news. That day had begun the trek southward, and D'zan was proud to ride in his company.

Four days later the vanguard discovered the mass of debris and wasted ground where proud Zaashari had recently thrived. There was nothing left of it but piles of crumbled stones. Tsoti pointed to where the hill-fortress had stood. The ground there now was flat and littered with black dust.

As the sun fell low beyond the sea, rotted corpses rose dumbly from the rubble and dirt. They stumbled toward the Mumbazans with gleaming dead eyes, and their grave-stench poisoned the air. Some were Zaashari folk, and some were the remains of Yaskathan soldiers. They grasped at the necks and limbs of living men, jaws snapping like vicious turtles. Tsoti sent warriors among them with spear and sword, but the dead men refused to die again.

"Flame," D'zan told the High General. "We must burn them. Only flame will set them free."

Tsoti drew his forces back and called for a cohort of archers, their arrows dipped in pitch and set alight. The Fangs of the Sky God never missed their shambling targets. In less than an hour every walking corpse was pinned and flaming. The reek of corrupt flesh was smothered by that of burning flesh. The dead things fell into heaps of ash and bone.

"This place must have been the center of the earthquakes we felt," said Lyrilan from his saddle. He never strayed far from D'zan, and his presence was a steady comfort. "There is nothing left here."

"Nothing but the dead," said Tyro, "who now have truly died."

"What forces must have been unleashed on this place . . ." Lyrilan mused.

D'zan shook his head. "The same forces that stole my father's kingdom. This place has the stink of Elhathym. They must have faced him here. There was a great battle, and these cursed dead were the result."

"Then where are Khama, Sharadza, and Iardu?" asked Lyrilan. "If they were triumphant, we should find them here. If not, where is Elhathym?"

"He's gone back to Yaskatha," said D'zan. "I saw him in a dream last night, as I often do, sitting on father's— on *my* throne. If he were dead, I would know it. He was *weakened* here, not defeated."

"He will march north again," said Tyro. He pulled his horse aside as a flaming revenant stumbled past and fell to the earth.

"We will not give him the chance," said General Tsoti, riding back from his parley with the archer captain. "This usurper has wiped Zaashari from the map. There were five thousand citizens of Mumbaza living here, and three thousand soldiers garrisoned in the citadel. It is all gone . . . This is a war not of defense . . . but *vengeance*."

"He has killed even more Yaskathans," said D'zan. "Death is the wine he drinks, the wind he breathes across the world. We fight him not only for Yaskatha's liberation and Mumbaza's sovereignty, but for all of civilization."

General Tsoti blinked his eyes beneath the brow of his golden helm. "You are your father's son, D'zan," he said.

The Mumbazan host made camp in the ruined valley. D'zan spoke with the High Sun-Priest about the ward on his greatsword. "This is an ancient symbol," said the ecclesiastic. "It is indeed a symbol of the Bright God, and we can mark it upon the shields and spears of our warriors. But the secret of its magic has been lost to us for centuries. I cannot say if it will have much power over these shadow demons."

"Perhaps if the men believe in its power," said General Tsoti, "that power will manifest. I have found that, in battle, what a man *believes* gives him the power of life or death."

So the Sun Priests worked their antique sigils on the shields and blades of the army. D'zan saw wisdom in Tsoti's words. He prayed to the Bright God to invest these marks of ink and ash with all the power of the one he carried on his own blade. Either way the Mumbazans would face whatever evils Elhathym cast at them. He made sure that Tyro and Lyrilan were also marked with the sun symbol. Lyrilan wore his gilded mail; now he carried spear and longblade instead of quill and parchment.

D'zan remarked on this when morning broke over dead Zaashari. The Mumbazans pavilioned in round tents assembled from hide and wooden hoops. He entered Lyrilan's tent as the Prince was pulling on his mail shirt.

"You no longer carry a manuscript," said D'zan. "Have you given up on writing my life's story?" He smiled to show his good humor.

Lyrilan strapped the longblade to his belt and tied his long curls behind his head. "Not at all," he said. "I simply realized I was going about it all wrong. The story has grown, D'zan. As much as I tried to stand outside its pages to chronicle its characters and events, I could not do it. I am a part of the story now, whether I like it or not. My mistake was in trying to write the thing down as it was happening. I need to *live* the story first, as you do. When it has finally ended, only then can I go back and write it. The Sea Beast taught me that. I will not ignore its lesson."

D'zan clapped him on the shoulder. "You are a good friend, Lyrilan. You could have walked away from this at any time. Yet here you stand. I will never forget what you and Tyro have done for me."

Lyrilan splashed cold water on his face from a bowl. "How could I walk away from such a compelling tale?" he said. "As for Tyro . . . well, he loves a good fight."

*

Four more days along the coast and the brown hills became the green plains of northern Yaskatha. Groves of cypress grew infrequently about the rolling landscape. Directly south, another two days' travel, lay the seacoast city where Elhathym sat on Trimesqua's throne. The tyrant would not allow a siege; instead he sent the Yaskathan legions northward to secure the border plains. From the crest of a high ridge, D'zan, Tyro, Lyrilan, and General Tsoti observed the massive host sent to thwart their advance.

Twelve legions of Yaskathans were assembled in vast four-sided formations spread across the green tableland. Their colors were silver and crimson. At their head flew the tree-and-sword banner, which Elhathym in his cunning had not sought to change. These men would fight for the flag of their nation no matter who sat upon the throne. If he had replaced that national emblem with one of his own creation, it would only dampen the morale of his troops. Their cavalry were as mighty as the Mumbazans', and more numerous: three-thousand mailed lancers mounted on chargers bred for battle. Thousands of footmen with pike, sword, and shield comprised the bulk of their forces, and a great cohort of archers was stationed as expected – in the rear of the host, where they could send volleys arcing over the heads of the forward ranks.

Advance scouts had reported these formations, so seeing them arrayed across the field was no surprise. Here would be the killing ground, the blood-soaked theatre of war. D'zan looked across glittering legions of his own countrymen and felt a pain in his heart, a sickening in his stomach. These were *his* people, and he rode against them today. If only they would break and rally under their true monarch, none would need to die. If he could win them over, with word or deed, thousands of Mumbazans and Yaskathans might live to see another sunrise.

The two great hosts lined up along the northern and southern ends of the plain, and D'zan looked down upon them both. Generals and Princes would observe the fight from the ridge-top, sending commands to their captains with horn, drum, and signal flags. He watched the plumed Mumbazans flow around him to fill the plain below, a flood of bronze and flesh.

The commanders were quiet. Tyro had determined to lead the northern cohort of three hundred men, but Tsoti bade him wait until the greater mass of the host was in position. Tyro sat patiently on his warhorse, eyeing the orderly rows of military splendor that would soon become a pit of seething, bleeding chaos. Lyrilan sat in silence near D'zan, his disciplined steed gnawing at the scrub-grass. D'zan spurred his own mount and it trotted toward the High General where he consulted with the six Adjutants. A flock of ravens from some distant grove scattered into the sky.

"General!" called D'zan. "Let me ride forth between the hosts before the battle. Let me fly the standard of my father before Yaskathan eyes. When they see me alive, some of them may join us."

"Too risky," said the general. "Stay on this high ground, Prince, where arrow and spear cannot reach you. It would not do to win back your throne and have you killed in the process. You must fight this war like a King, D'zan . . . not a foot soldier."

D'zan watched Yaskathan banners flapping in the breeze; they rose at regular intervals from the massed ranks of silver and crimson. Tsoti spoke with wisdom, yet his heart could not bear doing nothing while others fought for him. What kind of King would he be if he did such a thing? He sat brooding in his saddle when Tyro and the six Adjutants rode down the slope and took their places among the legions. Tyro's cohort guarded the southern flank.

Now there stood only Tsoti, D'zan, and Lyrilan upon the ridge, and a few mail-shirted servants bearing horn, flag, and flask. Well behind the ridge two legions of spearmen and a legion of cavalry lay in reserve. "Let them think we are weaker in forces," Tsoti had explained. "Never show your enemy everything." Although perhaps enemy scouts had already counted their exact numbers.

D'zan shifted in his saddle.

It was true that he must live through this to claim his throne. Yet he must do something *now*, or he would never be worthy of it.

He spurred his horse, galloping down into the corridor between the central formations. He ignored the shouting of the High General behind him, and the desperate voice of Lyrilan calling after him. If he would be a King, he must act like a King.

Riding at full speed he broke past the front cavalry lines and entered the no-man's-land between the two hosts. Grass and sod flew from his stallion's hooves as he pulled forth the Stone's great blade. He hoisted it toward the sky with his right arm. Alone, he rode toward the gleaming wall of Yaskathan soldiery, the emblem on their round shields also blazing on his chest.

In the heavy calm he reined his horse a short distance from the silver-crimson front line. In the shadows of symmetrical helms, ten thousand eyes blinked at his approach. A High General in armor of burnished plate sat upon a black charger at the line's center. D'zan could not recognize the man through the closed visor of his silver helm. A black cloak billowed from the commander's metal shoulders, and the legions sat restless and attentive at his back.

D'zan stood high in his stirrups, the greatsword's blade casting sunlight across their eyes, and he shouted: "I am D'zan, Son of Trimesqua, returned to claim what is mine by right of blood! You need not serve the tyrant usurper! Come across and join your King! I am D'zan! Rightful King of Yaskatha!"

He galloped north along the line and doubled back, riding south now and shouting his message twice more. A nervous mumbling grew among the Yaskathan ranks. Like a soft wind it began, gathering strength and volume, spreading from the vanguard toward the heart of the host.

The Yaskathan High General raised his right hand, sheathed in a bright gauntlet. In an instant an unnatural and pervasive silence fell across his legions. His black steed walked forward as if to treat with D'zan, and diamonds glittered along its mailed caparison. D'zan reined again to face him, and the general pulled up his visor.

D'zan nearly fell from his horse. The gaunt face of Elhathym stared at him from within the silver helm. The eyes were black without luster, as if they devoured the sunlight. He smiled and revealed white teeth, and D'zan thought of a lizard's smile before it devours its prey.

"Prince D'zan, the long-lost heir," Elhathym greeted him. "Welcome back. Many times I have tried to bring you hence, yet you resisted every one of my invitations. It pleases me that you have come now of your own will instead. Now you may accept your inheritance . . . by joining your ancestors in death." A metallic note rang loudly as he drew from his side a greatsword of black iron with a hilt of blazing silver. The sound of it wavered in the air above the hosts, so that every man on the plain heard it like the peal of some mystic gong.

It was like a clarion of thunder that begins a dreadful storm. War-horns sounded from both hosts. Legions of archers let their volleys fly. As the sky turned black beneath a rain of criss-crossing bolts, Elhathym's blade crashed against D'zan's sword. The shock of the blow traveled through D'zan's body, rattling his bones. He gritted his teeth against the pain. There was far more than human strength in Elhathym's arms; it was the strength of sorcery that drove his iron. D'zan turned his two-handed parry into a clever thrust, but Elhathym's silver breastplate turned away his blade. The sorcerer laughed and hacked at him. D'zan ducked beneath the killing arc.

Their horses spun in a circle as the blades clanged between them. D'zan breathed through gritted teeth while Elhathym laughed, his mouth a feral grin. The sound of arrows raining down upon upturned shields hung over their battle. Then both sides launched a second volley, and metal rang like a million drums.

Now the great cavalries charged. The Yaskathans galloped past D'zan and Elhathym, speeding to engage the Mumbazans in the center of the plain. The thunder of hooves rocked the earth and the odor of torn grass filled D'zan's nostrils. A fresh shock along his blade knocked him from the saddle. He landed on his back in the mud and pulped grass. His horse squealed as Elhathym hewed it down with a single stroke. It nearly fell on top of him, but he rolled away. The rushing hooves of a Yaskathan cavalryman almost brained him, but instinct jerked him backward. When D'zan regained his feet, Elhathym had dismounted as well. The clanging of bronze on bronze and the cries of men killing and dying joined the thunder-song of the horses' hooves. The field was a swirling chaos of spear, shield, and sword.

D'zan faced Elhathym in the eye of this mad hurricane.

He raised the Stone's blade high and brought it down on Elhathym's head. The sorcerer's blade was there to catch it, fast as lightning, and suddenly D'zan knew he could not win this duel. He had trained hard, but not for long enough. He had grown strong, but was not mighty. He had defied the wisdom of General Tsoti and now was beyond hope. He parried another strike from Elhathym's blade and screamed his guttural fury. Words were long gone; there was only the sound of his anger, tempered by despair.

Elhathym laughed and drove the point of his blade through D'zan's mail, a bolt of lightning through his heart. D'zan stood motionless for a single moment that seemed an eternity, impaled on the cold metal. It burned through his breast and burst from his back. The cold spread throughout his body, and his arms fell limp. They were useless things, hanging at his side like pieces of meat, but his right hand refused to let go of the sword hilt he had clutched so tightly for so many nights. The point of the greatsword lodged in the mire at his feet.

Elhathym drew back his elbow, and his black blade exited D'zan's body. The sorcerer's eyes blazed, twin stars of triumph swimming in dark lakes of malice.

D'zan's chin fell upon his breast, and he watched the crimson flow of his lifeblood spilling to the earth, staining his black-and-silver mail to gleaming red. Then he fell, face down in the muck at Elhathym's feet. His eyes somehow still functioned, and he saw clearly the silvered iron of the sorcerer's boots as one of them rose to his shoulder, flipping him onto his back. The cacophony of battle, the shrieks of wounded men and horses, the ringing of bloodied metal . . . all these things faded from his ears.

"Now, Prince of Yaskatha," said Elhathym, staring down at him. The world faded to eternal night and silence, but his words echoed with clarity. "Time for you to embrace your destiny, as you always wished. Rise now, D'zan, Son of Trimesqua, and lead your armies to victory over the Mumbazans. Your living soul I cast off like a heavy chain, Your bones and flesh now belong to me. Rise up and serve your King . . . "

In the mute darkness, D'zan rose away from blood and dirt and pain. He was no longer even cold. Elhathym's words faded. Something called him onward through the dark, toward a constellation of lights . . . a glimmering fog into which he fell with a great sense of contentment.

Why had his futile struggle been so important? Flesh and bone were such unimportant things . . . transitive . . . dancing dusts in a wind that blew forever. Now he rode that wind, and the memory of who he was and all he cherished began to fade, as the light and noise of the world had faded already.

Yet inside his tight pale fist, back on the blood-splattered plain, lay the hilt of the sword that bore the Sun God's sigil. And that same sigil was marked on his pallid forehead in black ash by the hand of that God's High Priest. D'zan had prayed over that sigil when he lived, asked the Bright God for his blessing and the protection of the ward that had come to him across the ages.

Something dark and ethereal tugged at his lifeless bones, seeking entry into that house of drained flesh. At the words of Elhathym, this dark spirit struggled to invade the young corpse . . . but could not enter it. D'zan felt this as a living man might feel a mosquito crawling across his forehead. It nagged at him, it sliced him with memories, stabbed him with anger that refused to subside. He turned away from the celestial lights and swam back toward the cold flesh that belonged to him and him alone. He had lost a kingdom, lost a father, lost a throne, lost his very life . . . but he would not lose his own bones to some foul thing that obeyed the whims of Elhathym. His rage blossomed, and the blackness of eternity became a universe of blood and flame. He would have cried out, but he was a disembodied soul and had no throat with which to scream. So he merely claimed what was his . . . the last vestige of his existence.

D'zan's corpse rose to stand before the outstretched hand of Elhathym, whose mouth was a hideous smile. D'zan glared at him with glazed eyes swiveling inside their sockets.

I am dead.

Yet here I stand with my enemy before me.

"Go now!" said Elhathym. "Take this steed and ride among your living troops! Lead them to victory in my name."

I exist under the power of his will, thought D'zan. *He wants me to conquer in his name, the last threat to his rule now turned into an asset. His final stroke of victory.*

Living, I defied him.

Dead, I must serve him.

The Stone's blade was still in his hand. He lifted it, and it seemed light as a reed.

"Yes!" said Elhathym. "Take up your ancestral weapon and fight!"

I must serve him.

D'zan, dead and yet beyond death, raised the greatsword high. The sun-sigil on his forehead, like the one on his sword, gleamed bright as a torch.

Elhathym laughed at the greatness of his new slave.

No.

He brought the sword down upon Elhathym's helm with all the terrible might of a dead man.

The helm cracked and the skull beneath it split wide. Elhathym's face slackened, and a black fluid that was more shadow than blood gushed from between his lips. He no longer laughed. His eyes bulged on either side of the iron blade. Astonishment gleamed in those bloodshot orbs.

D'zan pulled the blade free of Elhathym's skull and swept it with uncanny grace in a sideways arc, cleaving the sorcerer's body at the waist. His two halves fell into the muck where D'zan had lain. Neither half twitched, and there was no blood. Galloping horses trampled them to dusty fragments.

D'zan raised his free hand to his chest. He felt the jagged hole, the wound that had killed him. There was no heartbeat. He stared in awe at his milk-white hand. He stood in a pool of blood that was mostly his own. There was no more of the stuff in his body, or very little.

I am dead, yes.

But I serve myself.

I serve Yaskatha.

He climbed upon Elhathym's warhorse and raised his blade toward the sky. From his dry throat came a battle cry that froze mens' hearts even in the midst of killing and savagery. He saw their faces turn upon him with fear, wonder, and terror. Then he laid about him with the sword, slicing a path through the Yaskathans. The battle was in full swing, and there was no stopping it now. He must fight for Mumbaza and hope that his own people would surrender once they realized their Tyrant-King was dead.

Someone shoved a spear through his belly. He killed the man with a swipe of his blade, then pulled the spear free and tossed it aside. He felt no pain. His strength seemed limitless, and his blood was already spilled. Swords bit at him, and he brushed them aside. Arrows peppered him through the mail shirt, and he plucked them out like thorns.

Everywhere he rode, slashing and stabbing his foes (his countrymen) to death, and he sent up the cry in his hoarse, rasping voice: "Elhathym is dead! Long live the true King of Yaskatha! The tyrant is dead! King D'zan has come! Elhathym is dead!"

The news spread, and some Yaskathans began to surrender. When the Mumbazans called in their reserves, a general retreat was sounded. Tyro cut down a Yaskathan Adjutant who refused to let his troop surrender. D'zan laughed, but it sounded like coughing. The battle became a rout. Yaskathans either gave themselves to the mercy of the Mumbazans or fled across the plain toward their city. Most of those fleeing were cavalrymen. The foot soldiers were faced with the options of accepting quarter or trying to outrun Mumbazan arrows and horses.

D'zan took a fallen Yaskathan flag and raised it high. He ordered a prisoner to sound the horn of Yaskathan assembly. He galloped about the field, trampling or leaping over dead bodies, weaving through forests of spears planted in flesh and earth. His banner waved high as the assembly horn sounded. Many of the cavalry had ridden too far south to see or hear him, but the captured men and those who ceased retreating took up a cheer now.

"King D'zan!" shouted the captives. Tyro and his cohort joined them. The Mumbazans added their voices, and three retreating divisions rode back to the middle of the plain, where D'zan flew their flag from the back of his leaping stallion. It bucked beneath him and snorted like a bull, stamping the earth. Its eyes were flames, and it howled like a wolf as the cheering men gathered closer.

Now D'zan realized that the horse of Elhathym was not a horse at all, but some demon given a horse's shape. Still it served him, and he accepted its fealty without question. As he accepted his own dead existence.

The Yaskathans rallied about their rightful King and shouted his name. They were mostly glad to be alive, but also that the tyrant's rule was done.

"Long live D'zan!" they shouted, and a sadness fell upon him.

Tyro rode near to congratulate him. His green-and-gold mail was showered in the purple of drying blood. He carried a deep gash on one arm, and his face was blackened by dirt and sweat. Yet he smiled and hoisted the flag of Uurz next to that of Yaskatha.

Tsoti and Lyrilan rode down from the ridge to join the triumph. The banners of Shar Dni and Udurum rose alongside those of Uurz and Yaskatha. Soon D'zan would ride into the city and reclaim it in the name of peace.

He calmed his demon-steed and looked into the face of Lyrilan. The scholar's face fell from joy into deep worry.

"He is wounded!" Lyrilan shouted. He turned to the battle-maddened Tyro. "Can you not see D'zan is wounded? He has lost too much blood! We must get him to the tents!"

General Tsoti looked at him with a grave face and ordered men to bring a litter.

"No, I will ride," said D'zan. "I am . . . fine."

Lyrilan looked at him in horror. "You are delirious. You are white as death. You must rest! You have won, but you must rest!"

"I have won," said D'zan. He looked about him at the elated faces of the Yaskathans in their smeared silver mail and torn cloaks, some wounded and barely standing.

"I have won," he said again, bringing his horse close to that of Lyrilan. He reached out a hand and pulled his friend close to him. Close enough to whisper in his ear. "I have won, Lyrilan. But he has killed me."

Lyrilan looked into his eyes and understanding dawned on his lean face. The Scholar-Prince pulled his horse away, his eyes still staring at D'zan, speechless.

Now Tyro saw the mortal wound in D'zan's chest and turned to Tsoti, who also saw it. His friends stared at him with a strange aspect now. Their joy had turned to sympathy and worry. And now to something else entirely.

It was fear.

"Assemble a vanguard to take the city," said D'zan in his croaking voice. "I will not rest until I sit the throne again. Let the wounded stay and be tended. All who can ride, come with me. My own legions will aid us."

He swirled away from them on his demon mount and guided it into the midst of the Yaskathans, who knew nothing of his terrible wound and hailed him with a banging of shields, and prayers lifted to the Four Gods.

"D'zan!" they cried. "King D'zan! Long live King D'zan!"

The Yaskathans followed him, seven thousand strong, as he rode toward the city of his birth, and they chanted long life to a King who was already dead.

Living . . . dead . . . What does it matter?

They ride alongside their rightful king.

Thousands of Mumbazans followed with General Tsoti at their head, and the men of the other nations rode behind Tyro and Lyrilan.

After a league or so, the sweet smells of orchards and salty sea air replaced the battlefield stench of blood and death. D'zan marveled that he could still smell such things with his decaying nostrils. His hand wandered again to the gaping fissure in his chest. A numb red crevice.

Four Yaskathan Generals rode at his side. He pulled his torn cloak close to hide his death-wound. They congratulated and praised him. They told him of assassins and rebels who had tried several times to slay the usurper, all meeting with horrible deaths. They told him the people had never given up hope that he would return and set the kingdom to rights. Only one who was blessed by the Gods, the ordained ruler of the realm, they said, could slay the demon tyrant.

D'zan nodded and smiled, and said nothing.

Elhathym was not dead. By the sorcery they shared, the same sorcery he had turned against Elhathym, D'zan knew the tyrant lurked still in the House of Trimesqua. He had won back his people, but not yet his throne.

As the sun-gold spires of the city grew near, D'zan felt the sorcerer's presence seething inside the Palace of Trimesqua, where he must go to face it one more time.

There was no trace of fear left in D'zan's cloven heart.

He has already killed me.

In death, I have defied him.

In death, I will defeat him.

Now let him *fear* me.

29

Secret of the High Realms

At the top of the Great Earth-Wall, overlooking a sea of churning stormclouds, the three riders stopped at midday. They shared a meal of mangoes from the orchards of Mumbaza. The northern half of the world stretched away from the precipice, hidden beneath a blanket of mist and thunder. Gold sparks of lightning danced across the cumulus, yet here at the top of the continental cliff the air was warm and dry. The rising echoes of distant tempests reached their ears. They traveled the narrow strip of mossy ground between the sudden lip of the cliff and a dark wall of dense forest. To east and west the precipice reached as far as the eye could see, a dividing line between the lower world and the wilderness of the High Realms.

A fourth horse stood riderless, its flanks heavy with provisions. The four steeds nibbled at the green grass while Vireon, Alua, and Andoses stretched their legs and enjoyed the sweet southern fruits. At times the clouds below the crag parted, and vast swathes of green plain shone through, only to be obscured a moment later by the next bank of scudding clouds. The two Princes looked north across the roof of the Stormlands, but Alua's eyes searched the shadows between the red-barked trees and tangled skeins of undergrowth. There were no mighty Uyga trees here, but some of the rust-hued and black-boled hardwoods grew nearly as high, if not as thick in the trunk. The songs of birds and insects flowed from the deep thickets. Occasionally the growl of a hunting panther shook the foliage, or at night the far-flung howls of wolves.

Vireon turned from the precipice to Alua. She chewed the flesh of her mango while staring into the forest. It called to her, the wild freedom of its deep hollows and unseen groves. He felt it too. Yet while he could easily ignore the call of the hunter, she heard a more urgent call. He did not quite understand it, but he recognized it. She longed to roam the wildwood as an eagle longs to fly.

"The forest is haunted," Andoses had said on their first day up from the steppes. After three days crossing dry grasslands and two more scaling a series of escarpments, they had reached the western rim of the Earth-Wall. Their course now lay directly east, atop the cliff all the way to Allundra on the Golden Sea.

"Haunted by what exactly?" Vireon had asked. This was his first sight of the High Realms.

Andoses shrugged in his saddle. "Ghosts, spirits, the restless dead, I suppose," he said. "Legend says a proud people once lived there under the protection of a Forest God, but some plague or destruction fell upon them. The Mumbazans will not hunt there, nor the Yaskathans at its southern edge."

"It is beautiful," said Alua, already under the spell of the spreading trees.

"Nearly as fair as the northern woodlands," said Vireon. "Perhaps even more fair for its mysteries. What splendid game must lie within."

"Perhaps we'll snare a wayward hare, or take a quail with this Mumbazan bow," said Andoses. "But we'll do well to stay clear of those branches."

"Worry not, Cousin," said Vireon. "We'll move hastily across this high trail and get you to your crown. There is vengeance waiting for us. I am as eager as you are to grasp it."

"Twelve days should put us in Allundra," said Vireon. "Then a fast ship from its port is only a few days to Shar Dni. Would that we could fly there instead."

Six days of riding between precipice and forest had brought them here, where the Wall curved northward for several leagues. "This region is known as the Promontory," said Andoses. "A kind of peninsula that stretches north a while before doubling back to its eastward course. Here we must hold steady and cross a league or so of treacherous woodlands. However, there is a path here used by Royal Messengers. It should bring us safely through if we cross the stretch of woods by daylight."

Vireon fed the rest of his mango to the packhorse and rubbed its nose. He looked east into the thinly wooded peninsula of Wall. It was not the forest proper, but its shadows were no less murky. Alua wrapped her arms about his neck and laid her head upon his shoulder. The sunlight sparkled on her golden hair as it fell across his chest.

"Your cousin fears the wild," she whispered.

Vireon pursed his lips. "He is a city-bred Prince. Walls and towers give him comfort."

She smiled and kissed him. "I am glad *you* do not fear the wild, Vireon."

His lips lingered against hers until Andoses' subtle cough made him pull away. "Let us ride," he said. "A few hours of sun are left . . . We should cross these Promontory woods with ease."

Andoses made the sign of the Sky God at his chest. He nodded, but his nervousness was clear in the narrowing of his eyes, the deepness of his breathing. Vireon loved him and worried for him at times. In the past few weeks Andoses had become more like a brother to him than a cousin. Having him near made it easier to bear the loss of Tadarus, and the memories that haunted him each evening. How many times had he promised vengeance to his brother's ghost? Once he dreamed that Tadarus came to him on a black horse and offered him a golden crown. He could not hear what the dream-Tadarus said, but he smiled at Vireon the same way he had when he was alive. Vireon spoke to no one about the dream.

The horses picked their way through a carpet of moss beneath the red-bark trees. The path was broad and easy to spot, yet it was not well tended. The undergrowth was less thick along its route, and the steeds found their way naturally onto it, skirting thorn bushes, clumps of fern, and rotting logs thick with purple mushrooms.

The fragrance of the deep woods was strong here, and Alua breathed deeply. Her head turned always to the south as they rode, her senses drawn toward the flowering thickets and along the corridors of green shadow. A pale mist wound among the boles, and birdsongs sounded above. Andoses kept his eyes on the path, looking straight ahead. But Vireon found himself looking as Alua did, into the leafy depths of the High Realms. Something shadowy, almost like a man, flitted between the trees. Or was it only the mist? Alua gasped. She must have seen it too.

"Ride on," said Vireon. "We must reach the open way soon."

Their horses went from walking to trotting. From the corner of his eye Vireon saw a glimmering in the mist, a darting shadow. When he turned his head, there was nothing. Some trick of the forest air. Now he followed the example of Andoses, keeping his eyes focused ahead. He breathed in the fragrance of strange blossoms; huge blooms the color of honey opened along the sides of the path. A large insect buzzed by his head and disappeared into a broad flower. Some distance ahead the light of open ground formed an orange archway in the gloom.

Now they passed beneath the branches that formed that arch and rode beneath open sky once again. The precipice ran close on their left side, and the forest wall stretched away on their right, farther and farther away as they left the Promontory woods behind them.

At sunset they made their usual camp near the cliff's edge. Alua lit a small fire while Vireon tended to the horses. Andoses extracted cooking implements and provisions from the packhorse's bundles. He dropped onions, carrots, chunks of dried meat, and sprigs of herb into a pot, filled it with freshwater from a flask, and boiled up a hearty soup. They drank the last of the wine the Boy-King had bestowed upon them, then fell into drowsy slumber.

Vireon and Alua lay beneath a woolen blanket, the fire separating them from Andoses. Vireon slept lightly; several times each night a mouse or night-bird stirred him awake. Yet it seemed that nothing dangerous roamed this narrow way between Stormlands and High Realms.

Tonight it was no wood creature that roused him. It was Alua, slipping from the coverlet and running toward the black wall of forest. He called her name, but she did not hear . . . or chose to ignore him. He stood and pulled his sword-belt over his shoulder as she disappeared into the darkness between trees.

Andoses raised his head. "What is happening?" He blinked at the moonlight.

"Alua," said Vireon. "Stay here." And he was off, racing after her.

Andoses yelled for him to wait, but Vireon was already among the leaves now. Alua leaped through a moonbeam ahead, and he jumped across a wild hedge to follow. He called her name again, but she ran on. Some spell had grabbed hold of her. Or she truly hoped to lose him. He had chased her across the breadth of the northlands and into the White Mountains. She would not outpace him now.

She splashed through rills and streamlets, pounced over mossy heaps of rock, and tore through verdant thickets. The ground was uneven and dense with bracken. Up a slope she ran, then down its far side, dodging low limbs and hanging vines. The moonlight glimmered in her hair, and her pale skin was silver. Thorns and brambles tore her fine Udurum gown to shreds.

Now she became the white fox again, and her speed increased. Vireon whispered a prayer to the Earth God that she turn back and heed his call. But she raced ever deeper into the shadows of the forest. He could chase her for days, but Andoses must not be abandoned. He ran faster, the white fox a blur between the trees.

At last he climbed the far side of a hollow crested with a stand of silverbark and found her standing at the edge of a great and ancient ruin. Now she was a woman again, and she gazed upon the tumbled blocks of green stone, silent as a ghost. He joined her there, but she paid him no mind. Her eyes drank in the panorama of shattered flagstones thick with lichen and made uneven by sprouting weeds. Fallen pillars lay in pieces beneath shrouds of thick verdure. The forest here opened to the sky, and the full moon poured its gold across the bones of a primeval city.

Alua walked a winding avenue through the collapsed metropolis. Vireon followed, drawing his Giant-blade from its scabbard. They passed the husks of crumbled towers in vestments of blooming vine. Fragments of colonnade and arch stood heavy with curtains of leaf and hanging moss. It seemed that every fragment was made of pale jade. The stones had faded from emerald brightness to pastel green over the ages. In a broad plaza headless statues stood on blocks or lay in pieces among clustered ferns. Some of the figures were tall as Giants, but they bore no aspects of Uduru or Udvorg. These were the effigies of Men, garbed in baroque armor, hefting broken spears or the hilts of swords whose blades had gone to dust.

Curved terraces had become hillsides of wild growth, and fractured fountains of marble had ceased long ago to spill their waters. A high temple stood at the center of the ruins, its dome cracked and open to the night atop a series of terraced landings. Alua was drawn to this place. Vireon walked beside her, but she heard nothing of his whispers. He did not wish to raise his voice any louder in this place, for it held an aura of forgotten holiness. Dusty jewels lay scattered across the moss at their feet, treasures unclaimed for so long they had lost their gleam. Alua climbed the temple steps, and he followed.

A pale skull lay upon the highest step, secured to the stone by clinging lichen. It wore a helm of violet and gold blossoms. Alua glanced at it, as if she might pick it up, then she passed through the open arch of the temple gate. Its portals had fallen to dust long ago, and the high-walled vault within refracted moonlight from its round walls like dirty mirrors. She walked into that glow and a mass of tiny furred things skittered into the corners. Four massive pillars had once supported the dome, and three of them still stood. A dark form stood in the shadows across an expanse of toppled masonry.

She walked into the streaming moonlight and stood before an idol of some ancient Goddess. Vireon's eyes traveled up the slim figure of sculpted jade, over its naked breasts, and settled on the finely sculpted face. It was a beautiful girl with eyes of inset onyx, or obsidian. The icon stood intact but for a few hairline fissures in its slim arms and legs. The green Goddess held a three-pointed flame symbol in each of her open palms.

Vireon looked at the young face, then at Alua, and he knew.

She wept now. Her tears sparkled in the gloom as she stared up at her own face. There was no doubt that it was her. At the idol's feet sat a great round bowl, and a low altar also of jade. She waved a hand over the bowl, and a white flame rose up there, along with a deep sound that echoed through the ruined streets.

She fell to her knees, and Vireon put his arm around her.

"What is this place?" he asked.

She looked at him with drowned eyes.

"This was my home," she said. "These were my people . . . "

She looked again at the idol's face.

"I remember . . . " she whispered and sighed. "I remember it all now."

"Tell me."

"*Omu*," she said, her voice swelling with pride and sorrow. "This was Omu the Green City. I watched over them here like my own children . . . They worshipped me with sacrifices of blossom and herb. I was old even then . . . older than they could understand. I had not yet forgotten everything. I . . . I loved them."

He held her close as she sobbed. The white flame danced in its bowl, and Vireon felt a presence now in the temple. Something or someone had entered. He looked about, squinting. Alua lifted her head at his sudden intake of breath.

They wandered in through cracks in the walls, or the crumbled gate. Men and women with painted dusky skin, feathers tangled in their hair. Some carried spears of wood with triangular tips of jade. Their bodies were transparent as mist, their eyes sorrowful and yet somehow joyous as well. The moldy stones of the temple shone through their ribcages and faces. They were ghosts, every one of them. Of this Vireon had no doubt.

"The spirits of my people," said Alua, rising. "Children," she said to them. And a few of them now *were* children, walking unhurriedly with the rest to fill the temple. "Forgive me . . . I could not save you."

As she wept behind those words, the ghost-people went to their knees and bowed their translucent heads to the floor. They were silent as the moon, but their message was understanding. Forgiveness.

"Go now," she said. "Go and rest. You need not have waited for me all this time. Take your peace and know that I remember you. I remember Omu."

The phantoms faded from the world like pale smokes. She and he stood alone inside the sanctuary. Her eyes scanned the faded frescoes along the walls.

"Alua," he called to her softly.

"My name was Ytara," she said. "Though I had many other names."

"What shall I call you?" he asked.

She turned her eyes on him again, smiling a little now. "Call me Alua, for that is who I choose to be. It is more fair than all my other names."

"What happened here?" he asked.

She sighed and sat herself upon the fallen pillar. "Omu was a peaceful kingdom. How long I fostered them I cannot say, but when I found them they lived in woven huts. Over time they built this city from a hill of precious stone. It was a happy age. The laughter of children and lovers was as common as the singing of birds. Gentle rains fed the streams. The beasts of the forest looked to the People of Omu as friends and guardians. There is a word in your tongue to describe it. Paradise.

"Then the Pale Queen came, spreading darkness and contagion. Our waters dried up and our young ones died. She brought a horde of demons against our city and sought to drive us from the forest if she could not kill us all. She was as old as I . . . yet so very wicked. A selfish thing driven by her lust for destruction . . . a drinker of blood. I stood against her, but she cast me down. Her pacts with dark powers made her too terrible, and there was nothing more I could do. Rather than be her slave, I rode the flame as far as I could go. It carried me north, to a land untouched by her evil. There I roamed and hunted and forgot my pain . . . my name . . . my people.

"I forgot my power too. Until you came, Vireon. You awakened me from a long sleep. It was your love that brought me home . . . You have given me the gift of memory."

She kissed him then, long and deep. They made love on the temple floor, wrapped in the glow of the white flame. Her urgent cries echoed through the ruins, but there were no ghosts left to hear them.

"I remember the Pale Queen's name," she told him afterwards, lying in his arms.

"Tell me."

"Ianthe," she said. "Ianthe the Claw."

He held her tightly, and they slept for a little while amid the ancient stones.

In the hazy light of pre-dawn they ran laughing together until they regained the forest's edge and the camp of Andoses. The Prince had risen early and stoked a breakfast fire.

"Where have you two been?" he asked.

"To the Ruins of Omu," said Vireon. "Visiting with the spirits of a lost people."

Andoses' eyes grew large. "You never cease to amaze me, Cousin. Here . . . have some vegetables."

Alua ate none of the breakfast, but stood quietly and stared eastward. The direction they must go to reach the sea and passage north.

"Vireon," she called to him. "You spoke of vengeance yesterday." A gust of rising wind caught up her blonde locks and tossed them savagely about her shoulders.

"For my brother," said Vireon.

"I, too, seek this," said Alua. "Though I had forgotten it. Now this desire has returned with the rest of my memories."

Vireon quaffed a bowl of steaming broth. "We seek two things that are one . . . intertwined, like our fates." He went to Alua and pulled her close.

"She must pay for what she did," Alua whispered.

"As must he."

"I sense them now," she said. "North and west . . . "

"Shar Dni?"

"It must be. They are no longer in Khyrei."

"Then we must travel faster," he said.

"Yes."

Andoses eyed them curiously as he stamped out the morning fire. "Shall we ride?" he called. He had not yet saddled and burdened the horses, waiting for Vireon's strong arms to help.

Alua took Vireon's hand and led him to stand beside his cousin.

"This way is too slow," she told them. "These mounts are too tired. We must ride the flame to Shar Dni."

Andoses looked at him. Vireon nodded.

Alua spread her arms, and white flames erupted from her palms. She cast the fire about them in a burning ring that floated in the air like smoke. Then another, and another, until they stood cocooned in a sphere of blazing whiteness. Vireon and Andoses shut their eyes against the brilliance. There was no heat, only a pleasant warmth that replaced the cool of morning.

Alua grabbed them by the hands. Now the globe of white flame rose, and Vireon felt his feet leave the ground.

She is a sorceress, he thought. *This power is the substance of her memory.*

The flaming sphere rose into the sky, hurtling eastward. Vireon could see nothing, but he felt great winds rush past the globe. He remembered a comet he and Tadarus had seen as young boys, a spark of light rushing across the starlit sky. That must be how they looked from below, if any could see them against the blue vault of sky.

The smell of seawater met his nostrils, and he knew they flew now above the Golden Sea. At what great speed, he could not guess. The hand of Alua was cool and strong in his own. The hand of Andoses was sweaty and warm. After a while came the gradual sensation of sinking. The white flames faded and their feet met the earth again, ever so gently.

Vireon opened his eyes, blinking. Alua smiled at him. Andoses smiled too, and gave a quick laugh. They stood upon damp green grass atop the western heights of the valley containing the River Orra. The Valley of the Bull. Andoses stared past Vireon's shoulders toward the city. The laughter died on his lips.

Vireon turned and saw the charred walls of Shar Dni across the river. Red fires danced like crazed Giants, and pillars of black smoke rose from the streets. They were not the ritual smokes of the temples. The holy pyramids were piles of rubble; slim towers stood ablaze. The stench of burning flesh hung over the valley, and the bridge to the Western Gate was gone, great chunks of it lying in the river. The Orra ran black with blood, or oil, or both. The husks of burned ships lay along its banks, tilted on their sides like dead fish.

In the harbor a fleet of black warships flew the emblem of the white panther.

30

Stone, Glass, and Crystal

True to his word, he placed her in his throne room between two fluted pillars. She was a statue of white granite flecked with gray, and even a discerning eye would see her as no more than a finely crafted sculpture. Yet the only eyes in the great hall were Elhathym's, and he knew she was a slave of living stone. He had restored her to human height and would keep her in this petrified state until it pleased him to do otherwise. Or he might simply forget about her, until her thoughts grew thick and dull as the granite of her body. For now she lingered fully conscious inside her stone form, imprisoned but aware of everything that passed in the royal chamber.

What had once been a sun-bright dome where the Yaskathan Kings held feasts, rituals, and entertainments was now an austere vault of gloom. Tapestries of black wool obscured the soaring window casements so that no sunlight could intrude on the usurper's court. Statues of former Kings and Queens had fallen to mounds of dust in their niches. Three great braziers burned with eldritch fires that never waned and required no oil or tender. The rich carpets and wall hangings depicting the histories of Yaskatha were gone, replaced by drapes of crimson fabric stitched with the hair of corpses. A pile of bleached skulls sat where the Vizier's podium used to stand.

The Great Hall of Trimesqua was now more tomb than throne room. About the royal dais concentric rings of sigils, wards, and runes were carved into the marble floor. Elhathym sat and brooded in the jeweled throne at their center. Near his chair stood a tall mirror of murky obsidian, its frame embroidered with tiny carved demons. Often he stared into the volcanic glass, and Sharadza saw and heard the things that he saw and heard there.

At times he trailed a finger along her chin or breast, anticipating a delicacy he would devour later. His touch brought a rush of fear into her stone heart. But always he wandered into the shadows, or back to his throne to mumble incantations and stare into the enchanted glass. Terrified servants or cautious generals entered through the chamber's high doors. Elhathym spoke with them in tones of menacing calm, or raged and brutalized them, giving orders that were followed to the letter. Once he killed a trembling cup-bearer with a touch of his finger. The man had spilled drink at his feet. Other servants hauled his corpse from the chamber, and there were no more clumsy servitors. Mostly the tyrant sat in his mausoleum throne room alone, but for the mute presence of the stone girl between the pillars.

After several days of captivity she became aware of the dark jade nestled at the center of her granite being. It was the amulet given to her by Indreyah the Mer-Queen. She had forgotten it, but had worn it when Elhathym's sorcery overcame her own. The words of Indreyah echoed in the chambers of her stone brain.

And if you wear it while you sleep, we may speak together in dreams.

As an entity of living rock, she could not truly sleep, but neither was she fully awake. She lingered somewhere along the line between Life and Death, near the drowsy kingdom of Sleep. She pulled her attention away from the tyrant's bleak hall toward the crossroads of Dream and Death. The shard of jade thrummed inside the granite effigy. Elhathym's attention was elsewhere, so she hoped he could not hear it.

She swam through the dark emerald waters of dream, across aqueous gardens thick with anemone and iridescent schools of fish. The coral palace opened before her, and she saw the Sea Queen on her oyster-shell throne. Her silvery scales were phosphorescent, and she turned the amber slits of her eyes toward her visitor. Here Sharadza was no longer stone, but neither was she flesh and blood. This was her dream-self, an extension of her bodiless consciousness. And this was not truly the Mer-Queen's hall, but a dream place created by their thoughts.

"Princess," Indreyah greeted her with a pearly smile. "It pleases me to see you again. You have learned to use the trinket I gave you."

"I have," said Sharadza. "There is little else I could do in my present state. I seek your aid."

"Let us walk in the gardens as we did before," said the Queen. Now they stood among the waving sea-plants and gliding manta rays of her aquatic courtyards. Sharadza told her of Iardu and Khama. She spoke of the confrontation with Elhathym that had killed them both and left her a prisoner of stone in the conquered palace of Yaskatha. Indreyah listened intently, strands of green-black hair swirling in a halo above her heart-shaped face.

The orbs of the Queen's eyes grew wide when she heard Iardu's fate. "You say the Shaper . . . Iardu . . . is dead?"

Sharadza bowed her head. Dream tears floated like diamonds from her eyes, rising like bubbles of air. Iardu had loved Indreyah, and perhaps she had once loved him. Sharadza hated to be the bringer of bad news. Yet what other news was there in these times?

"No," said Indreyah. She looked toward the distant surface of the sea as a land woman might stare into the sky. Perhaps her senses extended far beyond the roof of her sunken kingdom. She seemed to observe some distant vista or scene before turning back to Sharadza. "No. Iardu cannot be dead. If he were, I would feel it. We once shared a bond . . . that I cannot explain. We are linked in subtle ways that have more to do with spirit than flesh. He might eventually perish in some distant eon, but he lives now. This I can tell you without doubt."

Sharadza told her about the black void spewing from Elhathym's mouth, and Iardu's plunge into that vortex of darkness. It had utterly consumed him. She saw it herself. Unless . . .

"Iardu lingers *somewhere*," said the Mer-Queen. "Perhaps he is imprisoned as you are. You must find him if you can. Tell me more of this Elhathym."

She told Indreyah about the enchanted mirror. "He keeps it near his throne and peers into it every day. It brings him visions. I could not understand most of these, but I did see the Empress of Khyrei reflected there, and I heard her speak to him. There were flames, and bloody shadows swirled about her . . . the Spirits of Vakai."

"Did you hear their words, child?"

"He demanded she return something to him . . . some *things* he had given her. She refused, saying she needed them for her own plans, and he grew angry. Next I saw him conjure an image of Uurz in the glass. Emperor Dairon assembled his legions there, preparing for war."

"You are clever," said the Mer-Queen. "Here is what you must do. When Elhathym next leaves his chamber, you must take command of this mirror. It is a Glass of Eternity. Only two are said to exist in this world. Concentrate your will upon it, and it will show what you wish to see. Use its power to find Iardu."

Sharadza stepped over the coils of a lazy octopus crossing the garden. "But I am caught in a cage of granite," she said. "How can I—"

"Give me your hand," said Indreyah. "Sorcery is driven by willpower. Elhathym's is far greater than yours, so he keeps you locked in this granite form. That is his will. Yours must only be greater than his and the spell will break." She held Sharadza's dream-hands and put her scaled forehead against the girl's own. "My will added to yours, child . . . through the power of our dreaming minds . . . together we may bend the elements to our will."

The dream garden fell away and she was again inside her granite body. She looked not at the throne room but inward, harnessing the consciousness of her intent, focusing her will as the sculptor focuses on his marble block, or the painter his canvas. Gradually the cold stone grew warm and soft, pink replacing granite, black curls falling across her shoulders. The musty grave-scent of the chamber entered her nostrils, and she felt some invisible presence remove itself from her. The dreaming connection with the Mer-Queen was broken, but she was flesh and blood again.

Upon his high seat Elhathym stirred and turned his head from the black mirror. She caught a glimpse of glinting metal in the glass, a sea of spears that could only be an advancing army – legions in war formation. In a blink she turned herself to stone again before his dark eyes fell upon her. He came down the dais then and his dark robes shifted, hardened into the plates of a dark armor. He spread his hands and pulled strands of shadow into the shape of a great black sword. He walked near enough to impale her with the black blade, but he only caressed her stone cheek. Stone by *her* will now, not his.

"I must ride among my legions to finally kill the Son of Trimesqua," he whispered. "When I return from the field of battle, I will grant you fleshly form, and we will celebrate my victory. If you please me, I will keep you as my Queen . . . not that faithless whore of Khyrei."

He kissed her stone lips, took up a helm of silvered metal, and walked through the chamber doors. They slammed shut behind him.

She willed herself to flesh again the moment he was gone, wiping a hand across her lips. She crept across the floor, stepping between the concentric runes and sigils, up onto the dais, and stood before the Glass of Eternity. Miniscule gargoyles peered at her from the intricate frame of blackened wood. She brought an image of Iardu into her mind, and closed her eyes, concentrating. When she opened them again, the surface of the mirror swirled with darkness. It was like Elhathym's vortex-mouth, the void into which Iardu had fallen. The mirror grew darker, all light fading from its slick surface, and now it was an oval of dull black.

There . . . in the center of the darkness . . . a blot of pale orange, growing larger as she looked upon it. It took the shape of a red-garbed figure, careening toward her as if falling sideways toward the mirror. A blue flame danced on his chest, illuminating the face of Iardu. His eyes opened wide and he seemed to see her through the glass. He slowed and floated nearer, as if swimming through a sea of black ink that did not stain or drown him. He spoke, but she heard no sound from the glass.

"Iardu . . . " she whispered. He floated now on the other side of the mirror, as large as if he were in the room with her. He shouted soundlessly. His hand reached forward, but could not break the invisible plane between them. "Iardu!" she shouted. If Elhathym lingered nearby, he might hear her. But she must reach Iardu. And if not now, then when?

He mouthed something, again and again. She tried to read his lips.

Pull . . . me . . .

True?

Pull . . . me . . .

Through.

Pull . . . me . . . through.

Her fingers trembled as she raised them to the surface of the glass. It was like a window, and he floated just outside it. She touched it with the tip of a single finger, and it rippled like ebony water. Iardu hovered behind the ripples.

Pull me through, he mouthed.

She took a deep breath and pushed her hand into the mirror's liquid surface. *Cold . . . terribly cold.* The mirror tugged at her. She set her feet firmly on the marble. Now her entire arm was inside that dark void. Something grabbed it and she almost screamed. But it was only Iardu, his fingers locking about her wrist. She stuck her other arm through, and he took her other hand.

She pulled, straining against the gravity of the mirror and the void beyond. It was like lifting someone out of hole in the ground, but Iardu's weight fell horizontally instead of vertically. She leaned back on her heels and pulled his arms through into the Living World. His head came next.

"Good!" he panted. "Keep pulling, girl! Almost there!" She saw now the lacerations along his body, the dried blood. His iridescent robe was ripped in a dozen places. The marks of the death-vines lay across his flesh like black tattoos, or bruises. She pulled, and finally he fell through. They tumbled across the dais together, catching their breath. Then he stood and waved a hand before the mirror. The dark universe faded, and the opaque shimmer of obsidian replaced it once more.

She sprang up and wrapped her arms about him. "You're alive!" she said stupidly. Her eyes welled with tears. "Thank the Gods . . . "

He hugged her fiercely. "Of course," he said. He patted her back and pulled away. "He only hurled me into the Void of Vakai. Still, he might have kept me there forever if not for your assistance. He has some elemental connection to the place. I believe he has spent ages there, perhaps trapped as I was. This explains his mastery of the Vakai and his skill at drawing them into our world – to the extent that none at all are left in the void. It stands empty."

She wiped her eyes. "Khama burned them away before he died. Yet there are more . . . I believe they are in Khyrei, serving Ianthe."

As if waking from a dream, Iardu started and looked around curiously. "Where are we?" he asked.

"Elhathym's throne room. The one he stole from Trimesqua."

"Where is he?"

"Gone to slay D'zan," she said. "He will return soon."

"Does he know you are here?"

"He thinks me a helpless statue . . . keeps me as a toy."

Iardu smiled. "Amazing! Thanks to you, Sharadza, we have regained the element of surprise." His eyes darted across the carved runes circling the dais.

"What can we do?" she asked.

"Look . . . See these markings about the throne. This is Elhathym's seat of power. His physical form is only a construct, a frame of congealed shadow to house his immortal essence. Here that essence must return to restore itself. This is why he can never be slain by physical means. He simply constructs a new body to wear like a suit of clothing."

Iardu stared at the great throne now, peering at its golden arms, velvet-lined back, the jewels set along its surface. He reached a hand to pluck a single jewel from the burnished metal, like picking an olive. Then another stone, and a third. In his palm now lay three blue opals.

He breathed on the jewels and waved his free hand above them, and he sang in a low, tremulous voice. Two of the gems expanded, flowed like glistening water, and grew tall in his palm, until an opal decanter the size of a wine bottle stood there. He picked up the third opal and used it to cap the crystal flask. Now it was a sealed vessel and fine enough to carry the wine of a King.

"What is it?" she asked.

"A trap."

He removed the opal cork and set the decanter beneath the throne, centered between its four golden legs.

Two quiet hours passed in the tomb-throne room, and Sharadza stood in her granite statue guise at the exact spot where Elhathym had left her. On her shoulder crawled a black ant that was Iardu, and he muttered precise instructions in her ear.

She felt Elhathym's presence before she saw him. He did not enter the hall through the great doors, but manifested as an invisible presence on the velvet cushions of the throne. At first he was glimmer of emptiness in the gloom, then a man-shaped phantasm, translucent as a ghost. Over the course of several long seconds the substance of his body grew darker and more substantial. His ethereal face was an expression of bitter anger as it solidified. When his form reached the consistency of a dense smoke, it began to sink toward the floor, wafting between the legs of the throne toward the mouth of the opal decanter.

At first he did not notice this, so consuming was his rage. But then his half-solid hands grasped the arms of his seat as his legs became columns of black vapor streaming into the decanter.

Iardu leaped from her shoulder, and she took fleshly form again. As they raced toward the dais, Iardu waved a hand and the throne became a pebble of gold. It fell through the black vapor into the bottle with a tinkling sound. Now there was only Elhathym, his lower half streaming into the opal container. His arms flailed, his clawed hands grasped at the air, and he belched a deep moan like the grinding of monoliths.

Sharadza did as Iardu had told her. Standing on the right side of the dais, she stared between her fingers at Elhathym. Opposite her, on the left side of the throne, Iardu did the same. She poured every ounce of her willpower along her arms, into her fingers, and thrust it against the phantasmal sorcerer. Iardu's will joined with her own as the Mer-Queen's had earlier. It was like pushing against a wall of heavy stone that threatened to fall back and crush her beneath its inevitable weight.

Elhathym writhed and howled and struggled against the gravity of the opal decanter-prison that drew him inward. The lower half of his body was already trapped, nothing but black mist inside the bottle, but from waist to head he floated nearly solid. His arms reached now for his assailants. He roared and pounced like a tiger as his left claw wrapped around her throat, his right around Idaru's. She almost fainted, so deadly cold was his touch . . . colder even than that void from which she had pulled Iardu.

She shivered and whimpered, but refused to lose her concentration. A trickle of blood ran from her nostril and crawled across her lips.

Iardu's teeth were gritted above the strangling claw. "Ignore the pain," he shouted. "Force him in! He is sorely weakened! We'll not get another chance – force him in!"

Elhathym's responded in the guttural howls of a beast. He slavered and ravenous sounds arose from his gaseous throat. His claws squeezed tighter about their necks. Sharadza could not breathe. A red haze clouded her vision . . . His talons sank into her flesh . . . She bled across his iron-hard fingers as the shadow-smoke of his torso swirled and drew toward the decanter mouth. The bottle shivered and rocked beneath him, drawing him into its tiny, self-contained void.

Now Elhathym laughed, and his substance reversed itself.

He began flowing *out* of the bottle-prison.

Sharadza wept, knowing Iardu's ingenious trap was a failure.

Elhathym grew larger and more solid, and she felt her neck about to snap in his grip.

The chamber doors crashed open. A contingent of Yaskathan warriors marched into the dim hall, crimson cloaks billowing from their shoulders. The silver of their armor was tarnished with dried blood. At their head strode a fair-haired youth without a helmet. His black mail was purple with gore from chest to knees, and he hefted a greatsword in both hands. His skin was milk-pale and bloodless, his eyes rimmed in darkness, his mouth set with determination. The sigil of Yaskatha on his chest had been cloven in a recent battle.

He vaulted to the top of the dais and a gleam of sunlight burst from a mark on his forehead. A golden flash rippled along his blade as he thrust it deep into Elhathym's nearly solid breast. The sorcerer howled with fresh agony. Sharadza saw now that it was Prince D'zan who wielded the bright blade. Elhathym's claw fell away from her throat. She sucked in stale air, coughing.

Elhathym flowed once more into the decanter now, his corporeal form lost completely. He was no more than a writhing black vapor . . . a fog of hate being drained from the world.

She breathed in deep gulps as she forced him down, down. Iardu laughed and squeezed his hands into fists. Elhathym gave a final screech of defiance, his hands grasping at the mouth of the bottle until they faded and were drawn inside. His shoulders and head flowed downward into the crystal prison, dripping like black blood from the blade that impaled him. D'zan raised his blade, staring at the decanter with unblinking eyes.

Iardu moved quickly, stuffing the opal cork into the top of the bottle.

"Sharadza!" he called.

Already she stood before the Glass of Eternity. She focused her will on it, ignoring the gashes on her throat, the chill of pain. The glass became a pool of utter darkness, as it had before. Iardu stepped up and hurled the sealed decanter toward the mirror. With a soundless ripple it passed into the empty dimension beyond. She watched it spinning there like a meteor of blue crystal. It grew smaller and smaller as it tumbled into that sea of ultimate dark, and then she could no longer even see it. Iardu waved a hand, and the mirror faded to dull obsidian.

"Your Majesty." Iardu bowed to D'zan. The Prince had watched their actions with no trace of emotion on his pallid face. He did not look well at all. His blood loss must be severe.

Suddenly she feared for him.

"Would you be so kind," said Iardu, "as to destroy this looking glass?"

D'zan stepped atop the dais. He brought his blade down upon the mirror with both hands, shattering it to bits. The noise of its breaking filled the throne room and deafened Sharadza momentarily. As if a whole world of mirrors had died instead of one.

Thousands of gleaming shards lay scattered in the gloom.

D'zan pointed his blade at the marble floor. He stood wordless and still on the throneless dais. The warriors who had entered after him tore the black shrouds from the windows. The golden light of early evening fell into the chamber, chasing shadows from the door.

Iardu worked a spell above the barren dais. The white marble flowed upward to take the form of a high-backed chair engraved with the sword and tree of Yaskatha.

D'zan gave the Shaper a silent glance, then sat heavily upon his new throne.

The Men of Yaskatha fell to their knees, bowing at last to their rightful King. Now their voices raised in salute: "Long live D'zan! Long live the King!"

The sound of metal boots filled the outer corridors, and more Yaskathans came rushing in to hail their monarch.

"Long live D'zan! Long live the King!"

Sharadza watched the young King's pale face. His eyes were sunken in pools of shadow, and there was no joy in his gaze. He did not smile, or weep, or look upon his people with cheer.

She saw then the gaping wound in his chest . . . the hole where his living heart had beaten.

King D'zan sat with sword across his knees, tranquil as a sculpted icon.

"Long live D'zan! Long live the King!"

31

Vengeance

The survivors of the night's blood-feast gathered in the withered courtyard outside the Sharrian palace. Most of the city's men were dead, so the majority were wailing children and weeping mothers, huddling in miserable clusters. Masked soldiers roamed the city tossing thousands of drained corpses into bonfires. The horde of Vakai had drank their fill and sunk into the cracks between the city's stones, or fled to hide in cellars and tombs until sunset. At daybreak the Khyreins had claimed the massacred city for Ianthe. They burned the dead and rooted out the living, herding them like sheep into the royal gardens. A bounty of perhaps three thousand slaves for hauling back to Khyrei.

After sating his own thirst on the blood of panicked Sharrians, Gammir found the bloodless corpse of Omirus slumped on the Sharrian throne. The Vakai had entered the palace before him and taken the last of the royal blood for their own pleasure. It was a small price to pay for conquering the kingdom in a single night. Gammir kicked the corpse away with the heel of his boot. He wondered why Omirus wore no crown, only the golden circlet of a regent. No matter; the Khyreins would scour the palace vaults until they found the crown Ammon had worn. It must sit upon

Gammir's own head. He would claim the Valley of the Bull as his own, a colony of Khyrei. In time he would grow a new city to replace the old, as Vod had replaced Old Udurum with New. From Prince of Khyrei to King of Shar Dni. His rise had been faster than he ever expected.

Perhaps he should change the city's name when he rebuilt it. Shar Dni was dead. He might give it her name: Ianthe, City of Shadows. That might please her.

While he sat upon the Sharrian throne and legionnaires poured through the palace looking for loot and prisoners, Ianthe walked the corpse-littered streets and called lightning down upon the Four Temples. The thunder of their destruction, one collapsing pyramid after another, brought laughter spilling from Gammir's mouth. His chin and chest were stained with the wine torn from living veins. The smell of roasting flesh wafted through the high windows of the palace. He breathed deeply the savory aroma . . . the tang of overcooked Sharrian pork. Not unpleasant, but his appetite was only for the rich red fluid, and his belly was full. For the first time since he mastered the Power of the Blood, he was satisfied.

She had taught him so much since then. The weeks spent with her in the sanctuary of her High Tower were an interval of dark bliss. Ancient texts and words of power he had learned, and the gates of deeper sorceries opened before him. There was so much more to learn . . . and so much time in which to do it. Tonight they would send the Vakai horde to Uurz, ridding themselves of northland opposition. Not long after that would come the sweet pleasure of draining Udurum dry. He relished the promise of blood from men and giants. His lying mother would die then, or perhaps he might keep her as a slave . . . Make her pay for betraying his true father. Yes, that would serve his taste for irony – a Queen reduced to serving a King whom she had rejected as unworthy of her own throne. Unless Ianthe wanted her blood . . . He could deny her nothing.

The Khyreins found the treasure vault of Ammon, and they brought him chests of gold, silver, and jewels, pouring them into mounds before his throne. Caskets of sparkling jewelry, strings of pearl, gemmed statuettes . . . a hoard of wealth glittered at his feet. Among these treasures they also cast the severed heads of Sharrians found hiding in the palace.

The white panther came stalking through the gates. She picked her way through the treasure-mounds to join him by the throne. He ordered a great chair brought from some other chamber and Ianthe took her human form to sit beside him. It was easy to imagine she was not his grandmother at all then, but his young and lovely queen. All these riches had been gathered for her pleasure. Perhaps it could be that way if he convinced her of his regal presence. His power would grow to rival hers . . . then he would be her equal. Then he might claim her as his own, just as he did this slaughtered capital.

"How do you enjoy your new kingdom, Sweet Boy?" she asked him.

He met her dazzling dark eyes with his own. *One day she will be mine.*

"I find it amusing," he told her. "I quite enjoy this game of blood and fire."

She laughed and his skin tingled. "These baubles are of some interest," she said, poking at a mound of jewels with her toes.

"They are yours," he said.

"You will need most of this to rebuild this pile of refuse into a city worthy of your rule," she said. "Still . . . I may take a choice stone or two. To remind me of this day's sweetness. Did you drink your fill?"

"Oh yes," he said. "And you?"

"The blood of priests pleases me most," she said. "Nearly as much as the crumbling of their temples."

He frowned. "Their Gods came not to help the Sharrians. Why endure the presence of such useless shrines? They should thank you for ridding them of these reminders that their Gods care nothing for them."

"*We* are their Gods now," she said.

"Well, then . . . " he reflected. "We must build a temple!"

They laughed loudly, and the sound of it drowned the noise of weeping slaves in the courtyard.

The palace doors exploded as a great globe of white flame crashed into the throne room. Gammir shrank against his throne beneath the terrible glare. The sphere broke into bolts of radiance hurtling throughout the hall.

Vireon came leaping from the fireball, greatsword raised behind his head, handsome face snarling with hate.

When Alua's fireball broke apart, its sorcerous momentum hurled him toward vengeance. Even before his feet touched the floor, Vireon swung his blade in a downward arc at Fangodrel's head. But the Kinslayer cringed beneath the bursting flames, and Vireon's sword bit into the gilded chair-back instead of the traitor's skull.

Vireon growled. The Kinslayer's mouth was dark with dried blood, as was his black mail shirt. This was no longer his half-brother, no longer even a man at all. It was an evil thing, a blood-drinking demon. As he pulled the blade free of the throne, Fangodrel squirmed like a shadow from the chair.

Alua wreathed herself in white flame and fell upon Ianthe. They shrieked at one another like vicious eagles, and in the corner of his eye Vireon saw the Khyrein become a pale and massive panther, snapping ivory fangs. He did not see Andoses, but heard him in the clang of swordplay at his back. He had refused to stay upon the ridge. Andoses fought the masked murderers with naked steel. The conquering of his city had driven him mad with rage. He shouted a Sharrian war cry, and Khyreins died on his curved blade.

The Kinslayer slithered across the floor like a black eel and rose to his feet, hoisted by shadows spewing from cracks between the flagstones. The demon things glared at Vireon with eyes red as blood and hot as fire, stretching liquid arms toward him. These were the fiends that had drunk his brother's life. He sliced into them with the Giant-blade, but it was like cleaving smoke. They rushed upon him like a torrent of black water, fangs and claws taking on the hardness of onyx. Fangodrel stood behind them, shouting.

"You saved me the trouble of finding you, *Brother*!" said the Kinslayer. He spat this last word as if it were venom. "Always too stupid to know what was good for you."

Vireon dove through the coalescing shadows, aiming the point of his blade at Fangodrel's heart. But the demons grabbed him and he could not move. A wolf-like maw opened above his throat. A blast of white flame tore the shadows from his body like wisps of crackling paper. They howled and he shut his eyes. Alua's flame would not burn him, nor anyone she wished to protect. But the demons could not stand it.

He staggered backward as white brilliance filled the chamber. More shadow-things rushed up from the floor, seeking to escape through windows and doorways. They burned away to nothing in less than an instant.

Fangodrel too burned in the flames. His dark mail melted in the sorcerous fire. His pale skin shriveled and blackened. He howled like a wounded child.

Alua screamed, and the flames died instantly. The white

panther clasped her in its jaws, tearing and tossing her as a hound rends a captured hare. The flames wreathing her body dripped away, and her red blood splashed the piles of gold and jewels.

Vireon screamed her name. He would have gone to slay the panther, but Fangodrel flew upon him. A crippled husk sheathed in crackling, melting skin, the Kinslayer wrapped bony hands about his neck and bared yellow fangs in a desperate hiss. Even the tongue within was charred.

"Your blood will restore me," rasped the burned thing. "I cannot die . . . "

Vireon hurled him against the floor with a crunch of bones. He raised the blade high.

"I curse you, Vireon!" spat the Kinslayer. "Your children will be born into shadow—"

Vireon did not hear the rest of the curse. His blade sheared off the Kinslayer's scorched head, which rolled like a black melon into a pile of bloodied gold.

"For Tadarus!" Vireon stamped the blackened skull into ashes.

The white panther screeched and tossed Alua's limp body across the room. Andoses rode on its singed back now, his scimitar buried to the hilt in its flank. Crimson gushed from the wound, even as Alua's blood dripped from the ivory fangs. The great cat bucked and twisted, but Andoses held on, twisting the blade deeper into its side.

A dozen Khyrein swordsmen rushed at Vireon, their faces those of bronze devils. He cut them down two at a time, and those beyond hesitated as their Panther-Queen writhed and danced with the Prince of Shar Dni astride her. Now Andoses lost his grip on the sword-hilt and fell among the scattered wealth. Vireon raced toward the roaring panther, while Andoses rolled to his feet and pulled a dagger from his belt.

The panther swiped a massive claw at Andoses. It tore through his flesh and sent him careening against a fat pillar with terrible force.

Vireon came at it from behind, but it swirled and cast blue lightning from its eyes, blasting him through a tall window. He fell steaming among the terrified Sharrians in the courtyard. More masked Khyreins fell upon him as he rose from the trampled ground. He grabbed them by the heads and arms, tossing them aside like dolls. He found the Giant-blade lying amid a group of terrified women and took it up again, turning toward the palace.

The white panther burst from the hall now, trailing white flame. Alua held its thrashing tail in her fists, sending torrents of fire along its hide. Khyreins and Sharrians fled in horror as the Beast-Queen sped across the courtyard, roaring, dragging Alua behind her.

The sunlight dimmed as a host of shadows flowed up from the streets, tombs, and low places of the city. They converged like a black storm upon the white panther. They lifted her into the sky, swirling about her like a cloud of darkness filled with crimson embers. Alua floated now in the sky among them, bleeding and burning. Then her scream met Vireon's ears.

"*Nooooo mooooore!*"

She exploded with pale fire, burning the horde of shadows to oblivion in an instant. The flash blinded Vireon. All those in the courtyard covered their eyes with hands, forearms, or shields. Some fell to the ground, calling upon the Four Gods. Shrieking spirit voices filled the luminous sky. Vireon could see nothing.

"Alua!" he shouted into the brilliance.

Thunderbolts flared along the ground, tearing the earth, igniting trees and hedges. Slaves and soldiers alike fled, running blindly across the grounds. Sharrians and Khyreins were united in sheer terror of rampant celestial forces. The sky fell into silence while chaos poured across the slain city.

Vireon's sight returned gradually. White spots of flame still danced in his vision. Alua lay upon the charred ground, naked, torn, and bloodied. A few tiny flames danced along her limbs. He ran to her.

"Alua . . . " He raised her into his arms, where she lay limp and senseless. The panther's fangs had gashed her slim waist and marred her tender breasts. He cradled her cheek against his own, the water of his eyes spilling across her hot skin. She grew cooler, and a throng of awed Sharrians gathered about them. The distant calls of Khyrein captains rang beyond the palace walls. They were the commands of retreat.

Alua coughed and opened her eyes. She smiled at him weakly and spoke his name.

"Is she . . . "

"She is gone," he told her. "You have taken your vengeance. We both have."

Yet why does it feel so hollow? he wondered. *I wanted only to kill Fangodrel, to avenge Tadarus. Yet now* both *my brothers are dead and I feel . . . I feel only love for this dying girl.*

"Do not worry for me," she whispered, pushing him gently away. She conjured a small flame into her hand and touched it to her torn flesh. She sucked air in through her teeth as the lacerations and punctures closed one by one. When she was done, not even scars remained on her snowy skin. He helped her to stand, and the Sharrians brought the cloak of a dead Khyrein to cover her nakedness. She was so very weak, but alive. His heart sang.

They looked across the smoking city, through the broken city wall, and saw the black fleet begin to sail away. The Sharrian survivors cheered him, asked his name, and cheered again. Then they fell quickly back to mourning their multitude of dead. The invaders were departing, their Queen and Prince were slain, but Shar Dni was broken and ruined. Its people would be refugees now.

Vireon found Andoses in the throne room, lying bloody among the treasures of his royal house. He called for water, and a woman rushed off to get it.

"Cousin!" There was no answer. He felt the shifting of splintered bones beneath his hands. "Can you heal him?" he asked Alua.

She poured the white flame along his body, but it was too late. "His bones . . . " she whispered. "The blow was too great . . . or I am too weak." She wept quietly.

Andoses' eyes fluttered open. Vireon carried him to the throne and sat him upon it.

"You are King now, Cousin," Vireon told him. "This was your father's throne."

Andoses smiled, then coughed blood.

"Too late," he whispered. "When the kingdom dies . . . the King must die too."

"You were both King and Warrior," said Vireon. "You saved Alua. I will look after your people. Go now and join your father."

Andoses grew very still upon the throne. His eyes stared beyond the shattered windows into some unknown land, and he died.

So this is the cost of vengeance. The price that a Prince must pay to be a King.

Vireon wept in the cool shelter of Alua's arms . . . for his cousin, his brother, his father, for Shar Dni.

"It is too much," he whispered.

It is too much . . .

32

Beginnings (Kings and Queens)

The streets of Yaskatha boomed with song and cheer. Months of misery and fear were replaced by a flood of goodwill and wild celebrations. D'zan's name rang through the avenues, plazas, and orchards. Well-wishers and skeptics flocked into the city from outlying farms and villages. Wine and ale flowed in rivers, men carried girls on their shoulders, and children stuffed themselves with the sweetmeats of vendors made generous by joy. D'zan had not yet emerged to walk among his people, and tales of his battle wound explained his immediate privacy. The Yaskathans wrote verse about him and sang his praises. The legend of his vanquishing Elhathym grew wilder with each telling.

In the midst of this jubilation, Sharadza sat with Iardu in a grove of the palace gardens and wept. She gazed into a pool below a sculpted fountain. Atop the water gleamed a vision of Vireon and Alua kneeling before the throne of dead Andoses. Iardu put his arm about her shoulders. She had learned the spell of scrying from him, though she already regretted looking toward Shar Dni. So much death ... An entire city, more or less, murdered in a single night.

Poor Andoses. He looked so pitiful slumped in his father's throne, a pile of broken bones and punctured flesh. The headless corpse of Fangodrel lay nearby, blackened and shriveled. Sharadza had watched it all, helpless to give Vireon aid. Unlike the Glass of Eternity, the enchanted water could not be used as a gateway, only a window. She could look across the world, view any scene she wished, yet was powerless to affect it from so far away. She felt useless.

All the suffering and devastation of the Sharrians . . . It was the very thing she had tried to prevent. War and death had come despite her intervention. Iardu had been right all along. War is a tide that flows where and when it will. A storm of tragedy too great and powerful for any man or woman to control. The Khyreins had struck first and decimated the Sharrians; Elhathym had struck first and annihilated Zaashari. Perhaps if she had not rushed off to save the world, the attacks would have been postponed. Perhaps Shar Dni might still exist today. Andoses might still be alive . . . and the people of Zaashari . . . and D'zan. What a piteous thing this handsome Prince had become. Dead, yet undying, what future could he have among the living?

What difference have I made at all?

What if I had done nothing?

"Dry your tears," said Iardu, patting her shoulder. "It's not as bad as all that."

She glared at him. His eyes gleamed in their myriad colors. The blue flame guttered low on his chest. His robes had been restored, but the dark bruises on his skin remained.

"My cousins are all dead," she reminded him. "My aunts, uncles . . . an entire city!"

"No," he said. "Thousands of women and children survive. See them milling in the courtyard there. Vireon is their hero, their savior. Alua is their new Goddess."

Sharadza watched them in the ensorcelled water. Grimy faces

bright with tears stared upon Vireon and Alua, raw hope glimmering in their eyes. Among the smoking ruins of an empire, those people refused to give up. Surely Vireon would take them to Udurum. And there he would be King. What of Shar Dni? Perhaps, over time, it might be rebuilt as Udurum once was. Yet there were no Giants to rear its new walls and raise its towers. No, it would remain a haunted ruin.

Iardu waved his hand and the watery view shifted to the open sea. The black ships of Khyrei sailed southward. What must those captains and soldiers feel in their hearts now that their wicked Empress was gone? Which one of them would rise to replace her, and bring more war in some distant year?

"Their fleet is leaderless and vulnerable," said Iardu. "If you wish, I might summon a hurricane and drown them all."

"No!" She shook her head, a mass of black curls twirling. "There has been enough death. Leave them be."

"As you wish," he said. "Perhaps they will choose a more peaceful way of life without Ianthe the Claw driving them to conquest."

She heard the doubt in his words. He did not believe them himself.

"What about D'zan?" she said. "What has happened to him?"

Iardu dispelled the image with a dip of his finger into the pool. The vision turned to ordinary ripples. Songbirds trilled in the cypress branches, and the smell of citrus hung heavily about the garden. Somewhere inside the palace walls D'zan sat or wandered wordless and grim, a prisoner of his own dead flesh.

"Elhathym killed him," said Iardu. "Yet his spirit refused to abandon his body. By embracing death instead of running from it, he defeated his enemy."

"How could he do this?" she asked.

Iardu shrugged. "You saw the gleaming sign on his forehead, the mark of the Sun God. His belief in this power made it real.

This is the sorcery that *all* men are capable of working . . . the magic of Faith. They give credit to the Gods for their own works. Try to tell them this, however, and they call you Heretic." He smiled.

"What will become of him?"

"His physical shell will continue to rot and decay with his spirit trapped inside. Eventually, he will be a dried, animate skeleton. The people will fear him and call him worse than Elhathym. Unless . . ."

"Unless what?" she asked. "What can we do?"

Iardu stared into the green leaves dappled with sunlight. The Flame of Intellect blazed on his breast. "Did you know that the hair and fingernails of corpses continue to grow even in the grave?"

They left the gardens and entered the palace. Servants and soldiers were busy removing all trace of Elhathym's brief reign, cleaning for the coming feasts and the official coronation of the young King. Sharadza and Iardu found D'zan sitting still upon his throne, from which he barely moved at all. In the last few hours the throne room had regained much of its grandeur. Fresh tapestries of Yaskathan ancestry lined the walls. Dust and blood and bones had been scoured away, and the Vizier's podium was restored to its rightful place. The throne that Iardu had conjured from marble had been set with a fresh coterie of jewels. Beams of sunlight showered through the vertical casements.

D'zan wore a silver breastplate engraved with the sword and tree, a crimson cloak, and leggings of white silk tucked into tall black boots. On his sallow face sat a slim crown of gold studded with six emeralds and a single brilliant red opal. His eyes sat like heavy stones in the center of black sockets, and the flesh grew tight about his skull. The hole in his chest was completely covered by the corselet, and gloves of dark leather hid the pallid skin of his hands. As before, the greatsword lay across his knees, oiled and gleaming bright as his crown.

Iardu climbed the dais and spoke to him in whispers. At length D'zan sighed and nodded. He arose and followed them into the garden. There he gave an order, in a voice like sand on stone, that his two guests and he not be disturbed.

The Shaper found a secluded glade rimmed by blossoming pomegranate trees. Here D'zan lay down upon the grass, the sword on his chest pointing toward his feet. His gloved hands wrapped about the hilt like a slain hero fit for burial, which in many ways he was.

Sharadza let Iardu lead the spell. She played the role of student and protégée.

He plucked a single strand of D'zan's brown-blonde hair from his head and breathed upon it; he gathered naked sunlight in his right hand and invested it into the strand. Then he offered it to Sharadza, who poured her own breath upon it and pricked her finger with a pin so that a single drop of her blood fell upon the hair.

Iardu let go of the strand and it floated down to the green sward next to D'zan. Now Iardu sang over the strand in the grass, and Sharadza watched in awe. The hair grew into a rope, then wound upon itself to create an oval. Drops of white fire fell from Iardu's hand upon the oval and it melted into a shape like that of a newborn baby.

As Iardu sang, he made the sign Sharadza had been waiting for. She poured a ewer of fresh water and another of seawater over the infant sculpture. The substance of hair became flesh, and it grew longer and more solid. Iardu dropped a shard of white bone upon its belly, and the flesh rippled, taking the bone into itself. Now the shape lying near D'zan was that of a young boy, the hardness of bones filling its limbs. Soon the young boy was a young man, a twin to D'zan before his death. Its eyes were closed as if in sleep.

Sharadza took D'zan's sword from his cold hands and wrapped the new body's warm fingers about its hilt. Then she took the crown from the rotting head and placed it on the fresh one. Now Iardu bent over the rotting corpse and pulled something miraculous from its mouth – a glowing orb large as an orange and blazing brightly even in the sunlight. He held it out to Sharadza. She took it in her hands gingerly, as if it were a delicate crystal. It hummed, warm and beautiful in her cupped palms. She knelt and dropped it into the open mouth of D'zan's new body.

His new eyes opened. They were sparkling, and as green as her own.

He sat up, inhaling air with freshly molded lungs. She glanced at the corpse and saw that it was now truly lifeless . . . only a husk of dissolving skin and muscle. These two were twins – one living, one dead. She put her arms around the new D'zan. He could not speak or see yet – while Iardu stripped armor and clothing from the empty corpse. She helped D'zan then to stand in his new body, and he blinked at her, voiceless. His eyes gleamed at her. They had been dark before, but now they were bright as emeralds.

They helped him to dress in tunic, corselet, cloak, leggings, and boots. By that time he had regained his voice. He spoke his first words to Sharadza, an intimate whisper.

"You are beautiful," he said. "I wanted to tell you this since I first saw you."

She smiled at him and could do little else. He stood on his own now, a proud young King restored to health and vigor.

"Thank you, Shaper" he said, taking Iardu's hand. "Now that I live again, my kingdom will live. I will never forget what you have done this day."

Iardu's shoulders sagged a bit, but he seemed chipper. "Thank me later with some of your fine Yaskathan wine. Now you must bury this corpse to complete the spell."

He produced a silver shovel for D'zan, who proceeded to dig a grave between the pomegranate trees. Sharadza and Iardu kept an eye out for passers-by. It would not do to have anyone witness the burial of their new King. Even if it was the new King himself that dug the hole.

D'zan rolled his former body into the hole and covered it with dirt. Iardu waved a hand and thick grass grew across the mound. Sharadza tossed a few flower petals on the unmarked grave, and a patch of golden magnolias sprouted there.

Every grave must have some marker.

She embraced D'zan, then Iardu. She wiped at her eyes. "Life from death . . . This miracle soothes my heart." Something in D'zan's eyes made her want to linger near to him. Perhaps it was because her own blood had played a small role in his rebirth. Or it could be the verdant green of his eyes? Suddenly the urge to kiss his warm pink lips overwhelmed her. She turned away and faced Iardu instead.

"I supposed we must carry the grim news of Khama's death to his family."

Iardu smiled. "There was no time to explain before now . . . but Khama is not dead."

Her mouth fell open. She turned to stare at handsome D'zan again. He grinned, his white teeth shining.

"Elhathym merely caught the Feathered Serpent in a prison of earth," Iardu said. "What better way to capture a Creature of the Air? Khama is of the Old Breed. We do not die so easily."

Sharadza beamed. "Then let us go to Zaashari and free him."

Iardu glanced at D'zan then back at her. "No . . . no, you stay here for a while, Princess. I will go alone to free Khama. Then I'll return to my island."

"Why?" asked Sharadza.

"There is a certain stone there that I've kept too long . . . a splendid pearl that belongs to someone else. I think it is time I returned it."

Sharadza hugged the Shaper, squeezed him in the way she used to squeeze her father's neck. She kissed his cheek. "You should visit her," she said. "Don't just drop it in the sea."

Iardu smiled. His eyes glimmered. He turned to D'zan and motioned to the hidden grave. "If these bones are ever found, you must declare them a fallen soldier whom you loved well. No one must know what Elhathym did to you. Or what I have done to reverse it."

D'zan embraced him as well. "All the riches of my kingdom are yours for the asking. What would you have from me?"

Iardu rubbed his beard, cocked his head. "A bottle of wine would suit me best."

D'zan called for a servant and Iardu had his wish. He kissed Sharadza's forehead, then soared into the sky as a red eagle. They watched him ascend until he was only a speck in the blue vault. Then he disappeared behind a pearly cloud.

Sharadza turned her gaze earthward again and found D'zan kneeling on the grass before her. In his open palm lay a ring of white gold set with three fiery stones.

"Sharadza, Princess of Udurum," he said, gazing into her eyes. "Every kingdom needs a King . . . and every King needs a Queen. You held my soul in your hands even before I died and was reborn. Will you be my Queen?"

She stared not at the golden bauble, but into his eyes of glittering green.

Lyrilan walked into the Royal Library of Uurz and felt himself at home. The journey from Yaskatha to Murala had taken nearly a month, with frequent stops along the coast to avoid winter storms. In those tiny villages and desolate stretches of coast, he had found a peace that was wholly unlike the peace of Uurz, or any of the cities he had visited. The simple fisher-folk of the coasts were unconcerned with wars, sorcerers, or the many evils abroad in the world. He wondered what secret they knew that allowed them to enjoy a day-to-day existence without the benefits of city culture, the written word, or the thoughts of history's great men. They told folk tales around warm hearth-fires and showed him scattered ruins where the heroes of old fought monsters. Half their tales were lies or distortions of actual history, but that made them no less compelling. Some of them he would write down one day.

First he must write the story of D'zan as he had long intended. Upon the rolling sea for weeks, he often stared at the dark waters, thinking of his lost and incomplete manuscript rotting away on some sandy sea bed. It was better this way. How could he be objective and consider the whole story while he was stuck in the middle of it? Trying to write the chronicle of King D'zan's rise to power was impossible while he shared that adventure himself. Only now, with months and a thousand leagues between him and those wearisome days, could he see it all clearly enough to set it down in ink.

It was a tale of Princes, Kings, Sorcerers, a Princess and an Empress, a Boy-King and a Giant-King. The death of Shar Dni wove tragedy into the narrative, not to mention the betrayal and seduction of Fangodrel the Bastard. The rising legend of Vireon the Slayer began inside D'zan's tale. Tales often grew from other tales – like buds from the branches of trees. Tyro played a starring role, though not as great a one as he had imagined.

Tyro had expected a war of years, and the Battle of Yaskatha had not sated his lust for glory. He had tried to convince D'zan to march upon Khyrei, but the King of Yaskatha had other, sweeter endeavors in mind. So Tyro returned to Uurz with his battle fever still burning . . . No tragic fate had befallen him, only a minor wound quickly healed. He would continue to look for war where he could find it. Someday, sooner than Lyrilan or Tyro would like, their father would pass away and they would rule as Twin Kings. Lyrilan would have to balance his brother's lust for war as the voice of peace. He did not look forward to those days.

Dairon had greeted his sons with pomp and splendor when they returned, and his joy was even greater when he learned there was no longer a need for his legions to march south. He mourned the death of Shar Dni, but he rejoiced at the death of the Khyrein Beast-Queen. "Let them rot in their filthy jungle," Dairon said. "We'll not spill our blood unless they forget their place again." Naturally, Tyro felt otherwise. Father declared it was time for Tyro to marry. A good woman would cool his warrior passion. Lyrilan was not so sure.

The wedding of D'zan and Sharadza was a spectacular affair. Lyrilan would save its description for the closing scene of his book. It would make a fine and uplifting coda to a tale of death and grim sorcery. The rain of flowers from the golden heights, the silver parade of soldiers trailing crimson, the black horses thick with hanging jewels, the opulence of the bride's gown and her crown of jewels . . . All these details lingered vivid in his mind. Now, however, he must cast his mind back to the day he met D'zan, a frightened, nervous lad who smelled of horseflesh and ate like a starved orphan. Or perhaps he would reach farther back and begin with the Prince's early years . . . the tales of his father's conquests. Whichever he chose, the tale would really begin when the dark stranger came to Yaskatha.

Outside the librarium's high windows, raindrops glistened in the sunlight and a rainbow glimmered above the Palace of Sacred Waters. Somewhere in the city bards sang of ancient lovers, and storytellers spun sagas of war and doom. Wine poured and flowers bloomed. Plowmen planted the fields beneath the rushing clouds of spring. Uurzians lived, loved, died, hoped, dreamed, wept, and laughed. A thousand thousand stories unfolded like the petals of numberless flowers, composing a pattern whose complexity was too great for a single mind.

The only way to make sense of nature's grand design was to isolate the threads, follow the individual strands in the weave of the world. To capture the essence of life itself on parchment with a spell of ebon ink. One tale at a time.

He picked up his quill and dipped it into the flask of dark fluid.

He thought of his friend who had lived, died, triumphed, and lived again, and he pictured the King and Queen of Yaskatha lying in some shady bower. They would have many heirs to read this story.

In the brazen haze of daylight, he touched quill to page and began his spell.

The broad streets of Udurum were full again. Not with bustling and rowdy Giants, but Sharrian refugees eager for homes and work. They carried bags of gold and precious jewels from the treasury of their dead city, placed into their hands by Vireon the Slayer. Spring warmed the black walls of the city, and the Sharrians walked humbly through lanes built by Giant hands. They spread their wealth gradually among the folk of Udurum and forged lives for themselves the way Giants used to forge steel here.

Vireon looked across his city from a balcony on the high tower of Vod's palace. His mother had gone south to visit her daughter and new son-in-law in Yaskatha. She had given him the crown before she left, and Udurum applauded her choice. Even the fiercely proud Uduri knew the city would be stronger with Vireon as its King. The Giants who went north might even return when they heard the tale of King Vireon whispered about their cold fires.

Shaira lingered long enough to bless his marriage to Alua. Shar Dni's fall and the murders of her entire extended family, brothers, sisters, nephews, nieces . . . it had all been too much for her. The lines of worry marred her face, and the burden of Queenship must come off her shoulders. So Vireon took the weight of the crown, made Alua his Queen, and now his mother would know at least a little happiness. She would have many grandchildren. He expected she would live out the remainder of her life in warm, sunny Yaskatha. It reminded her of Shar Dni as she had known it in her youth. He would visit her when duty allowed it.

Now Udurum had both King and Queen again. Alua turned her natural wisdom to the fields and orchards. The blooms of spring had never come so thick and vibrant. Vireon watched the dancers of the spring festival in the streets below, and the lilting music filled his ears.

She came from the tower to join him on the terrace, wrapping her cool arms about his chest from behind.

"Shall we go down and join them?"

"It is expected," he said.

"What troubles you? This should be a time of joy. The frost fades and the earth sends forth its bounty. Speak to me."

He breathed deep of the sweet northern air. Along the southern horizon, the Grim Mountains looked tiny and insubstantial, black fangs crowned by white mists.

"At times . . . I still think of Tadarus," he told her. "And the other one."

She knew of whom he spoke, as she knew he could never again say the name.

She kissed his mouth softly. "The past is set in stone . . . the future is a mystery . . . but the *now* is what you wish it to be. Your memories honor Tadarus. Let that honor give you joy."

He held her in his arms while warm winds danced about the tower.

He said nothing of Fangodrel's last words, the hatred he spat as his scorched head flew from his shoulders.

My blade interrupted that curse . . . stole it from his lips.

I reject his curse.

It is only the reminder of a sad revenge.

The only true curse is that of memory.

Alua was right. He must forget the one and honor the other.

I reject his curse.

They entered the tower and lay together, the melodies of the festival wafting in through the windows. Later they went down into the streets and sampled the delights of spring.

He still did not understand Love.

Or Sorcery.

But this simple joy in a world filled with sorrow . . .

Perhaps this was the beginning of Wisdom.

Epilogue

Shadows and Glass

It took far longer than he imagined. His body congealed from mist to mud and finally to cold, weary flesh. He awoke in the center of runes and sigils carved into the floor. He blinked but could not raise his head. Here, in the highest chamber of the thorny tower, he knitted together a body from fluid strands of shadow. The windows were curtained, so he could not see the passage of days outside, but it must have been many. Eventually, after an eternity of gnawing hunger, he rose from the frigid floor and stood on two legs.

The second ring of runes lay empty.

Where was she? Ianthe should have manifested here at the nexus of her power. She had given him this knowledge, helped him carve the runes. On her shelves the skulls and tomes were cluttered and dusty. The great desk and its chair were empty but for the usual piles of scrolls and moldering volumes. The decanters and bottles along the walls stood festooned with cobwebs.

She had never returned.

She must be truly dead. Annihilated by Vireon's bitch.

He shivered at the memory of his burning agony. That was his physical body ... The first death was the most difficult – so

Ianthe had told him. This new body was a shell, a creation of his will and the power of the blood. His belly ached for more of that red wine.

Now the pale ghost of Tadarus stood where Ianthe should be.

"You are avenged," he told it. "Vireon has killed me. You may go now."

And the ghost was gone.

He stared at the blank spot on the basalt stones where she *must* appear. He wept a few tears, then remembered the Glass of Eternity. He approached it, bending its obscure surface to his will. A blur of colors and shapes swirled inside the flat pane, taking no form he could identify. The more he concentrated on Ianthe, the less he recognized. There could be only one answer . . . The Empress was dead and he was now Emperor of Khyrei. Or would be when he descended from the tower and laid claim to the throne. A city of ignorant, loyal slaves awaited him.

Perhaps this was not such a terrible loss.

He turned from the mirror and glanced at the books of antique lore, the texts of inscribed sorcery. He would miss her tutelage even more than her kisses. There was so much more to discover in the labyrinthine kingdom of sorcery.

Something drew his eyes back to the glass. It swirled now of its own accord and turned to solid black. A starless void hung open before him. A distant hum rang in his ears.

Something gleamed in the darkness . . . a star? No, a mote of azure crystal. It fell toward the mirror, hurling end over end, growing larger. He recognized it as a wine bottle crafted of delicate gemwork. Opal or sapphire. Curious, he reached through the mirror's surface and let it fall into his hand, grasping it by the slender neck.

He pulled it through the rippling glass and studied it. It sang with power, raising the hairs on his new arm. Something dark swirled inside, and the sound of a pebble or small gem rattled against the inner surface.

A whisper seemed to come from the jeweled cork, slipping out like vapor. He held it closer to his ear. Could this be Ianthe?

Now he heard the voice clearly.

Gammir drew his head away from the crystal and frowned.

"Fool," he said to the sealed decanter. "How I hate you. If and when she returns, she will belong to *me* . . . and only me."

Without another word he hurled the bottle back through the mirror and watched it spin away into the vast sea of nothingness. Soon the void faded and the mirror stood dull and opaque as before.

He turned away from the Glass of Eternity, cloaked himself in a robe of jeweled shadow, and descended the spiral stairs.

There was still so much to learn, and so much time in which to learn it.

Dramatis Personae

Vod the Giant-King—Ruler of New Udurum, City of Men and Giants; slayer of Omagh the Serpent-Father; sorcerer and living legend.

Queen Shaira of Udurum—Wife of Vod; Sister of Ammon; former Princess of Shar Dni; Mother of Fangodrel, Tadarus, Vireon, and Sharadza.

Prince Fangodrel of Udurum—Shaira's first son; named after Vod's father; born during the reconstruction of Udurum.

Prince Tadarus of Udurum—Shaira's second son; named after Shaira's father; born one year after Fangodrel.

Prince Vireon of Udurum—Shaira's third son; born one year after Tadarus.

Princess Sharadza of Udurum—Only daughter of Shaira and Vod; sister of Fangodrel, Tadarus, and Vireon; born several years after Vireon.

Prince Tyro of Uurz—Son of Dairon; twin brother of Lyrilan; swordsman of renown.

Prince Lyrilan of Uurz—Son of Dairon; twin brother of Tyro; scholar and scribe.

Prince Andoses of Shar Dni—Son of Ammon; Nephew of Shaira; Cousin to Fangodrel, Tadarus, Vireon, and Sharadza.

Prince D'zan of Yaskatha—Son of Trimesqua; lone heir to the throne.

Olthacus the Stone—Personal bodyguard to Prince D'zan; veteran of the South Island wars.

Elhathym—Usurper of Yaskatha; ancient sorcerer and necromancer.

Ianthe the Claw—Empress of Khyrei; former wife of Gammir; a known sorceress.

Gammir of Khyrei—Former Emperor of Khyrei; a known sorcerer slain by Vod the Giant-King during the rescue of Shaira.

Omagh, Father of Serpents—Ancient progenitor of Serpents; slain by Vod the Giant-King.

Fangodrim the Gray—Uncle of Vod; Brother of Fangodrel the First; Great Uncle of Fangodrel, Tadarus, Vireon, and Sharadza; a leader among Giants.

Dairon, Emperor of Uurz—First Emperor of the New Blood; former Captain of the Uurzian Legions; father to Tyro and Lyrilan.

Indreyah the Sea-Queen—Ruler of an ancient kingdom beneath the Cryptic Sea; a known sorceress.

King Trimesqua of Yaskatha—King of Yaskatha; veteran of the South Island wars; father of D'zan.

King Undutu of Mumbaza—Twelve-year-old Boy-King; son of Umbrala.

Queen Umbrala of Mumbaza—Mother of Undutu; reigning Queen-Regent of Mumbaza.

King Angrid of the Icelands—Lord of the Frozen North; ruler of the Udvorg clans.

King Ammon of Shar Dni—First Son of Tadarus; brother of Shaira; father of Andoses.

Iardu the Shaper—Master of Shapes; a known sorcerer reputed to live on an island in the Cryptic Sea.

Acknowledgments

A colossal "Thank You" to the following fine people for the following fine reasons:

Howard Andrew Jones—for believing and for speaking up about it. (And for being an all-around great guy.)

Bob Mecoy—for listening, for spot-on advice, and for being a fantastic agent. (He's a Magic Man.)

John O'Neill—for his support and encouragement, and for all the great artwork in BLACK GATE.

The Scribes—for invaluable feedback on the first four chapters. (Keep writing, guys!)

Tanith Lee—for her sheer imagination and endless inspiration.

Darrell Schweitzer—for showing me the path and how to walk it. (Sensei!)

John and Evelyn Waggoner—for a supply of inexhaustible love.

Wanda Jane Allgood—for reading to me when I was little, for buying me all those books, and for making damn sure her son got an education. (Love ya, Mom!)

extras

meet the author

John R. Fultz lives in the Bay Area of California but is originally from Kentucky. His fiction has appeared in *Black Gate*, *Weird Tales, Space & Time*, *Lightspeed*, *Way of the Wizard*, and *Cthulhu's Reign*. His comic book work includes *Primordia*, *Zombie Tales*, and *Cthulhu Tales*. When not writing novels, stories, or comics, John teaches English Literature at the high school level and plays a mean guitar.

interview

***Seven Princes* is your first novel. What was the impulse behind this project?**

After years of writing short stories, and cycles of related short stories, it was only natural to move into long-form works (i.e., novels). There was a time when you could make a living writing only short stories... alas, those days are gone. Fantasy lives and breathes today in the form of novels (and series of novels). Originally, I wrote a novel called *Child of Thunder*, which told the story of Ordra, also known as Vod—the Man Who Was a Giant and the Giant Who Was a Man. In retrospect, it wasn't quite right, so I moved it forward twenty years in the future and used everything that I had built in *Thunder* as backstory for *Seven Princes*. I was partly inspired by the way Tolkien used his decades of Middle Earth history (later collected as *The Silmarillion*) as a solid and deep foundation for the Lord of the Rings. Those books are so wonderful and rich because they have this entire panorama of history to draw upon. It makes the invented world seem fully fleshed out, and readers love discovering the depths of a fantasy world as they go. So the story of Ordra/Vod eventually comes out in *Seven Princes*, and everything Vod did sets the stage for the conflicts and situations that comprise this novel. For years I talked about my "big fantasy novel"—now it's here. Or it will be in January 2012.

The book has a particularly mythic tone. Do you see it as being different from where fantasy is headed as a genre?

I'm not sure... it seems fantasy these days is segmented into different types, or sub-genres. You've got epic fantasy, sword-and-sorcery, heroic fantasy, urban fantasy, contemporary fantasy, surrealism, slipstream, and the list goes on. I believe that *all* fantasies draw on myths, some just "dress it up" more in modern-day clothing (Gaiman's *American Gods*, for instance). I prefer fantasy set in a secondary world (I always have), and that's the milieu in which I operate best. I'm glad to see these types of "big fantasies" coming back into style—witness the huge success of Martin's A Song of Ice and Fire and *Game of Thrones* on HBO. So the question about where fantasy is headed—it's anybody's guess. However, I think interest in fantasy fiction is peaking right now, thanks to writers like Mr. Martin, Mr. Gaiman, and many others.

Some have commented that my work hearkens back to the "old school" or "traditional" type of fantasy. In a way that's true, but I'm also trying to do something new with it. It's not pastiche, or repetition, it's simply my vision coming through on the page. A writer's sensibility is, I think, determined largely by his or her influences... what you've read most and where your passions lie. You write what you love. That said, writers like to stretch themselves too. For me, the whole epic/heroic fantasy realm is where I've been heading since I began reading fantasy as a kid in the late 1970s. Some have also called my work "sword and sorcery" but nobody can give a solid definition of what that actually is. For me, the bottom line is that I just Do My Thing and let my passion for storytelling lead me where I need to go.

There is room for all types of fantasy in today's market, and epic fantasy is a broad playground. The difference between a fantasy world and our world is that in the fantasy world the myths are *real.* In our world they're usually metaphors or symbols...abstractions meant to invoke truth. In a fantasy world, myths live and breathe and weave spells over mortal kingdoms. I guess my mission is to find the humanity inside the myth...therein lies a great fantasy tale.

Who/what would you consider to be your influences?

I could write a whole book answering this question, but I'll try to contain myself. Lord Dunsany was perhaps the inventor of the modern fantasy tale. His work never ceases to inspire me, and his novel *The King of Elfland's Daughter* is an immortal classic. His gift for speaking with clever metaphor and concise imagery is stunning, even a hundred years later. Fantasy writers should study his works the way classical composers study Mozart and Bartók. I'm also a big Robert E. Howard and H. P. Lovecraft fan, but Clark Ashton Smith is my favorite of the old-school *Weird Tales* writers. In my opinion Smith invented the whole dark fantasy genre. He had the lost cities, the sorcerers, the creatures from beyond space and time, the mummies, the vampires, the decadent dying empires of Zothique, and the primordial ooze of Hyperborea. As an eleven-year-old I remember discovering Smith's work in some anthology (probably one of Lin Carter's Ballantine adult fantasy series), and seeking him out in every new and used bookstore I could find. In the 1990s I was thrilled when Necronomicon Press released the *Book of Zothique* and the *Book of Hyperborea.* Both are wellsprings of sheer inspiration that I turn to again and again, just like the Dunsany stories.

Tanith Lee is also one of my biggest influences, no doubt about it. Her Tales of the Flat Earth are my favorite, but the Secret Books of Venus, the *Secret Books of Paradys,* and the

Lionwolf trilogy are also up there. Everything she writes is brilliant and inspiring. Reading Lee's work is like drinking fine wine...you get to savor every well-crafted sentence and soak up the dark beauty that only she can invoke. She is amazing.

Anyone who knows me knows how passionate I am for the work of Darrell Schweitzer, especially his *Mask of the Sorcerer* novel, but also his hundreds of amazing short stories. He's often considered a "stylist" who produces a Dunsany-like effect in his best tales, and that can be very true. But he's also a bit of a surrealist in his inventive approach to sorcery and magic...I'd call him a metaphysical fantasist. Any single one of his story collections is worth its weight in platinum.

In the past ten years I've been drawn wholeheartedly to the work of A. A. Attanasio (his Arthor series), R. Scott Bakker (his Prince of Nothing series), and George R. R. Martin. Martin set a new bar for deep characterization, one that brings readers and characters closer than most other writers are able. Thomas Ligotti is also an all-time favorite of mine—the greatest living horror writer for my money—even though he doesn't write much anymore. His stuff is pure weird perfection.

I'll only mention two more authors, both of whom are science fiction icons: Robert Silverberg, whose book *Worlds of Wonder* helped set me on the writing path way back in college (circa 1989)—*Nightwings* is one of my all-time favorite novels; and William Gibson, whose work taught me economy of language and brevity of style. His prose is the epitome of coolness. I'm still amazed at how much detail Gibson packs into a scene with so few words. And his tightly woven plots are superb. The Sprawl and Bridge trilogies are my favorites.

There are *many* other authors whose praises I could sing, but these are probably the most central to my own experience. My favorite Tolkien book is *The Silmarillion.*

Do you have a favorite character? If so, why?

Wow, asking me if I have a favorite character in *Seven Princes* is like asking a father of twelve if he has a favorite child: Hard to answer! I have a particular affinity for Vireon, I suppose. He is the young warrior, supernaturally gifted, who charges head-first into vengeance with no idea what that really means and how it will change him. Without giving anything away, his growth across the first book (and beyond) is something I enjoy chronicling. Vireon also has a special bond with Nature, so there's something very pure about the character.

I also have a real soft spot for Sharadza, who is perhaps the heart of the book—its female lead. She is headstrong and determined, especially in her pursuit of sorcery and her desperate desire to save her doomed father. She is also the conscience of the book…the one who tries the hardest to prevent the atrocity of war. She is the youngest, but in some ways she is the wisest. Like Vireon, she often dives in with good intentions and goes beyond her depth.

Then there's Iardu the Shaper, an ancient sorcerer who has spent thousands of years subtly (and unsubtly) molding the world into a vision that has grown unclear even to him. I like writing Iardu because he is the font of all things ancient, mysterious, and magical. Yet he's not the only sorcerer character in the book, and more sorcerers arise as the series continues. Iardu is there, sometimes behind the scenes, sometimes right in the middle of the action, pulling strings and weaving the fates of Men and their kingdoms. He is a storyteller. He knows far more than he ever admits, though sometimes his cosmic wisdom spills out. There's a lot to love about this character—has he given up on the human race, or can the fires of his ambition be rekindled? That's part of the story that fascinates me and, I hope, will fascinate the readers. Each book in the series will reveal more about the Shaper and his role in historic and current events. Some see Iardu as a benevolent shepherd, while others see him as a scheming manipulator. Both are probably true because people are complicated. Especially ancient wizards.

When you aren't writing, what do you like to do in your spare time?

I listen to music constantly. Mostly hard rock and blues, but I love just about everything. Huge Black Sabbath fan. I love reading (when I can find the time). I'm a huge comics fan, so I get my weekly comics fix whenever possible. Brubaker's *Criminal* is my current favorite. I also love movies, though finding time to watch them has been a challenge lately. I play guitar, something I've been doing since I was fifteen. As a full-time teacher, I get most of my reading/watching done in the summer... which is also when I get most of my writing done. I also love going to see live music—I'm hitting the Soundgarden reunion tour in SanFran this July, then heading down to Southern Cal to see Kyuss and The Sword in early October. My biggest musical goal right now is to see the Black Keys perform live—I will make it happen! I also blog for www.blackgate.com on a semi-regular basis, as well as maintaining my own blog at http://johnrfultz.wordpress.com.

introducing

If you enjoyed
SEVEN PRINCES,
look out for

SEVEN KINGS

Book Two of the Books of the Shaper

by John R. Fultz

1. Three Lives

The colors of the jungle were bloody red and midnight black.

Whispers of fog rustled the scarlet fronds, and the poison juices of orchids glistened on vine and petal. Red ferns grew in clusters about the roots of colossal carmine trees. Patches of russet moss hid the nests of sanguine vipers and coral spiders. Black shadows danced beneath a canopy of interwoven branches that denied both sun and moon. Toads dark as ravens croaked songs of death among the florid mushrooms. Clouds of hungry insects filled the air where red tigers prowled silent as dreams.

Death waited for him in the jungle. There was nothing else to find here. No refuge, no escape, no safety or comfort. This place offered none of those, only a savage end to suffering and a blinding slip into eternity. Tong expected to die here, and he welcomed it. He would die a free man, his knees no longer bent in slavery. He ran barefoot and bleeding through the bloodshot wilderness.

Yes, he would die soon. But not yet. He would take more of their worthless lives with him. This was why he fled the scene of his first murder and entered the poison wilderness. It was not to save himself from the retribution of his oppressors. He fled so they would chase him into this scarlet realm of death. The dense jungle and its dangers gave him precious time. Time to steal the lives of the men who chased him. He would survive just long enough to kill them all; then he would give his life gladly to the jungle and its cruel mercy.

Only then would he allow himself to seek Matay in the green fields of the Deathlands.

Already he had claimed a second life, leaping from the trees like a wild ape, plunging the blade of his stolen knife into a soldier's soft throat. The company of nine Onyx Guards had been foolish enough to sleep that first night about a small fire. They had assumed their prey would be sleeping as well, somewhere ahead of them on the crude trail Tong's passing had created. Some had stripped the plates of black bronze from their chests, arms, and shins. They had even removed the demon-face masks that hid their humanity. For the first time in his young life, Tong saw the raw, sweat-stained faces of his oppressors, the masters of whip and spear and disemboweling blade.

Their flesh was as pale as his own, their eyes and hair the same black. As far as he could see, there was nothing that physically separated him, a slave, from these tormentors of slaves. Nothing except their actions. Far more than enough to damn them all. While the night watcher's back was turned, Tong pounced. His short blade ripped the life from a sleeper's chest as his hand clamped over the dying man's mouth. His entire weight pressed against his victim's chest; he watched the man die slowly. When the man's twitching eyes closed forever, Tong stole his curved saber and a bag of rations. He slipped back into the night, ignoring the winged vermin that gnawed his skin and stung at his blood-smeared hands. He ran south, toward the mountains of fire at edge of the world, making sure to leave an obvious and clumsy trail.

In the morning they found the dead soldier and followed Tong deeper into the jungle. He ran as he ate from the stolen food bag. Salted pork and dried apricots. The vegetation of the jungle was poison, as were most of the creatures who lived here. So finding anything edible was next to impossible. After days of starvation and pain, the meal sent waves of fresh energy coursing through his limbs. The fire of his hatred burned hotter, and he laughed as he leaped over a coiled viper that bared its dripping fangs at him.

O, Pitiful Gods, let them follow me, he thought. *I will lead them all into death.*

He ran until exhaustion fell upon him like a black cloud. He slept in a hollow depression between two great tree roots, on a bed of ruddy lichen. He called Matay's name in his sleep, and he dreamed she was near, reaching for him like she did on the day of her death. Rising from the jungle filth, he reached out and grabbed only a fistful of lichen. A colony of red ants crawled across his body, feasting on the dried blood of his lacerated skin. His chest and back were a maze of fresh welts, the work of razor-edged fronds, biting insects, and patches of sharpgrass. He uprooted a fern and used it to brush the ants from his body, wincing at the pain of beating his own wounds in such a way.

Pain was good, he decided. Pain would keep him from sleep... keep him wary... keep him ready to kill.

He climbed a tree as high as he dared, not far enough to breach the lofty canopy, but high enough to see a great distance across the leagues of crimson undergrowth. He waited there until he saw his pursuers, just at the edge of his vision, cutting their way through the jungle. They reminded him of the marching ants he had wiped away, except these black ants were far more vicious and cruel.

The upper mass of the tree's branches rattled. A great black bird flew from its nest and burst through the canopy. A ray of orange sunlight fell through a hole the bird's passing had made. It warmed Tong's face and shoulders. He recalled Matay's love of the golden sun, how she watched it sink beyond the fields every evening. Sometimes she even halted her work, forgetting the harvest as the glory of sunset burned across the sky, amber and scarlet sinking into purple. More than once her sun-gazing had drawn the whip of the Overseer. Yet it was her daily ritual to watch the sun sink beyond the walls of the black city and into the Golden Sea, where ships sailed to and from mysterious lands. Somewhere in that walled hive of barbed towers the Undying One sat on his throne of blood and tears, dreaming new tortures for his people.

Matay's eyes saw well beyond the ramparts of oppression. She discovered freedom in the splendors of dawn and dusk.

Tong recalled the morning after their first night together. She had awoken wrapped in his arms inside the wooden shack only to slip away from him into the chill of dawn. He lay on his side on the woven sleeping mat and stared at her sleek body as she pulled on the rough-spun, colorless garment that all female slaves wore. The blackness of her hair shimmered with silver as the first rays of morning peeked through the ragged window.

"Where are you going?" he asked. "We can sleep awhile longer before the work horn blows…"

She paused before the door curtain and looked back at him with sparkling eyes. Her smile was the one she would wear in all his future memories. "I want to watch the sunrise," she said. She held out her small hand, soft and warm. "Come with me…"

He joined her that day and nearly every day after for six growing seasons, staring into the gray sky as the face of the sun set it on fire, burning away the last shades of night and making way for the brilliant blue of daylight sky. They sat on a log outside his narrow hut, enjoying the most precious part of the day, the part when they were not yet driven to toil and sweat in the fields, when the whips and clubs of the Onyx Guard and the Overseers had yet to appear between the rows of windswept corn. It did not take him long to understand why she valued the beauty of the sunrise, and why she stopped every evening to watch the sunset. Dawn and dusk. These were the only two things she possessed that slavery could never take away or destroy. This awareness was a gift she had given to him, long before she gave him the more precious gift that grew inside her belly.

I wish I could see Matay's sunrise one more time. Tong stared at the ray of light slicing through the red shadows. He climbed to a lower position in his tree. The path he had so carefully lain would lead them directly below his perch. He need only wait. He may never feel the warm glow of sunrise on his skin again, but he would know the hot blood of his enemies running along fist and fingers. He drew the long saber from its scabbard and crouched like a panther on a wide branch above the trail.

Soon the noise of the masked ones rang through the glade, the swishing of blades, the falling of stem and branch, the tramp of metal-shod boots through mud and moss and rotting leaves. Tong's own boots were mud-caked leather, torn in several places by thorn and brush and stone. The boots of a slave. His feet were cold and his toes tingled against the red bark of the tree. He decided it would be good to meet his death in a pair of soldiers' boots. Eight such pairs drew nearer to the tree that sheltered him.

He would wait until the last one passed below, then drop and kill the man, drag him into the undergrowth and steal his boots. Then he would march out to face the remaining seven at once and kill as many as he could before they brought him down. He was no swordsman, but his arms were big and powerful, the arms of a man used to laboring all day every day for twenty-three years. The masked ones had their armor, but they were frightened of him. They were cowards beneath their devils' visages, impotent beneath their shells of black metal. Only black ants, marching.

His time in the jungle had made him wild and desperate, hungry for blood like the vipers and the tigers and the flying insects. All things here were hungry for blood. He was becoming one of them.

He could wait no longer.

Dropping from the wide branch he fell directly toward the last soldier in line, saber pointed downward, hilt grasped in his clutched fists. His knees hit the man's back, knocking him forward. He drove the sword's point into that familiar soft spot between corselet and helmet; the same vulnerability his knife had discovered earlier. Half the blade's length sank into the man's body with a crunching of bones and a vertical spray of hot blood. The soldier cried out as he died, but his masked face was pressed into the mud. In the constant mélange of jungle noises, crying birds, whirring insects, the cutting of foliage and tramping of armored feet, the sounds of this man's death was lost to his companions. The last of them disappeared among the fronds as Tong twisted the heavy blade.

Dragging the body into the undergrowth, he exchanged footwear as he planned. The new boots were tight yet warm on his aching feet. He lifted the bronze helmet with its welded mask from the dead man's head and placed it on his own. Let one of their own demon-faces be the last thing they see as they die. He took what else he could from the body (a few more bits of dried food) and rolled it into a stagnant pool. A viper glided through the black water and wrapped itself around the corpse. Tong caught a glimpse of himself in the surface of the water. A pale, broad-chested devil with a leering face of black death, twin horns growing from his temples. His mouth was a fanged grin and his eyes were invisible behind narrow slits. He grinned beneath the mask and walked back to the trail, the bloody saber in one hand, his knife in the other.

He stalked after them in resolute calm, ready to face the triumph of his death. Ready to end this parade of suffering and toil called life. To find a better place among the spirits, where surely she waited for him. As for these Onyx Guards, they were city dwellers. Those who dwelled inside the walls of the black city did not share the beliefs of their slaves, who could only stare from afar at the ebony towers. The men Tong killed today, their souls would sink into the Hundred Hells that the city's priests venerated, there to feed the ranks of true demons or be judged and made into demons themselves. Tong did not care what they believed. He only knew they would not be in the bright meadows of the Deathlands, where milk and honey fed the spirits of earthborn slaves.

There in the glow of a new sunrise, he would meet her again. Matay. And the one she carried in her soft, round belly. His son, who was never born into a slave's life as his father was. At least he was spared that. Yet his son had also never breathed the fresh air of morning, never held the sweetness of the sun in his eyes, never known the touch of his father's hands, his mother's breast, the lips of a girl he would one day love. A slave's life was not much, but even that mean gift had been stolen from Tong's unborn son.

The Overseer on that awful day had been a youth himself. Tong heard it in the quavering, too-high voice that came through the mouth slit of the fanged mask. Perhaps nobody had told him that pregnant slaves should be given extra periods of rest in the latter half of their term. Tong was working on the far side of the field when he saw the glittering of the black-lacquered club rising and falling in the sunlight. He raced through the rows, kicking dirt behind him, ignoring the whips of other Overseers who tried to shout him down. He even knocked one of them over in his headlong rush to reach Matay before the fifth and sixth blows fell.

There was no sixth blow, however. The youth in the devil-mask stood over Matay's bloodied body. She lay still among the rows of green and yellow plants, lines of scarlet spilled like whip marks across her white frock. Her skull had been split open, the bones of her face shattered. A clump of her beautiful hair hung from the end of the dirty club. All these things fell starkly into his vision as he threw himself to the ground and took her in his arms. She was still warm then, yet her heartbeat was fading. Her sweet face blurred as his eyes welled, and he called her name. Suddenly, as if she had turned to weightless mist in his arms, he knew that life had left her completely.

"Up, Slave!" cried the young voice, ripe with nervous power. "Get back!" Now he applied the whip, striking Tong across the back. One, two, three times. Tong never knew how many more times it fell, leaving red trails across his back and shoulders. He stared into the unkind eyes peering from within the mask. There must have been other Overseers, other soldiers, other slaves rushing toward them at that point. Yet Tong never knew.

His fist grabbed the whip that plied his flesh and he pulled the armored youth off his feet. The Overseer fell against the dirt with a heavy sound, his body squirming next to Matay's still one. Tong did not remember climbing on the man's back, or wrapping the leather whip about his exposed throat. He only remembered pulling, twisting, tightening. The sound of the cruel youth's gagging filled his ears. The metal helmet was knocked away in the struggle, but Tong's weight held the Overseer against the earth. Pulling, gnashing teeth, squeezing, and snapping. The flesh of the neck gave way as boiled leather bit into it. Finally, an explusion of breath as the Overseer died.

The next thing he remembered was the terrified face of his cousin Olmai, standing over him with arms full of green corn husks. His mouth was an open cave of darkness, like a tomb. "Run!" he begged Tong. "Run now! They are coming!"

He would have stayed there and taken Matay's body in his arms again, but Olmai kicked at him, pushed him into the cornstalks. "Run, fool! Make for the tree line! Go!"

After that, there was only running... panting... bleeding... hunger.

Rage.

And the deep red jungle whose poisons were nothing compared to the venom in his heart.

Now he marched after the seven masked soldiers wearing one of their own fanged faces, carrying two of their own blades, wearing the solid boots of a man no longer a slave. He had killed three of them now, but it was not enough. He marched toward Vengeance and its smiling sister, Death.

The whir of a black arrow caught his ear and the shaft took him in the right breast, just below the collarbone. If he had run into a wall of stone headfirst, he could not have been more stunned. Two more shafts followed from the left and right, one taking him in the left leg, the other piercing his side. Now the masked ones came screaming toward him, sabers raised, horned helms grimacing in the red gloom. He fell on his knees in the muck as the rushing forms surrounded him. The blades of swords and spears gleamed dully as they pressed near to his skin, and a fourth arrow clanged off his stolen helm. The Onyx Guards laughed while Tong gasped for air inside his mask.

They had fooled him. They let him take their rear guard, then circled about to pin him down with arrows. The chase was over. He had thought he was stalking them now, but they had snared him instead. Already he felt the poison of the arrowheads rushing into his blood, making his arms heavy. The saber and knife fell from his numb fingers, dropping like useless stones into the mud. The weight of the helm was terrible, so that he could no longer keep his head up. He fell backward to a chorus of metallic laughter. The circle of blades moved closer about him, sneering devil faces hovering behind them.

Someone barked an order, and someone else reached down and plucked the stolen helmet from his head. A high-ranking Overseer stood above Tong, marked by the black whip with a golden handle that hung from his belt. "Stupid, stupid, Slave," he said, though the demon lips did not move. His eyes blinked through the slits of the mask. "What did you gain from all this? A few more days of misery and starvation?" He kicked hard at Tong's belly with a filthy boot. "Eh? What did you gain?"

Tong's voice was a rasping groan, like the ripping of a delicate fabric.

"Three..."

"Eh? Speak up, Slave!" said the Overseer. He kicked Tong again, striking near the arrow protruding from his side. A wave of agony made Tong shiver. The poison froze his blood and his limbs.

"Three..." he moaned again.

"Three? Three what?" The demon mask hung low before his face now, the Overseer kneeling to mock his prisoner.

"Three lives."

Tong used the last of his strength to force his lips into a smile. He would die a happy man, knowing he had taken three of the Onyx Guard with him. Let the Overseer understand this.

The demon face stared down at him, saying nothing. The Overseer rose and uncoiled his whip. "Tie him to that tree," he ordered. "I'll flay the life from him piece by piece. We'll carry his carcass back in pieces to fertilize the fields."

Hands gripped his arms and legs, hauling him up from the earth. They rustled him toward a crimson tree bole thick with russet moss. He had seen slaves whipped to death. He knew his demise would be a long and lingering process. Yet his eyes welled not with sadness. He wept with joy as the soldiers dragged him across the glade. Death was coming to greet him. He need only cross a river of boiling pain and she would welcome him into her domain.

Matay...

He wanted to call out her name, but his tongue would no longer move.

They slammed him chest-first against the tree, rattling the three arrows still in his flesh. His cry of pain was a gagging moan. One man gathered rope from a shoulder pack while the other two pulled Tong's arms about the tree trunk.

Behind him, the Overseer cracked his whip, warming up his arm for a slow execution.

Now the men stopped silent, the rope gone slack in their hands. Masked heads turned to the left and right, and the sound of the whip fell into silence. The soldiers stared at something behind Tong. Something had come out of the jungle. No, there must have been several things, though they did not make a sound. The Onyx Guards were silent, but the sound of their metal blades sliding from scabbards filled the glade. The three archers, who had come into the glade after the capture, nocked fresh shafts and drew taut their bowstrings. Tong's limp body dropped into the muck, his head fell back across his shoulders, and he saw the beasts.

They might have been hunched apes, long of arm and squat of haunch, yet they were entirely without hair or fur. They ringed the glade, at least thirty of them, though perhaps more lurked in the scarlet foliage. Their skins were white as bone, supple as leather. They crouched atop clumps of rock or fallen trees, lifting great flat hands that ended in vicious claws, working silently in the air as if speaking with their fingers.

Most shocking of all, their heads were lizardine ovals with no eyes at all. Where eye sockets should have been grew instead a pair of white, curling horns like those of a ram, tapering to points on either side of their skulls. Their mouths were impossibly wide and full of sharp teeth. Above the mouths sat slitted noses like those of bats, flaring and pulsing as they sniffed the jungle air. The beasts' arms and legs were mightily muscled, their bellies lean and flat. It was not clear if they had dropped down from the trees, rose up from the ground, or simply lumbered into the glade. They moved quickly, silent as white mists.

The seven masked soldiers stood wrapped in a precarious calm before this strange audience. From his place among the gnarled roots, Tong saw a white blur leap across the glade, then another, and another. A helmeted head rolled across the ground like a melon and bumped against his shoulder. The men behind the masks were screaming. At first they bellowed rage and warnings. In a matter of moments, as clouds of warm red mist erupted into the air, raining down upon Tong's face, their screams turned to cries terror and pain. Soon a heavy silence replaced them.

Tong managed to raise his head a bit. He moaned softly at the pain of his pierced flesh. The white creatures crouched among the bodies of the dead men. Scarlet stained their long claws and bony chests. Tongues descended from their fanged maws to lick at the bronze faces of corpses. At first he thought they were lapping up the blood, that they would devour the dead men and himself. He only hoped they would kill him before eating him. Yet the eyeless ones seemed only to explore the men's faces and armor with their weird pink tongues like curling tendrils. Their tongues moved more like curious fingers than organs made for tasting.

Now they gathered about Tong, sniffing at him and sliding their tongues across his skin. Tongues wrapped about each of the arrow shafts and pulled them from his body in quick, painful jerks. Fresh blood welled from the ragged holes. The eyeless faces drew near to his own, and he heard them sniffing. He must smell like a wild animal dying of infected wounds. Perhaps his stink would drive them away, and he would lie here and die at last.

The shadows of the jungle converged to flood his brain, and the beasts lifted his useless body. He hung weightless in the grip of their powerful hands, and their claws unavoidably pricked his skin. Blood spilled from his poisoned wounds as awareness spilled from his mind.

The creatures raced in bounding, graceful strides through the scarlet wilderness.

He did not believe they were carrying him toward the green fields of the Deathlands.

THE DRAGON'S PATH

Daniel Abraham

All paths lead to war . . .

Marcus's hero days are behind him. He knows too well that even the smallest war still means somebody's death. When his men are impressed into a doomed army, staying out of a battle he wants no part of requires some unorthodox steps.

Cithrin is an orphan, ward of a banking house. Her job is to smuggle a nation's wealth across a war zone, hiding the gold from both sides. She knows the secret life of commerce like a second language, but the strategies of trade will not defend her from swords.

Geder, sole scion of a noble house, has more interest in philosophy than in swordplay. A poor excuse for a soldier, he is a pawn in these games. No one can predict what he will become.

Falling pebbles can start a landslide. A spat between the Free Cities and the Severed Throne is spiraling out of control. A new player rises from the depths of history, fanning the flames that will sweep the entire region onto the Dragon's Path—the path to war.

"Prepare to be shocked, startled, and entertained."

—*Locus*

"It's as if Clint Eastwood went to Narnia."

—*Kirkus*

THE MAGICIAN'S APPRENTICE

Trudi Canavan

In the remote village of Mandryn, Tessia serves as assistant to her father, the village Healer. Her mother would rather she found a husband. But her life is about to take a very unexpected turn.

When the advances of a visiting Sachakan mage get violent, Tessia unconsciously taps unknown reserves of magic to defend herself. Lord Dakon, the local magician, takes Tessia under his wing as an apprentice.

The hours are long and the work arduous, but soon an exciting new world opens up to her. There are fine clothes and servants and—to Tessia's delight—regular trips to the great city of Imardin.

However, Tessia is about to discover that her magical gifts bring with them a great deal of responsibility. For a storm is approaching that threatens to tear her world apart.

"Some excellent reading to be had."
—Robert N. Stephenson on *The Novice*

"A wonderfully and meticulously detailed world, and an edge-of-the-seat plot, this book is a must for lovers of good fantasy."
—Jennifer Fallon

THE BLACK PRISM

Brent Weeks

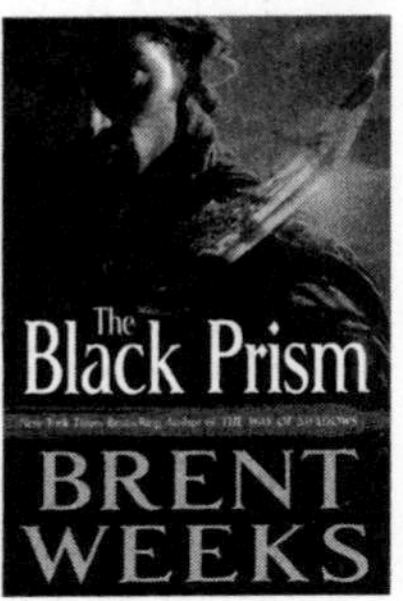

Gavin Guile is the Prism, the most powerful man in the world. He is high priest and emperor, a man whose power, wit, and charm are all that preserves a tenuous peace. But Prisms never last, and Guile knows his time is short.

But when Guile discovers he has a son, born in a far kingdom after the war that put him in power, he must decide how much he's willing to pay to protect a secret that could tear his world apart.

"It is a truly visionary and original work, and has set the bar high for others in its subgenre."
—graspingforthewind.com

"Weeks manages to ring new tunes on…old bells, letting a deep background slowly reveal its secrets and presenting his characters in a realistically flawed and human way."
—*Publishers Weekly*

THE DWARVES

Markus Heitz

For countless millennia, the dwarves of the Fifthling Kingdom have defended the stone gateway into Girdlegard. Many and varied foes have hurled themselves against the portal and died attempting to breach it. No man or beast has ever succeeded. Until now . . .

Abandoned as a child, Tungdil the blacksmith labors contentedly in the land of Ionandar, the only dwarf in a kingdom of men. Although he does not want for friends, Tungdil is very much aware that he is alone—indeed, he has not so much as set eyes on another dwarf. But all that is about to change.

Sent out into the world to deliver a message and reacquaint himself with his people, the young foundling finds himself thrust into a battle for which he has not been trained. Not only his own safety but the life of every man, woman, and child in Girdlegard depends on his ability to embrace his heritage. Although he has many unanswered questions, Tungdil is certain of one thing: no matter where he was raised, he is a true dwarf.

And no one has ever questioned the courage of the Dwarves.